MAIDEN

'Say goodbye to your modesty!' Aisla crowed and tugged Ea's pantalettes down.

Elethrine felt a hot flush rise to her face as the girl's pert white bottom was laid bare. Aisla raised her hand and planted a heavy smack on it, making the soft nates wobble delightfully. Another harder smack made them part a little, giving a glimpse of jet-black hair and wet, pink flesh. Two hand marks showed pink against the white skin of the small girl's bottom. A shiver went right through Elethrine at the sight, making her want more of the same; a tiny, round bottom, red all over and parted to show the girl's most intimate secrets. Not just framed by a tangle of dishevelled clothing either, but on a nude, shamed girl.

'Naked!' she ordered.

By the same author:

THE RAKE

MAIDEN

Aishling Morgan

This book is a work of fiction.
In real life, make sure you practise safe sex.

First published in 1999 by
Nexus
Thames Wharf Studios
Rainville Road
London W6 9HT

Typeset by TW Typesetting, Plymouth, Devon

Printed and bound by
Cox & Wyman Ltd, Reading, Berks

ISBN 0 352 33466 5

Contents

KORA

MUND

Mundic Roads

HAI (GLASS COAST)

Red Parch (Ara Khum)

CYPRAYA

APRINA STATES

Ryna Sea

Ergan Deep

Aeg Roads

AEGMUND

Five Hundreds of Longpine

DWARVEN KINGDOMS

LAI

YTHAN

Khum

VENDIOME EMPIRE

APRAYA

Eigora

ORETEA

1

Demoiselle

Elethrine peered down from her window high in the castle's tallest turret. A noise had attracted her attention. Far below in the blockyard, a ring of youths had surrounded a girl and were teasing her by singing a song that was always guaranteed to bring the blushes to maidens' cheeks. Elethrine listened to the words drifting up with a trace of irritation, knowing that had she not been the daughter of a baron, she herself might be subject to such cruel taunting:

Here's the dirty goblin, hop, hop, hop,
Down with his trousers and out with his cock,

Now you'd better run girl, far, far, away,
'Cause if you let him catch you, he'll put you in the
    hay,

See how big his cock is, all green and fat and long,
And there's no good in telling him, he doesn't
    know it's wrong,

He'll lift your skirts and split your drawers as it
    begins to swell,
He'll put it in your maidenhead, your bottom ring
    as well,

He'll squeeze your tits and smack your arse, and if
    he's in the mood,
He'll make you suck and lick his balls, and other
    things so rude,

1

He'll fill you full of thick white cream, in every
   single hollow,
He'll stain your clothes and soil your face, he'll
   even make you swallow,
And when he's done he'll steal your clothes and
   leave you shamed and bare,
With jism up your bottom, and jism in your hair,
But if you run and tell your men and ask them to
   go searching,
It's like as not they'll strip your rump and tie you
   for a birching,
'Cause they all know that girls can run as fast as
   needs may be,
But goblins can't, and never could, and so it seems
   to me,
That girls who walk where goblins live and whistle,
   laugh or sing,
Know well what fate waits there for them and
   hunger for its sting.

The ditty trailed off, leaving the youths laughing and the
girl hiding her face in shame. The knowledge that her
rank made her immune to such coarse behaviour
pleased Elethrine, yet also left her with a faint sense of
missing out on something; as if it might actually be
enjoyable for the poor girl below to be tormented with
the thought of what would happen if the goblins caught
her. The song was no joke either. Sometimes it actually
happened, and when it did – Elethrine's nurse assured
her – the poor victim was sore for a week. Sore where,
Nurse Anaka had not made clear, but Elethrine could
imagine, and found her hand moving involuntarily to
the front of her skirts.

   The thought made her shiver, a naughty sensation
that immediately filled her with utter mortification.
With a disturbingly warm feeling in her belly, she turned

away from the window. In her mind she made a note to have the youths whipped, not for teasing the hapless maiden, but for disturbing her, the Demoiselle Elethrine, only daughter to Dakarmoth, twelfth Baron Korismund. In reality, of course, their punishment would be for causing the disturbing thoughts that had made her belly warm and set her throat fluttering, but that was hardly something that could be spoken of.

Anyway, it was a silly rhyme. Especially the ending, as if any girl would actually let herself get caught on purpose, knowing she would be put through such an ordeal. Besides, it wasn't even accurate. Goblins didn't wear trousers, everybody knew that. In fact, a pouch of uncured leather was the only thing they wore, if that. Trousers were hardly practical with their shape, which Elethrine knew, because she had seen one. A woodsman had caught it in a net and brought it into the keep, intending to use it for sport. Forbidden to go near it, Elethrine had sneaked down at night and peeped through the keyhole of the room in which it was bound in an iron cage. One glimpse had been enough. It had been no more than one third the height of a normal man, deep, rich black-green in colour and covered in warts and wattles. The face had been set in an expression that was somehow unutterably lewd and also fierce, which had terrified her, but not nearly as much as what it had between its stubby, bowed legs.

Never having seen a naked man, she was unsure of the anatomical details of their secret places, yet knew enough of male animals to know that they were very different from girls, and ruder. What was between the goblin's legs was far ruder than anything she could have imagined, and hardly secret, being barely constrained within the crude pouch of stained leather. The outline of the penis had been clearly discernible, a great, fat thing that squirmed and writhed obscenely in its sack as if determined to burst free. It had been huge too, out of

3

all proportion to the goblin's body. Beneath it the balls had also shown clearly, bulbous globes larger than hens' eggs.

Elethrine had stared entranced, until, perhaps catching her scent, the grotesque beast had moved its hand purposefully towards its pouch. She had screamed and run, not stopping until she was safely in her room with the door locked behind her. There had also been a curious scent, although she had scarcely been aware of it until it was gone. It had been compelling, making her want to do things the very thought of which brought blushes to her cheeks.

In the morning the goblin was gone, which caused an uproar that ended with the Baron banning them inside the castle walls. It had never been found either, and for the next three months two veteran pikemen had guarded her door night and day. That had been in addition to her purity girdle, which she wore anyway to ensure that she remained chaste until the day she was taken in wedlock by a highborn Mundic who was strong and cunning enough to achieve her.

She sat down on her bed, remembering the gross sight and the disturbing dreams that had followed for weeks afterwards. Always it would be the same. She would be picking flowers in one of the meadows above the castle. It would be quiet and still, and then she would hear a rustling in the long grass. Somehow she would know what it was, and run immediately, down the hillside in a blind panic. In reality, goblins were easy to outrun, their short, bow legs making them incapable of any speed. In her dream they were as fleet as the finest horses, while she was clumsy and slow. Always they caught her, and always in the big cherry orchard, where, under the shelter of the blossom-hung trees, they would pull her to the ground. Her skirts would be thrown up, her bodice torn apart. They would fumble open the strings and catches of her petticoats and chemise,

4

tearing what wouldn't come easily. They would open her drawers and burst her corset, breaking the lock. They would rip open her pantalettes to expose her final barrier – her purity girdle.

Only she wouldn't have it on. Their monstrous cocks would be out of their pouches, their obscene balls swinging beneath them. Lying on a bed of her ruined clothing, her precious tuppenny would be open, vulnerable, as the biggest, ugliest goblin got down between her legs, its gigantic, hideous penis ready to deflower her. The others would be molesting her, some holding her thighs apart, others using their long spatulate fingers to explore her body, several pawing at her naked breasts, one trying to get its penis to her mouth, one with a finger sneaking towards the most intimate part of her bottom . . .

And then she would wake up, always an instant before she was deflowered. She would be sweating and breathing hard, and always, always, her tuppenny would be wet and warm. Her purity girdle stopped her touching herself there, which was just as well, as without it she knew that she would try to do what her giggling maid had told her was possible.

The maid, Nurse Anaka's daughter Aisla, was a tall, lithe girl with the flame-red hair colour known in Mund as 'peasant red'. Elethrine herself, like most nobles, had hair of a rich, yet pale blonde, which made her stand out from the tawnys and reds of the peasants and artisans. When Aisla had hinted to Elethrine of the pleasures of playing with her tuppenny, Elethrine had ordered the poor girl to do it, not believing it was possible. Aisla had protested, but under the threat of a paddling, had agreed. Blushing furiously, the maid had raised her skirts, opened her single pair of drawers, pulled apart her pantalettes to reveal a neat, pale pink tuppenny. With her eyes closed in embarrassment, Aisla had started to rub at the little bump towards the top of the soft pink centre. As she played, her embarrassment had faded, until she was lying with her thighs spread wide, breathing deeply as her fingers worked in the wet, fleshy folds between her legs. The maid had popped her breasts out of her bodice after a while, feeling them and sighing and arching her body in a pleasure that was obviously no pretence. At the end Aisla had cried out as if in pain and called her mistress's name, only to revert to coy blushes within the minute.

Elethrine had watched the display with the warmth between her own thighs becoming increasingly urgent. By the end she had felt so discomfited that she had ordered Aisla to strip to her underwear and kneel on the bed with her haunches up. Elethrine had then opened the maid's drawers wide to get at the full breadth of trim bottom. The position had left Aisla's tuppenny and bottom ring showing, to Elethrine's delight, and she had taken further pleasure in describing to Aisla how she looked. Elethrine had then beaten the poor maid across her bare buttocks, using a wooden rule, then a hairbrush and finally the thin cane that was kept for her own discipline. Far from soothing her nerves, the act of beating her maid had only served to heighten Elethrine's discomfiture. The harder she beat, the worse it had become, until Aisla's bottom had become the colour of a ripe cherry and the unfortunate maid was crying into a pillow. Finally Elethrine had had to abandon the process and, feeling very odd indeed, had ordered Aisla to draw her a cool bath.

The memory made Elethrine feel much the same, filling her with an urge near to desperation to get her purity girdle open and see if she could do the same as Aisla had done. Unable to resist, she quickly checked to make sure that nobody was coming up the stairs. Confident of her privacy, she began to massage her breasts, feeling the full globes of flesh under her straining bodice. Naked, they were heavy and each one filled a hand, as she knew from feeling them at night

6

when her linen gown could be pulled up for access. Leaving her breasts she stroked her hands down the trim line of her waist, delighting in the gentle, elegant curve. Lower, her hips flared, supporting a bottom that was perhaps a shade fatter than she might have liked. The heavy cheeks were sensitive though and she cupped one in each hand and stuck them out as if awaiting punishment. The feel of her bottom in her hands made the need to try and get at her tuppenny even stronger and she began to pull up her skirts at the front. Lifting her dress and three petticoats left her drawers showing, at which point she hesitated. Exposing the lock to her purity girdle meant unlacing the front of her drawers and then the front of her pantalettes beneath. To undo them would be the work of a moment, but to do them up again was a very different matter. If she was caught trying to open her purity girdle the result would be a hasty upending over her bed, the exposure of her bottom and the application of twelve agonising strokes of the cane, which always hung above her bed to remind her that she was not beyond discipline.

Even as she paused, listening carefully, she caught the sound of the door at the bottom of her staircase being opened. Frantically rearranging her skirts, she just managed to adopt a demure, ladylike pose by one of the windows when the door opened. Elethrine turned, discovering to her annoyance that it was not Anaka but Aisla, who not only would not report her but who might have been made to help.

From nowhere the thought that Aisla might have been made to help with more than getting the purity girdle open came into Elethrine's head, sending furious blushes to her cheeks at the very idea of what she had so briefly imagined.

'What do you want?' she said rather curtly, trying to rid herself of the image of the maid's delicate features pressed against the soft golden curls between her thighs.

'Your father commands your presence, mistress,' Aisla answered hastily. 'In the great hall.'

'Why?' Elethrine demanded, irritated at the summons.

'I don't know, mistress,' Aisla replied. 'Father awaits you at the foot of the tower stair.'

'Your father, I take it?' Elethrine replied. 'Oh well, I suppose it must be important then. Stay in your room, I may want you later.'

'Yes, mistress,' Aisla answered.

Elethrine made a final adjustment of her dress and started down the stairs, meeting Aisla's father, Uroth, at the bottom. Greeting him with a curt nod, she set off towards the great hall. The gigantic Uroth walked steadily behind her, his great steps easily keeping up with her brisk pace. As master-at-arms and armourer, Uroth was not the normal person to escort her, and as she passed through the tall, dim corridors of the keep and crossed the cloistered courtyard, she was wondering at the reason for so much ceremony.

The great hall opened off the cloisters, and Elethrine walked through the high door, Uroth remaining at the entrance. The scents of smoke, dust and old wood struck her as she entered. Walls of rough-hewn granite of the deepest grey rose on either side, set with high, arched windows and half-covered by the banners of the various nobles of Korismund. What had once been rich, deep colours highlighted with cloth of gold and silver lacquer were now faded and thin with age. Above them the soot-blackened roof beams reared to a peak that was lost in shadow, the dull light from the high, stained glass windows providing only hints of grotesquely carved faces bearded with cobweb.

An enormous grate ran the length of the room, deep with the cold ashes of the previous night's dining and ringed with tables. At the far end a vast wooden throne rose to half the height of the room, its back fantastically carved and worked with polished stones – garnet, dark malachite, jet, blood-stone. On the throne sat a tall, grim figure, his black cloak and armour of dull steel worked with the arms of Korismund, a crimson rose held in a clenched steel fist. A great banner hung above his head, showing the same arms, as did the shield fastened to one side of the throne. A massive sword hung on the opposite side, its worn leather grip showing that it was not merely ceremonial. A coronet ringed his head, bright in contrast to the grey of his hair and long beard.

'Why so formal, father?' Elethrine said cheerfully, giving the smallest of curtsies as she approached.

'For good reason, child,' the Baron replied. 'As you know, Talithea, Princess of Mund, will be coming here to take formal betrothal with Kavisterion, Prince of Ateron in Aegmund.'

'Indeed, father.'

'Her outriders are here and she will also be here within the hour,' he went on. 'It is necessary that we receive her with due protocol.'

'Within the hour?' Elethrine echoed. 'I thought she was coming this evening. I must change, bathe, have my hair set! Where is my maid?'

'Calm yourself, little Pommette,' he continued. 'All that in due course, but first there is something important I must tell you.'

'What is that?' she replied, trying not to sound too impatient.

'As you know,' Dakarmoth rumbled, 'being a somewhat remote barony, we have tended to stay with the old traditions.'

'Yes, father,' Elethrine replied, conscientiously.

'And thus,' he continued, 'being of the fourth rank, and noble, we are entitled to names of nine letters in length.'

'Yes, father,' Elethrine repeated.

9

'Yet,' he sighed, 'as you may not know, some two hundred years ago, some modernist clique in the royal court – led by King Galaitharion XI himself, I believe – reduced the number of ranks to nine, abolishing the four ranks of peasants and decreeing that all peasants are equal and might have names of four letters. Artisans might all have five, regardless of rank; the thaneclan, squires and reeves six, nobles seven and royals eight, again regardless of rank. Foolish, I know, yet the upshot is that Princess Talithea has a name of only eight letters, as you may have noticed.'

'Indeed, father,' Elethrine answered. 'I had thought it because her family are descended from Thane Etharion . . .'

'So is ours, impertinent child,' Dakarmoth interrupted.

'Your forgiveness,' she said meekly.

'Granted,' he answered. 'Now, we must observe protocol . . .'

'Of course,' she put in.

'Exactly,' he continued. 'We must observe protocol, and so, for the duration of her stay, you must shorten your name . . .'

'Father!' Elethrine exclaimed, scandalised by the suggestion. 'Then, then, should it be eight letters, I would be thought no more than of the rank of a thane!'

'Seven letters,' her father corrected her.

'Seven!' Elethrine shouted. 'Me, be thought a member of the squires! Never! I could never! Oh, for shame!'

'Elethrine!' Dakarmoth boomed in a voice redolent of thin canes and sore, female bottoms.

Elethrine shut up hastily.

'But, father,' she continued after a pause, her tone now thoughtful, almost wheedling, 'the Prince of Ateron is named Kavisterion, a name of eleven letters –'

'He is of Aegmund,' Dakarmoth interrupted her, 'and frankly little more than a barbarian, although it is

10

clearly an important move on the part of the king to join his line to ours. No, this evening at the ceremony of betrothal, you shall be announced as Ethrine, which, when all is said, is a pleasant name.'

'A pleasant name for the daughter of a squire,' Elethrine retorted.

'Silence!' her father roared. 'Do as you are told or I shall call for Nurse Anaka and a cane!'

Elethrine bowed her head meekly although she was seething inside. From long experience she knew that the Baron was as good as his word and that if she resisted she would end up bent over the table with her skirts up and her purity girdle off for a dozen stinging strokes of Nurse Anaka's cane. The nurse had little sympathy with tantrums and might even pull her victim's pantalettes open and inflict the caning on the bare bottom. With her buttocks on show, the humiliation would be worse than the pain, yet she would still be announced as Ethrine. The difference would be that she would have a fresh set of smarting cane stripes on her bottom to remind her of her disobedience.

It was pointless to double an already intense shame, so she curtsied politely to her father and left the room, breaking into a run as soon as the heavy doors had clanged shut behind her. Her blood was boiling in her veins and she mounted the steps to her tower full of determination to take her temper out on someone.

'Aisla!' she yelled as she reached the doorway of her maid's room. 'Draw my bath and fetch Nurse Anaka for my key.'

'Yes, mistress,' she heard as she carried on up the steep, spiral stairs.

In her room she glanced out of the window that looked out across the countryside of Korismund, fiddling with the laces of her dress rather than wait for Aisla to help her. To north and south stood the high grey ramparts of the mountain range known as the

11

Spine, a natural barrier that separated the Kingdom of Mund from barbaric Aegmund. Korismund Keep stood in the pass which it had been built to defend, perched on an outlying crag high above the dense woods that covered the lower slopes of the mountains. To the east she could see fields and orchards, the village that shared its name with the keep, and the road leading out across the broad, mountain-ringed bowl that was the Barony. She could see no sign of an approaching party of horsemen, yet knew that her preparations would take longer than the Princess and her guard would need to cover the distance from the furthest visible point of the road.

'Aisla!' she called back over her shoulder as she struggled with the complicated set of laces that held her bodice shut.

There was no response, increasing Elethrine's fury despite the knowledge that her maid would be fetching Nurse Anaka. A moment later she heard the lower door close and footsteps on the stairs.

Elethrine grabbed her hairbrush, intent on taking her anger out on her maid's bottom even if a dozen Princesses were approaching the castle. She began to smack the brush meaningfully on her palm as the door handle turned, knowing the shock Aisla would get on discovering she was to be spanked for nothing.

'Now . . .' she began, only to discover that it was not Aisla, but Nurse Anaka, coming through the door.

Elethrine hastily returned the hairbrush to the table and greeted her nurse with a smile. Nurse Anaka – Aisla's mother and a big, strapping woman with a no nonsense look about her – gave Elethrine a single curious glance, curtsied briefly and came into the room.

'Aisla is drawing your bath,' the nurse stated. 'I will help you undress.'

'Thank you, and please hurry,' Elethrine replied.

'Hurry does not become a Demoiselle,' Anaka remarked.

'True,' Elethrine admitted as the nurse took over the process of unlacing her bodice, 'but the Princess Talithea will be here for her betrothal within the hour and I should greet her.'

'Nonetheless, Pommette,' Anaka continued, using Elethrine's pet name as she always did when her charge was letting her enthusiasm run away with her, 'you must be properly presented.'

'Indeed,' Elethrine agreed, 'which is why we must hurry. Now, while Aisla bathes me, you must lay out my dress in the deep blue Jhai velvet, chemise, corset and under-dress in the royal-blue silk, silk petticoats of lake blue, blue-grey and powder blue, white silk drawers and my new coral pink pantalettes. Stockings of –'

'But, Pommette,' Nurse Anaka interrupted, 'nobody will know what colour you petticoats are, much less your drawers and certainly not your pantalettes!'

'I will know,' Elethrine replied, 'and don't call me Pommette in company. I'm not a child and it's an embarrassing pet name.'

'It's a pretty name,' Anaka replied defensively as she undid the key-buckle on Elethrine's chemise.

Elethrine sighed as her breasts burst free of restraint, drawing a mild noise of rebuke from her nurse. The chemise and bodice held them tight against her chest, giving her figure a smooth line of which she was proud. Nevertheless, it was always bliss to have her chemise undone to let them return to their natural shape, and also to have her nipples pop out as the cool air touched them.

'You can be such a wanton girl,' Anaka said, mildly.

Elethrine didn't reply, quite aware of the strength of her body's responses, and simultaneously pleased and ashamed. Nurse Anaka took no notice, instead turning to one of her favourite topics, the decline in the old traditions of the kingdom.

'I don't really hold with this betrothal business,' she

13

began with a phrase that Elethrine had heard perhaps a dozen times since the news that there was to be a formal agreement to marry between Prince Kavisterion and the Princess Talithea. 'In my day he'd have had to carry her off and ravish her like everyone else.'

'Theiron and Ateron are nearly a thousand leagues apart,' Elethrine pointed out.

'All the better,' she continued. 'Think of the glory of having a prince ride a thousand leagues for your sake.'

'Two thousand leagues, by the time he'd got back,' Elethrine said. 'The marriage also makes an important alliance.'

'That's true,' she admitted. 'Still, I always think ravishment is so much more romantic. Who knows, some day some bold thane may come and take you in your bed, risking everything for your beauty and the chance to become Baron Consort.'

'Ha!' Elethrine laughed. 'There is no thane in Mund so stupid. First he would have to break into the keep, then get the key to my purity girdle from your apartment and risk facing Uroth in single combat. Should he survive – which I doubt – he would have to defeat a guard or two, batter down my door, ravish me, descend the height of twelve men to the blockyard and escape with me across his shoulders. Name me the idiot who would so much as consider the feat?'

'I don't know. Still, it's a nice thought,' Anaka responded.

'Indeed,' Elethrine admitted, 'but it is also most unlikely. No, I shall consider the suits that are put to me and hold a jousting contest or something modern.'

Nurse Anaka tutted disapprovingly and went back to the task of loosening Elethrine's clothes.

With the dress and corset off, it took Nurse Anaka's practised fingers only minutes to strip Elethrine for her bath. As always the sensation of having her purity girdle removed was more blissful even than the unlacing of her bodice. Scampering naked down the stairs to her bath also produced a deliciously naughty feeling of freedom very different indeed to the shame of having her bottom exposed for punishment.

In the room below, Aisla had Elethrine's bath ready, a great oval tub filled with steaming, lily-scented water. Aisla stood by it, as naked as Elethrine herself as she would be using the water once her Mistress had finished. The sight of Aisla nude set off the same dirty, guilty thoughts Elethrine had had before, and she climbed quickly into the bath to hide the flush that rose automatically to her face and chest.

In the bath it was worse, with Aisla's bare breasts swinging naked inches in front of Elethrine's face as the maid soaped and scrubbed. They were big for such a slim girl and kept touching Elethrine's arms and her own breasts – once even her face as Aisla leant across to reach for a fresh vial of scented bath oil. Minutes before Elethrine had intended to spank Aisla, but as the maid bathed her the urge to punish was rapidly being replaced by the urge to caress.

Elethrine shut her eyes, trying to think about something other than the soft, full breasts that were pressing against her upper arm or the dainty, gentle fingers that were working soap into her belly. It was no good. Aisla's fingers were going lower, one hand soaping the subtly rounded undertuck of her tummy, then working the lather into the curls between her thighs.

'Could you lift your bottom a little please, mistress?' Aisla asked.

Elethrine responded, trying desperately to keep control of herself as Aisla's hands slid down between her thighs and under her bottom. One hand began to rub at Elethrine's tuppenny, the other at the sensitive skin of her bottom. Elethrine moaned, lost to pleasure as Aisla's fingers slipped between the lips of her tuppenny

15

and found the little, hard bud in the middle. Aisla giggled, one long finger slipping between the cheeks of Elethrine's bottom, finding her anus and poking a little way into the tight ring.

'Don't stop!' Elethrine sighed.

'Now, now, mistress,' Aisla chided, gently. 'It's not the first time I've bathed you. It doesn't do to get so excited.'

'I don't care,' Elethrine breathed. 'Just carry on rubbing like that.'

Aisla made a little tutting noise and made as if to take her hands away.

'Please!' Elethrine begged, hotly.

'I'd better do it for you then,' Aisla replied, 'but be quick, if mother came down . . .'

Elethrine moaned again, abandoning herself utterly to whatever was going to happen. Aisla increased the urgency of her rubbing and slid the finger that had been cleaning Elethrine's bottom ring deep inside the hole. An exquisite feeling began to build up as Aisla's mouth found hers and they began to kiss, lightly at first and then with their tongues twinned together. Aisla's breasts pressed against Elethrine's chest, their nipples hard in mutual pleasure. The muscles of her bottom and thighs began to move of their own accord, wriggling against Aisla's hand and squirming on the finger that was up her bottom. The feeling was becoming unbearable, as if she was about to burst.

'Girls!' A shocked voice rang out from the doorway, shattering Elethrine's blissful state.

Aisla jumped back, leaving Elethrine with a view of Nurse Anaka standing in the doorway with an expression of absolute outrage on her face.

'We – I –' Aisla stammered.

'Strumpets! Dirty, wanton little strumpets!' Nurse Anaka declared. 'Out of the bath, Elethrine! Over the bench, both of you!'

16

'Not naked!' Elethrine retorted, horrified by the sheer indignity of what her nurse was demanding.

'You'll get your formal caning later, in proper style,' Anaka stormed. 'For now, over the bench with both of you, you wanton little sluts, and if you're in your birthday suits, then you should have thought of the consequences before allowing your filthy lust to get the better of you.'

'But . . .' Elethrine began, determined not to suffer the terrible indignity of a naked beating. 'Nurse Anaka, beat Aisla nude if you must, but my father would never permit me to suffer a punishment suitable only for a peasant girl.'

Nurse Anaka paused, her face red with fury. Aisla was already bent over the low wooden bench with her bottom raised for punishment. Her tuppenny and anus were on full show in a nest of dark ginger curls, a position that Elethrine was determined not to be put in. The bench normally served as a seat for Elethrine while she was dried, but was also ideal for girls to be beaten over. Nurse Anaka looked at her daughter, who gave back a look of utter misery and contrition. For a moment the big woman seemed to waver, then her expression hardened.

'No,' she said brusquely, 'you need a sharp lesson, Demoiselle Elethrine Korismund, and being beaten like any common peasant girl may just teach it to you. Should you object, we may happily take the matter before your father, otherwise get over the bench next to Aisla. I shall use a strap on your naughty behind and no more need be said. Well?'

'I shall not!' Elethrine stormed.

'I think you shall,' the nurse replied. 'Otherwise I shall recommend that you be taken out to the blockyard this afternoon. Once there I shall strip your haughty little bottom, whip it well and leave you there for the rest of the day. What is more, I shall get a clerk to write

17

your crime out and have it pinned to your upturned skirts. Then how much will your precious dignity be worth?'

'Father would never permit it,' Elethrine began determinedly, only to stop at the thought that her father might very well permit such a degrading punishment if he were told that she had allowed her base lust to carry her away enough to make love to her maid.

'And think,' Nurse Anaka continued. 'The Princess Talithea visits at any moment. Think how it would feel if the first she saw of you was your blushing red bottom. Now what's it to be?'

'Very well, Nurse Anaka,' Elethrine said, suddenly feeling very crestfallen, 'you may beat me naked.'

The tears were starting in her eyes as she got out of the bath and padded reluctantly across the floor. Aisla looked back at her, the maid's big green eyes full of sympathy. Elethrine tried to smile but felt her mouth curl down at the edges into what she knew was a singularly pathetic and hang-dog expression. She sank slowly to her knees and bent forward, going down over the bench into the same rude position as her maid, bum up and cheeks open, hairy tuppenny and pink bottom ring showing to the woman who was about to beat her.

Nurse Anaka left the room, leaving the two girls with their bums up and ready, not daring to move. Elethrine heard the door to Aisla's room open and then close, and a moment later Nurse Anaka returned, holding the broad leather strap that was normally reserved for Aisla's bottom. Elethrine shut her eyes tight, trying not to whimper and make a display of herself. There was a whistle and then the smack of leather on girl flesh and a squeal from Aisla. Elethrine winced, fought the urge to get up and run and then yelled out loud as the strap came down hard across her naked bottom.

'Ow, Nurse!' she protested an instant before the sound of Aisla's second smack and the resulting squeal rang out.

Elethrine squealed again as the strap once more struck her bottom, the tears starting in her eyes as the pain and shame of being strapped with a belt in the nude became too much for her. Aisla was crying too, a snivelling, sobbing sound suddenly broken by a yelp as the strap hit her. As Elethrine braced herself for the next smack she heard a distant trumpet, sounding from well outside the walls of the keep. The beating stopped abruptly, leaving Elethrine profoundly thankful for what presumably heralded the approach of the Princess's retinue.

'We will finish this later,' Nurse Anaka announced, slightly out of breath from the exertion of taking the strap to the two girls. 'For now we must hurry.'

Both girls got up, hurriedly wiping their tears and rubbing briefly at smarting bottoms before running upstairs. Elethrine stood patiently as she was dressed, trying to ignore the fact that the ignominious beating had done nothing to lessen the hot, urgent feeling in her tuppenny. In fact it was worse, as if adopting such a rude pose and then having her buttocks smacked up to a rosy pink glow was no different than being touched more tenderly. From the swelling of her tuppenny after previous beatings she knew that it happened, but it was now stronger by far.

A second trumpet fanfare announced the arrival of the party at the gates as Elethrine was being laced into her corsets. Glancing towards the south window of her room, she saw the men on the walls start to work the mechanism that controlled the portcullis.

'Hurry!' she urged, as she stepped into her dress while Aisla was still working frantically at the corset laces.

Neither woman answered, but both increased the pace of their work, so that they had Elethrine's bodice half-done by the time a third fanfare announced that the Princess was actually within the walls of the keep.

'You must greet her in the Maiden Garden,' Anaka

19

said as she began to pull Elethrine's hair into a jewelled net.

'I know that!' Elethrine snapped, forgetful of what had just been done to her in the panic of the moment. 'Aisla, put some clothes on, quickly!'

Aisla scurried away, Elethrine getting a last glimpse of her bare white back and pink bottom as she left. Slipping her feet into shoes as Anaka finished her hair, she tried to calm her breathing, knowing that she was far from the cool, decorous young Demoiselle that she wished to appear before the Princess.

Finally she was ready, with the wet parts of her hair artfully concealed in curls and tucks and no more than a mildly uncomfortable damp feeling between her legs. Aisla greeted her at the door, her simple dove-grey dress chosen to complement Elethrine's magnificent gown of rich blue velvet.

Together they walked to the rear door of the Maiden Garden, a tiny walled garden exclusively for the use of highborn women. Normally it was a peaceful, private haven for Elethrine, somewhere she could go to be alone as her mother seldom used it and neither Aisla nor Anaka could enter without her or her mother's permission. Protocol, however, demanded that she greet the Princess there, which seemed to Elethrine something of an invasion of her privacy.

To her relief the garden was empty, but no sooner had she arranged herself on an iron bench in a posture that suggested she had been there all along, than the main door opened and a page ushered a girl of much her own age into the garden.

Elethrine rose and curtsied formally, taking in the appearance of the Princess as she did so. Talithea was slim waisted, full at chest and hip and perhaps half a hand breadth shorter than Elethrine. Her hair was almost white and was bound into a complicated system of plaits and coils that framed an oval face with features

20

of exceptional delicacy. A scattering of freckles across the bridge of her tiny, upturned nose softened a look that would otherwise have been too formal, the whole creating a beauty not far short of Elethrine's opinion of her own looks. Her dress was a deep crimson and even richer than Elethrine's, while slippers of golden leather peeped from under the hem.

'Princess Talithea Mund, third daughter of Utharion V, King,' Elethrine spoke in the correct formal address between their respective ranks. 'I give you welcome to Korismund.'

'Demoiselle Ethrine Korismund, daughter of Karmoth, Baron, I accept your welcome,' the Princess replied.

Elethrine choked down her immediate flush of anger at the contraction of her name and her father's, instead completing their formal introduction and asking if Talithea would care to take refreshment in the Maiden Garden.

When Aisla had left to fetch an infusion of pear blossom, Elethrine attempted less formal conversation, choosing as her topic the dark-leaved, purple-flowered roses, the cultivation of which was something of an obsession among Mundic horticulturists.

'Most fine,' Talithea replied evenly, then paused before continuing, 'for an outland Barony, very fine indeed. Of course in the Royal Botanical Gardens at Theiron we have had pure black flowers for some time now.'

Elethrine found herself bristling but went on trying to be polite.

'You are fortunate in Prince Kavisterion,' she suggested. 'He is a great warrior and exceptionally handsome.'

'He is a monstrous, hirsute oaf,' Talithea responded, 'and a barbarian; broad but rather less tall than your maid and with hair of a colour that suggests more than

21

a touch of peasant blood. He has the manners of a troll and something of one's appearance. Still, one of my rank has little choice in these matters. You, of course, are more fortunate.'

'My nurse,' Elethrine replied, desperately trying to find a topic that the Princess was unable to turn into an insult, 'hopes that I will be ravished, in the old tradition, but I have little hope that any thane would dare the attempt.'

'Indeed,' Talithea answered, 'it is hard to imagine a man of real quality considering the reward worth the risk. Still, perhaps if you were to wear your hair in a more fashionable style and try a little more make-up, you might tempt a man of moderate ambition.'

For a moment Elethrine could find nothing to say but found herself wondering what the consequences would be if she and Aisla were to sit on the haughty Princess and give her a dozen well-deserved cuts of the cane across her thighs. Talithea was relatively small, and Elethrine was sure they could do it and that it would not take many more goads to make her lose her temper completely. At that moment Aisla returned with the infusion and also a companion, immediately reducing the tension.

The newcomer was quite unexpected, being a tiny girl, although quite obviously mature. She stood no higher than Elethrine's chest and was pale skinned with a great amount of jet black hair, a rarity in Mund. Pert breasts constrained within her bodice and neatly rounded hips showed that she was not the child she would otherwise have seemed. Her manner was grave and pensive, her clothing black in every detail.

'May I present Ea, apprentice to the witch Aurora,' Aisla announced, bobbing slightly to Elethrine and Talithea. 'Ea, I present the Princess Talithea Mund, third daughter of Utharion V, King, and my mistress, Demoiselle Elethrine Korismund, daughter of Karmoth, Baron.'

'Elethrine?' Talithea demanded, turning in sudden outrage.

'We hold by the old traditions in these outland Baronies,' Elethrine replied, rather pleased that Aisla had made the mistake of giving her proper name.

'No matter,' Talithea responded, suddenly gay again. 'I shall call you Trina to remind you of your place.'

Elethrine opened her mouth but shut it quickly, sure that whatever retort she made it would only meet with a still more biting response. Short of physically punishing Talithea there was nothing she could do, and the consequences for her would undoubtedly be worse by far.

'So what is this?' Talithea continued in an amused tone as she turned her attention to the newcomer. 'A witch's apprentice, you say?'

'The apprentice to Aurora, who can summon a demon with a single motion of her hand,' Elethrine said, hoping that association with the powerful witch would impress Talithea. 'She is due to stand witness to your betrothal.'

Talithea made no reply but stepped forward.

'She is extraordinarily small,' the Princess remarked as she walked around the witch's tiny apprentice, studying her as if she were a moderately interesting piece of pottery.

'Possibly she is half-elf,' Elethrine suggested, glad that Talithea had found a new mark for her bitter tongue.

'Elf!' Talithea replied with a sharp laugh. 'Whoever heard of a lordly elf condescending to speak to a mere human woman, never mind take her to wife! Especially as, with a name so short, her mother would have to be the lowest of pariahs.'

'It is rumoured,' Elethrine said, mindful of propriety, 'that elven girls have sometimes surrendered to woodsmen, or possibly been taken unawares. They are without doubt winsome, after all.'

23

'Sheer fancy!' Talithea snorted. 'No, she is more likely half-dwarf.'

Aisla laughed, a nervous titter promptly silenced as Elethrine turned to look at her. Ea raised her eyes, and Elethrine found herself staring into them. The apprentice's gaze was more than a little disturbing, her eyes large and lustrous with irises as black and shiny as the pupils. The suggestion that she was half-dwarven was absurd; halflings of dwarven lineage were invariably squat and broad, almost as much so as dwarves themselves.

'Or even half-goblin!' Talithea continued, oblivious to Ea's expression of mounting fury. 'Perhaps on her mother's side!'

'I am one-eighth-part nymph, if you must know!' Ea answered in a hiss, the appalling and impossible insult finally stinging her into refute.

'Oh, look, she is angry! How droll!' Talithea laughed as Ea turned to her. 'Still, we cannot have a lowborn halfling daring to answer us back, can we?'

'Indeed not,' Elethrine answered, unwilling to dispute the Princess despite her caution.

'Then have your maid spank her,' Talithea continued in an amused tone. 'By hand − it will teach the little frippet an important lesson.'

Elethrine hesitated. Having Aisla spank Ea would certainly be amusing, especially as the indignity of a hand spanking was bound to make the tiny apprentice thrash and squeal most beautifully. It was also hard to resist Talithea's forceful personality, yet there was something about Ea that made her nervous. More importantly, seeing Ea punished in such a humiliating way would do something to reduce her own feelings at the way Nurse Anaka had treated her.

'May I speak, mistress,' Aisla put in meekly.

'You may,' Elethrine answered, grateful for the interruption.

24

'Thank you, mistress,' Aisla continued. 'Please forgive my presumption, but might I not strip her nates, the better to bring her punishment home to her.'

'Excellent!' Talithea laughed. 'Bare-bottomed, over the knee of a mere maid! That will truly teach her not to be impudent to her betters! Yes, do it!'

Elethrine felt a rush of anger. Talithea had no right to give Aisla a command, Princess or not. She had also manoeuvred Elethrine into a difficult situation. For Elethrine to support the order would be an admission of her inferiority to Talithea, while if she countermanded it she would look weak. There was only one option that allowed her to retain her dignity, which was to make the punishment more degrading still.

'Yes,' Elethrine said in her most haughty tone, 'do it, but do not merely strip her bottom, strip her naked.'

'Naked?' Aisla asked in obvious alarm.

'Naked,' Elethrine repeated, 'and do not answer me back, or you shall be served the same way.'

'Yes, mistress,' Aisla replied hurriedly.

Elethrine raised her chin, aware that the game had gone far further than they had intended but determined to carry it through. To strip a girl naked and spank her by hand was a punishment considered so degrading to the victim that it was normally reserved for the daughters of peasants, and then only in private. Talithea was looking a little shocked, which pleased Elethrine immensely. Even when Nurse Anaka had beaten Aisla and herself she had not gone so far as to do it by hand, although she had subjected them to just about every other possible degradation.

Ea looked as horrified as was to be expected. Her face, always pale, had gone white. Her little mouth was open in disbelief and her eyes were wide and staring. As Aisla advanced on her she backed away, but instead of the rush of tears that Elethrine expected, the apprentice began to chant and make patterns with her fingers.

Elethrine swallowed hard. She had once seen Aurora summon a great black demon with the body of a monstrous toad and recognised similarities in the apprentice's chant and hand movements.

'Silly child,' Talithea remarked, but her subsequent laugh sounded more than a little strained.

Ea's voice rose to a scream as Aisla backed her into the corner of two tall yew hedges.

'Come quietly,' Aisla remarked firmly, reaching out to take Ea by the arm.

Elethrine relaxed. Whatever invocation Ea had been attempting had evidently failed. She felt her pulse calm and a smile came to her face as Aisla dragged the struggling apprentice away from the corner towards a heavy iron bench. As Aisla got a firm grip, Elethrine and Talithea exchanged glances of malicious delight at the prospect of seeing a naked spanking, their initial antipathy forgotten. Ea fought hard, pulling Aisla's hair out of its net into a cloud of red-gold, an action that caused the maid to give a cry of annoyance and redouble her efforts. A moment later the apprentice's dress was being hauled up over her head, revealing her petticoats and corsets, as black as her dress and worked with purple embroidery and ribbon. With a brisk motion the maid knotted Ea's dress over her head, rendering her helpless. Elethrine felt a disturbing, yet familiar, warm sensation between her legs as Aisla set to work at the stripping, tearing the tiny girl's chemise-bodice open to reveal two breasts not much larger than the halves of a big plum, yet surprisingly womanly.

Ea gave a scream of pure outrage at the exposure of her breasts, but with her dress up she could do nothing. Elethrine laughed at the girl's consternation, glancing once more at Talithea to find the Princess watching the stripping with an expression of rapture. Aisla had pushed Ea onto the wet ground and turned her bottom up. The maid's face was set in mischievous delight as she took hold of Ea's petticoats and began to pull them out from under her corset. Ea kicked and thumped at the ground with her fists as her drawers were exposed. Aisla laughed and whipped off the petticoats, all three at once. Ea began to chant again, her muffled voice pure fury as Aisla began to interfere with the strings of her drawers.

Elethrine found a hard lump in her throat as she watched Ea's legs kick. They were pretty, and sheathed in black silk. A froth of lace, also black, hid the more interesting parts of her trim figure, but Aisla had opened the drawer string and was about to expose it all.

'One . . . two . . . three . . . and off they come!' Aisla chuckled wickedly and pulled Ea's drawers down and off, revealing a pert bottom covered only by black silk pantalettes.

'More black, how pretentious,' Talithea remarked, the hauteur of her voice failing to conceal the underlying lust. 'And silk too, quite inappropriate.'

'Pull them off, Aisla, and throw them to me,' Elethrine said, 'they'll make a nice trophy.'

'No!' Ea screamed and then yelled out another word which Elethrine didn't understand.

Ea was kicking and bucking frantically, putting every effort her small body could muster into trying to prevent Aisla from inflicting the ultimate indignity on her and pulling down her pantalettes. Elethrine found herself grinning and desperately trying to resist the temptation to push against the front of her dress so that her tuppenny rubbed on her purity girdle.

'Say goodbye to your modesty!' Aisla crowed and tugged Ea's pantalettes down.

Elethrine felt a hot flush rise to her face as the girl's pert white bottom was laid bare. Aisla raised her hand and planted a heavy smack on it, making the soft nates wobble delightfully. Another harder smack made them part a little, giving a glimpse of jet-black hair and wet,

27

pink flesh. Two hand marks showed pink against the white skin of the small girl's bottom. A shiver went right through Elethrine at the sight, making her want more of the same; a tiny, round bottom, red all over and parted to show the girl's most intimate secrets. Not just framed by a tangle of dishevelled clothing either, but on a nude, shamed girl.

'Naked!' she ordered.

'Naked! Stark naked!' Talithea echoed frenziedly.

Once more Ea screamed, using the same word as before as her pantalettes were pulled free of her ankles. A scream of utter fury sounded, not from the struggling girl, but from high above. Elethrine looked up, and screamed herself.

High above the castle, a grotesque shape was tumbling towards them in a tangle of wings and other, indeterminate body parts. Elethrine found herself frozen to the spot, her eyes locked on the horror as it untangled itself and the head became apparent, followed by the rest of the thing. Elethrine immediately wished it had stayed hidden.

Vast, leathery wings supported a bony body from which stubby legs and a short, flattened tail stuck out behind. Yet it was the head to which Elethrine's eyes were riveted. The skull was an explosion of bony spikes, from the centre of which two great red eyes stared angrily down, likes the eyes of some nightmare owl. A long beak protruded from between these eyes, with two high-set nostrils on top and a quadruple row of spine-like teeth lining the open jaws.

She heard Talithea echo her scream as the ghastly apparition went into a dive, directly at them. Ea was gabbling frantically, a sound of which Elethrine was barely aware as the demon landed with a rush of air and a great crash of its wings. She heard Aisla scream and then a gigantic claw gripped her body, crushing her against Talithea. Ea screamed out once more and the great demon responded with a furious croak. Its wings beat down and Elethrine was being lifted, whirled high into the air, the walled garden and then the castle itself shrinking with distance beneath her. The shout of a guard and Ea's triumphant yell reached up to her and then, mercifully, everything went black.

2

Exile

Several times Elethrine regained consciousness, only to faint again as the realisation of her predicament returned to her. On each occasion she was vaguely aware of the landscape far below – sea, a great bay, a land of woods and rivers, desert and, on the last occasion, a great arid plain dotted with tiny figures.

The next time her senses returned it was with the shock of being deposited into a snow bank. As her eyes jerked open she caught one final glimpse of the appalling demon, only to see it vanish to a point against a sky of absolute blue. For a long time she lay shivering in the snow, the nightmare journey still fresh in her mind. Finally it was the sight of Aisla's face, full of fright and concern, that brought her back to full sensibility.

'Mistress?' Aisla asked.

Elethrine managed a nod, then pulled herself to one elbow, her need to show strength in front of her maid overcoming her shock.

'The snow is cold, mistress,' Aisla continued. 'We must move down the mountain.'

'Mountain?' Elethrine replied groggily.

'We are on a mountain, a big mountain,' Aisla told her.

'Somewhere on the Spine?' Elethrine asked.

'No, mistress, I don't think so,' Aisla answered quietly.

Elethrine sat up fully. In front of her a long snow-covered slope descended to a belt of evergreens, just as did the upper slopes of the Spine. Beyond the pines, though, the scenery was unlike anything in Mund. The trees gave way to a plateau of sparse blue-green vegetation and rock, which rose again and then ended abruptly at a lip which ran from horizon to horizon in a near straight line. Beyond the lip there was nothing, only the blue of the sky, the haze of distance and a curious area of pale dun colour quite unlike anything of her experience. A glance behind her showed the bulk of a mountain, with others to either flank and yet others, even greater, beyond.

'Where are we?' she managed.

'I don't know, mistress,' Aisla answered. 'I thought perhaps with your better teaching . . .'

'Nothing in my lessons spoke of a mountain range that ends in thin air,' Elethrine replied. 'Could it be the edge of the world?'

'No, mistress,' Aisla said. 'What you see is a great cliff, below which is a plain. I saw it from the air.'

'You stayed awake?' Elethrine asked. 'Through that!'

'Yes, mistress,' Aisla said. 'I awoke several times. We have crossed Aegmund, the Aeg Roads and lands beyond that sea which I know nothing of. We are far to the south.'

Aisla broke off, looking ready to cry, which made Elethrine feel stronger, despite the knowledge that the maid seemed to have taken less shock then she at the experience of being snatched and carried by the demon.

'Come then,' she said, getting to her feet and then suddenly remembering the Princess Talithea.

Elethrine looked around as Aisla began to brush snow from her dress. A blotch of crimson in a deep drift a little way up the mountain side showed where the Princess lay, apparently still insensible.

'What of the Princess Talithea?' she asked Aisla.

31

'I do not know, my first duty being to you, mistress,' Aisla replied.

'Then we must see to her,' Elethrine announced, her authority beginning to return along with a hint of satisfaction that the sharp-tongued Princess had proved the weakest of the three of them.

Talithea lay in the snow, her red dress and pale hair spread out around her. Shaking her produced no response, and Elethrine finally managed to rouse her by rubbing snow in her face. Her immediate response was outrage, and then shock as her memory came back to her. In the end Elethrine and Aisla had to help her to her feet. She was weak as they set off, pausing frequently to rest, but by the time they reached the tree line something of her normal personality was beginning to reassert itself.

'I can manage on my own,' she said sharply. 'Now hurry, we must return to Korismund Keep before Prince Kavisterion arrives.'

'I fear there is little chance of that,' Elethrine replied. 'We are not in Korismund, nor yet Mund, nor yet even on the continent Kora. We appear to be somewhere in the centre of the continent Apraya.'

'Apraya!' Talithea snorted. 'Nonsense, look at the sun. We have been gone no more than three or four hours.'

'With respect, Princess,' Aisla replied, 'it is the afternoon of the third day following our bewitchment.'

Talithea stopped, to stare blankly around her as if becoming aware of her surroundings for the first time. As the Princess looked around, Elethrine also took stock. The trees, while superficially similar to the pines and spruces of Mund, grew less straight and had foliage shaded a tone more towards blue. The sky was also an impossible rich blue and absolutely cloudless, a condition almost unknown in Mund. Finally there was the lip of the cliff and the great chasm of shimmering air beyond it, a sight quite out of character with the clear, cool vistas of Mund.

Slowly Talithea's expression of bewilderment faded, to be replaced by a commanding and determined look.

'Very well,' she announced, 'so we have been flung to the wilds of Apraya. In that case we shall demand an honour guard, return to Thieron and impose justice on the brat Ea. Come.'

She set off through the trees, Elethrine and Aisla following with considerably less confidence. Beyond the trees a thin stream ran across their course with the plateau beyond it. They paused to drink and wash before continuing, each girl stripping nervously, Elethrine and Talithea to their purity girdles, Aisla nude. Talithea made the greatest fuss, insisting that the others kept careful watch with their backs turned while she went through the laborious process of undressing without help and washed herself.

Proceeding, it became possible to see white shapes on the horizon, possibly human. These were in ones, twos and occasionally small groups, distributed along the top of the cliff. The girls approached cautiously, aiming for a lone figure and finding it to be a thin, sinewy man with skin the colour of a hazelnut shell and a great beak of a nose. He wore only a loose white robe and was staring fixedly out over the cliff.

'Aisla,' Elethrine said as they came close, 'from his clothes this is clearly some local peasant. Speak to him and establish in what land we are and in what direction lies the nearest keep or town.'

'Very well, mistress,' Aisla replied and walked on, coughing gently when she was directly behind the man.

He turned, his expression at first one of mild curiosity, then of astonishment.

'Good peasant,' Aisla said, ignoring his apparent surprise. 'I am Aisla, an artisan of Korismund, and I desire information.'

When she spoke the man's eyebrows rose high onto his wrinkled forehead, showing even greater surprise. There was a long silence before he replied.

'You are not snow-dryads then, come to ensorcell me?' he said, his accent strange yet by no means incomprehensible. 'Nor the daughters of frost titans?'

'Neither,' Aisla replied.

'Nor yet some exotic breed of nymph, escaped from your owners?' he queried.

'Certainly not!' Talithea snapped, forgetting propriety.

'We are from Mund, far to the north,' Aisla explained. 'Perhaps you saw the great demon that carried us?'

'Indeed!' the man replied. 'An eighth arc of the sun or more ago. It flew directly over my head, causing great alarm both to myself and to those on the plain. They take it for an omen and have disengaged from battle. But who, or what, are you, to be transported by demon, and with such strange clothing?'

'We fell foul of a witch,' Aisla explained, 'and find ourselves banished to this strange land. Perhaps you can tell us where we are and advise us on how to obtain a guard for the journey back.'

'Remarkable,' the man said, 'and a fine tale. Give me the details, that I may amuse and astonish my fellow villagers, and in return I shall give my best advice as an elder. But who are your companions?'

'Very well,' Aisla replied, 'we thank you. My companions are my Mistress, the Demoiselle Elethrine Korismund, daughter of Dakarmoth, Baron Korismund. Also the Princess Talithea Mund, third daughter of King Utharion V.'

'Remarkable,' he repeated. 'I am, simply, Ghutanisip.'

'That is a fine name,' Elethrine said, surprised by the implication of the long name. 'I apologise if we have

34

been discourteous by not speaking, but from your dress we thought you merely a peasant. From the length of your name I understand you to be a noble of high degree.'

'Your remarks puzzle me,' he answered, 'and I suspect that our customs differ somewhat. My clothing is simple and practical for the heat of the plain. As to my status, I am a village elder, no more.'

'Your rank is perhaps similar to that of a squire . . .' Elethrine continued uncertainly, 'whom I might speak to. Princess?'

'I feel it best to remain aloof,' Talithea replied.

'As you wish,' the man replied. 'Yet if you have a long journey ahead of you it would seem ill advised not to converse with those you meet. Personally I will speak to any who will lend an ear.'

'Then I would be happy for your advice,' Elethrine replied.

'Come close to the edge then,' he suggested, 'that you may observe the battle while we talk.'

'What battle is this?' Aisla queried.

Elethrine walked forward until she could see down onto the plain below. On it, two armies faced each other, the individual men appearing the size of ants.

'Observe,' the old man said, 'to the left are the men of the great city Oretes, to the right those of Imperial Vendjome. In the distance, where the smoke rises, is the city Reites, which has changed ownership twelve times in my lifetime. At present it is held by Vendjome, and the Oreteans seek to take it. The Vendjomois have, however, sprung a cunning trap, striking here to the south in an effort to encircle the Oretean forces. Unfortunately for them they have come up against a small Oretean force intent, so I suspect, on a similar manoeuvre. This is much to my annoyance as it has meant evacuating the village until they finish their dispute.'

35

'And to which realm do you owe allegiance?' Elethrine queried.

'Neither,' Ghutanisip replied. 'Both realms claim the Glissade Mountains as theirs, and both send tax gatherers. When they do we simply retreat to the mountains and throw rocks down at them. If they burn the village then it is little loss and indeed reduces the spread of pestilence.'

'These mountains are the Glissades then?' Elethrine asked. 'I have never heard the name.'

'Then you are from far indeed,' he continued. 'But see, when your demon appeared they were engaged in a fine disagreement, and now they prepare to restart. Presumably both have taken new auguries. Observe those in the purple cloaks, they are a detachment of the Imperial Guard of Vendjome. Unless I am mistaken, they intend to attempt to break through to the tent of the Oretean general, which is guarded by squares of dwarven mercenaries.'

'They will not succeed,' Aisla said, her voice showing more than a little excitement.

'How so?' Ghutanisip demanded.

'Each square is a double line of pikemen with a squad of archers in the interior,' Aisla explained. 'They can hold against the heaviest cavalry.'

'Remarkable knowledge for a young girl,' Ghutanisip replied.

'Her father is armourer and master-at-arms,' Elethrine explained. 'But, putting the battle aside, how would you advise us to travel north in safety?'

'Your friend with the extraordinary hair has hinted at it,' Ghutanisip went on. 'Note that the Vendjomois also employ dwarven mercenaries, who are notoriously tough. When the battle has finished, simply follow the stream down to the plain, engage a hand of mercenaries at a price higher than that the Vendjomois are paying and give them your instructions.'

36

'By what route would you advise?' Aisla asked. 'And why is my hair extraordinary?'

'What price should we offer the dwarves?' Elethrine added.

'Only one route is possible,' Ghutanisip explained, 'as I thought the whole world knew. Travel east and north to the Ephraxis River, then up it as it flows through the Eigora Khum. Beyond that I have no knowledge save that dwarves come from that direction and so should not be adverse to returning. As to your hair, once I travelled to Vendjome itself, and in the market I saw two girls with golden hair who were the marvel of all and sold for six hundred gold imperials the pair.'

'Sold?' Elethrine asked in shock.

'Sold,' Ghutanisip repeated. 'They were slaves. Other tales of golden-haired maidens exist in plenty, and, as you may know, elves have white hair rather like that of your quiet friend. Hair the colour of the metal copper I have never heard of, and doubtless all three of you would fetch high prices in Vendjome. Should you wish to avoid slavery I strongly advise covering your heads until you have secured the protection of a dwarven guard. Once you have, then you will be safe enough. As to price, I understand that they ask one imperial a week of the Vendjomois, which is roughly the worth of a goat. It is a high price, but should you be unable to match it, an offer of pleasure should sway the balance.'

'Pleasure?' Elethrine demanded.

'Pleasure,' Ghutanisip said. 'If you, Aisla, have knowledge of dwarven warfare, then you will also know that they are partial to the use of the mouths of human girls, their own women being somewhat short in the throat and sharp toothed to boot. The opportunity of mouth service from three girls of your height and appearance should weigh heavy in the scale.'

'What! Kiss a dwarf! There!' Talithea exclaimed. 'Never!'

'What of you?' Ghutanisip asked the others with a shrug.

'Indeed not!' Elethrine responded. 'Even Aisla is of too high a status for such a thing.'

'Then why are her cheeks the colour of the setting sun?' he asked with a smile.

'I –' Aisla stammered as all three of them turned to look at her.

'Out with it girl,' Elethrine demanded.

'I – I –' Aisla managed, blushing crimson. 'When that troop passed through last year and they stayed in the shippen, they tricked me into coming to them by asking for more bread and then offered me some pretty stones – serpentine, jade and tiger's eye. I, er . . . took them.'

'And?' Elethrine demanded.

'Sucked each one's cock,' Aisla admitted, speaking in a whisper and looking shamefaced at the ground.

'Each one's? There were thirty of them!'

'Sulia the Milkmaid was there too,' Aisla said, defensively.

'So you sucked the cocks of fifteen dwarves!' Elethrine exclaimed. 'Had I known, you would have been in the blockyard for a week, you slut! Sulia also. Well, I hope you enjoyed the taste, because it seems likely that there will have been a further five dwarven men to satisfy before we see Korismund again! Slut!'

'Yes, mistress,' Aisla said, quietly.

Elethrine turned away, pretending to study the battle below but thinking how Aisla must have felt as one dwarf after another presented his cock for her attention. It was a disgusting thought and must have left her looking as if she had been used by goblins, with come all over her face, in her hair, on her hands and down her front. Elethrine shivered, half-disgusted, half wondering what a dwarf's cock looked like, or any cock for that matter.

On the plain the Vendjomois Imperial guard were

moving out from between the wings of their army at a trot. Their pace increased to a canter and then a full gallop as they closed on the massed squares of dwarves. The charge looked magnificent, with their lances and armour gleaming in the sun and their purple cloaks streaming out behind them.

As Aisla had predicted, they might as well have charged the cliff and Elethrine estimated that only around half rode back the way they had come, leaving the stubborn dwarven formations hardly disturbed.

'Gallant, but foolish,' Talithea commented.

'True,' Ghutanisip agreed, 'but if you wish to reach their camp by sundown I would advise starting off. Should some disaster occur you can always turn back, but if the Vendjomois retreated in good order you might find it hard to keep up.'

'Indeed,' Elethrine agreed, 'and I thank you on behalf of us all and of Mund, wishing only that we could reward you in some way. Perhaps you would accept this ring?'

'Keep your trinket,' Ghutanisip replied, 'but remember your half of the bargain. You must tell me how you came to fall foul of the witch, and while you are about it – as you are so ready to order Aisla to provide intimate service to dwarves perhaps she, or yourself, would care to oblige me?'

'I . . .' Elethrine began, horrified by the suggestion and the casual way he had proposed it but filled with the urge to see what his cock looked like. She was, after all, a long way from home and nobody need know, while it could be argued that honour demanded acceding to his request by way of payment.

'Very well,' she said instead. 'Aisla, perform your duty as you have already disgraced yourself by far worse actions.'

Aisla grimaced but made no protest and a glance at Talithea showed that she seemed rather to like the idea

39

of making Aisla suck the man's cock. He was grinning and was already pulling up his robe, revealing skinny legs, then his penis and a round, wrinkled scrotum. Elethrine swallowed at the sight, feeling a little scared even though it was no threat to her. Dark brown and smaller than the goblin's, Ghutanisip's cock had already begun to swell, moving sluggishly as Aisla got to her knees in front of him.

Elethrine watched in mingled disgust and fascination as her maid reached out and touched the old man's penis, then took it between fingers and thumb and began to pull at it. She leant forward, seemed to hesitate, then opened her mouth wide and quickly gulped it in. As she began to suck his expression changed from lechery to pleasure, and his weather-beaten old face was fixed on the sight of his cock going in and out of the beautiful girl's mouth. His cock was soon rock hard, protruding from her mouth as she tickled the underside of his balls. Her position left her bottom high, filling Elethrine with the urge to beat her while she sucked as a punishment for her wantonness.

Occasionally she would pull back to lick at the tip of his erection, showing what Elethrine considered suspicious expertise. When she did this Elethrine got her first look at an erect penis, finding it both irresistible and terrifying. A long brown shaft supported a bulbous head of glossy, red-brown flesh with a ring of almost black meat below it. It looked both powerful and obscene, a very suitable thing for poking into girls' secret places. The very knowledge that it was designed to go inside her tuppenny made her shiver, yet she knew that it was what she badly needed.

As his excitement increased he took Aisla by the hair and circled the base of his erection with his fingers. She made no move to stop him as he began to masturbate into her mouth, but put a hand to her bodice and began to stroke at her breasts through the material. Aisla's eyes were shut, either in shame or pleasure as she kneaded her breasts and Elethrine found herself feeling increasingly uncomfortable. There was a strong urge to get down beside Aisla and share the stiff little cock, but it was an urge she knew she had to resist, especially in front of Talithea.

Nevertheless it was hard, and she was almost at the point of forgetting herself when his cock suddenly jerked and Aisla gasped and sucked her cheeks in. Then something white was dribbling from around the sides of the maid's mouth and Elethrine knew that he had come inside it. A strong shiver passed right through her as her maid pulled back and then obligingly licked the remaining come from the old man's cock. She sat back and gulped, quite clearly swallowing her mouthful.

'Disgusting slut!' Talithea remarked, but Elethrine caught the catch in her voice.

Ghutanisip listened to a somewhat abridged version of their story from Elethrine, occasionally raising his eyebrows or making an appropriate remark. In the end he thanked them, suggested that witches were better left alone and added the comment that nobody would believe him.

They thanked him and left, Elethrine feeling more than a little disturbed as they followed the stream. As Ghutanisip had said it would, it followed a long gully that came out at the cliff bottom a good league to the east of the Vendjomois camp. From the top of the gully the descent looked dangerous, a jagged path among crumbling pinnacles and great boulders that appeared to defy gravity. With little choice in the matter they started down, Elethrine finding that the path, while difficult, was no worse than the mountain tracks along the Spine.

'How much wealth do we command?' she asked as they came out onto a broad ledge above the stream.

'I carry no coin whatever,' Talithea replied, 'as is

suitable to my rank. Still I have seven rings, four of them with fine stones. Moreover, we can give bond of payment on reaching Thieron.'

'In my experience dwarves prefer hard coin,' Elethrine answered. 'Yet I also have rings and perhaps together we will have enough. A gold imperial must be small if one buys only a single goat. Aisla, what is the price of a goat at home?'

'Perhaps a one twelfth thalar piece,' Aisla replied uncertainly.

'My dark-emerald ring alone cost eighty thalars,' Talithea put in.

'Which,' Elethrine replied, calculating quickly, 'would be nine hundred and sixty goats, and thus sufficient to pay a hand of dwarves for one hundred and ninety two weeks, or three years, thirty eight weeks and four days – surely enough to travel a distance far greater than three days by demon. We need perhaps twelve weeks, so my band of red-gold should suffice for their payment. Excellent, we need not fear for our virtue; not even yours, Aisla, though you may be sure that I intend to punish you severely for your disgusting behaviour.'

'Yes, mistress,' Aisla replied nervously.

'Perhaps you should do it now?' Talithea suggested.

'You are right,' Elethrine agreed, realising that nothing would soothe her inner feelings of nervousness and anger more than taking it out on the unfortunate maid's bottom. 'Aisla, get over that rock and stick your bottom out. I shall spank you with my slipper.'

Aisla gave them a single miserable look and bent over the rounded boulder Elethrine had indicated. Talithea watched as Elethrine lifted the maid's dress and petticoat. Aisla gave a little sob as her drawers were pulled open and her bottom exposed, a sweet orb of girlish delight with a puff of deep red hair showing between her thighs.

'Part your legs,' Elethrine ordered as she bent to remove her dainty leather slipper.

The maid sobbed again, a sound combining both misery and passion. As her feet came apart so her thighs opened, exposing the pouted rear lips of her tuppenny, the centre of which was pink and distinctly moist.

'As I thought, she is excited, the little slut,' Talithea said.

Elethrine said nothing but brought the slipper down hard across her maid's naked bottom, making the cheeks bounce and quiver. As always, punishing Aisla was deeply satisfying, yet it also never failed to bring the heat to her own sex. The maid squeaked as another slap landed across her bottom but raised herself on tiptoe and pulled her back in, adding the exposure of her anus to the humiliation of her position.

Incensed by the lewdness of Aisla's display, Elethrine grabbed the maid around the waist and began to belabour the squirming buttocks with hard slaps of the slipper. Aisla was soon squealing and kicking, thrashing her bottom beautifully while Talithea watched the beating with an expression of utter delight. Finally Elethrine decided that she was satisfied and stood back, leaving Aisla bent over the rock, sobbing loudly and massaging two cherry-red bum cheeks. Between them her tuppenny was an open pink oval, like the centre of a small tart and clearly ready for entry.

'You truly are a slut, Aisla,' Elethrine remarked with satisfaction as she put her slipper back on. 'You may cover your shame now as we had best press on.'

Aisla hastily covered her bottom and followed the others, snivelling slightly from her spanking but quickly becoming more cheerful. The act of beating her had increased the confidence, not only of the punishers, but also of the punished.

'There is also, of course, a somewhat delicate problem,' Elethrine said after a moment.

'Indeed,' Talithea replied. 'My key is at the bottom of my matron-in-waiting's strong box.'

'And mine on a ribbon around Nurse Anaka's neck,' Elethrine added.

'Possibly dwarven troops travel with some sort of Matron?' Talithea suggested.

'She would also need to be a locksmith,' Elethrine pointed out, glumly.

'They must have an armourer, mistress,' Aisla said.

'And so we must lift our skirts and split our drawers for the attentions of a dwarven smith?' Elethrine snapped back. 'The humiliation would be unendurable. Besides, he would be bound to mount us. How could he resist?'

'I would willingly drain him of jism first,' Aisla offered. 'For the sake of your chastity.'

'For your own pleasure more like,' Talithea laughed. 'Do not forget, girl, we have seen you with your mouth engorged with cock. And don't think we didn't notice that you were unable to resist playing with yourself.'

'Still,' Elethrine broke in, 'your offer is a worthy one.'

They fell silent, turning their attention to negotiating a cluster of boulders that linked the ledge to a stretch of ground that led to the cliff base. A league to the east rose the characteristic square tents of a dwarven encampment. As Ghutanisip had also predicted, the two armies were breaking apart as dusk fell, yet the Vendjomois showed no disposition to break camp. Mindful of his comments on the Vendjomois habit of slave-taking but reluctant to suffer the shame of covering their hair, they stole carefully along the base of the cliff, keeping in the shadows until they came close to the dwarven encampment. A single sentry guarded it, leaning on a pike.

Unlike Ghutanisip he showed only mild curiosity, a typically dwarven trait. On learning that they wanted to hire mercenaries he simply called up a companion and instructed him to take the three girls to the tent of the Stipulator. This proved to be the second largest tent and was crowded with dwarves. At the rear a heavily scarred, grey-haired dwarf sat behind a trestle. To his side was a squat, balding dwarf with a sheet of charta in front of him and an exaggeratedly long stylus in his hand. Elethrine had Aisla perform introductions, a ritual that caused no more than a flicker of surprise to cross the Stipulator's features. She then stood forward, preferring to conduct the negotiations herself rather than trust to Talithea's high-handed attitude and uncertain temper.

'So, Demoiselle, what do you require?' the Stipulator asked.

'A hand of mercenaries for a period of three months or more and the services of a smith, preferably female,' Elethrine answered.

'I doubt that there is a female dwarf within a thousand leagues,' he answered. 'We do, however, have a smith in tent L5, whose services you may command at the usual scale of fees. As to mercenaries, we are currently receiving one gold imperial of Vendjome per week. Should you be able to better this offer, there will be no difficulty.'

'Indeed we can,' Elethrine replied pulling her red-gold ring free. 'We estimate that this finely engraved band of red-gold should be more than adequate payment.'

The Stipulator's eyebrows rose before he turned on Elethrine a most undwarven look of incredulity.

'For five men? For three months? Why, there is less gold than in a single imperial.'

'It is a work of art,' Elethrine explained, 'and cost twenty gold thalars, which, from what you say, are perhaps twice the size of an imperial and we feel worth perhaps twelve times as much.'

'You gave perhaps forty weights of gold for one weight in a different shape?' he asked in disbelief. 'I have always thought humans lacked sense, but this is ludicrous. Let us weigh your gold and we will come to a sensible price.'

Reluctantly Elethrine and Talithea removed their rings and placed them on a small scale that stood by the clerk. In total they weighed as much as five imperials.

'There we are, a simple, honest and indisputable measure,' the Stipulator declared. 'The gold entitles you to one hand for a week at Vendjomois wages. The stones are also valuable and being girls you will of course wish to give service and thus outbid our current employers.'

'One week!' Talithea exclaimed. 'The red-haired maid can give service – but one week!'

The Stipulator shrugged.

'Surely we can reach a settlement,' Elethrine went on. 'In Mund our fathers will provide as much gold as you care to ask.'

'Payment is accepted only in advance,' the clerk spoke for the first time. 'What if a guard were to fall in combat? What use then all the gold in Mund?'

'I advise giving details,' the Stipulator said, 'so that a notice may be posted in the mess hall. If you are for Mund then it may be that some of our number will accept a lesser price to guard you as far as Ar-Kian or perhaps even Utan, from which you may take ship for Aegmund. To reach either would take a month or more, but who knows. You are young, beautiful and appear healthy, so you might tempt. Give the clerk your details.'

'Very well,' Elethrine sighed, turning to the clerk who was already picking their names out on the pale surface of the charta.

'Five gold imperials,' he mumbled, 'five jewels, and the service of three exquisite human maids.'

'One maid,' Talithea interrupted. 'I am a princess and do not so debase myself.'

'Nor I,' Elethrine answered.

'One?' the clerk responded. 'Your expectations are extravagant. Your offer might tempt two guards, just

46

possibly three if she could serve with mouth, cunt and anus each night. But a hand? Never!'

'Then we shall have three guards,' Elethrine replied, shivering at the clerk's crudeness.

'Impossible,' the clerk answered. 'During the course of hostilities between Vendjome and Oretea no group of less than one hand may travel abroad – by order. Five imperials and the services of your fine maid might pay your way as far as Gora-Jome on the Ephraxis, but there you would certainly be taken as slaves immediately our contract ended. The Vendjomois are a greedy, lustful and not altogether honourable race.'

Elethrine paused, trying to come to terms with the idea of accepting one or more dwarven cocks in her mouth every night for perhaps two months. The idea at once disgusted her and filled her with longing, yet that of slavery with terror and defiance. She glanced at Talithea, finding the Princess biting her lip in uncertainty.

'Very well,' she said quietly. 'I offer what you call mouth service.'

'And I,' Talithea added, in an almost inaudible whisper.

'Not cunt?' the clerk asked in a voice loud enough to be clearly audible throughout the tent.

'We are maiden,' Elethrine answered.

'I am not sure that I understand the concept,' the clerk went on. 'You take life partners don't you? Does being maiden mean that you can only accept your life partner in your cunts?'

'Yes,' Elethrine answered, blushing furiously.

'The first to do so becomes the life partner,' Aisla explained. 'It is a great honour for both man and maiden, but for a noble or royal maiden to submit to someone not of her rank is unthinkable.'

'Aha,' the clerk replied, evidently not understanding at all. 'So you can only take pleasure up your bottoms before finding a life partner – I'll put that down.'

47

'No!' all three girls exclaimed in unison.

'That is the most dirty and debased of acts!' Elethrine added.

'It is?' the Stipulator put in. 'Several human women of my acquaintance take great pleasure in it.'

'Yet it is still unthinkable,' Aisla explained.

'So you enjoy it, but it's unthinkable?' the Stipulator asked, sounding greatly puzzled.

'Yes, I mean no,' Elethrine stammered and then shut up hastily before admitting to the unpardonable sin of enjoying the thought of the penetration of her anus.

'So will you do it or not?' the clerk asked testily.

'No,' Elethrine replied.

'Very well,' the clerk answered, 'but I hold little hope for your expedition if you persist in taking such a prissy attitude. May I at least put down that you will strip for their pleasure?'

'Certainly not!' Talithea answered.

'No,' Elethrine said, 'yet I will have Aisla serve bare breasted at meals.'

'Good, but still not sufficient,' the clerk went on. 'Anything more?'

'Perhaps it would amuse them to watch Aisla beaten?' Elethrine asked uncertainly.

'Indeed it would,' the clerk answered with an appreciative glance to Aisla. 'I still doubt that your offer is sufficient, yet you are beautiful and so we shall see.'

'And what of the armourer?' Elethrine asked.

'Tent L5, as I said,' the Stipulator replied. 'What is the job and how will you pay?'

'Is that not a matter between us and the armourer?' Elethrine asked, blushing at the thought of explaining her intimate needs in front of thirty or so dwarves.

'Not at all,' the Stipulator explained. 'We agree the price and you take a docket to the armourer.'

'We, er, we need our purity girdles removed,' Elethrine managed.

48

'And this is a job for an armourer?' the Stipulator queried.

'They are locked,' Elethrine said, blushing crimson, 'and made of brazen mesh with a heavy lock of iron at the front.'

'Mine is silver,' Talithea put in, with a curious mixture of pride and embarrassment.

'Silver?' the Stipulator asked, drawing a nod from Talithea. 'Then let us set the rate of work at two weights of silver and the balance can be added to the offer for your guard hand. The brass will perhaps cover some of the cost of your food.'

'Very well,' Elethrine said, glancing quickly to Talithea for approval. 'Might we also eat?'

'There is gruel in the mess hall, free for all,' he answered. 'Wine and meat may be had at a surcharge.'

'Thank you,' Elethrine said, withdrawing with a curtsy judged appropriate to her estimation of the Stipulator's rank.

'Let us eat first,' Talithea said as they left the tent.

'No, please,' Elethrine replied, 'if we must undergo this undignified ordeal let us get it done quickly.'

'In other words you are at risk of soiling your undergarments,' Talithea replied shrewishly. 'Come then, it is bad enough to have to present our bare tuppennies to a dwarven smith, let alone with soiled pantalettes to add to our disgrace.'

They set off, Elethrine hurrying despite the prospect of the humiliating experience she was about to undergo. Not only was there the problem of having her purity girdle removed and of the intimate exposure such an operation would entail, but of whether to order Aisla to slake the smith's lust first and thus risk making a mess of herself. Finally she decided that she had no choice, as she was certain that any male presented with the sight of her bare pink tuppenny would be quite unable to resist mounting her on the instant unless he was

49

physically incapable. Even if Aisla drained him it was a risk. A virile male might manage to have her anyway, yet she had no choice.

They quickly found tent L5, each row and column of the encampment being clearly signposted. Inside was a forge and a massively built dwarf whose head came close to the level of Elethrine's bodice. He accepted the docket without question, read the task description, grunted and asked Talithea to lie on the table.

'One moment,' Elethrine interrupted, 'for reasons of our own we feel it necessary for my maid Aisla to offer you mouth service before you commence work.'

'That is uncommonly generous,' the armourer answered, looking up in mild surprise. 'She is a great beauty, and I gladly accept.'

'Go on, Aisla,' Elethrine ordered, trying to ignore her unworthy feelings of delight at the prospect of seeing her second-ever penis and of watching her maid suck it.

Aisla got down on her knees and went through a similar procedure to that which she had used to thank Ghutanisip for his advice. The smith's cock came out of his trousers and into Aisla's mouth, stiffening rapidly to a stubby thickness that she was barely able to get her lips around. As before, she used her tongue and lips with an agility and skill that looked to Elethrine suspiciously like the result of long experience. It was certainly effective because, almost before Aisla had got into the rhythm of her task, he filled her mouth with an extraordinary quantity of thick sperm, most of which spurted out to run down his shaft and onto his great, hairy balls. As Elethrine stared open-mouthed at the sight she became aware of a scent – rich, musky and reminiscent of something that she could not bring to memory. Aisla dutifully licked the come up and swallowed, then stood up with her eyes twinkling, a mischievous little smile on her lips.

'Strumpet,' Talithea remarked, which Elethrine

thought unfair as the Princess had watched the entire process in fascination.

'Don't forget you'll be doing it yourself soon enough,' Elethrine answered, causing the blood to go straight to Talithea's face.

'I shall not simper and smirk afterwards!' the Princess retorted, hotly.

'Right now, these girdles,' the smith said, defusing what might otherwise have flared into an argument.

'Quite,' Elethrine said, 'now I must ask that you wear a hood or something while you work.'

'Work blindfold?' the smith demanded. 'In such a sensitive area?'

'I . . .' Elethrine began and then stopped, abandoning her reserve in her desperation to get the girdle free. 'Very well, it seems I must show myself to you, but be quick.'

The smith merely shrugged and indicated a broad, low bench. Elethrine sat down with her legs to either side and then lay back. As the bench was designed for dwarves the position left her feet on the floor and her knees up. With a flush of pure shame she spread her thighs and began to pull up her skirts and petticoats, her only consolation being that they were her best and of a quality too fine for Talithea to make any barbed remarks.

Elethrine saw that Talithea was watching with interest. Unable to bear watching them inspect her tuppenny, she closed her eyes and pulled open her drawers and pantalettes, exposing the lock of her purity girdle.

'Mm,' the smith said, 'this is a dwarven lock, not easy to pick. Mm, no, it will be easier to cut the brass chain links.'

'Very well, but quickly, please,' Elethrine answered.

A moment later she felt a pressure against her belly and heard the snick of a link being cut. The sound

51

produced a sharp pang of shame, and lust. Her purity girdle was being cut off, and not by some lust-crazed thane unable to resist her beauty but by a squat, dwarven smith who smelt of oil and charcoal. As another link snapped, and then a third, her shame intensified. She could feel the moisture of her tuppenny and knew that the others would see how excited she was – possibly they would even smell the aroma of hot, aroused girl when the heavily padded girdle was pulled free from between her legs. Worse still – as the cutters continued their work – was the knowledge that had the dwarf mounted her she would have done nothing to resist but merely spread her thighs wider to accommodate him in her virgin tuppenny.

Elethrine kept her eyes closed but was unable to stop her lust rising as the girdle was cut away. It was something she had always dreamed of, having her girdle removed prior to ravishment by the man bold enough to take her. Now she knew just how willing she would have been, probably helping instead of putting up the resistance that protocol required. She moaned aloud as the final link snapped, her brain a welter of lust and need. The smith pulled the girdle down, exposing her swollen, wet tuppenny for all to see. Elethrine moaned again, wondering if the dwarf would manage to have her. He had, after all, removed her girdle and so it was his right. She wanted his lovely, fat cock rammed home inside her, stretching her, tearing her maidenhead . . .

Talithea's giggle brought Elethrine sharply down to earth and she got up, her face crimson with blushes. A moment more and she would have asked the smith to mount her. The knowledge made her burn with shame. As she smoothed her skirts the smith indicated the bench to Talithea. Elethrine went to stand by Aisla, unable to resist watching the Princess have her purity girdle removed.

As Elethrine herself had done, Talithea shut her eyes.

She was also blushing and clinging onto the bench, too full of chagrin to lift her own skirts but instead allowing the smith to do it. He did so without fuss, showing none of the triumph or curiosity that a normal man would have had while pulling up a girl's skirts. He was, however, wearing a grin that was more than a little lustful, and Elethrine wondered if Talithea was going to be mounted.

The Princess's underwear was magnificent, filling Elethrine with jealousy. The crimson dress hid an underskirt of dark, rose pink, which in turn covered four petticoats, each of a paler pink than the last and heavily trimmed with lace and, in one case, fur. Beneath that, her drawers were made of heavy silk, embroidered and coloured the most delicate coral. When the smith pulled them apart it was to reveal pantalettes of pure white silk of an even heavier grade. These came open to reveal a purity girdle fashioned of silver chain and closed with a lock that appeared to be solid silver.

Talithea lay spread out on the bench, breathing softly, her legs wide to show off the pale skin of her inner thighs. The smith rubbed his chin, for a moment put his hand to his crotch and then turned to the work bench, taking not the cutters but a thin nail. This he inserted into Talithea's lock, wiggled, twisted and then withdrew as the catch sprang open.

'Human locks – rubbish,' he muttered with satisfaction as he pulled at the lock.

It came apart, exposing Talithea's sweet, bare tuppenny. Elethrine gasped, partly a reaction at the indecency of seeing the Princess spread-eagled so rudely and partly at the sheer beauty of Talithea's sex. The mound was covered in pale blonde fur as soft and fine as duck down. The lips formed a neat, bulging purse and were slightly swollen, hinting at the contents. Rudest, and most appealing, was the way Talithea stayed in place, clearly expectant of being mounted and entered.

Elethrine waited with her breath held. Talithea was surely more than any man could resist and the smith was bound to whip his cock out and mount her at any moment. The idea of watching the Princess's maidenhead taken appealed to Elethrine immensely, more even than the thought of seeing the haughty young woman's bottom stripped and beaten.

'Come on then, you're done,' the smith said jovially, breaking the spell.

Talithea closed her thighs and sat up in a hurry, her face crimson with blushes. Elethrine – feeling more disturbed than ever – made a hasty exit in search of some privacy.

3

Protectee

Elethrine reined in her camel with some difficulty. All day they had ridden across a vast, flat plain broken only by the occasional shallow water course and copses of a curious tree with leaves like sword blades.

Ghutanisip had been right about travelling with dwarves, and as they had proceeded Elethrine had become more and more grateful for the old man's advice. Several times on the road they had passed groups of soldiers, each one of which had cast curious, lustful eyes at her, Talithea and Aisla. None, however, had dared to dispute their right of passage, even though the squares of raw silk that they had been persuaded to use to cover their hair did little to hide their foreign nature. Elethrine could see only too well that, without the pentagon of heavily armed dwarves that surrounded them, things would have been very different.

At first the idea of escorting them north had been received with only moderate interest, but as soon as they had walked into the mess hall that had changed. Finally the hand had had to be chosen by prestige of arms, a process that had resulted in a bodyguard that satisfied even the Princess.

At the apex of the pentagon rode the hand leader, Karogan, a massive, grey-haired dwarf whose breadth of shoulder exceeded his height. Second, and normally a hand leader himself, was Turilan, while three warriors,

Umajan, Rilan and Harthistan made up the rest of the group. Each carried a crossbow, a heavy axe, several knives and an assortment of personally chosen weapons.

The sun was already reddening when Karogan called a halt, for which Elethrine was glad, despite her unease at what was coming. All day the dwarves had acted with consummate professionalism, neither teasing the girls nor making ribald remarks to one another. Yet the price of their passage included mouth service and even if her honour code had not obliged her to keep her compact she would have been in no position to break it.

Turilan was sent to scout the area while the others prepared a camp in the centre of a thicket of blade tree. Elethrine dismounted, resisting the urge to rub at her sore bottom where it had been bouncing on the camel's back for the entire day. The riding position also left the beast's spine pressed into her tuppenny, which had simultaneously been aggravating and arousing.

'Note,' Karogan addressed her as he fixed the tether of his camel to a tree trunk, 'how the fallen blade leaves tinkle when walked on. To approach us noiselessly is an impossibility, and there will be two guards on watch at every point of the night.'

'We thank you for your service,' Elethrine replied, 'which is fine indeed.'

'Standard dwarven routine,' Karogan replied dismissively.

'What of our service?' Aisla asked from behind Elethrine.

Elethrine turned a glance to her maid, whose tone had been perhaps a little too eager. Aisla immediately cast down her eyes.

'Have patience,' Karogan replied sternly. 'First we must set the guards and eat, then you may take your pleasure of our cocks for as long as you please. But explain to me while the pot comes to the boil: Why is it that you do not want your cunts filled?'

Elethrine felt herself colour up and turned to Aisla for help.

'In Mund,' Aisla explained, 'protocol prevents ladies of royal and noble birth from surrendering to their natural urges until taken in wedlock, as do their purity girdles, normally. As an artisan I am subject to no such restraints and may pleasure myself at will, and you also.'

'Not if you wish your bottom to remain un-blemished,' Elethrine warned, shocked at Aisla's open flirting.

'Sorry, mistress,' Aisla said, hurriedly.

'Go on,' Karogan said, 'I do not pretend to understand human thinking, which seems muddled to us dwarves, yet I am prepared to try.'

'Lowborn men and women of Mund pair as they please,' Aisla went on. 'They hold no land and so it matters little who they take to partner, although I would think it a shame to wed any but another artisan. Among the seven ranks of highborn: reeves, squires, thanes, barons, earls, princes and full royalty, any man may aspire to any maiden, so long as they are able to ravish her successfully.'

'Ravish her?' Karogan asked.

'I shall explain,' Elethrine interrupted, feeling that Aisla was making the explanation too simple. 'My mother is the High-Demoiselle Seraphinia, and the daughter of a barbarian earl from the west of Aegmund. When my father desired to wed her, he scaled the walls of the Earl's keep, defeated three men-at-arms, climbed the central tower, broke the lock of her purity girdle with his sword point and ravished her on her bed. It was a fine deed and did her great honour.'

'I am surprised anybody ever lives to marry,' Karogan suggested.

'On the contrary,' Elethrine replied haughtily, 'it ensures that only the strongest and cleverest produce children, thus retaining the strength of the nobility and royalty of Mund. Still, it is true that I have seen twenty winters and am still maiden. None have yet dared attempt me.'

'Recently, and in the more civilised parts of the kingdom,' Talithea put in, 'betrothals have become common. Indeed it is quite the fashion. I am betrothed to the Prince of Ateron in Aegmund.'

'A weak choice that will surely see the downfall of the Kingdom,' Elethrine answered, drawing daggers from Talithea's eyes.

'Extraordinary,' Karogan said. 'I will never understand humans. We simply mate as we please, and look to our offspring as seems appropriate. Still, an interesting tale that has made me forget my hunger while the stew readies.'

They ate in shifts, always with two dwarves patrolling the edge of the copse of blade tree, despite the lack of any evident danger. The meal consisted of a rich stew of spiced meat and barley, eaten with chunks of coarse bread. As they had promised, Aisla served bare breasted, blushing as she exposed her full chest but clearly proud at the compliments she received. Her breasts were large and heavy: full, firm globes of pink flesh topped with rose-pink nipples. Aisla's slim frame made them seem larger still, and more prominent. As the meal progressed Elethrine became increasingly nervous at the prospect of what honour obliged her to do afterwards. At last the pot was scraped dry and she was left sipping at a rich red wine with a hard knot of tension in her stomach.

When the moment came, it was with a suddenness that startled Elethrine. Karogan simply opened his mail shirt, undid the thongs which held his trousers together and pulled aside the pouch beneath, exposing his genitals. Elethrine squeaked in alarm, quite involuntarily. His cock was thick and a ruddy brown, the wrinkled skin moving slightly as the fat balls beneath it squirmed in their sack. There was also a curious scent, earthy and somehow familiar. The thought of putting the obscene thing in her mouth horrified her, yet also filled her with a strong sense of need. Instead of demanding it sucked immediately, he began to stroke it as he looked up to Elethrine.

'Well now,' he pronounced cheerfully, 'as you can see, I am ready for my entertainment. Let me see. Elethrine, I think I would enjoy watching you punish Aisla while Talithea attends to my penis.'

'Very well,' Elethrine answered, glad that the fat brown cock in his lap was not destined for her mouth, or at least not immediately. 'Aisla, come across my lap.'

Aisla, already bare breasted, came over with her head hung meekly, accepting Elethrine's order without question, despite having done nothing to earn a beating.

'I shall beat her with this,' Elethrine announced, reaching for the big wooden spoon that had been used to serve the food as Aisla knelt by her knees.

'Excellent,' Karogan retorted. 'Make it hard, I want to see the pale skin of her buttocks turn red and hear her yells.'

'And I also,' Harthistan put in. 'Do it well.'

Elethrine glanced towards the speaker, finding him with his cock also out and erect in his hand. Feeling weak in the presence of so much excited masculinity, she pulled Aisla smartly across her lap. The maid lifted her bottom obligingly as her mistress began to fiddle with her skirts.

'Come, Princess, to work,' Karogan ordered, flourishing his cock at Talithea.

Elethrine turned, finding Talithea standing with an odd look in her eyes. Walking slowly, almost as if entranced, she crossed to where Karogan was sitting, knelt for him, opened her mouth and took his cock in.

'That's my girl,' Karogan said happily as the Princess's cheeks sucked in as she began her work.

Despite her surprise at Talithea's easy acquiescence to something that should have horrified the delicately nurtured Princess, Elethrine found herself wishing it was she who was sucking so lovingly on the dwarf's stout penis. Still, having her beautiful maid across her knee was something, and she determined to explore Aisla's bottom while she beat it. A weak voice in the back of her head was telling her that this was not only an improper reaction to the very necessary task of discipline, but also an odd one. She ignored it, instead making short work of exposing the maid's trim hindquarters.

Aisla made no protest at the undignified lifting of her skirts, nor at the opening of her drawers and pantalettes, a procedure that in the past had always had her snivelling with shame and begging to be let off her punishment. Elethrine had never paid any attention to such protests, but now found their absence annoying. She wanted Aisla to blubber and plead while her bottom was smacked, and she wanted it because she knew that it would add to the warm feeling between her thighs. Aisla's bottom was bare, a sweet pink peach that Elethrine longed to smack. Raising the spoon, she brought it down hard across the maid's naked buttocks, making her jump and squeak in shock.

A surge of delight went through Elethrine at Aisla's reaction. She had always enjoyed beating her maid, but this was more intense, more satisfying and made her tuppenny tingle more than ever. Again the heavy spoon smacked down, making the soft, girlish nates bounce and wobble. Once more Aisla squeaked, to her mistress's delight. Another smack fell and Aisla's thighs parted to give the dwarves what Elethrine knew would be a fine view of wet, pink tuppenny and wrinkled, brown bottom ring. Grinning in delight, Elethrine set to work to punish Aisla properly, spanking her with an excited fury that quickly had the hapless maid kicking and squalling while she made a most undignified display of her most intimate secrets.

As Elethrine beat Aisla, Talithea sucked on Karogan's cock, displaying the same wanton eagerness as Elethrine felt. His cock was hard in her mouth as she licked and sucked at it, frantic in her eagerness to enjoy the taste of excited male dwarf. Then, to Elethrine's amazement, Talithea began to pull up her skirts, exposing layer after layer of silk, lace and fur petticoats until her fancifully embroidered drawers were exposed, with her full bottom stretching the material out in an enticing ball. Still sucking voraciously on Karogan's cock, the Princess pulled her drawers wide, exposing heavily flounced pantalettes that did nothing to hide the contours of her magnificent bottom. The split of the pantalettes was open, revealing a hint of blonde fluff and creamy bum-cheek, a display of immodesty so flagrant that Elethrine could scarcely believe that it was the shrewish, demure Princess Talithea who was doing it.

Her own response was little different though, and as Aisla kicked and yelped her way through her beating, Elethrine found herself wanting to make an equally rude display of her own behind, perhaps even opening her pantalettes and offering her virgin tuppenny to the dwarves' lust.

Perhaps it was the sight of Aisla's soft, hot bottom and the scent of excited girl. Perhaps it was the sight of two dwarves nursing thick erections while a third fed his penis to Talithea. Perhaps it was the strange, earthy smell in the still evening air. In any case, Elethrine could feel her lust rising as it had never done before and knew that unless she acted quickly she would be committing an utterly degraded act by offering herself for entry to a squat, dwarven soldier.

Finishing Aisla off with a volley of hard smacks, she selected her target, choosing Harthistan, who seemed on the edge of explosion. Aisla squeaked as she was pushed to the ground and landed with a bump, her red bum stuck up rudely towards the waiting dwarves. Shaking too hard to walk, Elethrine scrambled over to Harthistan on her hands and knees. Even before she reached him she was gaping for his cock, desperately in need of it in her mouth. Then it was in and she was sucking frantically, her senses filled with the strong taste of male dwarf. Harthistan groaned and gripped her hair with a strength that Elethrine knew she had no chance of resisting had she wanted to. Her head was pulled hard down, his cock bumping against the back of her throat. Then it jerked and her mouth was full of something salty and thick. Even as she realised that her precious, pretty, virgin mouth was full of dwarf's come she was swallowing. Harthistan groaned again, his cock giving another jerk as it was pulled from Elethrine's mouth. The second spurt of come caught her full in the face, splashing her nose, cheeks and neck to dribble down onto the blue velvet of her bodice.

As he pulled away with a long exhalation of breath Elethrine sank back onto her haunches, her need greater than ever. The taste of come in her mouth was the same as the curious scent she had noticed before, and now that it was stronger she realised with utter horror what it reminded her of. It was the same scent that had pulled her towards the captive goblin, back in Korismund, or at least very similar. Tears of shame welled up in her eyes as she realised what she had done, but her lust was still there, as strong as ever. The dwarves, however, were busy elsewhere – Karogan still with his erection in Talithea's mouth, and Umajan mounted on Aisla with her long legs high and wide around his squat brown body.

Elethrine watched the frantic movement of the dwarf's muscular little buttocks as he fucked Aisla, imagining herself in her maid's place, hot red bottom pressed into the ground, naked breasts flaunted for all to see, face set in an expression of bliss, dwarven cock working in and out of her open tuppenny. Unable to resist any longer, she began to crawl towards Karogan and Talithea, intending to offer her maidenhead to the hand leader's swollen penis on which the Princess was sucking with such relish.

Talithea's bottom was in front of her, plump and bulging inside the frilly pantalettes with a hint of blonde hair protruding from the split to hint at yet more intimate secrets. The sight made Elethrine waver in her intent, the Princess's luscious sex suddenly as welcome a target as the dwarf's cock.

The hesitation saved her maidenhead. She reached a trembling hand out to pull Talithea's pantalettes aside, intent on exploring the Princess's bottom while she begged Karogan to take her. Suddenly the dwarf groaned and his penis jerked in Talithea's mouth, the next instant a gush of white sperm spurting out from around her lips. Elethrine sank back, her hand touching the frills of Talithea's pantalettes, her mouth open in an 'O' of disappointment.

Talithea sat up as Karogan pulled his penis from her mouth, leaving her with sperm running down her chin. As the dwarf sat back Elethrine found herself coming forward, her eyes meeting Talithea's then moving to a dribble of come hanging from the Princess's nose. Somewhere in the background she heard a loud grunt and Aisla's scream of ecstasy, a noise serving to increase her need for Talithea. They came together, their lips opening to share each other's mouthfuls of thick, salty semen. Eagerly, earnestly, they licked each other clean of dwarves' come, until both were slippery with saliva on their faces and necks.

Even as she swallowed her last mouthful, Elethrine's overwhelming lust for sexual contact began to fade. Slowly she began to wonder why she was licking

Talithea's face so wantonly, then she pulled back, filled with embarrassment and shame at her own behaviour. Worse still was the knowledge that is was the musky scent that had overcome her reserve, a scent similar to that of goblins and one that she knew she would be unable to resist.

The situation remained the same as they made their way across the great plain. By day they would ride within the protective pentagon of dwarves, shielded from the attentions of the Vendjomois. By night they would eat and then submit themselves to the lust of their guards. Despite Elethrine's inability to control herself while under the influence of the dwarves' scent, she managed to retain her maidenhead simply because she had not offered it as part of the original bargain and so the dwarves refrained from taking advantage of her excited state.

Little else was left to her in the way of modesty. On one night she took all five of them in her mouth in turn, swallowing their thickly scented come until she was delirious with need. She also allowed her breasts and bottom to be fondled, both by the dwarves whose penes she was sucking and by the other girls while they also were in the grip of sexual need.

By mutual consent no mention was made during the day of their nocturnal behaviour, an agreement that allowed Elethrine and Talithea to retain at least the pretence of propriety, although both knew that they would be as eager as ever for the feel of dwarven cocks and taste of dwarven come in the evening. There was also the matter of feeling each other, which they did with abandonment while under the influence of the dwarven musk but avoided mentioning altogether during the day.

Before supper on the third day, Elethrine found herself alone for the first time since their arrival in

Apraya. They had set up camp beside a dry gully and she had used this as shelter in which to relieve herself. Squatting with her dress and petticoats up, her drawers and pantalettes open and her bare tuppenny gushing a golden stream, she had been thinking of the coming round of cock sucking and wondering how it might feel to allow a dwarf to come between her breasts. With a flush of guilty delight she realised that at last she had the opportunity to play with her tuppenny and see if she could experience the same exquisite feelings of climax that Aisla had shown her.

As soon as she had shaken away the last drops of pee she began to rub at her clitoris as Aisla had done but with the urgency of possible discovery. Her mind turned to the thought of cocks and hands and the taste and feel of come in her mouth. The previous night she had had a really good feel of Talithea's bottom, massaging and stroking the full, bouncy cheeks through just the thin cotton of the Princess's pantalettes. The temptation to split the pantalettes and kiss Talithea's anus in a gesture of abject submission had been there, or even to ask for a spanking.

That would be it, she thought as she began to rub harder. To be spanked across the Princess's knee, spanked with her bottom bare in front of the others, her cheeks parting to show her wet tuppenny and her tight bottom ring, spanked as if she were some ill-behaved maid whose exposure and punishment were meaningless. Better still, she could be stripped nude and passed round for spanking, being beaten bare-bottomed by each of them while she masturbated in a rude, dirty, wanton display of her sex.

For the first time in her life Elethrine came, screaming out her ecstasy as her clitoris burned beneath her finger. Even as her climax hit her it was accompanied by a great wave of utter shame for her degraded fantasy. Then a clatter of pebbles startled her and she spun round to find Turilan standing at the top of the bank with his axe ready in his hands.

'You screamed?' he asked in puzzlement, casting about for an assailant.

Then his eyes lit on the glistening juice on her fingers and his swarthy face broke into a wide grin. He turned away, laughing and leaving Elethrine with her face scarlet with blushes. Nevertheless, that evening and the next she masturbated while she gave mouth service, coming secretly with her hand down her drawers.

On the morning of their fifth day in Apraya they came within sight of the city of Fujome. At first it appeared as a smoky blotch on the horizon, then as an irregular line of watery violet far off across the plain. Gradually the details of its high wall and even taller towers and domes became clear. The land also became lusher, and presently Elethrine made out the high, single sails of boats on what was presumably a river.

'Fujome,' Karogan announced, turning in his saddle, 'and the river Phætes beside it. Here we shall renew our stores and prepare ourselves for the journey across the Eigora Khum to Gora-Jome and the great Ephraxis.'

Elethrine nodded in response and turned her camel on to a road that ran towards the gates of the city.

'Cover your hair,' Turilan remarked from beside her. 'It is unlikely that any will dare accost us, yet it is wise not to tempt providence.'

She obeyed, twisting her hair into a loose bun and winding the square of raw silk around it. Beside her Talithea and Aisla did the same, the maid without hesitation, the Princess with reluctance.

They entered the city through a high portal of solid marble, the points of the arch meeting at what Elethrine estimated to be the height of perhaps as many as twenty tall men. To either side bartizans projected from the walls, with fierce, helmeted faces visible through the arrow slits and strange metal tubes projecting from holes. An officer stepped out, causing Elethrine a moment of unease, but after a brief word with Karogan he allowed them to pass. Elethrine briefly met his eyes, finding a look of pure lust that made her blush. She felt sure that had their guards not been with them she would have been put on the ground and ravished, regardless of onlookers, and probably by the entire guard once the captain had finished. He made no move though, merely eyeing the heavy axe at Karogan's belt.

'They know better than to meddle in dwarven affairs,' Turilan remarked dryly, as they passed into the main street of the city.

'I wish to bathe and change,' Talithea announced. 'Is it possible to purchase new clothes?'

'Possible it is,' Karogan replied. 'The city is famed for its bazaar, yet knowing your scruples you might wish to consider before changing into local raiment.'

Elethrine saw immediately what he meant. The place was busy, men and women thronging the marble paved edges of the broad street. Their clothes were silk and in every colour she could imagine, yet even those women who appeared richest were scarcely decent. A length of light silk seemed to be the standard garment, wrapped around the chest and hips. Some were worn so as to leave one breast bare, others tight across the full, rounded bottoms that seemed characteristic of Vendjomois women. A few wore short skirts, loose trousers or shorts, but in all cases the thin silk did little to conceal their figures.

'It seems that washing my clothes must suffice,' Talithea sniffed.

'You looked little more decent with your pantalettes on show,' Elethrine remarked, unable to resist the dig at the Princess's behaviour when overcome by lust.

Talithea shot her a furious glance and opened her mouth to speak, only to think better of it.

'Eurlan's Inn hard by the sentinel tower seems the

most sensible choice for accommodation,' Karogan announced. 'The prices are reasonable and it is staffed by dwarves and halflings, who ask fewer questions than most.'

'Very well,' Talithea answered him, 'so long as I may sleep in comfort.'

Karogan answered with a grunt and they turned down a side street, the magnificent marble-faced houses immediately giving way to dwellings one or two stories shorter, and considerably less impressive. The inn proved to be close to the wall and overlooked by a tall tower. The squat building stood in its own compound, with stables to the rear. Elethrine dismounted gratefully, intent on washing the dust of the journey first from her mouth and then from her body.

'Aisla,' she ordered, as Rilan took her camel, 'go and find out what facilities exist for bathing and the washing of clothes.'

Aisla curtsied and hurried into the inn after Umajan; Elethrine, Talithea, Karogan and Turilan following at a more sedate pace. The inside proved cool and comfortably furnished, while smells of frying fish, onions and other foodstuffs helped to create a homely atmosphere. Elethrine sighed, feeling safer and more relaxed than at any time since their violent abduction from Korismund.

Karogan ordered drinks, first water and then mead, which Elethrine accepted gratefully, joining the dwarves on a padded leather bench and sipping at the rich fluid while her body slowly relaxed. Before Elethrine had finished her drink, Aisla returned to announce that a bath was being drawn and that their clothes would be washed while they bathed. Rising gratefully to her feet, she followed the maid up a flight of broad stairs, Talithea beside her.

She bathed, taking her time, and then took her meal in her room, Aisla serving her and Talithea while their clothes dried in the hot, arid afternoon air. Finally she crawled into the bed and collapsed into a deep, dreamless sleep. At some point during the night a hand on her shoulder shook her gently awake and a cock was offered to her mouth. She sucked, slowly and sleepily, until whichever dwarf it was came in her mouth. As a second took her by the hair and fed his erection to her she was vaguely aware that Talithea and Aisla were giving similar service, but was quickly asleep again as soon as she had swallowed.

When Elethrine awoke again, it was to bright light of a different quality to that which had filled the room when she had first gone to sleep. After a moment of disorientation she realised that she had slept through the entire night and that it was morning. Aisla was sprawled beside her, while Talithea still slept in the bed opposite. Rubbing the sleep from her eyes, Elethrine sat up, glad of the long sleep. Having wakened the others and dressed, she made her way down to the main hall of the inn to find the dwarves in conversation with a group of men.

One of these, an obese man whose short stature and ruddy-brown skin colour suggested that he was half-dwarf, was in earnest conversation with Karogan. The other three had the yellowish-brown skin typical of the Vendjomois and none looked at all prepossessing. One was lean, relatively tall and carried a somehow predatory air, another was older, grey-haired and paunchy while the third was heavy-set, youthful and apparently not of the fastest wit.

'Demoiselle Elethrine,' Karogan greeted her, 'this is the merchant Ayapan, Kaulak of Teahjome, Mausac and Ulak, noted soldiers, if not currently in service. Men, I give you the Demoiselle Elethrine, who has a title too long to easily remember, and with her are Talithea and Aisla, the first a Princess. All three are of Mund in the far north.'

'Mund?' the man who had been introduced as Ulak remarked.

'To the north,' Elethrine explained, 'across the Eigora Khum and many other lands and seas besides.'

'I had thought the northlands an icy waste inhabited by giant yellow-haired barbarians,' Ulak said in disbelief.

Unable to resist the effect, Elethrine pulled at her head scarf and shook out her mane of rich, pale blonde hair. Ayapan's eyes opened in amazement, as did those of the soldiers.

'We are not giants though,' she said.

'Nor barbarians, save in Aegmund,' Talithea added.

'Barbarism is relative,' Ayapan the merchant replied, 'as is size. You stand over a head taller than I, and your friend perhaps close to two heads. Your men folk must be taller still, so you are surely giants.'

'I think not,' Elethrine answered stiffly, 'and as to barbarism, I have seen nothing in Vendjome to impress me. Come Karogan, we should be pressing on.'

'There is a change of plan,' Karogan replied. 'Ayapan is a nymph merchant and has asked us to guard his precious merchandise. Kaulak here has been guarding him since leaving Gora-Jome, but twice they have been troubled by bandits. Ayapan wishes a more secure guard.'

'That is his difficulty!' Talithea snapped, her voice rising above the protests of both Elethrine and Aisla. 'You are hired to guard us!'

'Do not fear,' Karogan responded evenly, 'we will return your payment less only our actual expenses. Also, Kaulak has agreed to serve in our stead.'

'What?' Talithea demanded hotly. 'You are not merely going to desert us but leave us in the care of this wolf-faced vagabond! Where is your honour!'

'My honour demands that I serve my kinsman first,' Karogan replied calmly. 'Ayapan is son to my uncle's cousin and so may fairly claim our protection.'

Talithea continued to protest, with Elethrine and Aisla adding occasionally to the debate, but Karogan stood firm and they were eventually forced to accept the change of guard.

4

Slut

Leaving Fujome, they rode out to the north, headed for
the city of Gora-Jome and the Ephraxis river. The
countryside was lush and fertile, with the broad Phætes
a placid expanse to one side and watermeadows and
orchards to the other. Farms and villages were
numerous, and the peaceful, rich air of respectability
served to calm Elethrine's nerves. The road was busy,
and although their dress aroused some curiosity, with
their headscarves to hide their hair it was less than
before and nobody sought to interfere with them. As
before they received lustful glances, but the men of
Vendjome seemed timid and unable to act on their
impulses. Nor were the guards the trouble that she had
anticipated. Kaulak rode ahead, Mausac and Ulak to
either side and a little behind, each sitting proud and
upright with their lances held at ease. Scraps of crimson
cloth at the lance heads bounced and waved in the light
breeze, marking the three men as paid guards. Despite
the occasional remark to compliment their figures, the
guards had not molested them. Evidently the men of
Vendjome were not as incapable of controlling their lust
as she had suspected.

They made good time, and before noon had reached
a village where the Phætes swung away to the east and
with it the main road. Having filled their waterskins and
checked their supply of food, they struck off on the

smaller road that led out across the Eigora Khum and
ultimately to Gora-Jome. At first the countryside
around them was moderately lush, fields of wheat mixed
with orchards and pasture, watered by numerous
irrigation canals. As the heat of the day reached its full,
burning peak they came to a low scarp which marked
the edge of the river's flood plain. Beyond it the land
was dryer and grown with vineyard, olive grove, blade
tree and copses of a strange tree with feathery foliage
that Elethrine did not recognise. After an hour's ride
another scarp marked the start of more broken, hilly
land rich with the scent of wild thyme and sage. A third
brought them out onto the true desert.

'Eigora Khum,' Kaulak announced, reining in his
camel, 'or at least its edge. Gora-Jome is close to two
hundred leagues east. North, you will find nothing but
rock and sand and more rock for six, perhaps seven,
hundred leagues.'

'A lonely place,' Mausac remarked with a light,
somehow cynical laugh.

Elethrine looked at the parched, lifeless waste with
distaste. She had thought the Oretean plain arid, but it
teemed with life beside the Eigora Khum. She turned,
giving what she hoped was a last look at the Phætes
valley, glanced at Talithea and Aisla and then set her
face to the desert with determination.

For another four hours they rode, largely in silence,
until they reached a group of broken rocks at the
summit of a low hill. The sun had begun to fall into the
west, throwing long shadows from the rocks out across
the desert ahead, a flat expanse of pale, yellow sand
marked only by rounded dunes. Kaulak dismounted
and signalled that they should do the same, briefly
tended his camel, and then sauntered over to them.

'Here will do as well as another place,' Kaulak
declared, 'and besides, it would be foolish to camp out
among the dunes for fear of storms.'

73

'Why so?' Talithea asked with her usual haughtiness. 'There are perhaps two hours of light left, and I would like to make the best time possible.'

'And wake up under the sand,' Mausac laughed, 'if at all. No, my pretty, we rest here tonight. Besides, sand makes a poor surface for the pursuit of erotic pleasures, tending to instability.'

'Grains also frequently lodge in awkward places,' Ulak agreed as he slipped from his camel.

'Do not call me "my pretty", and what erotic pleasures do you intend?' Talithea demanded hotly, although the hauteur of her voice showed an underlying alarm.

'My maid will be available for such services, should you insist,' Elethrine addressed Kaulak, 'but the Princess Talithea and myself are highborn and do not dally with hired soldiers, nor any others for that matter.'

'Are you virgin then, to so resent the pleasures of the flesh?' Kaulak responded in genuine surprise. 'Life is short, and we travel together in this lonely place. Is it not natural that we should together take pleasure in the natural abilities and senses of our bodies? This is my philosophy.'

'I know nothing of your philosophy,' Elethrine replied proudly, 'and I am indeed maiden.'

'And I likewise,' Talithea added. 'We are the unwed daughters of king and baron, how else could it be?'

'The unwed daughters of our high-placed men are notorious for their excesses,' Mausac said in surprise. 'Ulak, do you not recall Zinjana, daughter of the Governor of Arijome, and how she satisfied the troop of Captain Orik?'

'So I do,' Ulak replied, following his remark with a satisfied sigh.

'It is so,' Kaulak assured the girls, 'and at the inn you stated that while within the rule of Vendjome you were prepared to accept Vendjome customs. The Panjandrum lays claim to the entire Eigora Khum – though for no obvious purpose – so, by your own argument you should take joy in coupling with us. Any girl of Vendjome would approach our offer with abandonment.'

'There is a great difference between covering one's hair and surrendering one's maidenhead,' Elethrine answered.

'You speak of joy,' Talithea put in hotly. 'Do you take us for strumpets that we should give ourselves to our base needs so easily?'

'You admit to the need then?' Kaulak replied, shiftily.

'Indeed,' Elethrine answered as the blood rushed to her cheeks, 'it is nature, though hardly a fit topic to discuss with hired guards.'

'To suggest that we surrender to you with abandonment is to insult us,' Talithea put in.

'In our land it would be an insult not to invite you to couple,' Ulak responded, and then turned to Aisla. 'For myself though, all day I have been watching the roundness of your bottom as it bounced with the motion of the camel and wondering how it would feel in my hands. You seem less reserved than the others and I have often wondered how it would feel to take pleasure with a woman of height greater than my own. Will you couple with me?'

Aisla giggled, and glanced at Elethrine.

'A sensible idea,' Elethrine stated, 'and when you have finished, your comrades may take their turns.'

'Not so,' Mausac interjected, 'for, beautiful though Aisla is, her passage will be swimming with Ulak's sperm and loose, whereas yours, if you are truly maiden, will be tight and running only with your own sweet juice.'

'Sir!' Elethrine and Talithea exclaimed in simultaneous outrage at the intimacy of his remark.

'Let us cease bickering,' Kaulak said tiredly. 'The

proposal is this: when we accepted the task of guarding you over many hundreds of leagues of barren or dangerous land, we assumed that the nights would be spent in blissful indulgence in each other's bodies. Without such comforts the journey is simply not worth undertaking, nor would you have our true loyalty, having so rudely insulted us. So, either give in to the feelings which you admit to or we will return to Fujome and you may proceed as best you can.'

Neither Elethrine nor Talithea responded, both struck dumb by the treachery of their guards.

'Come, come,' Ulak said, sensing their despondence, 'all day you have sat with your sweet cunts spread over the spines of camels. If you are not aroused you cannot be human!'

Elethrine blushed deeply, horrified by his knowledge of something that had been an embarrassing secret for most of the day. Her tuppenny was moist and sensitive, which she knew meant that it was ready to accept a penis even if she wasn't.

'We must speak apart,' Talithea said formally and tugged on Elethrine's dress.

Elethrine and Aisla followed her into the shadow of a tall rock well out of hearing of the three guards. Elethrine saw that Talithea's face was flushed as she lifted her veil.

'It seems,' the Princess said resignedly, 'that we have been tricked, which is perhaps not dissimilar to ravishment.'

'Indeed not,' Elethrine agreed. 'We have only two choices, surrender or be abandoned in the desert.'

'Then we had best surrender,' Talithea suggested with a tone than Elethrine found suspiciously close to anticipation.

'What?' Elethrine demanded. 'Surrender our maidenheads? To common soldiers?'

'Kaulak's previous rank is equivalent, perhaps, to

76

that of thane,' Talithea replied, 'and to be ravished by the thane of an enemy state might be thought a natural fate for either of us, and not without honour. To be tricked into ravishment is perhaps a little less acceptable, but still . . . I would surrender to Kaulak.'

'How can you say this?' Elethrine retorted. 'What of your chastity? What of our return to Mund? When it is discovered that you are not pure you will be sent to a celibentuary. Your life will be one of shame and drudgery – working stripped, at scrubbing floors and serving, spanked bare each dawn, tattooed as a harlot!'

'Not so,' Talithea answered. 'When we reach Thieron I will wed Kaulak, who, in truth, appeals to me more than Prince Kavisterion.'

'What then of me?' Elethrine demanded, furiously. 'That leaves me with Mausac, I suppose? A coarse, overweight oaf! My modesty recoils at the very thought!'

'There speaks the girl who swallowed the jism of five dwarves!' Talithea laughed. 'You are modest indeed!'

'To save my maidenhead!' Elethrine retorted.

'Ha! Your eyes were shut in bliss! You licked Karogan's organ clean as if enjoying a stick of iced peach juice! You allowed Umajan to fondle your breasts while you sucked on him! You are a strumpet Trina, face it.'

'Me? Who wants to spread her thighs for a disgraced soldier? And as for the dwarves, who allowed her skirts and petticoats to be lifted, took down her own drawers and showed off her pantalettes for their pleasure?'

'Mistress, Princess, please!' Aisla interrupted. 'They are harnessing the camels!'

Elethrine turned to find that it was true. For a moment she stood irresolute, half terrified of what would come if she accepted the guards' offer, half wanting to do exactly that. Kaulak was adjusting the girth straps of a camel, Ulak checking the level of a water skin. Mausac had already mounted, his paunch bulging out between his open legs and the long scar on his face reflecting an angry red in the setting sun.

'Mistress,' Aisla spoke softly from behind her, 'this Mausac is no noble, it is true, but see the scars on his face and arms. He must be a warrior of note, and so perhaps worthy.'

Elethrine swallowed, grateful for Aisla's encouraging words but still uncertain. Yet all around them the Eigora Khum stretched away, parched rock and sand with no trace of life or water and little shade. Had she been alone, she told herself, honour might have demanded running into the desert, but she had a responsibility to Aisla as her maid and fealty to Talithea as a Princess of the House Royal of Mund. Besides, as Aisla said, Mausac was the warrior of a strange race, to whom she could submit without complete loss of face.

'Very well,' she said slowly, 'let us go to them.'

They walked towards the three men, Talithea in front, Elethrine wondering if by some clever trick she might not escape defloweration.

'Kaulak, Thane of Teahjome,' Talithea addressed the lean ex-officer. 'I, Talithea, Princess of Mund, submit myself to your lust. Do with me as you will.'

'Aha!' Kaulak declared. 'I knew it was simply a matter of allowing you to find an excuse. Come, let us commence before the sun falls and I can no longer admire your beauty.'

He turned to pull the blanket from his camel, favoured the others with a grin and, taking Talithea's hand, led her off among the rocks. Ulak smiled at Aisla and accepted her hand as well, leaving Elethrine faced with the still-mounted Mausac.

'Do you have any rank at all?' she asked, hopefully.

'None to speak of,' he answered, scratching his nose with the tip of a finger. 'I was made a leader of twelve during the siege of Reites, but demoted for drunkenness shortly after.'

'And how many have you slain in fair combat?' she persisted.

'Fair combat?' he queried. 'Well, that is hard to say. I and three others planted the petard that brought down the tower at Bome-Remore, which must have killed a hundred or more. I was an archer with Captain Orik when we ambushed a troop of Oretean cavalry in a gully and I must have taken a dozen at the least. Then there was the molten lead at Reites –'

'I mean in single combat,' Elethrine explained, 'or a mêlée perhaps.'

'Perhaps fifteen, perhaps twenty,' Mausac shrugged. 'But should we not be talking of love rather than war?'

'We do talk of love,' Elethrine replied. 'I seek to discover how great is the dishonour of being ravished by you, as you are determined to have me. If you have truly slain twenty men face to face, then it is no dishonour at all.'

'No?' Mausac queried, then continued. 'I do not pretend to understand you. Vendjome girls are, by and large, alarmed by my scarred countenance and take little pleasure in my prowess as a soldier. Still, if you must know, when they breached the wall at Reites I slew a general.'

'A general?' Elethrine queried.

'One who commands an army,' Mausac explained.

'In Mund any noble might command an army,' Elethrine replied. 'Yet it is a great feat of arms for a common soldier. Perhaps it is I who am unworthy of your attentions.'

'Not at all,' Mausac insisted. 'And, during a skirmish in the Glissades I slew a man in mail and armed with an axe, using only my teeth.'

'Was he highborn?' Elethrine questioned.

'I didn't ask him,' Mausac answered with a grin. 'But enough talk of blood and battle. Come.'

'I fear I am scarcely worthy of being taken by such a

great warrior,' Elethrine faltered as Mausac dismounted.

'I don't mind,' he assured her, taking her hand and pulling her gently towards the rocks.

Elethrine followed with a lump in her throat and a strong tingling feeling between her legs. As they passed between the two towering rocks, Elethrine heard gasps and moans of pleasure, and, coming into a small flat area, she came upon a sight that set her pulse hammering. A camel blanket had been laid down on the hard ground, and on it knelt the Princess Talithea. Her dress and petticoats had been thrown up over her back and her drawers and pantalettes pulled open to expose the full, creamy-skinned peach of her bottom, her anus a dark, puckered spot between them. Her breasts had been pulled out of her bodice and swung bare beneath her chest. Her tuppenny was swollen and moist, the taut skin of her maidenhead visible, all but blocking the entrance to her vagina.

Kaulak was at her head, his erection in her mouth as he fondled one dangling breast. He grinned up at Mausac and Elethrine, then, with a curious, shuffling gait moved behind Talithea. Elethrine watched with her mouth agape as his long brown penis was put to the Princess's hole. Kaulak found the entrance and gave a shove. The Princess's maidenhead broke and she gave a curious cry, both a sob and a squeal. Then his cock was in her and she moaned, opening both eyes and mouth wide as for the first time a penis filled her vagina.

Kaulak moved, mounting himself on her more comfortably, his organ still deep in her previously virgin vagina. He began to pump vigorously, with his legs cocked apart in an obscene position that left his lean, dark buttocks wide and showed his balls as they smacked against Talithea's sex. With her bodice and chemise unfastened, her rounded breasts slapped together as she was ridden. The greatest shock to

Elethrine, though, was the expression on Talithea's face which, after the initial shock, had passed to absolute bliss. Her eyes had shut but her mouth was still wide, with a dribble of spittle running from one corner. With each push into her she made a little moaning noise, expressing pure ecstasy.

'Not so prim now, eh?' Mausac laughed as they passed.

Kaulak grinned up at them, then changed his posture slightly, placing his hands on Talithea's buttocks and pulling them open and revealing her anal opening and the juncture of his penis and her vagina. Elethrine shivered and hurried on, feeling still more nervous but also deeply aroused by the sight of Talithea's submission.

'Eager for our own coupling?' Mausac suggested with a laugh as he followed her between the rocks.

The disturbing sight of Talithea and Kaulak was quickly hidden from view. Talithea, Elethrine realised, had been eager for penetration – desperate even – and so had needed only a moderately worthy excuse to surrender her maidenhead. She herself, after exploring the pleasures of her own body with the dwarves, was also eager, but not so wanton as to submit so easily.

Elethrine found herself alone with Mausac in a clear space among enormous boulders. The sun showed between two of these, illuminating Mausac as he struggled with the buckles and straps of his belly harness. He was grinning broadly as the harness fell away to expose his great belly and the bulge of his organ beneath his kirtle, the red sunlight giving his face the look of a lustful, gorging demon.

Elethrine sank to her knees, her jaw shaking as he lifted the kirtle to expose himself for her. His organ reared up, rigid with blood, the shaft a rich-brown colour with the head protruding from the thick foreskin, red and shiny. A leathery sack, richly grown with hair and bulging with two plump testicles, hung beneath it. As with the dwarves, she felt immediate repulsion coupled with a strong desire to take the obscene thing into her mouth and suck it. Forcing herself to overcome her distaste, she moved forward and took hold of his balls with one hand and the shaft of his cock with the other.

Mausac groaned as she began to masturbate him into her face, then nudged his organ against her lips. Elethrine closed her eyes and gaped wide, surrendering herself to having her mouth used once more. As her lips closed on his shaft she tasted his organ, a rich, salty flavour less earthy than the taste of dwarven male. He groaned and took her by the hair, starting to use her mouth as Kaulak had been Talithea's vagina. Elethrine began to suck at his head, squeezing it between the back of her throat and her tongue each time he pushed in.

'Patience, little one, or I'll spend in your mouth,' he groaned.

Elethrine only sucked the harder and started to lick at the underside of his shaft. He gave a grunt, said something she couldn't understand and then came in her mouth. She gagged as her throat filled with sperm, swallowing frantically but not fast enough to prevent his last, ecstatic push from forcing sperm out between her lips and his cock to dribble down her chin and onto the front of her bodice. Twice more he jerked, smaller spurts of jism erupting into her mouth and then across her face as he withdrew and took himself in hand to squeeze out the last of it over her nose and cheeks.

'I'm sorry,' he said, hoarsely. 'I couldn't last. Like Ulak, all day I have been admiring the way your bottoms fill your dresses, and it is a wonder I didn't come before.'

'Pray do not apologise,' Elethrine said, sitting back and then swallowing the rest of the sperm in her mouth. 'As I said, I am scarcely worthy of your attention, and it is perhaps best that you spend your seed in my mouth or hand.'

'Nonsense, nonsense,' Mausac assured her. 'Later I shall take your maidenhead gently and then we shall try some interesting erotic combinations, such as the Goblin and Dog, which Kaulak and your friend Talithea were enjoying with such gusto.'

Elethrine shivered at the thought, and also at the disgusting description of the sexual position in which Talithea had lost her maidenhead. Her mouth was full of the taste of come and her sex felt hot and wet, yet she had made Mausac spend and was still virgin, while her need was not so strong that she would be unable to resist completely abandoning herself.

'I shall fetch a blanket,' she offered, rising to her feet.

'Good idea, the nights are cold, even with a lustful companion,' Mausac answered. 'Also the ground is hard.'

Elethrine moved off through the rocks in the failing light. The urge to find a quiet spot and play with her tuppenny was close to irresistible, yet the fear of one of the men finding her and taking advantage of her condition overcame her lust. Instead she chose her route carefully and presently found herself peeping out from between two rocks at Kaulak and Talithea. He evidently had more self control than Mausac, or possibly his position at the head of the column had left him less stirred by the girls' physiques. In any case, he was still going strong, and had Talithea laid out on the ground with her thighs up high and spread wide, a position almost as rude and perhaps even more yielding than the one she had been in before. Her clothing was completely dishevelled, with her breasts fully out of her chemise and her drawers and pantalettes stretched taut between her ankles behind Kaulak's rapidly humping back.

A wave of malicious delight swept through Elethrine at the sight of the haughty young Princess being ravished so thoroughly and evidently enjoying it so much. She, Elethrine, the Demoiselle, had had the calm and intelligence to retain her maidenhead if not her dignity, while Talithea, the Princess, had surrendered completely to her basest lusts. Only the look of utter rapture on Talithea's face marred Elethrine's delight, as while it showed what a strumpet the girl was, it also hinted at pleasures far beyond anything Elethrine had experienced.

Shaking herself, she moved back into the deepening shadows and returned to her task of finding a blanket. The camels were seated, passively chewing the cud, and they made no move as she pulled both her own blanket and Mausac's free. From somewhere among the rocks she heard Aisla's distinctive giggle and a grunt of passion from Ulak. Feeling pleased with herself yet slightly left out, she returned through the rocks, thoroughly wet between her thighs and reasoning that if Mausac chose to ravish her later then she would have little choice but to part her thighs for him rather than make an unseemly fuss.

On reaching the open ground where she had left him, she found him huddled on his side, snoring and deeply asleep. Elethrine spread her blanket with a mixture of relief and disappointment. She lay for a while as the light died from red, through crimson to purple, listening to Aisla's excited giggles, Talithea's soft moans and the men's grunts and sighs. Finally Talithea and Kaulak went quiet, but the last thing Elethrine heard before sleep was Aisla's giggle as she feigned reluctance to Ulak's suggestion that she strip naked.

Elethrine awakened to the gentle pressure of Aisla's hand on her shoulder. The first flush of dawn was coming up in the east as she sat up and accepted the waterskin from her maid.

'Was it –' the maid began and trailed off, looking anxiously at her mistress.

'No,' Elethrine replied, glancing to the still snoring

hulk of Mausac, 'it was not. He came once in my mouth and then fell asleep. I am still maiden.'

'I am pleased for you,' Aisla replied, although her tone suggested otherwise.

'Impudence could earn you a whipping,' Elethrine answered tersely, although she knew that it was her frustration and not her maid's manner that was annoying.

'Sorry, mistress,' Aisla said meekly. 'I sought only to comfort you.'

'I am very well, thank you,' Elethrine answered, 'which is more than can be said for Talithea, who behaved with the wantonness of a nymph and must surely now be filled with shame.'

'She seems pensive but not unhappy,' Aisla answered. 'We had best be underway. Kaulak wishes to be well out into the dunes before the full heat of the day sets in.'

'Fine,' Elethrine replied, 'just let me have some more water. My mouth tastes truly dreadful.'

As Aisla passed her the waterskin again, Kaulak appeared between two rocks, his skinny frame instantly recognisable in the dimness. He greeted the girls and gave Mausac a friendly kick, producing only a grunt and a muffled curse.

Within half an hour they were underway, none speaking as they picked their way carefully down the slope towards the yellow dunes. The day was windless and threatened to be hot, with the cool night air rapidly dissipating as the east flushed turquoise and jade with the coming of dawn. For two hours they rode without pause, the dunes becoming ever higher and more regular, like enormous waves. In each trough they could see nothing but fine yellow sand to all sides, and from the crests only an endless succession of similar dunes. There was no sign of any track whatsoever, and after what seemed an eternity of dunes, Elethrine started to worry.

'Are you sure of your way, Sir Kaulak,' she asked finally, judging the honorific address suitable for someone who had taken the maidenhead of a Princess.

'So I am,' Kaulak laughed, turning back to her. 'We ride due east. It is near to solstice and so the sun must be always to our left. If we keep this pace for twelve hours we shall either arrive at Gora-Jome or strike the Ephraxis a little way to the north or south. Do you not find your path this way in your native land?'

'Mund is a land of mountains and hills, woods and rivers and no two views are the same,' Elethrine replied. 'Also, the sun is always in the south, but not always visible.'

'Not visible? How can that be?' Ulak demanded.

'Clouds cover it,' Elethrine explained. 'Indeed, they often cover the whole sky.'

Her answer evoked a snort of disbelief from Ulak but cautious acceptance from the older Mausac and Kaulak, who had been in the east of the empire. The debate continued, softening their thoughtful mood of the early morning. Given a chance to air her education, Talithea quickly began to cheer up, although Elethrine was sure that thoughts of the shame veil and the celibentuary could not be far from her mind. The thought brought a new alarm to her own ponderings, and during a break in the conversation she pulled her camel up beside that of the Princess.

'Talithea,' she said softly, 'you and I must make a pact.'

Talithea turned a hopeful glance to her.

'As you doubtless heard,' Elethrine continued, 'Mausac did not take me last night, yet it seems hardly credible that I will reach the end of this journey without being forced to accept the same fate as you did.'

'True,' Talithea sighed.

'What was it like?' Elethrine asked, suddenly unable to restrain her curiosity.

'Exquisite, beautiful, too beautiful for words to describe, yet also dirty,' Talithea answered. 'That seems odd, yet until you do it you will not know. What pact do you suggest then?'

'That we, or just you, if by some miracle I am not ravished,' Elethrine continued, 'visit a witch before returning to our homes. There are several in the wilds of Aegmund and northern Mund who have little or no contact with other humans and are said to look with sympathy on soiled girls. With your maidenhead restored you could return to Thieron in pride, and you may rely on Aisla and myself to say nothing if you give the same covenant.'

'How would we pass through Mund unrecognised?' Talithea demanded with a trace of temper.

'In Aegmund we might pass,' Elethrine suggested.

'There is a flaw in your plan,' Talithea responded. 'We cannot travel through the wilds of Aegmund without a guard for fear of goblins, wild beasts and so forth. Yet we cannot command a guard without revealing our rank. The first noble holding we reached would demand to have their matrons inspect us for chastity and we would fail. Still, I readily accept your offer in the hope that luck will favour us, and suggest an exchange of names to seal the pact.'

'Very well,' Elethrine replied with a slight blush, 'my pet name is Pommette, the little apple, for the shape of my bottom, and yours?'

'Mine?' Talithea laughed. 'My sisters call me Snivels for my temper, but I prefer Moth for my pale hair and quiet movements.'

'Thank you,' Elethrine responded and fell silent, feeling a new sense of intimacy with the Princess.

The journey continued, the group pausing only briefly to take water and food, then once more setting off across the Eigora Khum. At length a line of low, sun-scorched hills appeared ahead, which they reached with the sun already throwing their shadows well to the front. The ground became rocky once more, then broken by dry ravines and finally a cliff, at the edge of which Kaulak reined in his camel.

'Perfect!' he called back. 'Too perfect even, for while we have come to Gora-Jome in a near straight line, we must now skirt the cliff.'

'Where is the city?' Elethrine asked in puzzlement, only to swallow her words as her camel came to a halt beside Kaulak's. To either side the cliff curved, forming a great bowl of land, formed of barren yellow rock all around but a carpet of green in the middle. Two features broke the green, the majestic sweep of a river, besides which the great Phætes seemed a mere trickle, and a tumble of yellow structures within high walls which she took to be the city of Gora-Jome.

'To the north, where the cliff is broken,' Kaulak explained, pointing to a distant gap in the cliffs, 'is where the Ephraxis comes down from the desert. It passes through a sheer gorge some two hundred feet deep and close to a league across. Where the valley opens out is a tithing post, which we must pass if we are to travel north. It will not be easy, as the captain might well view you three as exotic contraband.'

'Exotic contraband!' Talithea snorted.

'Restricted goods, if you prefer the term,' Kaulak continued. 'Trade laws forbid the export of human slaves –'

'Slaves!' all three girls interrupted in horror.

'What would pale-skinned girls with blonde hair, let alone red, be but slaves?' Mausac put in.

'This is so,' Kaulak said, 'there are truly but three social classes in Vendjome: the imperial family, free citizens of the Empire and slaves. In theory the son of a dung gatherer might rise to govern a city, but slaves are slaves and you three are clearly not born of Vendjomois stock.'

'I would sooner die!' Talithea declared.

'I also,' Elethrine echoed.

'Likewise,' Aisla added.

'Be calm,' Kaulak continued, 'there is a simple solution. Trade in nymphs is commonplace, and we three could easily pass as traders taking exotic nymphs to the north. Very exotic nymphs, it is true, but there are often new breeds on the market.'

'Nymphs!' Talithea snorted, but without the vehemence of her previous retort.

'Your beauty and colouring are sufficiently exotic to pass,' Kaulak went on, 'although your size is a problem and the trade normally comes down the river rather than up. Still, there is no law against inept merchants and so we should pass unmolested. Who, after all, would think that three ex-soldiers would be escorting three Mundic ladies up the Ephraxis? What, after all, would you be doing here in the first place?'

'I have a simpler plan,' Talithea put in. 'Rather than endure the indignity of pretending to be nymphs, why do we not simply ride north to beyond the gorge and pick up a boat there?'

'Not impossible,' Kaulak said with a shrug, 'but the gorge runs sheer for some two hundred leagues and barge captains might well be suspicious of travellers in the middle of the Eigora Khum and refuse to pick us up. A worse hazard is the sandstorms, which would bury us should one blow up in the three days it will take to reach the northern extremity of the gorge. Then there is the problem of Ythan, the country to the north of the desert. I understand that it is not a friendly land and that travellers without treaty passes from the Vendjome authorities are likely to be taken as slaves without question. Still, I am Kaulak and without fear. You may choose which plan to attempt.'

'Yours will do,' Talithea admitted, grudgingly.

They listened as he outlined the details of his plan,

then set off once more, heading south to where the cliff slowly declined to meet the bank of the vast Ephraxis. A ferry took them across, to where Kaulak led them into a dense copse of the same feather-leafed tree Elethrine had seen near Fujome.

'You must wait here,' he instructed them, 'while Ulak and I sell the camels and purchase the necessary elements of your disguise.'

The two men disappeared among the foliage, leaving Elethrine to wonder once more as to whether they could be trusted. It seemed likely, as it would have been far more convenient to have sold them as slaves in Fujome than to travel to Gora-Jome for the same purpose. Despite her reasoning she felt nervous as the shadows lengthened and dusk began to fall. Mausac had demanded that Aisla suck his penis and then had gone to sleep quickly, with a satisfied expression that further relaxed Elethrine's fears. Only when it was fully dark did Kaulak return, bearing a lantern and driving a strange combination of cart and cage pulled by a single ox.

'This is all I could get,' he explained, 'not that I got a bad price for the camels, but we need money for our passage and Ulak took some to buy food. He'll be at the inn. Come you three. I thought to find you already stripped and perhaps entertaining Mausac.'

'Do we have to disrobe now?' Elethrine asked, looking at the cage with feelings of both shame and trepidation. 'It is terribly undignified and surely not necessary until the morning.'

'You would cause comment in the city,' Kaulak answered. 'It is truly best this way, although a pity, as I had hoped we could take pleasure together tonight.'

'Oh, right,' Elethrine answered, quickly deciding that a night in a cage was a small sacrifice next to the loss of her maidenhead. Kaulak, she was certain, would be less easy to satisfy than Mausac had been.

'So,' Kaulak declared cheerfully, 'off with your clothes, and we will cover the cage with blankets if your precious "modesty" is disturbed.'

'Yes, please,' Talithea replied as Aisla began to unlace the front of Elethrine's bodice, 'and please also turn your head while we disrobe.'

Kaulak responded with a grunt of amusement. Elethrine undressed with a mounting sense of shame. As each layer of clothing fell away she felt a little more vulnerable and a little less self-confident. The removal of her chemise to expose her breasts gave her a strange feeling, as if she were doing it for the benefit of men, despite the fact that Mausac was still asleep and Kaulak had given her no more than the occasional curious glance as Aisla assisted with the more complicated fastenings of her underwear. When down to her drawers and pantalettes she had Aisla hold a blanket up, yet she still had to force herself to pull down her pantalettes. Once they were off her feelings of vulnerability reached a peak and she hugged the blanket tightly around herself while Aisla went to assist Talithea. Finally all three were nude under their blankets and huddled in the corners of the cage.

'Pretend to be asleep,' Kaulak advised as they set off, 'otherwise folk will think your behaviour strange for nymphs.'

Elethrine followed his advice, keeping one eye open as the cart bumped over the rough road into Gora-Jome. The cage wagon was parked in a stall that formed part of the inn's stables. A large area, it was evidently designed for such purposes and, as the girls peered out from under their blankets, another, similar wagon was moved into the stall adjacent to theirs. Inside were true nymphs – lithe, brown-skinned females of exquisite, delicate beauty and perhaps two thirds the height of their Vendjomois handlers. While the eyes of the nymphs showed intelligence, their entire being seemed

91

given over to lust. As their cage wagon was moved into place they postured and preened, casting enticing looks at the men and posing to display pert breasts and sweetly rounded bottoms in clear invitation. Simultaneously horrified and fascinated, Elethrine watched as the nymph merchants took turns to enter the cage. Each was immediately swarmed over, the nymphs licking and groping, eager for their owners' cocks. The men laughed at the antics of the beautiful females, pulling their cocks out to be sucked and teased to erection. Each fucked two nymphs while the remainder chattered excitedly and did their best to stimulate the ones being entered. It was done with the nymphs bent over, their pert brown bottoms raised to accept entry from the rear. When the merchants' cocks were in them they came quickly, giving excited squeaks and rubbing at their vulvas. Once each had been serviced the merchant would pull out and finish himself off into the mouth of another nymph, all of which were clearly eager for their share of cock. By the time the last nymph had come and the last merchant had had his sperm swallowed, Elethrine felt deeply disturbed and knew that her own tuppenny was moist and swollen. Resisting the urge to masturbate or to order Aisla to lick her between the legs, she curled up beneath the blankets and eventually managed to sleep.

Her dreams were powerfully erotic, involving being taken roughly from behind by a fat Vendjomois merchant, flaunting her naked bottom for the amusement of a great crowd of dwarves and accepting rear entry from Mausac in the hot desert sand. Twice she awoke, trembling with passion, and finally had to sneak a finger between her legs to bring herself to an urgently needed, but thoroughly shameful, climax over the thought of being used in the way the nymphs had been.

Despite Elethrine's suspicions of Kaulak's honesty, the remainder of the night passed without incident and she woke to a bright dawn and the clamour of the city.

The three of them stayed huddled under their blankets, both from modesty and the cold, not moving until Kaulak appeared with bowls of gruel. Checking that nobody was near, he leant close to the cage.

'Remember,' he said as he passed the steaming bowls through the bars, 'you are nymphs. Say nothing, merely twitter and giggle while making doe eyes at the men. If somebody touches you –'

'I could never behave so!' Elethrine interjected, recalling the lewd posturings of the brown nymphs.

'You must,' Kaulak answered.

'Could we not simply pretend to be asleep?' Talithea asked.

'For the guard point, yes,' Kaulak continued, 'but you cannot sleep all the way to Dry Ulan. Besides, the guards may wish to inspect you.'

'Inspect us!' Elethrine exclaimed, thinking of the intimate inspections given by Nurse Anaka.

'To ensure that the cargo manifest is correct,' Kaulak explained. 'Look, just smile and simper at the guards. Beyond the tithing post the ship master can be persuaded to continue – at the point of our swords if necessary.'

'Very well,' Elethrine sighed. 'I shall try, but it is all highly undignified.'

Kaulak made an unreadable gesture and stepped away.

Some time later he returned, along with Mausac and Ulak. The three girls feigned sleep as the cart moved out into the street, feeling intensely vulnerable in their nakedness despite the covering blankets. No challenge came on the way to the docks, nor as the barge was loaded. Elethrine risked a peep as she heard someone call for the cart to be put aboard. They were on a dock of yellow stone worn slick with years of use. Along its sides large sailing barges were moored; broad, shallow-draughted vessels each with a single tall mast. Beyond the barges the Ephraxis stretched away towards the high cliffs that marked the entrance to the canyon in which the river flowed through the Eigora Khum. As she looked back towards the city she found herself looking straight into the eyes of a longshoreman, who gave her the same sort of smile she might have bestowed on an exceptionally pretty cat.

She smiled back and hid herself hurriedly, not daring another glimpse until they were well out on the water. This time the view was even more alarming. A long, sleek craft painted in the gaudy purple and gold colours of Imperial Vendjome was pulling alongside them, a squad of soldiers standing ready at the gunwales. Hiding herself once more, she listened as the tithing officer spoke to the ship master.

One by one the items of cargo were checked and the correct levy of export tax collected, the tithing officer using a thoroughness and precision worthy of a dwarf. Finally their own berth was reached and Elethrine heard the tithing officer speak to Kaulak.

'Not slaves, I trust,' the officer asked with a laugh.

'Not at all,' Kaulak laughed back. 'Three nymphs, bound for Dry Ulan.'

'You are taking nymphs to Dry Ulan?' the tithing officer demanded. 'You would as well try and sell iron-work to the dwarves.'

'No ordinary nymphs,' Kaulak replied smoothly, 'but strange, wild ones captured in the high Glissades.'

'Remarkable,' the officer replied. 'I must see these nymphs that are so unusual that you take them north on the Ephraxis.'

'They are asleep,' Kaulak replied, 'and I would prefer to leave them so. The truth is, they are scarcely tamed yet and tend to become overly excited in the presence of males.'

'Their training will provide fine sport on the journey north then!' the officer laughed. 'But come, I must in any case confirm that they are nymphs, the captain is a stickler for precision.'

'Very well,' Kaulak sighed, but take care not to wake them.'

Elethrine closed her eyes and did her best to feign slumber as the blanket was drawn away from her. For the first time in her life her naked body was exposed to male eyes, and it was impossible not to tremble, while it took all her will power not to give in to her rising anger and shame.

'Extraordinary!' she heard the officer exclaim, amid a chorus of surprised murmurs from other onlookers.

'They are beautiful, certainly, but they are enormous! What hair though, pale as elf hair, brilliant, pale gold and gold-copper! And their skin, so white! You caught them in the Glissades you say?'

'High in the Glissades,' Kaulak confirmed, 'beyond Lake Phægron.'

'In Oretean held territory? You are bold indeed!'

'It is worth the risk. Ayapan the Merchant has already offered five hundred imperials for the biggest one.'

'As I would had I so much gold. She is magnificent. Never have I seen such breasts, and her bottom is a delight. Yet the others are nearly as fine, although the smallest has perhaps a weight or two excess flesh on her buttocks. Still, her purse looks moist and ready. May I test her?'

'I think better not –' Kaulak began, only to be cut off by Talithea's yelp of furious indignation.

'How dare you touch me?' the Princess yelled, as Elethrine turned and opened her eyes.

Talithea had stood up and pulled the blankets around herself, leaving Elethrine and Aisla completely nude. Stung with shame, both of them instinctively covered their tuppennies and breasts, an action that evoked almost as much astonishment in the onlookers as had Talithea's words.

'These are no nymphs!' the officer exclaimed, finally recovering his senses. 'What is the explanation for this?'

Kaulak acted promptly, driving his fist into the officer's face and leaping for the gunwale. An instant later he was gone, followed by Mausac and Ulak, all three diving deep into the water to avoid the crossbow bolts of the tithe collectors. Elethrine sat still, doing her best to cover her modesty as men clustered around the cage.

'Exotic slaves is my guess,' the ship master said ingratiatingly. 'Believe me, Officer Sarak, I had no idea of their true nature.'

'I accept your plea,' the tithing officer replied, 'so long as you waive all claim to them.'

'I accept,' the ship master replied, grudgingly. 'What then will you do with them?'

'They are now the property of the Imperial exchequer,' Sarak replied pompously. 'Regulation demands that they be taken to Vendjome and sold, their price to go towards our operating costs. Less commission for the capturing officer, of course.'

'Sold!' Talithea exclaimed. 'Enough of this nonsense! I am Talithea Mund, Princess and no slave! Free us on the instant!'

'This one has spirit,' Sarak laughed. 'It will augment her price, despite her fat bottom.'

Talithea lashed out, her nails coming within an inch of Sarak's face. Elethrine stood, mustering her courage with a prayer to her parents and earlier ancestors. Presenting her bare chest to one of the guards beyond the bars, she swallowed and then spoke in a steady voice.

'I choose death over slavery. Slay me cleanly.'

'I also,' Talithea added, quickly composing herself.

'What, and lose my commission?' Sarak exclaimed. 'Do you take me for an idiot?'

'I demand death,' Elethrine said haughtily. 'You shall never make me a slave.'

Sarak ignored her, instead detailing his subordinates to tie the three girls and bring them on to the tithe vessel. Elethrine did her best to fight and managed a few telling scratches before they overpowered her. Her hands were lashed in the small of her back, her legs were fastened together and a gag was thrust into her mouth, leaving her helpless and speechless. As she was lifted over the shoulder of one of the biggest guards she saw that Talithea had suffered the same fate, although none of the three men holding her was without bruises. Aisla though was locked in a wrestling grip with a squat guard. Elethrine felt a flush of pride at her maid's strength, but it was quickly extinguished as two more guards grabbed the struggling girl's arms and pinned her to the floor of the cage.

Soon they had been transferred to the tithe vessel and, in turn, to a fast river boat, which set off to the south under the command of Sarak. Numb with the magnitude of the disaster that had overtaken her, Elethrine could only lie on the floor of the cage, thinking in horror of the ultimate indignity that was slavery.

Two days later they came in sight of Vendjome. The capital was larger by far than any city Elethrine had seen before and straddled the vast Ephraxis as if it were a mere stream. The bright colours that characterised the Vendjomois taste were everywhere, houses tiled in turquoise and viridian, temples with domes of gold and silver inlay on vermilion tiles, shops with awnings of brilliant silk and, above all, a vast palace built of pink marble.

Elethrine took in the magnificent sight with a single miserable glance. They were to be sold as slaves, a fate too ignominious to think about. She was also still naked, without even a blanket to cover herself. The sole consolation was that she had been certified maiden, and that while Sarak and the other tithemen had taken every opportunity to indulge themselves with Talithea and Aisla, she had suffered nothing worse than sucking the men's cocks hard in preparation for her friends' vaginas.

Talithea and Aisla had been kept bound and entered in kneeling positions, their muffled protests quickly giving way to moans of pleasure as their tuppennies were filled with penis after penis. Elethrine had watched, torn as before between relief that she was not being served the same way and jealousy for the girls' obvious ecstasy.

Finally they docked at a quay of white marble and the cage was transported to a great circular building, which Sarak referred to as the Pelucidome. This proved to be open in the middle and lined with cages, into one of which the three girls were pushed before being untied.

5

Captive

For two days the girls were kept in the Pelucidome, allowed to sleep on rush mats in the rear cubicle by night but chivvied out for the inspection of potential clients by day. Elethrine found being caged deeply humiliating, although it was a fate she had always known might be hers if she were for any reason taken captive. When wars between the cities and fiefs of Mund and Aegmund had been common, captive girls would by tradition be displayed in wooden cages until ransomed or publicly shamed if no ransom was forthcoming. The higher born the girl the more prominent her display would be, and Elethrine had never been able to even think about the possibility without an inner shudder.

Yet, as the daughter of a baron, her display would have been a major spectacle and a great triumph for the victors. In the Pelucidome she was merely one more girl for sale, and treated no differently from any other. Indeed, from the aroma of their cubicle it seemed likely that previous occupants had been not human girls at all, nor even nymphs, but sheep or goats; a suspicion reinforced by the presence of a dozen large, black pigs in the pen next to their own. On the other side was a group of female nymphs; slight, brown-skinned creatures with huge, bright eyes and great bushes of crinkly, black hair. They would chitter and laugh, striking lewd poses in return for sweets and fruit from the people who

99

came to inspect them, a display which disturbed Elethrine deeply.

Elethrine, Talithea and Aisla did their best to remain poised and aloof, spending their time sitting cross-legged on the floor with their long skirts arranged to show not so much as an ankle. They were grateful for the return of their clothing, although they had overheard an overseer explain that it had not been done from a sense of decency but in order to tantalise potential customers and so push up their eventual price.

The interior of the Pelucidome was crowded, even at night when it was lit with a ring of rush torches. Despite the presence of several other groups of girls in the pens, the three of them received much the greatest attention and there was usually a good number of curious Vendjomois citizens peering in through the bars with expressions of lustful fascination. Few spoke directly to them, but marvelled at the colour of their hair and speculated on their bodies, notably how their breasts, bottoms and pubic areas would look naked. Many times attempts were made to goad, tease or bribe them into stripping but none succeeded.

On the evening of the second day Elethrine was sitting with the others, pointedly ignoring the attempts of a corpulent man in a turquoise silk robe to get them to display their bottoms. A commotion at the high doors that led into the Pelucidome attracted her attention and she looked up to see a dray entering. The superstructure was a cage, making it not unlike the cart in which they had been pulled through Gora-Jome. A group of female nymphs clung to the bars, chattering with excitement at the crowds and pressing themselves against the bars in the hope of caresses to their golden-brown skin. Two mules drew the dray, and as Elethrine watched a man stepped from behind them, Ayapan the merchant.

Immediately she was at the bars, calling to him, wildly hopeful that he might secure their release or that

Karogan and his warriors might be on hand to attempt a rescue. Ayapan looked over, saw them and began to saunter over, his expression showing no great surprise.

'Ah, I had heard that three northern girls were up for sale,' he said as he approached, 'and I had suspected it would be you. Evidently Kaulak failed to see you past the Gora-Jome tithe point.'

'He tried his best,' Elethrine answered, throwing Talithea a dirty look, 'but now we are safe once more, for surely you have come to release us?'

'Release you?' Ayapan answered, both astonished and amused. 'Far from it, I have come to buy you, should my purse stretch so far.'

'Buy us!' all three girls spoke together.

'Absolutely,' Ayapan continued. 'You are most valuable merchandise and will fetch a great price, so high indeed that I could not hope to make a profit, save perhaps in Oretes, and that unlikely. Yet you have other uses, for, let us say, a long term investment. As to releasing you, I am but a merchant, half-dwarven and of Ythan at that. How do you expect me to perform such a task?'

'Is not Karogan with you?' Aisla asked, hopefully.

'He and his fellows are drinking in a tavern,' Ayapan replied, 'and even they, veteran warriors though they be, could not bring you clear of Vendjome. Besides, why should they?'

The girls stayed silent, realising the truth of Ayapan's argument.

'And now I intend to join them, once my nymphs are secure,' he said. 'You will excuse me ladies, until the auction.'

He gave a low, mocking bow and left, Elethrine watching his globular figure as he walked away to remonstrate with a handler who had allowed one of the nymphs to mount herself on his penis. The girls sat back down, exchanging glum glances.

* * *

The following day dawned with the sky above the glass roof of the Pelucidome the unbroken expanse of blue that the girls had come to recognise as typical of Vendjome. The atmosphere around them, however, had changed. There were no casual onlookers, but only market officials and handlers, each busy about complex arrangements that were clearly a precursor to the auction.

'It is to be today then,' Aisla spoke, sadly.

'Be proud and show only contempt,' Elethrine replied with a good deal more strength than she felt. 'Slavery is a state of the mind and you will be free so long as your mind stays so.'

'Better to die honourably,' Talithea put in. 'Perhaps we could seize a sword from a guard and force them to slay us in fair combat.'

'They would catch us in nets,' Elethrine objected, 'as they did the bull-nymph that ran amok the first day we were here. No, have patience and we shall see Mund once more.'

Talithea started to reply but went quiet at the approach of an official. His scarlet robe and gold Pelucidome emblem showed him to be among the most senior, while his grey hair and sparse frame gave him an air of stern respectability. Elethrine turned to face him.

'I am Crizac, master auctioneer,' he announced as he reached the bars. 'Today I will be presiding over your sale and it is well that we understand one another in order that the best price may be obtained.'

'You may expect no co-operation from us,' Elethrine replied, coldly.

'Indeed, how dare you ask it?' Talithea suddenly stormed, abandoning her intention of remaining calm and dignified. 'You capture us, tie us, cage us and tell us we are to be slaves and then you expect our help in maximising our price!'

'You would do best to accept your new status as

slaves,' Crizac continued calmly. 'New slaves are often rebellious, but soon learn to respect the whip.'

'Not I! Never!' Talithea stormed.

'You will soon be putting your face meekly to the earth and humbly begging your master's touch,' Crizac replied. 'Meanwhile –'

He stopped abruptly to dodge as Talithea hurled an earthenware water jug at him. It shattered on the bars, showering him with fragments of pottery but doing no real harm.

'Be calm,' he said sternly, making a mark on the clay tablet in his hand, 'and listen well. You may hope to achieve your best prices from Izatak, the Imperial purchase agent, who may be identified by a white robe bordered in purple. You would do well to impress him as, should you succeed, you will become girls in the seraglio of the Panjandrum, a great honour for three uncouth barbar girls.'

Elethrine gave him her coldest look, which had no effect whatever.

'So,' Crizac continued, 'when you are ordered to strip, give him your full attention, expose your breasts for him, hold open the cheeks of your bottoms towards him –'

'Never!' Elethrine exclaimed. Talithea and even Aisla also added angry refusals.

'You would do well to heed my words,' Crizac went on. 'As I was saying, a good, open, yielding display of your sexes is essential, in particular your anal apertures, for which the Panjandrum has an especial taste.'

'Disgusting!' Talithea sneered.

'He is clearly depraved,' Elethrine added. 'I shall never adopt such lewd poses.'

'Should you not,' Crizac said dryly, 'it is likely that Izatak may limit his bids, in which case you may be purchased by other members of the Imperial family, wealthy merchants or senior officials. More likely,

103

should you appear sexually cold, you will be bought by priests, and I should here remark that no less than five temples have expressed the opinion that you would make fine sacrifices for the coming solstice.'

'Then let us die upon their altars,' Talithea declared. 'We shall never pose and flaunt ourselves as you suggest.'

'Oh, you will, you will,' Crizac replied, as he made another mark on his tablet and walked on to inspect the pigs in the next cage.

Elethrine stayed silent, comparing the prospect of making an unspeakably lewd display of herself with that of being sacrificed to one of the strange Vendjomois gods. Honour, she knew, demanded the choice of sacrifice, yet it was a poor way to die, suggesting submission to the will of an alien deity. Alone, she might have taken the other option, displaying herself before the crowds in the knowledge that no rumour of her wanton behaviour would ever reach home. In front of Aisla and Talithea it was simply unthinkable, not so much because of the shame of stripping and posing but because to do it would be an admission that she was a slave. Reaching a sudden decision, she turned to Talithea and Aisla.

'Princess,' she began, addressing Talithea formally, 'I was wrong to advise patience. Let us make a stand here and hope for a death of sufficient honour to buy us our places in the feast hall of heroines.'

'It is the only choice,' Talithea answered. Aisla nodded her acquiescence without hesitation.

They waited in silence as the auction was prepared. The centre of the Pelucidome contained only fences and other apparatus for controlling the stock, including a selection of whips. The auction itself was clearly to be held in the square outside, as a wooden platform had been erected across the door with a ramp leading up to it from the interior of the Pelucidome. Presently a junior official appeared to inform them that they were the last three lots and to attach red cards bearing numbers to the bars of their cage.

'We are to be auctioned separately then?' Elethrine asked in dismay.

'Thus the best price will be secured,' the official remarked.

'Who then is to be first?' Talithea enquired.

'You are second last,' he answered, 'the golden-haired one before you and the copper-haired one last. Thus the finest and so most precious will come at the end.'

He walked away, leaving Elethrine with a sharp pang of emotion. To be sold on the block was bad enough, but to be valued at less than her maid was mortifying.

The auction began, lot after lot being taken to the platform. The livestock went first, mainly pigs, goats and mandrills, ape-like creatures in which the Vend-jomois seemed to take particular pleasure. The nymphs followed – first the bulls, and then the exquisitely beautiful females, who giggled, tittered and struck lewd poses as they were led to the platform. Finally came the human slaves, mainly pretty girls with olive complexions and richly curled black hair, who Elethrine guessed to be Oreteans. Finally her own turn came and she braced herself for a final struggle and death in front of the crowds of Vendjome city.

Handlers approached, burly men of heavy physique and evident experience. Using nets and spears, they separated Elethrine from the others. She was stripped, rapidly and efficiently, such fastenings as they were unable to fathom out being torn or cut. Cursing herself for having revealed her intention not to strip to order, she allowed her beautiful clothes to be removed, reasoning that it was best to preserve her strength for a final, supreme effort.

To her further chagrin cuffs and close chains were attached to her wrists and ankles. Her hands were then placed behind her back and linked together. A linking chain was led from her wrist chain to that which joined her ankles. Helpless, she could only walk forward with small, precise steps. Fight was going to be near impossible, yet she determined to acquit herself as honourably as she might. She tilted her chin up, determined to show courage to the others and only disdain for her captors. As she reached the ramp the roar of the crowd struck her like a palpable thing, then doubled in volume as she stepped into the open air.

In front of her was a sea of faces, the whole great square of the city being thronged with people, thousands upon thousands, more than she had ever before seen assembled in one place. Everyone was looking at her, gazing on her naked body, calling remarks on the colour of her skin and hair, the shape and size of her breasts and hips, the length of her legs, the firmness of her belly and the look of the triangle of golden down that hid her tuppenny. Both anger and shame filled her, emotions so strong that the tears threatened to start in her eyes. Swallowing hard, she took the final step on to the platform and braced herself.

A spear point jabbed the soft flesh of her flank, distracting her for a moment. Then she heard the click of a lock and turned to see that she had been fixed to a pillar. Barely able to move her hands and feet and chained firmly in place, she resigned herself to the indignity of being sold naked, taking consolation only in the knowledge that they had not managed to make her acknowledge her own slavery.

In front of the platform two rows of seats had been positioned, evidently for the more important buyers. The white and purple robe of Izatak, the Imperial purchasing agent, was visible in the second row, next to a hawk-faced man with a bald head and cowled robes of golden cloth, who might possibly be a priest. In the first row of those standing stood Ayapan the merchant, flanked by the dwarven hand leaders Karogan and Turilan. The merchant gave her a knowing smile, each dwarf a formal nod.

To her side Crizac had stepped forward and was holding up his hands for quiet. A hush fell over the crowd, spreading slowly from the centre until the great square was mantled in silence, every eye fixed on Elethrine's naked body. Pride welled up inside her to join her feelings of shame and anger – pride that perhaps four thousand men and women should be feasting their eyes on her and evidently judging her beautiful. She tilted her chin up another degree, her determination to show no weakness growing with the new emotion.

'Parcel one hundred and five,' Crizac announced loudly, 'a magnificent girl-slave of barbarous Mund, golden-haired, white-skinned and as beautiful as the dawn. She has but twenty years and is firm and resilient of flesh. Regard the beauty of her lips and nose. Wonder at the colour of her hair, both of head and pudendum. See the fullness of her breasts and how they stand proud of her chest. View the roundness of her hips and the soft swell of her sex. As she turns and bends you may marvel at the magnificence of her bottom.'

Elethrine stayed still, ignoring the cue to flaunt her most intimate secrets.

'She is virgin in both cunt and anus,' Crizac continued, bringing the blood automatically to Elethrine's cheeks, 'as you will see when she displays her full beauty.'

Again Elethrine ignored him, then winced at the pain of a spear point being jabbed at her bare thigh. Reasoning that they would hardly damage her if it risked lowering her price, she maintained her haughty stillness.

'So,' Crizac announced, throwing her a brief glare of fury, 'who will bid for this paragon of exotic beauty? May I ask one hundred imperials?'

107

A gasp swept over the great throng at the opening price, many faces showing instant disappointment. Several had raised hands though, including both Ayapan and the priest seated next to Izatak. The purchase agent himself remained aloof, merely making a mark on the slate in his hand.

'Two hundred imperials?' Crizac called, at which the majority of the raised hands fell, but neither that of the priest nor Ayapan.

Elethrine stayed absolutely still, trying to keep her mind from the horrors of being sacrificed in some heathen temple. It was a better fate than slavery, but only marginally, and she wondered if she might not later have the opportunity of breaking loose and going down in honourable combat.

'Three hundred imperials?' Crizac enquired.

Several more hands dropped, leaving only Ayapan among those standing. The priest was still bidding, as were three evidently rich men in the front row. A motion caught Elethrine's eye, Crizac moving to speak into her ear.

'For the sake of your life, display yourself!' he whispered, urgently. 'The hawk faced man is Grauzod, High-Priest of Belime, god of war. If he takes you, your fate will be horrible beyond measure!'

'So be it,' Elethrine replied quietly, although trying to stop her lower lip from trembling.

'Fool girl!' Crizac hissed and turned back to his task. 'May I ask four hundred imperials?'

Two of the wealthy men lowered their hands, each shaking his head regretfully. Then Ayapan shrugged, smiled at her and also lowered his hand.

'I will pay four hundred and fifty,' the priest spoke, his voice a bass croak which sent a shiver through Elethrine.

The remaining rich man lowered his hand, his face showing a distinct flush of fear as he turned and caught the eyes of Grauzod.

'The bid rests at four hundred and fifty, with his venerance Grauzod,' Crizac said. 'May I ask more?'

For a moment there was silence. Crizac's voice had held a trace of pity and Elethrine found herself choking back tears, yet remained absolutely still.

'The throne pledges five hundred,' a quiet voice spoke.

'The bid rests at five hundred, with the Imperial throne,' Crizac said. 'May I ask more?'

Elethrine turned her head, unable to resist favouring Izatak with the smallest of smiles.

'Five hundred and fifty,' Grauzod spoke.

'Six hundred,' Izatak responded, calmly.

Grauzod shook his head, gave Izatak a cold look and sat back. Elethrine felt tension drain from her body that she had not realised was there. Relief flooded through her, overwhelming her feelings of shame and exposure. Suddenly exhausted, she allowed herself to be led to the side and chained to a post that also held two Oretean maidens. Beyond, other posts stretched around the curve of the Pelucidome, each with its chained group of girls, nymphs or livestock. Hers was the last post, and she had a clear view of the platform.

Talithea was next to be sold, and, like Elethrine, she was given no opportunity to disrupt the sale. Chained to the pillar, stark naked with every exquisite curve of her body on display to the vast crowd, she nevertheless maintained an air of regal calm that made Elethrine swell with pride. She also refused to pose on cue, merely tilting her chin another few degrees into the air.

The bidding followed a similar pattern to before, rising quickly beyond the reach of all but the most wealthy. Again the cruel Grauzod attempted to win the bidding, and again Izatak coolly pushed it beyond his means. Finally Talithea sold for six hundred and fifty imperials, a sum that had the assistant auctioneers in a froth of delighted calculation.

The Princess had shown no emotion whatever, but, as her chain was unclipped from the post, she suddenly hurled herself forward. The gesture was hopeless, yet Elethrine could not resist a yell of encouragement. Talithea landed across the front row, having aimed apparently for either Izatak or Grauzod. In any case it was the priest whom she struck as the chairs of the front row collapsed. The guards were moving even as her teeth sunk into Grauzod's arm, and they had grabbed her in the next instant. She was pulled back, spitting and thrashing, leaving half a dozen of the highest nobles of Vendjome sprawled unceremoniously on the ground and Grauzod with blood streaming down his arm.

Four guards were needed to drag her to the fixing post, and when she arrived Elethrine found her friend's eyes full of a berserk fury that faded only slowly once she had been fixed in place.

'Well struck,' Elethrine said quietly, when Talithea seemed a little calmer.

The Princess made no reply but gave Elethrine a blood-stained grin. Both turned at a sound from the crowd, finding that Aisla was now being led out onto the platform. At the sight of the maid's sleek figure and heavy breasts the crowd gave a great sigh of appreciation. Aisla shook her hair out around her head as she stepped forward, again drawing a deep murmur from several thousand throats. Crizac once more took his place, spoke quickly to Aisla and began to describe her virtues, although his audience seemed barely to hear. When the cue came to display, the maid, instead of remaining aloof, turned slowly and without losing a single iota of her elegance, bent forward slightly to allow a view of her bottom and a glimpse of the pursed rear of her tuppenny.

'She is a slut, your maid,' Talithea observed, her insane rage gone as swiftly as it had come on.

'True, yet it is her right as lowborn,' Elethrine

responded, 'and I wish her well, if only she may escape the attentions of Grauzod.'

The bidding rose with even more vigour than it had before. The five-hundred-imperial mark was passed with a dozen men still in contest, and four remained when it reached seven hundred, a level which the overheard whispers of the junior auctioneers indicated was unheard of. An enormously fat man in a splendid robe of vermilion silk backed out at seven hundred and fifty, leaving Izatak, Grauzod and an elderly man, whom Crizac had been heard to address as Jandrum.

Izatak shook his head and made a mark on his slate as Grauzod called out seven hundred and seventy-five. Elethrine felt a lump rise in her throat and gave a desperate signal to Aisla. The maid nodded to Crizac, and at his approach whispered in his ear. The master auctioneer moved to unshackle her wrists, reattaching her to the post from her ankle chain. Free handed, she turned again, once more presenting the crowd with her neatly rounded bottom. Parting her legs, she bent at the waist, exposing every detail to the audience. Her angle left her tuppenny thrust straight at Izatak, who gulped and hurriedly changed whatever mark he had made.

'Eight hundred,' he spoke.

'Eight hundred and twenty-five,' the Jandrum called hoarsely. 'Even the hair of her cunt is ginger!'

'Eight hundred and fifty,' Grauzod put in, his face contorted with a strange, vicious lust.

Aisla put her hands back between her legs, spread the lips of her tuppenny between two fingers and, quite shamelessly, began to masturbate.

'Nine hundred!' the Jandrum shouted, his bloated face purple with lust.

'Nine hundred and twenty-five,' Grauzod hissed.

Aisla swung her dangling breasts and pulled her back in to ensure a yet finer view of her open buttocks and the tight pink spot of her anus between them.

'Nine hundred and fifty,' Izatak said, doing his best to remain calm.

'Nine hundred and seventy-five,' Grauzod snarled, 'and beware my curse, man.'

'Better you beware the swords of the Imperial guard,' Izatak answered. 'One thousand imperials for the flame-haired wench, good Crizac.'

'The bid rests with you, Lord,' Crizac answered.

'Then I say one thousand and twenty!' the Jandrum called out.

'Then I call one thousand and forty!' Grauzod snapped.

Aisla, who had been masturbating with a lazy, lascivious motion more intended for display than to bring herself to a climax, began to rub faster. Moving the hand that had been holding her sex lips open, she let them close around her finger, then reached back. The crowd watched spellbound as she extended a long, slender finger, put it to the tight hole of her anus, rubbed and then quickly popped it inside. Elethrine heard her maid groan as the pretence of masturbation became real.

'One thousand and fifty!' the Jandrum declared.

'One sixty!' Grauzod countered.

'One thousand, one hundred!' Izatak yelled, finally abandoning his cool as Aisla started to come.

Her knees bowed. The muscles of her buttocks and thighs tensed. Her open, wet vagina contracted to expel a dribble of juice. She screamed and pushed her finger deep up her bottom and her anus squirmed around it. Her finger dabbed frantically at her clitty. She screamed again and then it was over. She slumped onto the wooden boards of the auction platform while the crowd stared in absolute silence.

'At one thousand, one hundred gold imperials, sold to the crown,' Crizac said quickly before any of the bidders recovered themselves.

112

None objected and Aisla was led, grinning, to the holding post where she joined her mistress and the Princess.

'You are a wanton little slut – but you did well,' Elethrine addressed Aisla as the maid's chain was clipped into place.

The formalities were quickly concluded and then Izatak came to claim his purchases. These also included two Oretean girls and a magnificent Cyprayan, whose discovery fractionally dented Elethrine's pride at her sale price. Evidently the Imperial purse was deep and it was a matter of pride that the most beautiful girls should grace the seraglio of the Panjandrum.

6

Slave

With both Imperial and Pelucidome guards covering them with spears and loaded crossbows, the girls were unchained and thrown gauzy pyjamas. These did little to cover their bodies, but Elethrine scrambled into hers gratefully, the decision to go down fighting abandoned now that the tension of being sold was past. Their chains were replaced with light fetters of pure gold. These joined their wrists in front, with leashes of fine chain running to wide holding rings.

Izatak took hold of their chain rings and set off, three guards falling into step behind him. Elethrine followed, full of chagrin and embarrassment. The gauzy pyjamas were only fractionally better than nudity, leaving her body visible for all to see. Glancing at Talithea, Aisla and the other girls, she found that, if anything, the pyjamas drew the attention to breasts and buttocks, enhancing but not concealing.

They were led out of the square and through the city, the crowds parting before the guardsmen and stopping to stare at the beautiful captives. Elethrine caught several remarks on her body and those of her companions, each making her blush. Jokes were also passed on the shape of their bottoms and breasts, and questions asked as to the price they had fetched.

After what seemed an endless march they reached the palace, a vast structure of pink marble topped with roofs tiled with pure turquoise and domes of verdigris-covered copper. A broad flight of steps fronted it, running up to a colonnade among the pillars in which stood groups of strange looking men. They wore yellow robes and were characterised by a uniform flabbiness of flesh and looseness of feature. It was towards them that the girls were led. At the head of one group was an older, stouter individual, his robe bordered with crimson.

'That is Apod, the chief eunuch,' the purchasing agent announced. 'It would be best to show him respect, as he will have direct control over you in the seraglio.'

'He shall never control me,' Talithea spoke up for the first time since the sale, apparently neither that nor the fight having cowed her spirit.

The purchase agent merely laughed and saluted the chief eunuch, who returned the greeting with a self-important nod.

'I believe the barbars are to be taken straight to the Presence,' Izatak said, handing the golden leashes to Apod.

'That is the case,' Apod replied in a pompous tone.

Izatak left without a word, taking the other girls with him. Elethrine and her companions were led into the palace of the Panjandrum of Vendjome. The colonnade gave on to a wall, its marble surface covered in a thousand intricate carvings, some showing scenes of a martial nature, some of what appeared to be religious significance and some of erotic acts in a detail that sent the blood to Elethrine's cheeks. A high door of beaten and polished copper inlaid with gold opened in front of them, a squad of Imperial guards at either side stood rigidly to attention as they passed.

'Speak no word to the Presence,' Apod instructed as they were led along a great corridor paved and walled in a marble of delicate pink veined with gold.

'I am the daughter of a king and I speak to whomsoever I please!' Talithea spat.

'It is unthinkable that a mere slave girl should address the Presence directly,' Apod retorted. 'Should you do so you will be whipped.'

He said it with a spiteful malice that told Elethrine that he would greatly enjoy the task. At his belt hung a quirt of braided leather, perhaps the length of her forearm and with a snake-tongued sting. It was stained black at the handle and along the last foot of its length, stains that she knew would have come from the sweat of its users and victims respectively. It looked painful, while its resemblance to the dog whips used in the keep added a pang of shame to the thought of having it applied to her bottom. Not only that, but there seemed little prospect of the eunuchs allowing them to retain what little modesty their pyjamas afforded. Indeed, she could see no reason why they would not be whipped nude, as they had been stripped before. Once more it looked as if Talithea's hot tongue might get them into difficulties.

At the threat of whipping the Princess went quiet, giving one nervous glance at Apod's quirt and then putting her chin up bravely. Elethrine put her head up as well, determined not to seem weak in front of her companions. Ahead was a gigantic door, as tall as the great gates of the keep and worked with fantastic carvings. To either side stood guards: massive, bearded men wearing the now familiar uniform of the Panjandrum's personal guard. These were evidently the elite of the elite, both stern, muscular and the tallest men she had seen in Vendjome, their spiked helmets reaching as tall as Aisla.

They paid no attention whatsoever as the eunuch and the three girls approached, not even deigning to glance at what Elethrine knew must be a display of breasts, bellies and legs as enticing to men as it was shameful for girls. A short flight of steps led up to the door, which Apod climbed to smite the door with his staff. There

116

was a pause, and then the door swung slowly open, the chief eunuch pulling the girls back into motion with a tug at their chains.

Elethrine mounted the steps as the doors opened, moved by some unseen mechanism, the existence of which was betrayed by the groan of pulleys and counterweights in the wall. Ahead was a vast chamber, set with pillars supporting the ceiling and a great dome whose apex was perhaps the height of twenty-five men. She found her mouth opening in awe and closed it quickly, instead looking staunchly ahead as they were led into the chamber. On all sides turquoise, malachite and cinnabar inlay decorated the walls, set in intricate webs of gold to no obvious pattern. Fountains stood on either side, crystal clear water tinkling into marble basins, the sound mixing with the light laughter of the numerous courtiers who lounged on great pillows of coloured silk. Their dress was as extravagant, and, to Elethrine's mind, as vulgar, as the setting. Brilliant colours abounded: viridian, copper-gold, fuchsia and vermilion most notably. Even the gauzy tunics and pyjamas of people who were clearly slaves looked rich and exotic. These were mainly girls, with a few effeminate youths among them. Without exception the females exuded sexuality, their oiled limbs and naked or near-naked breasts and buttocks showing a languid sensuality. Elethrine swallowed hard as she realised that her own gauzy pyjamas left her no more decent.

Nothing that she had seen came close to rivalling the chamber in magnificence, yet she set her chin high and walked towards the towering throne of what appeared to be solid gold that stood at the far side of the chamber. In it was seated a man who could only be the Panjandrum of Vendjome, the man who claimed an empire supposedly richer and more populous than any other. He wore a great headpiece of jewelled cloth of gold with an enormous ruby at the centre. His robes

117

were also of gold cloth and swept away from him and down the steps that led up to his throne. If his surroundings and clothes were impressive, the same could not be said for his body. He was small, squat and corpulent, with a round, bloated face red from over-indulgence. Dark, watery eyes looked out with little sign of intelligence, making Elethrine wonder if he was drunk or drugged. At one side of his throne was a beautiful boy, his pale skin and brown hair showing him to be a Hai from the Glass Coast region of Cypraya. He was naked, his body oiled and skin smooth. The ruler of Vendjome was stroking the boy's hair in a gesture of decadent lechery. At his other side stood a stately, dour man, his gaze as alert as his emperor's was slack.

'Look at the floor, unworthy chattels!' Apod hissed, furiously.

Elethrine glanced at Talithea, who still had her chin high. Resigning herself to the consequences of her arrogance, Elethrine followed suit, tilting her chin up another degree and noting that Aisla had also refused to look down. A sudden, sharp pain in her thigh told her that one of the eunuch guards to the rear had struck her with his quirt, yet it had been done surreptitiously and she guessed that the eunuch dared not discipline her openly in the audience chamber.

'Speak only to me,' Apod said, his voice full of his own importance. 'I shall speak to the vizier, who in turn will convey your words to the Presence. At the foot of the steps, kneel and put your faces to the floor.'

Elethrine made no move. To kneel as she had been ordered would be an admission of her place as a slave, and her refusal to admit it was the last bastion of her battered pride. Nor could she show weakness in front of Talithea and Aisla, both of whom had also stayed standing.

'Kneel!' the chief eunuch hissed.

Elethrine stayed standing and again the quirt lashed

118

out at her leg, a vicious blow aimed at the tender flesh where buttock met thigh. It stung, although the folds of her pyjama pants caught some of the impact. Although taut over the fullest part of her bottom they bagged a little lower down, providing welcome protection from the worst of the eunuch's malice. Twice more the quirt struck, applied across her bottom and then her thighs, and a muffled squeak from Aisla told her that the others were receiving the same beatings.

All three of them stayed standing, and the Panjandrum looked up. The whipping stopped abruptly, the assistant eunuchs having fallen to their faces on the marble floor. Elethrine look straight forward, directing her gaze a foot above the podgy emperor's head.

The entire audience chamber had gone quiet, the only sounds the tinkling of the fountains and a nervous titter from a slave girl. Slowly the Panjandrum's eyes came into focus and swung round to look at them. His face registered puzzlement and some annoyance, not apparently at their defiance but at having been disturbed.

'Who are these?' he asked the vizier by his side in a weak voice quavering with lethargy.

'Barbar slave girls from the northlands,' the vizier replied, 'purchased for the amusement of your Resplendence this very morning. Note the extraordinary colour of their hair and their great height.'

'Oh, yes,' the Panjandrum mumbled.

'I am no barbar girl,' Talithea announced, her voice unnecessarily loud from her apprehension. 'I am the Princess Talithea, third daughter of King Utharion V, and a free citizen of the kingdom of Mund.'

'As am I,' Elethrine added, 'the Demoiselle Elethrine, only child and heiress to Baron Dakarmoth of Korismund. Likewise my maid is my bondswoman and no slave.'

'Why do the pale-haired barbars shout so?' the

Emperor asked wheezily, ignoring them completely and addressing the question to his vizier. 'What do they say?'

'They express awe at your magnificence and wonder at your greatness,' the vizier said.

'Lord Emperor,' Talithea said. 'We make appeal to your Imperiality. Pray provide us with an honour guard that we may return in safety to our homeland, as my father would surely do should any daughter you might achieve have the ill luck to be thrown helpless upon the coasts of Mund.'

Again the Panjandrum took no notice, only looking at them with an expression of mild curiosity and then turning back to the vizier. Elethrine waited for his answer, sure that for all his apparent slackness of mind the ruler of the vast Vendjome empire must by definition have a strong sense of honour.

Moments passed, Elethrine's hope fading slowly to be replaced by further feelings of resentment and frustration at their treatment. She had been sure that if they could only communicate with someone of high status they would be treated as their own rank demanded, yet the more exalted the people they met the worse they seemed to be treated. A glance to her side showed similar emotions in Talithea's face, only stronger and less controlled.

'Why do they not kneel?' the Emperor asked finally, somewhat peevishly but slowly, as if the realisation that something was out of place had only just struck him.

'They have little wit,' the vizier answered. 'Their intelligence is perhaps of a similar level to that of a tame mandrill, a nymph or goblin.'

'Yes, I see,' the Panjandrum said slowly, 'yet beauty and simple-mindedness sit well together.'

'Deep is your wisdom, O Resplendence,' the Vizier simpered.

'I –' Elethrine started automatically, then stopped,

lost for words at the magnitude of the insults of both vizier and emperor.

The Emperor said nothing more, but began to study them in a lazy fashion, rather as if admiring statues; statues of a distinctly rude nature. Elethrine felt a blush rise to her cheeks as she realised the quality of his attention, becoming suddenly far more aware of the fact that the pyjamas did little to conceal her breasts, belly and legs from a gaze that was becoming increasingly lecherous. She began to tremble, wondering if he would simply ravish her on the floor, much as Sarak and his tithemen had ravished Talithea and Aisla, with no concern whatever for who was watching or what intimacies were displayed. Although scared, and physically repelled by the squat, flabby figure on the great throne, she was unable to resist a flush of pride at the thought of having her maidenhead taken by an emperor. He had also insulted her, a frequent precursor to ravishment. As a demoiselle she could fully expect squires, thanes and even higher nobles to want to take her, and she accepted the lust of the lower orders as inevitable, yet an emperor –

'Have them dance,' the Panjandrum spoke suddenly, as if reaching a momentous decision.

'Make them dance,' the vizier relayed.

'Dance,' Apod instructed.

'Dance?' Elethrine queried, taken aback by the sudden and bizarre request.

'Dance!' Apod repeated, more sharply.

'What would you have us dance?' Talithea asked, her voice showing puzzlement, temper and something of the demented rage she had shown at the slave market. 'A ten-step? A pavane?'

'And who would be our partners?' Elethrine added.

'The maidens' dance of spring might be possible, had we some flowers,' Aisla suggested respectfully.

'But scarcely appropriate,' Elethrine replied.

There was an awkward pause, finally broken by the chief eunuch.

'Possibly they are too ignorant to know the dances of lust?' he suggested to the vizier.

'Nonsense, sensual dancing is natural for girls, even nymphs do it,' the vizier replied before turning to the Panjandrum and continuing. 'O Resplendence, I fear that they are indeed little better than beasts, though beautiful, but perhaps they can be trained to give pleasure in due time.'

The Panjandrum merely gave a snort of doubt and disappointment. Elethrine felt her anger rising from the vizier's remarks.

'But see, O Resplendence,' the Vizier continued hastily, 'the bizarre and backward clothes which were found with them.'

As the Vizier spoke a curtain opened to one side and a servant emerged, his outstretched arms laden with their clothing. On the top lay a small tangle of frilled coral-pink silk – Elethrine's pantalettes. She felt the blushes rising to her cheeks as the Emperor reached out and touched them, feeling the silk between his fingers and then holding them up to inspect them with his rheumy eyes.

'Most curious,' he said. 'How are these worn?'

'How are they worn?' The vizier turned to the girls.

Elethrine said nothing, too ashamed to answer. Her cheeks were burning as her most intimate garment was held up for the inspection of the entire audience chamber.

'Answer!' the vizier demanded.

'It is not a matter to be discussed in the presence of males,' Elethrine managed after a pause.

'They serve to warm the neck and shoulders, O Resplendence,' the vizier addressed the Panjandrum. 'The fours holes are for the arms, torso and neck respectively.'

'Most curious,' the Emperor replied, poking his hand through the hole in the pantalettes that was designed to allow girls to pee in comfort. 'Have one dressed.'

The next instant Elethrine felt her pyjama pants pulled sharply down, baring her bottom, legs and belly on the instant. She gasped at the sudden exposure, a noise of alarm and shock. Before she could recover herself they had pulled her top up as well, exposing her breasts only to realise that the chains on her wrist shackles prevented her from being conveniently stripped.

'Not that one,' the Emperor said, 'the giantess with the flame hair.'

The eunuchs stopped interfering with Elethrine as quickly as they had began. Her top fell back into place, covering her breasts with the minimal modesty of thin blue gauze, but they left her with her pyjama pants in a tangle around her ankles. She felt a new flush of shame, aware that the partial stripping left her bottom cheeks and the furry triangle of her lower belly peeping out from beneath the hem of her pyjama top in a display that was somehow ruder than full nudity. It was impossible to decide which was more undignified: to attempt to pull them up with her wrists chained and give a still more revealing display of her bottom, or to remain standing with it all showing anyway. For a moment she squirmed in indecision, twice dipping as if to try and get her pyjama pants up, then deciding that Apod was holding the chain lead too tightly and that she would only succeed in assuming a variety of silly, rude postures that would doubtless amuse the on-lookers.

Beside her, Aisla had suffered the same undignified fate. Her rich green pyjamas had been pulled down and up, exposing bottom and breasts. A eunuch was fumbling with the key to her wrists' chains. Her face was flushed scarlet with blushes and she was making embarrassed little treading motions with her feet which set her breasts and bottom quivering. A eunuch pulled her pyjama pants away from her feet as the wrist cuffs unlocked, another quickly pulling her top away to leave her standing totally naked.

Elethrine felt sympathy at the sight of her maid standing nude for the inspection of the audience, but also pleasure that someone else had been stripped and a curious thrill that was clearly shared with the rest of the onlookers. Aisla's face and neck were flushed pink, even her rounded breasts having coloured up in her shame. Behind, her hair fell in a cloud of burnished red-gold, the longest strands reaching to the cleft of her muscular little bottom. It was a sight that Elethrine knew would stimulate male passion to an unbearable height, and Elethrine glanced up nervously, half expecting to find a forest of penes thrusting up from the men's robes, erect and ready.

She knew that in Mund, had a girl of Aisla's beauty been put naked in a room full of men, she would have been ravished on the spot. True, it would not have happened among highborn, but nothing in the behaviour of the Vendjomois nobility had led her to expect honourable restraint. Yet, perhaps out of deference to the Emperor, the men of Vendjome were bridling their lust. Their attention was fixed on Aisla's body, and one or two were fondling convenient slavegirls, but none were approaching or preening erect cocks.

Aisla dressed rapidly, clearly relieved to be covering her body in the familiar garments of Mund. In her hurry she fumbled with the catches and straps she was normally expert in fastening. She also dressed in Elethrine's clothes, which happened to be on the top of the pile. Finally she was fully dressed, a noblewoman of Mund in every particular save the tell-tale peasant red of her hair.

'Bizarre,' the Emperor remarked, indifferently. 'Have them put in my seraglio, I will amuse myself with them later. See to it that they are taught to kneel.'

'Never!' Talithea spat as the vizier relayed the order. 'I should rather kneel to the most base pariah of Mund! Ho, you with the body of a toad, how can such a one as you be called Emperor? Either ravish us as would a real man or give us to your guards.'

The Panjandrum threw a questioning glance to his vizier.

'She begs to leave your presence, for the light of your countenance blinds her, O Resplendence,' the vizier said. 'She also begs to be placed in your seraglio, there to be soundly whipped in order to instil in herself and her companions a true sense of her worthlessness should you ever condescend to use her miserable body.'

'My miserable body!' Talithea stormed, turning to address the vizier. 'You weasel-faced little –'

'Take them from the Presence,' the vizier ordered, 'whip them well, give them no food until morning and leave them chained in the seraglio.'

They were dragged away, Elethrine tripping over her pyjama bottoms, which then fell off, leaving her quite nude from the waist down. Talithea continued spitting curses until the great doors closed and cut off their view of the throne. Only then did the chief eunuch turn to her with a look of fury.

'Impudent trull!' he boomed. 'How dare you address the Presence! How dare you use such words! You may be fortunate your value is so high, or I would have you fed to the sacred mandrills!'

'Do it then, you sack of lard!' Talithea yelled back. 'I'll show you how a Princess of Mund can die!'

She struck out, hitting his face with the golden cuff at her wrist and drawing a high-pitched scream of pain and surprise. He came forward, his face red with fury and blood from a long cut across one cheek. One podgy arm came round in an open slap, only to meet Aisla's hands as Talithea's nails raked his face. Seizing her chance, Elethrine grabbed his free arm, twisting her chain around it and pulling to find him surprisingly weak for all his bulk. For a moment it seemed as if he would topple to the ground as the three of them pushed him back and then the guards reached them and they were pulled away. Elethrine struggled briefly in the grip of the two guards who held her and then gave up, realising that they were far stronger than the flabby Apod. The other eunuchs fluttered around, neither helping the guards nor seeing to their chief.

'They have spirit, these barbar girls,' the largest of the guards remarked as he subdued Aisla in a bear hug.

'Strong, too,' another answered as he tried to get a grip on Talithea's frantically waving arms. 'They would be interesting bed partners!'

'Careful what you say,' the leader put in. 'Remember that they are the Emperor's slaves.'

'I am no slave!' Talithea spat, kicking out but succeeding only in stubbing a bare toe on the guard's greave.

Elethrine noticed the great door begin to open, at which both guards and eunuchs came quickly to attention, the three girls dropping to the floor at the suddenness of their release. A small, dumpy man with a bald pate and a fringe of white hair appeared, his brilliant emerald robe and gold-traced sandals in odd contrast to the intense, intellectual expression of his face. Behind him came a taller, younger man wearing a kirtle of the same brilliant green and carrying a spear.

The small man glanced in surprise at the chief eunuch, then turned his attention to the guard leader.

'Serenity Astripod,' the leader said reverently, bowing while maintaining a firm grip on Elethrine's chain.

'What has happened here?' the little man answered. 'No, never mind that. Bring these three to my quarters before they go to the seraglio.'

126

'But, Serenity,' the leader protested, 'the Emperor will want them later.'

'Besides,' Apod added vindictively as he got to his feet, 'they are to be whipped, by the Emperor's own order.'

'By vizier Raugnak's order actually,' the small man answered. 'No, I must see them before they go to the seraglio.'

'But, Serenity,' a junior eunuch put in, 'they must be whipped, then tattooed, braceletted, washed and perfumed in readiness for the attentions of the Resplendence.'

'That can wait,' Astripod responded. 'Besides, I happen to know that the Governor of Sera-Jome arrives later, bringing a boy slave shipped in from the southernmost tip of Cypraya. He is said to have skin as black as jet and as smooth as velvet, and features both regular and beautiful. He also dances gracefully and is obedient. It will be days before the Emperor tires of him and wishes to enjoy his barbar girls.'

'But they must still be whipped,' Apod protested, vehemently. 'You heard how they dared speak to the Presence!'

'Very well, I shall whip them myself,' Astripod answered.

'But –' Apod began, only to be cut short by Astripod.

'Do not forget who I am, eunuch,' he said, coldly. 'Would you disobey the cousin to the Presence?'

'No, sire. Of course not, sire, I abase myself, your Serenity,' Apod replied hurriedly, then fell grovelling to the ground.

Talithea laughed, a sound of silvery beauty that Elethrine found disconcerting given their plight.

'Pig, toad,' the Princess taunted, kicking Apod with a dainty foot. 'Were my father here he would tear you apart with his bare hands, and your witless, bulbous emperor too.'

'See how they blaspheme!' Apod squealed from the floor.

'They shall be punished,' Astripod answered mildly as he took the golden leashes in his hand. 'Come, pretty barbars, we have much to learn together.'

As the chain pulled taut, Elethrine, Talithea and Aisla fell into step, with the young man behind them. Elethrine glanced at the Princess, whose face was flushed with anger but whose chin was still tilted up at a disdainful angle.

'First you shall provide me with some facts,' Astripod said, not troubling to turn to face them. 'Then I shall whip you and take my pleasure of you, an occurrence that you will not mention to any others unless you wish to undergo certain subtle and inventive tortures. And do not think to treat me as you did Apod. I am no eunuch and Aurac may be scrawny but he is strong and holds a well-honed spear. You will speak only when spoken to, obey orders promptly and address me as Serenity.'

'Yes, Serenity,' Aisla responded.

Elethrine said nothing, then hastily gave the same response as Talithea yelped from the application of a spear tip to one buttock. Astripod gave a brief snort of amusement as Talithea reluctantly added her reply.

They moved through a maze of corridors, all built of the ubiquitous pink marble but decorated with a thousand designs in coloured stone, exotic wood, stained glass and vivid paint. Many of the designs depicted erotic scenes, the detail and intimacy of which set Elethrine's insides trembling. All this was lit by torches set in braziers at frequent intervals, the dancing light making the copulating figures seem to move with obscene jerking motions.

Finally they reached a heavy door of black wood set with polished green gems, beyond which proved to be a spacious chamber with a window looking out, high over Vendjome city. Viewed from above, its sheer size was still more impressive than it had been before. Thieron, the capital of Mund and Talithea's home city, would have fitted easily between the palace and the distant wall.

'I see you gape in wonderment,' Astripod remarked, 'and so you should. Vendjome must seem magnificent indeed when compared with the wattle and daub huts of your native land.'

'I live in a castle built of stone,' Elethrine replied, 'and if it is not so large, its construction is every bit as fine. Also better able to withstand a siege. One day you will find that your ornamentation and fancy pillars make easy scaling for an enemy.'

'No enemy has approached Vendjome City for two thousand years,' Astripod laughed. 'But this is of interest, I had no idea that concepts such as defensive strategy were understood in the barbar lands. Still, we shall discuss that later. For now, observe this globe.'

He indicated a curious object, a sphere supported on a bronze tripod. Lines crossed its surface, some regular, some in complex patterns that gave it the look of a map. Elethrine noted the word Apraya on one area, and Cypraya to its side, apparently indicating the two great continents. To the north Kora was shown only as a vague coastline, with its interior marked as unknown.

'Why is it round, Serenity?' Aisla enquired, voicing the question that Elethrine had been too proud to ask.

'Because, pretty one, that is the shape of the world,' Astripod laughed. 'Now –'

'That's absurd. Everyone would fall off!' Talithea snorted, drawing a yet more condescending laugh from Astripod and a chuckle from his apprentice.

'I could attempt to explain,' Astripod said, 'but you would understand nothing of what I said. Anyway, we are not here that I may give barbar girls a lesson in physical philosophy – as well teach trolls the bass viola! No, what I wish to know is the detail of your continent

Kora, as its interior is a mystery to our geographers. Provide me with good detail and I will reduce the severity of your whippings.'

'We shall not,' Elethrine replied after an instant of hesitation. 'It is dishonourable to bargain for the reduction of a punishment.'

'It would also be foolish to supply you with details of our homeland,' Talithea added.

'Very well,' Astripod sighed, 'if you wish to be difficult then we shall see how your supposed honour stands up to the effect of Aurac's quirt across your naked backsides. Whip them, Aurac, the golden-haired one first.'

Wary of Aurac's spear, Elethrine allowed herself to be bent over the windowsill, a position that left her barely covered breasts dangling over Vendjome City while her naked buttocks were thrust high for the apprentice's attention. Turning back, she saw that Aurac had taken up a quirt similar to those used by the eunuchs. Once again she was reminded of its similarity to the dog quirts of Mund and felt an extra flush of humiliation at the thought of being whipped with it. She turned forward again, looking down at the city below her and tensing herself for her beating.

'A fine sight, eh, master?' Aurac said from behind her. 'I look forward to sheathing my phallus in her neat pink cunt, or perhaps driving it home into the warm rosebud of her arsehole.'

'As do I,' Astripod replied. 'Yet you cannot enter her cunt as she is virgin and even our resplendent cousin might notice if his pretty new toy were to be deflowered before he had a chance at her. If you want to have her, use her arsehole or breasts. Meanwhile I think I will fuck the carrot-haired beauty while I watch the whipping. Their bodies have inflamed me past reserve.'

Elethrine jerked and squealed as a line of fire leapt across her bottom without warning. Aurac laughed and

130

once more applied the quirt, smacking it viciously down onto the crest of one plump cheek. Elethrine yelped again despite her best efforts to remain dignified. She had never been good at controlling herself during punishment, especially when she knew just how quickly being whipped would bring the heat to her tuppenny. The indignity of her position made it worse as well, with both her friends and Astripod admiring her naked rear view and the risk that some of the men in the courtyard directly below might look up and be treated to a fine view of her ill-concealed breasts.

Sure enough, one of them looked up, then drew the attention of his companion to the sight above him. He laughed, passed a joke on the appearance of Elethrine's dangling breasts and shouted up to ask whether she was being fucked or whipped. She gave no reply save a gasp as the quirt once more slapped down on the soft flesh of her bottom, a response that drew laughter from the men below.

Behind her, Elethrine could hear the sounds of Aisla being entered by Astripod, first a wet smacking as she sucked him to erection, then a curious squelching sound and a moan as his cock went into her. The quirt began to fall rhythmically, striking one cheek after another, each blow burning into Elethrine's smarting bum flesh. Her whole bottom was warming and she could feel a trickle of wet on her inner thigh where her tuppenny had started to juice. As one of the men below made an obscene suggestion about placing his cock between her breasts she gave a sob of shame.

'See how her cunt opens!' Aurac declared. 'She may be virgin but she is ready for her first cock. Still, the one below is no fool. Her fat breasts will make a handsome slide for my prick.'

'Do it, then,' Astripod grunted.

Elethrine was pulled in from the window, her bottom burning but now thoroughly on heat. Aurac pushed himself into a kneeling position and placed his already erect cock between her breasts. She squeezed them around it and kissed the tip, lost to her need as his hard shaft began to move between the soft pillows of her breasts. Dimly she was aware of Talithea standing behind the two men, fiddling with the brass screw that held the globe on its tripod. Then her eyes lit on Aisla's face, which was set in ecstasy as the stout scholar humped her from the rear. While the blue velvet dress covered most of the maid's body, there was something incredibly exciting about the way it had been thrown up to gain access to her sex. Her drawers and pantalettes were down too, and Elethrine realised that she herself would have presented a similar picture if mounted for sex. Aurac groaned and started to come, a jet of white sperm erupting from his cock to splash in Elethrine's face and over her breasts. She stuck her tongue out, gaping eagerly for a mouthful even as Talithea raised the globe above Astripod's bald and sweating pate.

There was a rending crash and Astripod staggered back, his cock slipping out of Aisla's tuppenny, the globe an absurd parody of his head. He clutched at it briefly and then slumped down, unconscious. Aurac turned at the sound, the come still dribbling from his cock. The ecstasy on his face turned to alarm and then blankness as Talithea brought a brass telescope down on the back of his head. He too slumped unconscious, his cock sliding from between Elethrine's breasts to leave them slick with sperm. A burst of excitement expelled the dizzy, pleasantly helpless feeling that had been building up in her. Talithea was still holding the telescope, as if expecting further opponents, and her face was set in a manic grin.

'So,' she announced, 'now we take weapons, return to the great hall, slay the Emperor, go down in a welter of blood, the tale of which will ring down the centuries, and meet again in the feast hall of heroines!'

'No, no,' Elethrine objected, wondering once more about the Princess's sanity, 'we escape and return to Mund. Come Aisla, get up.'

Aisla was still kneeling, her bottom up and open as if her tuppenny were resentful of having lost the cock that had been pleasuring her. Her eyes were shut and her mouth open, an expression of dopey bliss that faded only slowly at her mistress's words.

'And give me some clothes,' Elethrine added, suddenly acutely conscious of her nudity and sperm-covered chest.

Aisla got up, blushing, and began to undo the blue velvet dress. Elethrine squatted down to wipe her breasts clean on the hem of the unconscious Astripod's robe, trying to think and ignore the tingling sensation in her nipples, the wet, open feeling of her tuppenny and the warm soreness of her bottom. Aisla peeled the dress off and gave it to her mistress. Elethrine pulled it on, immediately banishing the worst of her lust as she completely covered her body from view for the first time since the auction. The Princess was still toying with the telescope as Elethrine pulled her drawers on underneath the dress.

'We must leave, quickly,' Elethrine said, turning to study the maps spread out on the table.

'How?' Talithea demanded. 'We are in the middle of a gigantic palace in a still more gigantic city, near naked and instantly recognisable. Better that we go down fighting, as our fathers would wish.'

'Put the telescope down and listen!' Elethrine hissed. 'Aisla, give her my pantalettes and chemise, you must wear just a petticoat. Look, this map shows the city, in every detail, and this one the country and lands beyond. We may use them to get home!'

'Perhaps,' Talithea admitted, accepting the chemise and pantalettes from the now bare-breasted Aisla. 'But how do we get out of the palace?'

'By the roofs, once it is dark,' Elethrine answered, 'which it will be shortly.'

She turned away to look out over the rooftops of Vendjome but also to hide the fluttering of her heart. Aisla was strong, yet born to be subordinate, while Talithea, for all her urbane manner and fine education, was simply too crazed to take the lead. That left the responsibility and the task of escaping from slavery in a foreign city in Elethrine's hands.

Taking a deep breath and reciting to her mother the traditional prayer for a maiden about to embark on a challenging task, she turned back to the maps. As she did so an idea came to her, as if in answer to her prayer.

'The way out is simple,' she said with more confidence than she felt. 'In the streets we would be recognised instantly, yet we must have some time before our absence is investigated. Apod, the eunuchs and a few guards alone know we are here, and all have been warned to hold their tongues. So, we wait until dark, climb from the window, descend to the streets here . . .'

She jabbed her finger at the map of Vendjome City, indicating a jumble of small streets and alleys to the rear of the palace.

'. . . and make our way to here, the caravan terminus. Once there, we conceal ourselves among the cargo of a caravan and leave with it, thus evading detection. Our very obviousness is our safeguard, for they will think it easy to spot us and so be fooled.'

'What if they search each caravan as it leaves the city?' Aisla queried.

'Pray they will not,' Elethrine replied. 'Come now, let us make a rope.'

They waited until darkness had covered the great city. Then, using a rope contrived of two petticoats and the clothing of the unfortunate Astripod and his apprentice, they lowered themselves carefully from the window onto an ornate ledge some way below. With their hearts in their mouths they edged along the ledge to one roof, then another. Thus they descended, moving slowly and freezing each time a figure appeared in the courtyards and walkways below them. Finally they reached the street, a narrow alley where the smell suggested they were beside the palace kitchens.

They remained concealed behind a great bin of waste until the hubbub of the city had begun to die. Then, using the street plan and slipping from shadow to shadow, they made their way slowly to the caravan terminus. As they went, Elethrine found the deep shame and despair that had been building up in her ever since their capture ebbing away, to be replaced by elation, a fierce, wild emotion that gave her a sense of excitement and invulnerability. It was so strong that she had to struggle to keep herself in check against acting too hastily and she wondered if it was the same feeling warriors had when approaching battle. Talithea and Aisla were clearly in a similar state, their faces set in manic grins as time after time they risked exposure during dashes across open streets and along alleys. At last they reached the caravan terminus, to find a great yard illuminated by braziers and crowded with wagons, every one of which had at least one guard.

'So what now?' Talithea whispered, for once acceding to Elethrine's leadership without argument.

The disturbed cackle of a mandrill sounded some-where far off across the city, a sound entirely in keeping with Elethrine's mood. She paused before answering the Princess. To conceal themselves successfully among the wagons would be no easy task, yet it was one they had to face. Recalling remarks Kaulak had made on bribery, she decided on a plan. For all that she knew it was born more of desperation than common sense.

'We proceed thus,' she said, pulling the others back into the deep shade of a warehouse doorway. 'Two things I have noted while in Vendjome. First, like the

135

dwarves, they treat bodily pleasures as if they were a form of currency or barter. Secondly, men take more than one woman to wife – or whatever their equivalent. Therefore it seems that the poor and ill favoured must have little opportunity for pleasure.'

'All true,' Talithea responded. 'Gross, decadent, but true.'

'So,' Elethrine continued, 'we select the most ill-favoured among the caravan guards and offer our services for the duration of the trip.'

'Demoiselle!' Talithea exclaimed.

'Is that the voice of the girl who indulged in the position of the Goblin and Dog not so many nights ago?' Elethrine enquired.

'Kaulak is a noble and a warrior,' Talithea hissed.

'Kaulak is an opportunistic coward who fled at the first sign of danger,' Elethrine replied.

'I will serve as needs,' Aisla put in, softly.

'Slut!' Talithea hissed.

'You are she who always counsels the dramatic,' Aisla answered, for the first time speaking back to the Princess.

'I –' Talithea began in outrage, only to be cut short by Elethrine.

'Stop squabbling!' she hissed. 'We are a thousand leagues from Mund and under oath not to reveal each other's behaviour. Unless you have a better plan let us proceed.'

'I will not so soil myself,' Talithea answered, 'but let Aisla do it and you have my support.'

'You sucked dwarven cock eagerly enough,' Aisla said, spitefully.

'Aisla!' Elethrine hissed. 'Behave, or I shall spank you now, and a curse for the consequences when you begin to squeal and whimper!'

'Sorry,' Aisla answered, meekly.

'It seems I must do this myself,' Elethrine said,

knowing that she spoke sensibly but with a pang of shame for the fact that she was still on heat from her whipping, Aurac's treatment of her breasts and perhaps the thrill of escape. 'Aisla, give me your petticoat.'

Aisla stripped obediently, peeling the petticoat off her legs and passing it to her mistress. Elethrine made a shawl of it, hiding her golden hair and pale skin. Peering from the mouth of the alley, she selected her target. The guards were displaying little interest in their tasks, mostly talking together or seated on the wains, one or two actually appearing asleep.

'There is a difficulty,' Talithea's voice sounded softly from behind. 'How do we know whither the caravan is bound?'

'We don't,' Elethrine whispered back. 'Pray to every ancestor that you have that we chance well.'

Before Talithea could reply Elethrine slipped from the shadows. Her target was leaning on a wain no more than a hundred paces distant, a fat man, tall by Vendjomois standards. The light of the braziers revealed he had greying hair and a half-empty wine sack at his side. As she approached she heard him singing softly to himself, a song that bolstered her hopes of success:

When I had but a sapling I'd plant it anywhere,
In mouth or cunt or bottom hole of any strumpet
    fair –
For I had but to ask it and they'd willingly go bare.

And when I had a mighty tree I'd use it night and
    day,
To fuck the girls three at a time in each and every
    way –
For I merely had to show them it to know that they
    would play.

Then when I reached my middle time my bough
    began to fail,

137

A girl would come and tease me by wiggling her
tail,
So I'd grab her buns and come between to prove I
was still male.

But when I slow and my wood goes soft I'll find it
hard to rise,
The girls will laugh and run from me and refuse to
spread their thighs,
So I'll hide myself by the washing trough and take
them by surprise!

And when I'm gone and death has felled my once
mighty tree
That once I used to shake an arse and tremble a
dainty knee,
A cunt it has no memory, and they'll not remember
me.

For the last verse the guard's tone had changed,
indicating a degree of melancholy and sexual frustration. Elethrine smiled to herself, a grin of wicked
satisfaction which she quickly suppressed in case it was
the start of a berserk passion similar to those of
Talithea. No other guards noticed her as she slid into
the shade of the wagons and she reached her target's
side without being seen.

'Good man,' she whispered, causing the old guard to
jump and turn suddenly.

He opened his mouth to yell, but her hand had closed
over it, and as he saw her face in the shadow of the
improvised veil, his eyes became wide.

'The golden-haired barbar slave!' he exclaimed
quietly, as she removed her hand.

'I am no slave!' Elethrine hissed, and then hastily
controlled herself before continuing. 'I was captured
and sold, but I am no slave. Now I and my companions –'

'The copper-haired girl and the elfling?' he broke in.

'Yes, but for the sake of peace do not call the pale-haired one an elfling,' Elethrine answered, knowing that if there was one thing guaranteed to rouse Talithea's temper it was to suggest that her near-white hair came not from royal blood but from an elfin misalliance.

'But you are of the seraglio of the Panjandrum!' the guard quaked in terror. 'If I am so much as seen with you I will be fed to mandrills, alive! Even to look on a girl of the seraglio is death for such as I!'

'Be silent then!' Elethrine urged. 'Help us escape the city and nobody need know you saw me. Besides, we have a treat for you should you be of help.'

She reached out, pulling him back into deeper shadow and placing her hand softly on his crotch. The bulge of his cock and balls felt soft beneath the leather of his belly harness. He gave a sigh of pleasure and surprise at her touch and she felt his penis squirm under the leather.

'Think,' Elethrine teased, 'to be touched, there, by a girl of the seraglio of the Panjandrum himself, and with you I shall be warm and wanton, as I never could be to any who thought me not free.'

He swallowed loudly as her hand slipped into the side of his harness, finding his cock enclosed in a wrap of linen. She pushed the soft leather and linen aside, bringing his cock and balls out. They felt warm and full in her hand, a joy to handle, regardless of his age and physique.

'Will you do it?' she whispered.

'This, each night?' he queried, hoarsely.

'I give my oath on it, and the copper-haired girl shall play too,' she answered.

Elethrine began to tug at the guard's cock, bringing it slowly to erection. At first it felt soft and rubbery in her hand, then firmer and finally hard, so that she was

139

stroking a small, stiff cock as he sighed with the pleasure of being masturbated.

'Each night,' she whispered in his ear, 'until we reach our destination, and perhaps, if things go well, I'll kiss it too.'

'You will, and more,' he said as his hand closed on Elethrine's bottom.

She began to pull harder at his cock and made no objection to his rough fumbling of her bottom through her dress. His statement showed agreement if also a determination to squeeze the most out of the bargain. It was done, but she still needed to make him come, both for the sake of time and her own pride and pleasure.

'Think,' she whispered, remembering the pleasures males had wanted of her over the days in Apraya, 'each night for a week soft hands will caress you. Gentle mouths and tongues will suck and lick at your genitals. My friends will pose for you, showing breasts and bottoms, cunts and bottom rings. You saw the auction, think how Aisla of the copper hair bent to show her charms. Think of the lips of her soft, sweet cunt. Think of her kneeling nude, her cunt ready to receive you . . .'

The guard grunted and Elethrine suddenly found her hand wet with sperm. It had taken less than a minute to bring him off, a measure, she hoped, of the delicacy and finesse of her touch.

'So whither are we bound?' she asked, shaking her hand fastidiously and then wiping it on the linen of his underwrap.

'Rojome, on the coast,' he answered, 'with jars of honey and spices for shipment to Opina. You could hide in the great honey jars, which have already been sealed and will not be opened until the tithing point on Rojome dock.'

'Stay then, while I fetch my companions,' Elethrine replied.

7

Runaway

For nine full days the caravan made its slow way to the east and south. Elethrine, Talithea and Aisla huddled in the huge jars, naked and sticky with honey. Their clothes were folded among the personal possessions of Brissac, the guard. Sarod, the merchant who owned the cargo and that of several other wains, stayed in the more comfortable passenger wagons to the front of the caravan where there was less dust. Only occasionally did he saunter back to speak to Brissac, who each time assured him that all was well.

No others disturbed them and Elethrine's fear and apprehension slowly gave way to boredom. Naked, with her legs up and her tuppenny half immersed in what remained of the honey, she found it impossible to keep her thoughts from the newly discovered pleasures of her body. While the caravan trundled slowly across the great Vendjomois plain she learnt to masturbate properly, at first with shame and then with increasing enthusiasm as she discovered just how exquisite the sensation of her climax could be.

The first time, in the desert, she had been clumsy and in fear of being caught and taken advantage of. Now she could take her time, exploring each fleshy fold of her tuppenny to discover exactly what feelings a touch produced. She had always know that her clitty was the very seat of her pleasure and that it needed to be touched in order to reach the actual climax of her masturbation. The more subtle pleasures of her pubic mound, the outer and inner lips of her tuppenny and other areas were newer, everything having always been hidden by her purity girdle. Her anus in particular produced delicious sensations, especially as touching the tiny hole provided not only physical pleasure but a wonderful feeling of being rude, stronger even than that achieved by touching the taut skin of her maidenhead.

Each evening Brissac would wait until the caravan was quiet and then release them from their jars. The wagon was covered and allowed enough concealment for them to eat in safety and sleep stretched out on the floor. Only when dawn approached would Brissac wake and usher them back into the sticky warmth of the honey jars. Each night before they slept and when they rose, they would fulfil their bargain to Brissac. At first he contented himself with coming in the girls' hands, but as the distance from Vendjome increased so did his boldness and their sense of gratitude. On the third night he demanded that Aisla suck his penis, which she did. He then wanted his balls in one girl's mouth while another sucked on him, which was also granted by Elethrine and Aisla. On the fifth morning he fucked Aisla as she knelt naked and Elethrine played with his balls from behind. The scene so excited Talithea that she finally overcame her reserve and that evening allowed him to mount her in the same obscene 'Goblin and Dog' position in which she had had her maidenhead taken. By the seventh night all three were eager for his cock and Aisla allowed him the pleasure of her bottom ring, grunting and panting out her lust as she was buggered and her mistress held her head for comfort.

Afterwards Aisla admitted to the others that it was not the first time she had taken a cock up her bottom, and indeed that more than one man-at-arms at the keep had enjoyed her anally on a regular basis. She then explained how a girl might accept a cock in the anus without pain, a description so vivid that that night Elethrine masturbated over the thought of how it would have felt to allow Mausac, Brissac or even one of the dwarves to bugger her. The following night she was tempted to ask but could not face making such a dirty request in front of Talithea. Instead she acceded to Brissac's request that she smack and fondle Aisla's bottom while the Princess was once more mounted from the rear. Somehow the fact that they were performing for Brissac lessened the guilt of enjoying sexual contact with the other girls, and when Brissac had sprayed come across Talithea's naked bottom, Aisla and Elethrine licked her clean and finished by using their tongues to bring her to climax.

Finally the caravan reached Rojome, a port of white, marble mansions and palaces built around the curve of a great bay where two rivers poured into what the map marked as the Ryna Sea. It had an air of prosperity and, Elethrine was pleased to note as she peered cautiously from the honey jar, a far more cosmopolitan air than any of the other Vendjomois cities she had seen. While the great majority of the population were the small, yellow-brown-skinned Vendjomois, there were also many with skins darker still, others with straight black hair and a curious purple tinge to their skin and even a few fair-skinned, brown-haired individuals whose physiques somewhat resembled those of her kin.

'The dark-skinned ones are from the Aprina States and the jungles of central Cypraya,' Brissac explained that evening after Elethrine and Aisla had shared a long and grateful suck of his penis and swallowed his sperm. 'While those with tawny hair and powerful build are Hai.'

The caravan had pulled into a terminus and they sat together in the shade of the wagon, its front turned to a high wall. Elethrine and Aisla had given him his farewell suck while Talithea had played with her breasts for his pleasure. They had then spread the map out and fallen to discussion of how to proceed.

'We call Hai the Glass Coast,' Elethrine answered him, glancing at the map, 'and it is but two hundred leagues across the sea from Mund. If natives are here, then a link must exist.'

'So it does,' Brissac replied, placing a crooked finger on the map, 'goods from Hai come in on ships from Opina, and so it must be that a caravan route exists here, across the Ara Khum –'

'The Red Parch,' Talithea broke in excitedly, 'a great desert that was my limit of knowledge of the lands of Cypraya before now.'

'So we take ship for Opina,' Elethrine said. 'What sort of city is it, Brissac?'

'It is the greatest city of the Aprina States,' he answered, 'and by all accounts a place of high civilisation and luxury, though I have never been there. It is said that a council rules and that each citizen has a say in who takes a seat in council, a strange custom.'

'Do they take slaves?' Talithea asked, nervously.

'They do not,' Brissac replied, 'another bizarre custom. They are in many ways strange. Their women go bare-breasted and adorn their nipples with pendants of silver, gold or a strange, white metal brighter and heavier yet than silver.'

'Women of Vendjome go with little more than a transparent wrap over their breasts,' Elethrine stated. 'I see little difference.'

'They also make bombards capable of hurling shot over a league,' Brissac continued, 'and small ones that can be held by a man.'

'Bombards?' Elethrine asked.

'Did you not see them in Vendjome?' Brissac questioned. 'Tubes of black metal that hurl iron balls great distances. They are used in battle and to defend walls and ships.'

144

'I saw such devices on the walls of the cities,' Elethrine answered, 'but I had no knowledge of their use. They function by magic, I presume?'

'They function by a black powder that turns suddenly to gas when struck by a spark,' Brissac replied.

'Magic, as I thought,' Elethrine said with certainty. 'But no matter. If we approach a ship of Opina asking for passage, will the shipmaster accept us or ask awkward questions?'

'Better yet,' Brissac responded, 'declare yourself an escaped slave and demand sanctuary. They consider slavery an abomination for some reason.'

'So it is,' Talithea answered.

'Excellent,' Elethrine said, 'at last luck smiles on us; although I prefer to say that we are fleeing slavery than that we are escaped slaves.'

'He may make you work passage,' Brissac added, 'but he will take you, perhaps as cooks or laundrymaids.'

'There are worse fates,' Elethrine answered.

'Work as a menial?' Talithea snorted. 'Where is your pride, Demoiselle?'

'We have crossed a thousand leagues of hostile land,' Elethrine retorted, 'we have escaped slavery, we are together and we are unharmed – that is my pride.'

Talithea gave only a snort in response.

Elethrine breathed a long sigh as the sleek form of the Vendjomois pilot boat disappeared around a headland. They were free of the Empire of Vendjome. The shipmaster of the *Sea Chancellor* had accepted them without discussion, even with gladness, for the ship had taken on a large contingent of passengers and the cook had been more than happy to sign up three assistants. He had yet to attempt to make Talithea do any actual work, but that was a problem that could be faced in time. More importantly they were on a ship that flew the flag of Opina and so were free.

145

Heedless of the presence of Vendjomois passengers, she removed the headscarf of torn petticoat silk that she had been using to hide her hair and shook out her magnificent golden tresses, a display that immediately drew looks of surprise and lust from all around her. Talithea had already done the same, and Aisla now followed suit, leaving the beautiful maid in nothing but a truncated petticoat that barely covered her bottom. The fresh sea air blew Elethrine's hair out and she breathed in deeply, delighting in her freedom. Although Rojome was further south even than the point in the Glissades where they had originally been dumped, she didn't care. They were headed north, and that was what mattered.

A call from behind her made her turn to find a burly man with an oiled black beard and a heavy paunch coming towards her. With a pang of unease she recognised Sarod, the spice merchant, and then calmed herself with the knowledge that he could do nothing and had no reason to recognise her in any case.

'Greetings, lady,' he announced himself. 'Do you know, it is strange – I take ship for Opina, and on the ship are three maidens both beautiful and exotic. I have travelled widely, to Ythan, the Aprina states and even to the jungle kingdoms of central and southern Cypraya, yet never have I seen such girls.'

'I thank you for your praise, kind fellow,' Elethrine said, carefully.

'And yet,' Sarod continued, 'it is an extraordinary coincidence for, on the day prior to my departure from great Vendjome, three girls of strikingly similar appearance were sold at the Pelucidome auction to the seraglio of his Resplendence, the Panjandrum of Vendjome.'

'Such coincidences happen,' Elethrine remarked.

'So they do,' he went on, 'yet while we camped in the caravanserai at Iome a horseman who had overtaken us

146

brought a rumour of a most scandalous escape – the same northern beauties. Then, on arrival in Rojome I go to pay my tithes and discover that three great honey jars are near empty. Brissac denies knowledge of this and, indeed, it is hard to see how or why he would want to empty three honey jars. Yet I ponder what the reaction of the authorities in Anjome might be if they were to learn that three girls exactly resembling those escaped from the seraglio were on board the *Sea Chancellor*.'

'Anjome?' Elethrine queried.

'Anjome,' Sarod echoed, 'the most northerly port of the Sepia Coast, hard on where the Eigora Khum meets the sea. We touch there for cargo and supplies before crossing the Ryna Sea to Opina.'

'Hypothetically, then,' Elethrine stated, 'the authorities might be amused by the coincidence but make no investigation of a ship flying the colours of an independent nation famed for its skill in the production of bombards.'

'Alternatively,' Sarod responded, 'they might remark politely to the shipmaster that he is carrying two thousand, three hundred and fifty golden imperials' worth of the Panjandrum's personal property, stolen –'

'I am no man's property!' Talithea snapped suddenly and her palm smacked down on Sarod's cheek.

'Enough of circumspection, then!' he flared, angrily. 'You three will visit my cabin tonight, and I will take my pleasure of the elfling slut!'

Talithea lashed out again, but Elethrine caught the blow and pulled her friend back, smiling apologetically at several of the small, black-skinned Opina seamen who had turned to stare.

'I will speak to the shipmaster,' she informed Sarod. 'He seems a man of honour and will surely protect us.'

'Not so,' Sarod snapped, 'for while he espouses the fool doctrines of Opina as regards slaves, he values his cargo more highly than his moral scruples. So do as I say and perhaps, if you serve with energy and obedience, I shall forget to remark upon your presence when the tithing officer comes aboard at Anjome.'

'So be it,' Talithea declared later as they discussed Sarod's blackmail in their tiny cabin. 'I suppose one more cock in my tuppenny will make little difference, though to be had by a fat-bellied merchant is a disgrace greater even than Brissac or the soldiery on the Ephraxis.'

'Be assured that the knowledge will rest safely with Aisla and me,' Elethrine put in, glad that the Princess had at last acceded to the prospect of being taken by Sarod.

'I am,' Talithea responded, 'especially as he will doubtless pop your maidenhead either tomorrow night or the one after.'

Elethrine said nothing, but rose to her feet and nodded towards the cabin door. Sarod's cabin proved to be one of the largest, a square room set in the great sterncastle of the *Sea Chancellor*. They entered at his knock, to find him seated at a table with a goblet of golden wine in one hand and a peach in the other. At the sight of them he smiled, then indicated that they should lock the door. He then pushed his chair back and pulled his robe up, exposing spindly legs, a great round paunch and an ample set of genitals.

'Off with your clothes, girl, and bring me to readiness in your mouth,' he addressed Talithea. 'You others, play together on the floor and ensure that my view takes in plenty of cunt. Do not feel rejected though. As the nights go by, each shall have her share of cock.'

He spread his legs wide as Talithea shrugged off the chemise that had in any case barely covered her plump, young breasts.

'Crawl to me,' he ordered, as her heavily frilled pantalettes joined the chemise on the floor.

Talithea hesitated and then went down on her knees, incidentally providing Elethrine with a fine view of well-fleshed bottom and pouting, silver-downed tuppenny lips. The Princess crawled across the floor, breasts swinging and buttocks up high and open. Sarod grinned and held his cock out. Talithea reached him, took his balls in her hand and opened her mouth to be fed his penis. His face relaxed in an expression of bliss as she began to suck and Elethrine found herself shivering to see the haughty Princess nude on all fours with the penis of a mere merchant in her mouth.

Yet there was no denying Talithea's lust, and Elethrine knew that she herself would have sucked as eagerly once she got the taste of cock in her mouth and the excitement and humiliation of being nude into her brain. As it was, she had been ordered to play with Aisla, and she turned to her maid, wondering what to do. 'Plenty of cunt' the merchant had said, and so possibly a display of Aisla's pretty tuppenny might be sufficient.

Motioning Aisla to the floor and into a crawling position, Elethrine pulled up the shortened petticoat that formed the maid's sole concession to modesty. Beneath it Aisla's slender thighs and trim bottom were raised and open, providing Sarod with the display he had demanded. The maid parted her knees and put her face down, increasing the rudeness of her display. The scent of Aisla's tuppenny was rich in the air – a warm, excited musk that filled Elethrine with the urge to kiss and lick her maid between her thighs.

Trying to resist making such a wanton display, but unable to stop herself from touching, Elethrine began to stroke Aisla's bottom, rubbing the cheeks and giving the occasional light smack to make the maid's buttocks quiver. Aisla sighed from the attention and Sarod groaned and blew out his plump cheeks. Elethrine saw that the merchant's cock was now hard in Talithea's

149

mouth, a thick, dark erection around which the Princess's lips were stretched as she bobbed her head up and down on it. Leaning forward so that his fat belly pressed against Talithea's face, Sarod took a thick yellow banana from the bowl on the table and threw it to Elethrine.

'Spit on your friend's anus and stick this in it,' he ordered, once more lying back and easing his cock into Talithea's mouth.

Elethrine moved a little so that she could see the puckered pink orifice between Aisla's bottom cheeks. She knew that several cocks had been in it, yet it looked tight and dry, unready for penetration. Hardly knowing what she was doing she briefly placed the banana in her mouth, then spat directly onto her maid's anal aperture. Placing the fruit against Aisla's bottom ring, Elethrine pushed gently, getting a thrill of delight as the little hole opened to receive its load. Lubricated with spit, the banana went into Aisla's bottom ring, raising only a mild grunt from the maid as she was penetrated. Elethrine began to work it up, leaving it half inserted with a hand's width or so of thick yellow fruit in her maid's anal passage and the rest protruding obscenely from the taut ring.

'You show me your cunt also,' Sarod demanded, nodding to Elethrine.

Half-reluctant, half-eager, Elethrine turned and knelt by Aisla's side, raising her bottom until it was on the same level as the maid's. Reaching back, she began to lift her skirts, feeling the intense shame of thus exposing herself mingle with the pleasure of doing something so rude. With a final twitch she flicked the heavy blue velvet dress up onto her back, then swallowed and pulled open her drawers, displaying to Sarod the full white globe of her bottom with its centre of golden hair and pouting, plump tuppenny.

'Now, you two sluts,' Sarod rasped, 'rub yourselves while I fuck your friend.'

Elethrine's fingers trembled as she reached back obediently to find her tuppenny. It was moist and swollen, her clitoris a hard bump between the damp folds. She started to masturbate, a grunt from Sarod and a moan from Talithea telling her that the Princess had been mounted, presumably from the rear so that both of them could watch the two girls play with themselves.

Sarod took little time to come, but when he did, both Elethrine and Aisla were too far gone to do without their own orgasms. Knowing that she was no longer doing it because she had to, and feeling deeply ashamed of herself, Elethrine continued to masturbate, rubbing at her clitty with her thighs well splayed to ensure that her audience got a good look at what she was doing.

She heard Sarod chuckle, a derisive, knowing sound that only strengthened her lust and shame. There was a smack, as of a hand striking a soft bottom cheek, and the merchant said something Elethrine failed to catch. Then she felt a movement beside her and found that Talithea had crawled into position, leaving the three girls in a line, bottoms high and fingers working in swollen tuppennies as they masturbated together. The Princess came first, presumably as she alone had taken the merchant's cock in mouth and vagina. Aisla and Elethrine then came together. As Talithea's moans died to whimpers, each was squealing her lust out into the floor as the fat merchant laughed to see them make such a blatant display of their charms.

The next night followed a similar pattern, only with Sarod adding new variations to the game. Aisla was singled out for fucking and put into a variety of positions once she had sucked him to erection. Meanwhile Elethrine and Talithea were obliged to strip and adopt a series of rude poses, many of which involved touching each other. Finally their resolve snapped and Elethrine, who had been pushing grapes up the Princess's vagina, buried her face in the wet, juice-smeared mess and licked Talithea to her climax. She then took her own climax while Talithea whipped her gently with a quirt like those the eunuchs had used in Vendjome. Being naked and beaten, essentially with a dog whip, gave Elethrine one of the most intense and shattering climaxes she had yet had, while afterwards Sarod declared that the following night he would fuck Elethrine while Aisla and Talithea took turns to whip each other with the quirt.

The next morning found Elethrine in a state of supreme agitation. That evening she was due to lose her maidenhead and from the excitement she had known while playing with her friends she was painfully aware that she would quickly be too full of lust to play any clever tricks. Besides, she suspected that Talithea would happily hold her down for entry if need be.

As the day wore on she became more and more nervous, her thoughts constantly turning to the rough intrusion of a penis into her tight, virgin tuppenny and the tearing of her maidenhead. Finally she decided that the thought was unbearable, at least with Sarod, who was not only unprepossessing but a mere merchant, a class considered in Mund as of the peasantry and quite without honour. Even the ageing, scarred Mausac would have been better – at least he had been a warrior.

Determined on her course of action she began to assemble water skins and foodstuffs in their cabin, but waited until they had served the evening meal and the last trace of light had faded from the sky before presenting the others with her plan to steal one of the *Sea Chancellor*'s longboats. Aisla agreed without hesitation, but Talithea objected on the grounds that the ship was safe and reasonably comfortable, while Sarod had made no demands beyond his original blackmail. For a while they argued, becoming increasingly heated.

'It is but a trick!' Elethrine insisted. 'When we reach

152

Anjome he will simply hand us over and take whatever reward is being offered for our capture.'

'What, and lose out on our pleasure between Anjome and Opina?' Talithea queried.

'He values money above all else,' Elethrine said. 'Besides, what if he failed to report us and the authorities later heard that we had been on the ship?'

'True,' Talithea said, doubtfully.

'Come!' Elethrine urged. 'He might come to search us out at any moment!'

'So be it,' Talithea answered. 'Besides, I do not care to be subject to Aisla's dog whip while he uses you.'

'Thank you!' Elethrine said, gratefully. 'Now come!'

Together they hurried from the cabin and on to the deck. The night was dark and cool, stars alone showing in the great, clear dome of the heavens. Stealthily they crept to one of the *Sea Chancellor*'s boats, taking care to avoid the lazy attention of the lookouts at the stern and forecastle. Simple yet strong knots attached the boat to its frame, allowing for quick release in an emergency. The three girls loaded their provisions aboard, then climbed on behind them. With a silent prayer to her father, Elethrine tugged hard on one retaining loop even as Aisla did the same to the other. The boat slid into the sea, striking the surface with a loud splash. A cry of alarm sounded on the *Sea Chancellor* but they were already drifting clear, and as the girls managed to control the oars the gap widened, until presently they were beyond hope of retrieval in the dark.

Dawn found the boat rocking on a gentle sea, its sail set and pulling them slowly to the northeast, the presumed direction of Opina. Elethrine was in high spirits, enjoying the fresh sea air and grateful that the prospect of being deflowered by Sarod was now only a memory. Aisla also seemed cheerful, although Talithea was quiet and pensive.

'So, Moth,' Elethrine said cheerfully, 'you have sailed before. How do we find our direction for Opina?'

'By keeping the sun to the left,' Talithea answered. 'Without a compass and a better chart than our map, there is no way of being more accurate.'

'Well, I suppose we must strike land eventually,' Elethrine went on, 'and then we may simply follow the coast until we reach the estuary of the Cyazin, which the map shows as a river as great as the Ephraxis.'

'One thing,' Talithea said curiously. 'In the caravan did Brissac not say that the penalty for being found with a girl of the Panjandrum's seraglio was death?'

'Indeed,' Aisla agreed, 'for it is assumed that no man could resist such beauties and so would be automatically guilty. He said horrid penalties attach even to gazing upon the Panjandrum's concubines. Only the most highly placed and palace staff are exempt.'

'So if Sarod ...' Talithea began and trailed off, looking hard at Elethrine.

'Perchance Sarod has Imperial connections?' Elethrine hazarded.

'A merchant?' Talithea replied, her voice icy cold. 'So, Demoiselle, you have had me degrade myself utterly and all for no reason!'

'Not so!' Elethrine protested.

'Also,' the Princess went on, 'you have cast us on to the open sea for no better reason than the preservation of your precious maidenhead, even though you need not have feared for it had you used your senses!'

'I –' Elethrine began, only for Talithea to leap at her, red faced and furious.

She went down under the Princess's weight, losing her balance to sprawl in the bottom of the boat. For an instant Talithea's weight was on top of her and then she had recovered herself and managed to twist to the side. The Princess fell, landing on the duckboards with a thump and a curse. Elethrine grabbed an arm and

154

twisted again, her anger rising as Talithea's free hand caught in her hair. For a moment they were evenly balanced and then Elethrine's strength began to tell. Talithea's expression turned from fury to alarm as she was slowly forced over, the direction of Elethrine's pressure making it quite clear what was intended. The Princess was going to be turned onto her front, and once her bottom was uppermost her fate would be inevitable – a spanking.

'Right, you snotty little brat,' Elethrine hissed as she forced Talithea slowly over, 'I'm going to spank you and I'm going to spank your bare bottom, just as if you were some impudent peasant girl!'

'Never!' Talithea squeaked in fury and frustration, but she was already being pressed down and Elethrine's tiny pantalettes provided almost as little protection for her well-rounded bottom as they did modesty.

Elethrine sat up in triumph, only for the boat to pitch on a wave and the boom to strike her temple. There was a sharp pain followed by a moment of disorientation.

She heard Talithea's triumphant yell and found herself being toppled over, still dizzy from the blow. Before she could rally herself she had been pushed down over the rowing bench and mounted with her arm twisted into the small of her back. The Princess quickly looped rope around her victim's wrists and waist, securing her roughly to the rowing bench.

'Now let's see who gets the spanking,' Talithea crowed as she began to pull Elethrine's dress up.

'Aisla!' Elethrine managed as her head began to clear and the dress was lifted to expose her drawers.

'Would you strike a Princess?' Talithea asked Aisla, mockingly.

The maid hesitated, uncertain as Elethrine's bottom was exposed by the parting of her drawers.

'I'm going to enjoy this!' Talithea breathed as she wobbled Elethrine's bottom under her hand. 'Come,

Demoiselle, let us see how nicely your bottom reddens and whether you cry when you're punished!'

The Princess's voice was full of satisfaction and sheer lust, her anger having faded at her successful mounting of her victim. Elethrine found her breath coming quickly, shame and desire rising inside her as the first exploratory smack landed on her bottom. Another landed, harder, making her bum bounce and heightening her awareness that it was nude and showing to Aisla. Again Talithea smacked her, and again, laughing as she did it.

Elethrine sobbed, already feeling the warmth in her tuppenny as Talithea set to work spanking her. She had always had a sneaking desire to know how it would feel to be punished by the Princess and now that it was happening she knew that by the time her bottom was a burning ball of hot, throbbing flesh she would be whimpering and begging to be allowed to touch herself. Then she would raise her smarting bottom and masturbate in front of the woman who had beaten her, a shameless admission of her status and need for punishment.

'Aisla, please!' she gasped in a last, pathetic attempt to avoid disgracing herself after the punishment.

Talithea just laughed and paused in her spanking to pull Elethrine's buttocks apart.

'Look, Aisla,' the Princess crowed. 'Do you see your mistress's bottom ring? How tight and virgin it looks. How would you like to stick something in it, as she did to you? Come, fetch a banana from the provisions. Pop – in it will go, and we'll spank her together while she learns how it would feel to have a member up her bottom.'

'I – I really couldn't . . .' Aisla replied, falteringly.

'I shall do it myself then,' Talithea said and Elethrine felt her tormentor's weight shift as she reached forward for the bag of supplies.

Knowing that once the banana was in her anus she

would be totally lost to sensual pleasure, Elethrine gave a frantic jerk. Talithea squeaked in alarm and sprawled over the seat of the boat. Pulling free of her badly tied bonds, Elethrine was up in a second, twisting, grabbing for Talithea, catching the split of the Princess's pantalettes and pulling. There was a ripping sound and half of the Princess's bottom came on show. Elethrine pulled hard, sending the Princess fully over the seat and the next instant she was mounted on the helpless girl's back.

Without ceremony she pulled down Talithea's pantalettes, exposing the Princess's full, chubby bottom with its deep cleft and fleshy cheeks. Talithea gave a squeak of despair as Elethrine landed a meaty smack on her bottom, then a moan as her cheeks were cupped and squeezed.

'Now, Princess Talithea Mund,' she declared. 'I shall beat you, and when your fat behind is as red as a cherry and your tuppenny is awash with juice I shall push a banana up your bottom ring, just as you planned for me. Then you shall kneel and kiss Aisla's tuppenny, which should teach you some manners.'

The Princess groaned deeply and Elethrine set to work to spank her, slapping one cheek after another and occasionally pulling them open to inspect the state of her tuppenny. Talithea became more and more excited as her spanking went on, until she was moaning and pushing her bottom up shamelessly. Elethrine paused and once more opened her victim's bum cheeks, finding the Princess's tuppenny wet with white juice and all too clearly ready for entry.

'Pass me a banana for her bottom, Aisla,' Elethrine ordered, 'and once it is in, offer her your tuppenny to kiss . . . no, your bottom ring, from an inch or so in order that she does it willingly. Meanwhile, another twenty firm smacks will do her no harm.'

'Er – Mistress,' Aisla said haltingly, 'there is a ship approaching.'

8

Plaything

Elethrine paused in mid smack, leaving Talithea's reddened bottom quivering like a round, pink jelly. Looking up, she followed the direction in which Aisla was pointing to find a tall, triangular sail on the horizon. It was black and a black pennon flew from the masthead above it, neither bearing any insignia. As their boat rose on the crest of a wave she made out a long, low hull, also jet black. The ship was very different from the broad, heavily built *Sea Chancellor* and everything about it conveyed menace.

Talithea struggled up, the pain and indignity of her spanking set aside as she too focused on the approaching ship.

'Perhaps they won't see us,' Aisla said.

'They are coming almost straight at us,' Elethrine replied.

'Maybe they are simply traders,' Talithea suggested with very little hope in her voice.

'What matter?' Elethrine responded, bitterly. 'These southern men have no honour and think only of our value as slaves, be they supposedly honest merchants or the bloodiest of reavers.'

'I will not be a slave,' Talithea said, determinedly.

'Possibly they are not Vendjomois,' Aisla suggested. 'Possibly their customs are different and we might be ravished and taken to wife.'

'I do not care to be the wife of a corsair captain,' Talithea said.

'Better that than his slave,' Elethrine pointed out.

'True,' Talithea admitted.

'Let us try and get clear of their path in any case,' Elethrine said, 'and we had best cover our hair. Perhaps they will think us a simple fishing boat and too small to trouble with.'

They attempted the manoeuvre, only to see the ship alter course with a determination that destroyed Elethrine's last hopes of avoiding it.

'They will surely ravish us and make us slaves,' she said.

'Perhaps your time has come to surrender?' Talithea suggested, her remark showing that the recent spanking rankled despite the crisis.

Elethrine ignored her, picking up the boathook as the galley bore down on them. It closed quickly, the narrowing gap revealing its crew. Its deck was crowded, mainly with lean, dark-skinned men, small yet wiry with long faces and hawk-like features that gave Elethrine little hope of finding any nobility. There were also evident Vendjomois among the crew and black-skinned Cypraeans, yet two men stood out. The first, at the bow of the galley, was heavy set and pale-skinned with tawny hair. He stood well above the height of those around him and the hilt of a great, two-handed sword could be seen rising over his back. The second was larger still, and seemed to radiate power even at a distance. Large features and skin the colour of ash showed him to be of some race she had no knowledge of, while a crested helm and elaborate body armour marked him as captain of the galley.

As the galley closed Elethrine wondered if her time had indeed come to surrender. The appearance of the galley and its crew held a raw, masculine power that sent a shiver straight to the little bud at the centre of her tuppenny. To be taken by a man such as the captain would certainly be acceptable and she determined to make it clear that he was her mark before Talithea had a chance. Dropping the boathook, she determined on a different course of action.

Moments later the galley overhauled their boat. The sides touched and the girls found themselves looking up at a line of ferocious, yet surprised faces. In the centre was the captain, with the burly mate to his side.

'Do you talk?' the captain boomed, his voice unnecessarily loud even with the noise of the wind and the waves.

'Certainly we talk!' Talithea snapped back before Elethrine could contrive a more appropriate answer.

The captain exchanged a glance with his mate, the look containing both amusement and surprise.

'Know then that I am Irqual the Makean,' the captain announced, 'a warrior unequalled in all the world. Also the greatest of lovers, the –'

'To boast is easy,' Talithea said, to Elethrine's horror. 'True greatness comes with deeds, not words.'

For a moment a shadow of black rage passed across the captain's grey visage and his hand tightened on the hilt of the massive axe at his belt. Then his face split into a broad grin and he let rip a great gust of laughter. With a single hand he reached down and caught Talithea by her chemise, lifting her easily on to the galley.

Fired by hope, Elethrine lifted her own hand, to have it grasped by the burly mate who pulled her aboard with the same ease. Aisla followed and the three girls found themselves standing in a ring of fierce faces, many showing lust but none aggression.

'We thank you, noble captain,' Elethrine addressed the bulky Irqual in an attempt to show herself as leader among the girls. 'We had few supplies and were afeared of drifting forever on this bleak sea.'

'What were you doing out here in the first place?' the

160

captain demanded in curiosity. 'And of what race are you?'

'They are Mundics,' the mate put in, 'from Kora, across the sea from my own land of Hai, though the gods alone know what brings them to an oar-boat in the middle of the Ryna Sea.'

'We escaped from a Vendjomois trader who sought to make us slaves,' Elethrine explained, twisting the truth somewhat and allowing her tone to imply the unacceptability of such a thing.

'You are lucky, then,' Irqual boomed, 'for with us you'll get finer treatment than among the perfumed, effeminate men of Vendjome.'

'I thank you, captain,' Elethrine replied, taking his statement as implying that his people did not take slaves.

'I can see you'd fetch a high price though,' he continued, reaching out and quite casually taking one of Aisla's heavy breasts in his hand. She made no resistance, but allowed him to fondle her as if he were testing the quality of a melon. 'So, what are your names, ladies?'

'I am Elethrine,' Elethrine replied, deciding not to make an issue of her title for fear of kidnap.

'And I Aisla,' the maid giggled, as her nipple popped to erection under Irqual's thumb.

'And you, elfling?' Irqual demanded, turning to Talithea.

Barely before he had finished his question Talithea's hand had lashed out to land a stinging slap on the captain's cheek. He bellowed with rage and released Aisla's breast to grab at Talithea. He caught her chemise and it tore, baring her breasts and drawing a cry of indignation from her. Again her hand lashed out, her nails raking Irqual's arm even as he crushed her to himself.

Elethrine leapt forward by impulse even as she cursed

161

the Princess's stupidity in rising to what had not even been an intended insult. Irqual had pulled Talithea into a bear hug and Elethrine leapt onto his back, locking her arm around his bull neck even as Aisla rushed in to grapple him from the side. Irqual hurled himself sideways, oblivious to the weight of the three girls clinging to him. Talithea fell to the deck, Elethrine maintaining her perch as Aisla was flung to the side. Irqual roared in fury and swung his great arms up, even as the mate caught Elethrine around the waist. A moment later she was taken by a dozen hands and pulled back.

'She-cats!' Irqual roared. 'Put them over the bombards, stripped!'

Elethrine fought in vain as hands grabbed her gown. Despite her efforts it was quickly pulled up over her head and off, even as hands grappled her drawers to pull them down and leave her naked. Her arms and legs were grabbed and pulled wide, spreading her tuppenny open for all to see as she was carried towards the three fat-bellied, black-iron bombards that stood on the ship's sterncastle. As she went she saw that Aisla and Talithea had both been served the same way. Both were nude and struggling and both were destined to be strapped down for whatever punishment Irqual had in mind.

Elethrine cursed Talithea's temper as rough hands pushed her down over the barrel of the bombard. Her thighs spread involuntarily over the warm metal of the rounded chamber, sliding apart until her bare tuppenny was touching the surface. One of them pushed her back down, spreading her bottom for everyone to see as others began to lash her ankles to the carriage. Ropes were bound around her waist and the bombard, then tied off on her crossed hands, leaving her arms helpless in the small of her back. One dangling breast was taken in hand, making Elethrine tremble as she resigned herself to being ravished by thirty or so corsairs while strapped, naked, over the barrel of a bombard.

Her tuppenny was spread, wide and wet, an easy target for their cocks. She wondered who would be first, perhaps the blustering captain or his gross, uncouth mate. Or maybe they'd take Aisla and Talithea and leave her to the crew, adding the shame of being had by a commoner to her plight.

A hand grabbed one of her buttocks, squeezing and weighing it. A horny finger touched her anus, making her jump and causing her bottom to wobble, much to their amusement. A hand touched her tuppenny, the thumb right over the opening, and she realised that she wasn't even going to be allowed the dignity of having her maidenhead sundered by a cock. She clenched her teeth, waiting for the expected pain, only for the hand to be removed as the captain roared for the men to pull back.

'Get your hands away until I've made my choice, you filthy rats!' he shouted. 'You can all fuck until your balls drop off, but not my one, and not until they've had a damn good whipping for their nerve. Ha! How do you feel now, you three, with your fat female arses stuck up high and your cunts open wide? Ready for cock, eh? Well you'll get it, all you want, but not until Drathor here has brought the heat to your arses with a cat!'

Irqual stood back, and Elethrine turned her head to find the mate fingering a heavy whip with nine tails of braided leather. Aisla and Talithea were to either side, both with their naked bums in the air, just as she herself was, a thoroughly rude pose but a fine one to put a girl in for whipping.

Drathor scanned the three bottoms, selecting a target. Elethrine found herself shivering and kicking her legs in anticipation as his gaze settled on her spread seat. He stepped forward, took a handful of her bottom as if to test its weight and then stood away once more. Then the whip came down and Elethrine yelled as a fiery pain exploded across her bottom. Irqual laughed and slapped his thigh as Drathor once more raised the whip. Twelve hard strokes she was given, which left her bottom hot and throbbing. Drathor then served Aisla the same way, making the maid squeal and sob until her buttocks started to warm and she began to come on heat. Talithea was punished last and given eighteen hard, measured strokes that left her mewling and gasping on the barrel to which she was strapped, obviously excited and ready to be mounted.

Elethrine found herself breathing deeply and evenly. As with Aisla and Talithea, the whipping had brought the heat to her tuppenny and she felt ready for entry. Her bottom was a plump, hot ball of flesh, well smacked and throbbing, as it should be before her ravishment. The man who had beaten her was also he who was going to be the first to put his cock inside her. It was exactly as custom dictated – first the girl's ritual resistance had to be overcome. Then she would be whipped until her bottom was red and she was begging for entry. Finally she would be thrown down and entered, submitting herself joyfully to her future husband.

Yet she had always pictured the scene in her turret room at Korismund Keep, with some splendid Mundic noble standing over her with his magnificent erection straining out beneath his mail. Drathor, it was true, was obviously a great warrior, yet the situation was somehow strangely unsatisfying, perhaps because Aisla and Talithea alone would know how she had been taken.

Drathor himself evidently cared nothing for her qualms. He had stood back and, as Elethrine turned her head to see, she found that he was struggling with the crude fastenings of his trousers with a haste that suggested an uncontrollable lust. The others stood grinning around him, their eyes feasting on her naked bottom and the wet, ready tuppenny that she was flaunting for the mate's attention. She raised her bottom as Drathor's thongs came undone, her jaw trembling as she offered herself. He pulled his cock free, a massive thing, white and fleshy with a bulbous head already protruding from the thick foreskin. With his eyes locked on her naked bottom he began to masturbate.

'In the bull's eye, Drathor!' one of the others laughed, and threw something to the mate.

The others laughed and cheered, egging Drathor on to his task. The mate stumped forward, past Elethrine's waiting vagina and to her head, where he offered his cock to her mouth. She opened her mouth and took it in, starting to suck as she wondered if another would take advantage of her openness and mount her while the mate was busy in her mouth. His cock was big and made her gape, then gag as it was pushed roughly to the back of her throat. Several ribald remarks were made about her obvious willingness to suck, yet she was lost to the pleasure of ravishment and felt no more than a slight flush of shame that it should be done so publicly.

Drathor's great hand slapped down between her buttocks, applying something warm and greasy. She sighed around her mouthful of cock, grateful for the soothing feeling as the slimy substance was smeared over her freshly whipped bottom. From the smell she guessed it was some sort of fish grease, yet it felt pleasantly slimy on the hot, dry surface of the skin of her bottom. As his fingers began to caress her bottom, her sucking became more eager, a fully wanton response to the skill with which she had been brought on heat.

His hand was stroking her buttocks, then between them, the horny fingers rubbing her anus. Elethrine raised her bottom further, aware of the shame of her action even as she did it. Suddenly a thick, callused finger popped up her bottom, making her swallow and once more gag on the penis in her mouth. Somebody laughed and she realised what the expression 'bull's eye' probably meant. She groaned deep in her throat as his finger began to wriggle around in her bottom hole, stretching the ring in what could only be preparation for buggery.

It was too late. There was no point in protesting. Drathor was slipping his cock from her mouth. It reared up, wet with her saliva, the veins showing blue in the thick shaft. Then he was moving behind her. His finger came out of her bottom with a sticky pop. His penis was between her cheeks, hard against her soft, greasy flesh. The head was at her anus, pushing. She relaxed her ring and clenched her teeth, remembering Aisla's description of how to accept a cock in the bottom ring. Drathor grunted and she felt her anus stretch wide. She had the head of a penis in her bottom hole, then the neck as it pushed inside, aided by the liberal smearing of fish grease. She expelled her breath in a long, ecstatic moan as her back passage filled with cock, then began to grunt and sigh to the rhythm of his thrusts as he started to bugger her.

Her head was spinning, her whole world centred on the thick penis in her bottom and the breathless, dizzy feeling it was giving her. From the claps and whistles of the crowd she knew how her pleasure was showing, yet all she could do was writhe in her bonds, quite unable to get a finger to her tuppenny and indulge her need for the ultimate pleasure, and ultimate shame, of bringing herself to a climax while there was a penis up her bottom. Yet the way she was spread-eagled over the bombard meant that her clitty could touch the hard metal, just as it had in the heat of her whipping. Almost without knowing what she was doing she began to rub, bucking her hips and bottom in a movement of such lascivious delight that it drew a roar of coarse laughter from the captain.

'That's my beauty, come on my cock!' Drathor drawled hoarsely. 'Squeeze it out of me!'

Elethrine began to buck more frantically as her

orgasm approached. With each movement her tightly stretched anus pulled on Drathor's shaft, the straining ring drawing him in like a pursed mouth sucking. She could feel his pubic hair rubbing between her bottom cheeks and the coarse leather of his trousers touching the sore skin of her well-thrashed behind. He was still pushing into her, and each time a thrust matched her now frantic bucking, his balls would slap against her empty tuppenny. Her bound hands and ankles gave extra pleasure, reminding her of her helplessness and making every muscle strain with her rising climax. Then there was the hot, burning sensation of her freshly beaten bottom, a ball of pain that made a fine frame for her penetrated anus.

'Harder, deeper in me!' she begged, indifferent to her audience or the amazed stares of her friends. 'Bugger me! Hurt me!'

She came, screaming out her lust to the delighted watchers. The muscles of her sex contracted, hard, and her anus began to pulse, squeezing on the intruding penis. Drathor grunted, gave a final, hard shove and came up Elethrine's bottom, the rhythmic contractions of her stretched anus draining his sperm into her bowels. Once more she screamed, her mouth gaping in the vain hope of a cock being thrust into it at her very peak of ecstasy. Then it was over and she was subsiding onto the warm, sweat-slick metal of the bombard, blissfully happy and heedless of the utter shame of what she had just done.

It came back as Drathor pulled his cock slowly from her bottom. Her little hole closed, sore and throbbing, as his sperm trickled out to pool in her gaping vagina and then dribble down her tuppenny. Her bonds, which a moment before had added to her pleasure by giving her something to strain against during climax, now began to hurt, as did the cramped muscles of her arms and legs.

'Release me, I'll be good,' she said, softly.

At a nod from the captain two seamen came forward and began to work on her bonds. To either side of her the other girls were still strapped in place, their whipped bottoms thrust high over the fat bellies of the bombards. One man had his hand under Talithea's belly, and from the rapt expression on her face it was evident that he was playing with her tuppenny. Another was fondling the flesh of one of her breasts where it was squashed against the metal barrel, while a third was near her head and was stroking his cock in evident anticipation of her mouth.

Aisla, by contrast, had nobody within a good three paces of her. Nude except for the torn and dirty petticoat that had been raised to expose her buttocks for whipping, she looked good enough to tempt any man. Their lack of attention seemed curious to Elethrine until she saw the gigantic captain stride across the deck towards the maid. Clearly he had marked her for his own. Elethrine once more felt a flush of annoyance that her maid should be chosen over her.

Irqual lost no time with his prize, pulling his penis from his fly and thrusting it at Aisla's mouth. It was colossal, a great, fat thing the same curious ash grey as the captain's skin. Suddenly Elethrine was glad that it was not the captain who had taken her. The strain of accepting the mate in her bottom ring had been considerable and it now felt sore and strangely loose. Drathor's cock was big, but not by comparison with that of his chief, which was now being slid in and out of Aisla's mouth while her lips gaped around it like a baby bird attempting to manage an impossibly large worm.

As the last of her bonds came loose Elethrine struggled to her feet. Her dress and drawers were nearby, badly torn but still more or less intact. She reached for them more out of habit than to cover what had already been seen in every detail. For a moment she

168

wondered if the crew men who had untied her would want to use her, but none did and she realised that, like Aisla, she had been marked for exclusive use. As she sat down on the barrel of the bombard with a sigh of satisfaction and relief, Irqual pulled his cock free of Aisla's mouth. Elethrine watched as the giant went to the maid's rear and mounted her, sliding his monstrous cock into her vagina with remarkable ease. Aisla sighed and opened her mouth in an expression of contentment, then began to give little grunts of pleasure as she was ridden. For all Irqual's massive bulk, he stood perhaps no more than a hand's breadth taller than Aisla, which, Elethrine reasoned, meant that his cock was probably quite a good fit. The alternative was that Aisla's experience extended even further than she had already admitted to, and probably included accommodating the cocks of a good proportion of the male element of the keep's company.

A low moan drew Elethrine's attention to what was happening behind her. Talithea was almost invisible in a press of men. It was hard to see what was happening, but one of the larger men was certainly mounted on her and had his cock either up her vagina or her bottom ring. Two men seemed to be sharing her mouth, while her hands had been untied to allow her to stroke and fondle the cocks of others. As always after a good whipping, the Princess was exhibiting a wanton lust, yet, Elethrine realised, it was really no different from her own.

Only when Drathor had tired of watching Irqual fuck Aisla did he turn his attention back to Elethrine. Picking her up with ease, he threw her across his shoulder and made for the companionway to the stern of the galley. Elethrine made no resistance, but lay passively as he fondled her bottom through her dress. Doubtless, she thought, the sight of Aisla and Talithea being fucked had aroused him once more and once she had again sucked his penis to erection he would be ready to deflower her properly.

It didn't happen then, nor on the subsequent three days that the galley, the *Black Joke*, sailed steadily to the southeast. Instead Elethrine was used two or three times a day, always the same routine. Drathor would come down to the cabin and throw her across one of the wooden chimerae that supported his bed. Her dress would be pulled up and her drawers unlaced and pulled down. Drathor would then take the cat-o'-nine-tails to her bottom, not with his full strength but hard enough to bring her quickly on heat. He would masturbate while he whipped her and put his cock in her mouth once her bottom was hot and red. While she sucked he would grease her anus, using the same thick fish grease that he had the first time. Then his cock would go up her bottom and he would bugger her while she masturbated, always coming, so that the helpless contractions of her anal ring would draw the spunk fully from his cock. He showed no interest whatever in her tuppenny, nor her breasts, even when she offered them in the hope of having her nipples sucked. She accepted being buggered with a mixture of resignation and relief, enjoying her orgasms and grateful for the plentiful supply of fish oil that prevented her from becoming unduly sore.

When not providing sexual service, she and the others were allowed to wander the decks as they pleased, the crew apparently indifferent to the idea that they might pose any threat. Talithea had been appointed ship's whore and was seldom free from her task of servicing the crew in hands, mouth, vagina and anus. On the second day Irqual ordered that each man could take his pleasure with her only once a day, yet more often than not she was to be found on her knees in the main saloon, sucking on a seaman's cock while another rode her from behind and perhaps as many as four more queued for their turns. The attention seemed to put her in a sort of sexual haze, and by the evening of the second day she had abandoned her clothes altogether and even took her dinner naked and sat in a man's lap with his penis wedged firmly up her bottom.

Aisla, with only Irqual to satisfy, had more time to spend in Elethrine's company. While Drathor was both coarse and taciturn, Irqual was loquacious and affected a rough attempt at elegance. His routine with Aisla was to eat dinner with her as if they were man and wife, to have sex with her in a variety of different ways and then to sit and boast of his prowess while he downed flagon after flagon of strong red wine. It was from Irqual's boasting that Elethrine learnt that the *Black Joke* was headed back to the corsair's base after a long and highly successful voyage of raiding along the coasts of Vendjome and the Aprina States.

Home for the corsairs was Morin, a rock girt island somewhere to the south. The base was apparently approached by a treacherous channel and, according to Irqual, had resisted the attacks of both Vendjome and Opina for some three generations. This conversation was held on the evening of the second day as Elethrine and Aisla rested in exhaustion against the rear rail of the *Black Joke*'s sterncastle. Both girls had been well serviced by their masters and below they could hear the delighted shrieks of the drunken crew as Talithea was once more put through her paces. Two lookouts alone were visible, neither paying attention, while all around them the sea spread like glass with the sun sinking slowly towards the western horizon.

'This afternoon,' Aisla said, 'after Irqual had had me assume what he calls the position of the surprised armadillo –'

'The what?' Elethrine cut in.

'It means I have to curl up with my head down and

171

my legs well parted so that my tuppenny is over my face,' Aisla explained. 'An armadillo, he says, is a small animal that is able to roll itself into a ball for protection, like a hedgehog. It hurts my back a little but in the position he can use both my vagina and mouth without really moving. He likes to feed me my own cream and then have his balls sucked while he finishes off in me –'

'Aisla!' Elethrine interjected, shocked by the sheer wantonness of her maid's tone of voice.

'Sorry, mistress,' Aisla said, quickly.

'No matter,' Elethrine sighed, 'after all, I myself am buggered nightly and often in the afternoon. While Drathor may be less inventive, he is certainly no less dirty and I confess to taking pleasure in his antics. But you were going to tell me something.'

'Indeed, mistress,' Aisla continued. 'As Irqual was boasting of his raids along the coast of Cypraya he began to speak of a palace they stormed on an island far to the south. Apparently the owner was some sort of warlock – a death-seer Irqual called him – and he inflicted a lot of damage before Irqual killed him. The loot, Irqual claims, included a great carpet of blue and gold that will fly at the proper command . . .'

'And you feel we might use this to escape?' Elethrine finished, immediately sensing Aisla's drift.

'Perhaps, mistress,' Aisla continued, 'especially as the activating syllables are said to be woven into the pattern of the carpet.'

'A thought,' Elethrine admitted, 'yet I have surrendered to Drathor and expect to be taken to wife when we reach Morin.'

'Are you not still maiden?' Aisla asked.

'Indeed,' Elethrine replied, 'yet for all his perverse habits he is technically my master and honour commands me to respect him.'

'Yet we would never more see Korismund!' Aisla objected.

'Such is the burden of highborn honour,' Elethrine replied. 'Still, I am not yet taken to wife, nor even formally betrothed, although I offer my tuppenny willingly enough.'

She moved slightly uncomfortably on her sore bottom, feeling a trace of petulance at Drathor's wilful perversity.

'And what of Princess Talithea?' Aisla continued. 'Ship's whore is hardly an honourable estate for a Princess of Mund.'

'True,' Elethrine admitted, 'yet perhaps on Morin there is some other captain or great warrior who will want her. Alternatively we might persuade Irqual to relinquish you in favour of her.'

'He is not a man to be persuaded,' Aisla said. 'Nor do I think he would take a girl who has been so roundly used by thirty of so of his men.'

'Perhaps you are right,' Elethrine said after a pause, 'but we must wait to see what transpires on Morin.'

Late in the afternoon of the following day they sighted Morin, a jagged black crag low on the horizon. Elethrine watched as they approached, and as the island loomed closer she realised why the base had never been taken. They were headed for a small bay between great promontories of black rock which reached around to guard the inlet like the claws of a crab. At the summit of each stood a squat fortress, really no more than low towers but with three bombard barrels protruding from each, their deadly black mouth aimed out across the approach. Jagged rocks barred the entrance to the bay, and the *Black Joke* was forced to wait an hour until Irqual judged the tide high enough to make it possible to enter. Even then the galley had to be towed in by two rowing boats and Irqual himself took the depth soundings. Peering over the side, Elethrine twice glimpsed the pale shapes of rocks beneath them, scabrous ghosts that seemed insubstantial in the green water yet which she knew were quite capable of tearing the bottom out of the ship.

Finally they entered the bay and the bottom turned to a fine sand. The *Black Joke* was secured alongside a crude jetty of massive, rough-hewn boulders and a ramp was lowered to the ground. Many people had come out to greet the ship: corsairs like those aboard, girls marked both by beauty and a timid manner and a scattering of children. Only one of the females stood out; a plump, matronly woman with brawny red arms folded across her bulging chest and a look of stern disapproval on her face.

Irqual roared his greetings to those gathered on the dock and then began to throw down items of loot, boasting how he had acquired each as the men below caught it. Behind him men were dragging the loot up from the hold, carefully watched over by Drathor.

'See this,' he was saying as he held up a small casket of rose coloured wood, 'it contains a strange spice that makes the mouth burn. We took it from a village deep in the jungles of Cypraya. The locals cowered back at the very sight of us, and when Drathor belched, they fled!'

The people below laughed and a squat man caught the casket, stacking it among the rapidly growing pile of riches.

'And here,' Irqual shouted, 'taken from the dying clutches of some thrice damned death-seer, is a carpet that defies its weight and the weight of all that is placed on it! Nine good men died to take it and other things, but his spells were no use against my axe. I put it through him like a skewer up a rabbit's arse!'

Elethrine watched as he dragged the carpet out. It was large and woven of rich blue and gold, clearly an item of worth even if it did not fly. By careful questioning and a pretence of awe, Aisla had managed to establish that the corsairs had tested it and succeeded in getting it airborne, yet Elethrine was cautious of Irqual's boasting, as the deeds of arms he claimed were so fantastic that some, at least, had to be no more than hot air.

'And last,' Irqual was saying, his voice finally starting to become hoarse, 'just three days ago, in the sea off Anjome, we found three fine girls adrift in a boat. Ho, Omilla, take them to the girls' hut and smarten them up. They will serve at the feast tonight.'

As he gestured the three of them towards the gangplank, Elethrine began to feel a distinct sense of unease. She had been expecting to be announced as the intended wife of Drathor and certainly not as if she were part of the corsair's spoils. Yet the woman Omilla, the plump matron in the crowd, had been told to smarten them up, and possibly that and serving at the feast comprised some sort of pre-nuptial ceremony, rather like the ritual spanking of a girl before ravishment and again before the actual wedding ceremony in Mund.

With no more than a curious glance to Aisla and Talithea, she obeyed Irqual's instructions and Omilla's peremptory gesture once they reached the dock. The houses were no more than a hundred paces from the dock; long, low affairs with gable ends carved in the likeness of fierce beasts. The largest was in the centre, with a broad path leading down from its great doors to the dock. As they passed it, Elethrine glimpsed a long table set with trenchers and knives and various girls scurrying about performing preparatory tasks. All were near nude and all were beautiful, and as one bent to place a tray of fruit on the table, her short skirt lifted to display rounded, naked buttocks, each of which was criss-crossed with a network of thin red lines – clear evidence of recent punishment.

Omilla was headed for a different building, almost as large as the main hall but less ornate and set somewhat apart from the others. The woman walked with a fussy, somewhat irritated motion, as if to suggest that she had far more important work to do than see to the three girls. She walked fast, yet with their longer legs the girls had no difficulty in keeping up. They also had to duck to enter the building, which proved to be a long dormitory with perhaps as many as two dozen pallets arranged along either wall. Many of these had possessions beside them, but some, at the darkest and dampest end of the building, were vacant, and it was to these that Omilla gestured.

'Yours are the three at the end,' she ordered brusquely. 'They are to be kept tidy and no fripperies are permitted. Now strip.'

'I . . .' Elethrine began, intending to point out that there had been a mistake and that she was destined for the bed of the mighty Drathor, rather than what was evidently a communal dormitory for girls of no status whatever.

Omilla made no reply, but grabbed Elethrine by the ear so suddenly that she was taken completely by surprise. Thrown off balance, she was dragged to a chair, on which Omilla sat down. Elethrine managed a squeak of indignation as her arm was twisted forcefully into the small of her back. She knew exactly what was happening, as she had seen Nurse Anaka administer the same brisk, vigorous over-the-knee spankings to Aisla many, many times. It wasn't appropriate for her though – when she was beaten it involved a complex ritual of preparation and then the application of a cane or whip to her silk-clad buttocks. To be spanked bare-bottomed over a matron's knee was something that only happened to the lowborn, yet it was now quite clearly about to happen to her.

'No, not like that! I'm highborn! Aisla, help!' Elethrine squeaked, as Omilla threw up her dress.

Aisla stepped forward, but hesitated before the stern

176

fury of Omilla, her response ingrained from years of submission to similar punishments.

'No, not that, please not that!' Elethrine gasped as the dreadful woman pulled at her drawers, not opening them, but tugging them down, to effect the complete exposure of her naked bottom.

Elethrine gave a long squeal of despair as it all came on show: full, creamy buttocks, plump, pouted tuppenny lips with their puff of rich gold hair, and puckered pink anus, swollen and slightly open from repeated use by Drathor. Aisla took another, hesitant step forward, of which Omilla took no notice. Talithea was standing back, her pretty mouth open in a little 'O' of horror. To the Princess, Elethrine knew, being spanked bare-bottomed over a matron's lap was the ultimate indignity, far worse than taking any number of cocks into her body. True, they had done it to each other, but then they were more or less equals.

'You will obey me in all things,' Omilla was saying, her voice quiet and level, as befitted a matron about to put a naughty girl in her place. 'If you do not, this will be the result – or worse.'

From Elethrine's point of view there was nothing worse. Her dress was up, her drawers were around her knees, her bottom was bare and she about to be spanked by hand – spanked as if she were some common kitchen maid! She made one last, desperate effort to get free, kicking out and catching the woman's shin. Omilla took no notice, but only twisted Elethrine's arm more tightly into the small of her back. Elethrine gave a sob of resignation and stuck her bottom up as the pressure of Omilla's armlock dictated – far from happy about it but resigned to her punishment.

The spanking started, Elethrine feeling an enormous burst of utter shame as Omilla's hand smacked down full across her nude seat. Another fell, making her kick and buck her bottom in a way that she knew opened her cheeks and gave a fuller display of tuppenny and anal charms. She wriggled helplessly, overcome by shame, exposing herself more and more fully as the slaps rained down on her rapidly reddening buttocks. Finally her shame became unendurable and she started to beat her fist on the floor and burst into tears, giving in utterly to feelings stronger by far than when she had been quirted in the palace at Vendjome or flogged over the barrel of the corsair's bombard.

Only at the sight of her mistress's tears did Aisla manage to overcome her instinctive respect for the matronly Omilla. Stepping forward, she took a firm grip of the woman's spanking arm and pulled. Omilla pushed back, a preemptory move, as if brushing away a gnat. Aisla only pulled harder and then suddenly seemed to come alive.

With a jerk Aisla threw her weight backwards, unseating Omilla. Elethrine fell to the floor, to land with her red bottom stuck up and her thighs cocked rudely apart, the drawers having been kicked off one leg in her struggles during spanking.

Omilla had also landed on the floor. Rounding on Aisla, she spat a string of words with such venom and fury that the maid hesitated, but only for an instant. As the overseer tried to rise, Aisla threw a leg nimbly over her back, grabbed a wrist in each hand and pulled sharply sideways. Omilla landed back on the ground with a squashy sound and a curse, struggled again to rise but found Aisla's full weight on her back and her arms pinned up.

Elethrine had managed to get her drawers back on, and the feeling of submission that had been rising as she was spanked fled as she once more covered her bottom. Talithea also had come forward to help, finally snapping out of the obedient sexual trance she had been in since her first whipping from the corsairs. Together they quickly had Omilla's skirts up, exposing a fat pink bottom that quivered with the overseer's indignant struggles.

A delicious feeling of revenge came over Elethrine as she planted the first smack and watched the flesh of Omilla's big, round bottom wobble in response. Talithea planted a second, harder smack and for an instant Omilla's plump thighs opened to display the lips of her fat, hairy tuppenny.

Suddenly the door burst open. The scene froze: the three girls around Omilla, hands raised to smack the overseer's large, pale behind. In the door stood Drathor, his shoulders filling the frame and his face set in an expression of puzzlement and annoyance.

'What's this?' he demanded.

'We are chastising this impertinent woman,' Elethrine answered with as much certainty as she could muster. 'She seems to think us no better than the other serving wenches. Perhaps she does not realise that Irqual and yourself have singled Aisla and me out?'

Her statement had been delivered hopefully, almost pleading for Drathor to finally recognise their relationship.

'Singled you out?' Drathor asked. 'What fool's talk is this? You are slaves, like the others, and Omilla is the overseer. Do as she says, and be quick about it. Omilla, be quick, you have disturbed me with your yelping, so you had better have these girls ready.'

'Yes, master, immediately, master,' Omilla stammered as she got to her feet, the girls having moved back at Drathor's words.

'Slaves?' Elethrine managed. 'But –'

'Slaves,' Drathor answered, 'and you had best realise it. Had you not been my bed companion I would have you whipped just for speaking to me.'

'Do, master,' Omilla put in spitefully, 'they are in need of correction.'

'Tomorrow,' Drathor spat, 'for now they are needed

179

to serve. Now hasten. Oh, and leave on those ridiculous undergarments you wear, they will provide amusement.'

He left. Elethrine, stunned by the revelation that she held no special place among the corsairs, could find nothing to say and meekly took off her dress when ordered. Stripped to her drawers, with Aisla naked and Talithea in just torn pantalettes, she followed Omilla to the great hall, where the feast had already begun.

Men lined the long table, each with a trencher of coarse bread in front of him, a knife and a drinking vessel of glass or horn. There was no order whatsoever to the meal, drink skins mingling with platters of meat, fruit and pastries along the entire length of the table. Various girls poured and served, but were more often being groped or kissed by the corsairs.

Omilla stopped by the door and put her back against the first of the pillars that supported the roof. The annoyance had faded from her plump face, to be replaced by a look of self-satisfied superiority. Elethrine guessed that when their punishment came it would be long, hard and undoubtedly humiliating. In the meantime she could do nothing, and so copied Aisla in taking up a skin of drink and helping to keep the corsair's vessels filled.

At the head of the table Irqual was seated in a great chair of carved black wood. His trophies were ranged behind him, the blue and gold carpet among them. Elethrine glanced at it longingly, but could think of no way of securing it with some forty armed men in the room. Irqual, as usual, was boasting of his exploits, his voice a roar above the general clamour of the hall.

'Death flew from his fingertips,' he was saying, 'like the sparks of a fire, only blue. The man to my left fell, then the one to my right, their clothes burning. The death-seer was still some thirty paces away, maybe forty, and his hand was raised. His eyes looked into mine, red in black, the eyes of a demon. He knew he had me; indeed, he was laughing with delight. Then my axe took him in the midriff and his expression changed fast enough. Thrown from fifty paces it was, yet with enough force to hurl him back between the pillars of his palace. He cast no more spells after that, but as he lay dying he made a final prophecy. Looking right at me, and showing no pain whatever, he spoke that I would never be slain by the hand of man.'

Irqual paused to drain the contents of his flagon down his throat, then his voice once more roared out, the note of superstition quite gone from it.

'But I say he was a fake and could no more see the manner of men's deaths than I. It takes no death-seer to know that no man will strike me down, for there exists no man capable of the feat!'

His boast was greeted with a roar of drunken laughter and a great deal of clashing of cups and banging of knife hilts on the table. Elethrine looked away with a shudder of distaste. In Mund, boasting was considered vulgar and feats of arms were only ever related by witnesses, and then in the form of ritual sagas.

The evening progressed, with the corsairs becoming increasingly drunk and their attentions to the serving girls more lewd. Twice she and Talithea were made to show off the way their drawers and pantalettes split to allow access to their bottoms, which the corsairs found as amusing as the girls found it humiliating. Another girl was mounted on the floor, the other men taking little notice as their companion fucked her. Elethrine found hands groping her bottom or breasts each time she bent to serve, Drathor's right over her having apparently ended with their arrival.

At first she was sure that the night would end with her being ravished on the floor, yet as one man after another slipped into a drunken stupor, it began to look as if her maidenhead would survive one more night. Finally a man lapsed into unconsciousness while actually pawing her bottom. She looked around to find that only two corsairs remained sensible: Drathor, who had a skin of mead upended over his mouth and was clearly on the way out; and Irqual himself, who was still roaring boasts and threats despite his lack of audience.

Otherwise only the serving girls remained upright, and not all of them. Two were slumped over men – one with her breasts still smeared with the sauce her partner had poured over them – while a third was propped against a wall, looking dazed as she sipped at a cup of wine abandoned by one of the corsairs. The remaining three stood quietly together by the door, with Omilla the plump overseer seated beside them.

Irqual stopped shouting, becoming aware that there were only girls left to boast to. His eyes moved slowly from side to side, passing over the group by the door, resting for a moment on Aisla and then focusing on Elethrine.

'Ho, girl,' he boomed suddenly, 'Drathor is like to be insensible, so I will bed you tonight as well as your flame-haired friend, perhaps even the elven halfling too. Come.'

Elethrine stepped forward, her pulse increasing at the thought of finally losing her precious maidenhead. She knew from Aisla that Irqual was not one to allow himself to be manipulated or teased but would simply mount her and take her up her tuppenny without preamble. Every chance of honour seemed lost, yet just possibly she might be able to persuade him to take her as an equal and not as a slave.

'Have you ever seen a man such as I?' he demanded, flexing the massive muscles of his neck and arms as she approached.

'You are a great warrior,' Elethrine answered, trying not to tremble, 'and it is no dishonour to be ravished by you. Yet the protocol of Korismund demands that afterwards you take me to wife.'

'Wife?' Irqual bellowed. 'Wife? Ho, Drathor, have

you ever heard the like? The little slave wench wants to be my wife! Irqual takes no wife, little one, but he has many girl slaves, and each trembles with desire at the memory of her master's touch.'

'You would be a baron consort,' Elethrine said.

'Ha!' Irqual laughed, a sound of both disbelief and dismissal. 'But enough talk. Kneel, slave wench, and split those absurd drawers that I may have better access to your doubtless well-juiced cunt. Wife!'

'I will resist,' Elethrine said quietly.

'Resist?' Irqual roared, then let out a great booming laugh. 'Resist? Resist then, it will add sport to our coupling and perhaps I will beat your pretty bottom to teach you respect before I have you. Then I warrant you'll be eager enough. Resistance! Ha! You could not even lift my axe!'

'I can lift the arms of Uroth, Aisla's father, who stands a full head taller than you,' Elethrine said proudly, 'and he is also a greater warrior.'

'What?' Irqual roared. 'No such man exists! Go on then, try it, the effort will bring the blood to your veins and make you ready for the bedchamber.'

Elethrine reached out for the massive, sweat-stained shaft, gripping it with both hands. Finding the centre of balance, she bunched her muscles. Irqual's face broke into an amused grin as she lifted the axe from the table. Slowly she raised it to the level of her chin and then above her head, her arms straining at its weight. Irqual laughed at the sight, a great gust of mirth with his mouth wide and his head thrown back. Elethrine muttered a quick prayer to her father and brought the axe down directly on to Irqual's unshielded head.

Irqual's laughter broke off on the instant, to be replaced by total silence, which in turn gave way to a roar of fury as what had happened penetrated Drathor's drink-addled wits. Elethrine turned to find him half risen to his feet with his double-handed sword already in his hands. Aisla was in front of him, backing away with a trencher knife clasped in her fist. Drathor roared again and brought the sword around in a vicious arc. Aisla ducked and then came up as the sword passed her head, driving the knife up under Drathor's ribs at a low angle. For an instant his face registered horrified disbelief at the fate that had overtaken him and then he crashed backwards across the table.

Two strands of copper-gold hair fluttered down through the uncertain torch-light.

Elethrine looked up. Omilla had vanished. The other serving girls were frozen in place, starring in horror at the corpses of their masters.

'The carpet!' Elethrine called. 'Quick, Omilla will have gone for the ship guards!'

Talithea and Aisla were already moving towards the great roll of blue and gold carpet that was propped among the spoils of the corsair's raids. Praying that Irqual's boasts had not been idle, Elethrine grabbed a knife and slit the cord that held the carpet. It sprang open, Aisla grabbing it immediately and starting to drag it towards the door. Talithea joined her as Elethrine began to load her arms with food from the table, grabbing whatever seemed easiest to carry.

'Hurry!' Talithea called from the door.

'I'm coming!' Elethrine answered, clutching at a full goat's skin and starting to lurch towards the door under her burden.

Outside Talithea and Aisla had the carpet unrolled on the ground. The syllable that was supposed to activate it stood out clear in the middle, an 'X' and an 'I' woven in ornate letters. Somewhere in the night Omilla was screaming for help.

'We need more!' she gasped as she dropped her burden on the carpet.

'No time! Look!' Talithea answered, her voice filled with panic.

Elethrine glanced around. Down the slope the torches of the harbour illuminated the dock and four armed men, running. The nearest was no more than thirty paces away, his sword clasped ready in his hand.

'Xy!' she screamed, as she leapt onto the carpet.

Nothing happened.

'Zee!' Talithea tried frantically, still with no effect.

'X I!' Elethrine yelled as Aisla turned to face the man, her tiny blood-stained knife held in defiance of his sword.

Instantly the carpet was weightless, and rising on the slight breeze. The nearest man yelled, leaping forward and lashing out. The sword slashed the edge of the carpet, passing through so cleanly that he lost his balance. Aisla slashed at his head, missed and then they were out of reach, rising on the breeze.

The carpet rose, sailing high above the dock and the *Black Joke*, then out over the bay and between the grim black forts on the promontories. Drifting without control, they passed no more than fifty paces from one fort, Elethrine expecting the black mouths of the bombards to belch fire and death at any instant. Nothing happened and she finally felt able to expel her breath.

The carpet rode on the wind, gathering speed as it climbed. For a long while the girls said nothing, but looked back towards the lights of Morin and the figures outside the longhouse. The great moon illuminated the black cliffs, hanging like a pale, faint lamp over the scene, its lesser companion emerging slowly from one side as the girls gazed out in shock. Only when Morin had dwindled to a jagged black shadow on the moonlit sea did Elethrine regain her wits.

'Aisla,' Elethrine said quietly, 'you do your family honour. I shall stand witness to that blow.'

'And I to yours,' Talithea said, her voice trembling as she turned a final glance to the distant lights of the *Black Joke*.

9

Trollop

For days the carpet drifted. With no knowledge of how to control it the girls could only wait and submit themselves to the wind. Their general direction, at least, was north, which pleased them as, according to the map, they would eventually reach the Glass Coast, or even Mund itself. They had quickly discovered that dangling heavy objects over the side of the carpet caused it to descend, yet while they flew over sea the exercise was pointless. Instead they retained a comfortable height and prayed that the favourable wind would hold.

The shock of the events on the *Black Joke* and Morin wore off gradually, to be replaced by satisfaction at their escape and a deeper bond between them for having shared the experience. The initial excitement of flight also wore off, to be replaced by boredom, and they took to discussing their experiences, and most specifically their sexual encounters. This was aided by Elethrine's hastily snatched selection of supplies, which included mead, wine and ale but not a drop of water.

Feeling tipsy, safe and very far removed indeed from the strictures and protocols of Mund, they became increasingly honest about their feelings and increasingly excited. Elethrine even admitted that being hand-spanked across Omilla's knee had left her wanting to climax, which had left both the other girls in giggles.

'And when I spanked you?' Talithea asked.

Elethrine blushed and admitted that once Talithea had spanked her firmly she would have been more than willing to obey any orders that furthered her abasement.

'Even to kiss Aisla's bottom ring, as I intended?' Talithea said, softly.

Elethrine nodded, then continued, emboldened by drink and arousal.

'For perfection, perhaps,' she said, 'I would need to be naked and held tight around my waist. Then you could spank me and I am sure I would soon be ready to do whatever I was told.'

Talithea giggled and moved forward, beckoning to Elethrine.

'Come, Aisla,' she said, turning a bright, mischievous smile to the maid, 'let us see if your mistress would like to put her lips to your bottom ring. Off with your drawers, Pommette.'

Elethrine complied, her desire rising quickly as she stripped and got into position – kneeling – while Talithea took her tight around the waist. Her bottom was stuck well out, and as the Princess planted the first, gentle smack across her cheeks she sighed and called Talithea's pet name softly and eagerly.

Her bottom warmed quickly as Talithea's smacks became firmer and more purposeful. Being spanked nude was getting to her sense of shame, as she had known it would, yet now the shame was part of a build up of delicious sensations that were gradually making her want to take her self-imposed debasement further.

'I'm ready,' she sighed when she could no longer resist the delicious indignity of kissing her maid's anus.

Aisla giggled and moved round, presenting her trim, naked bottom to her mistress's face. Elethrine hesitated, her gaze locked on the tightly puckered spot of Aisla's bottom ring. For an instant, as her bottom bounced under Talithea's continued smacks, she wondered if she could really do it, and then suddenly she was, her lips pouting out to plant a wet kiss directly on the tiny hole in front of her. Aisla groaned and spread her thighs, immersing Elethrine's face deep between her buttocks.

'Lick it, you little slut,' Talithea said, as she turned her attention to turning the backs of Elethrine's thigh the same colour as her already throbbing bottom.

Elethrine sighed and began to probe Aisla's bottom ring with her tongue. She was in absolute ecstasy, nude, her head spinning with drink. Talithea had spanked her bottom and thighs and she was giving Aisla a token of utter submission – the licking of her anus.

'You're a naughty girl, Pommette,' Talithea giggled, as she tightened her grip and began to smack harder, again on Elethrine's bottom. 'How does it feel to be hand-spanked in the nude? How does it feel to know you're going to come while I smack your little buns? You know I can see your bottom ring – perhaps you'd like something in it while I punish you?'

Elethrine nodded and then went back to licking Aisla's bottom clean, revelling in the feel of her tongue in the maid's ring and the thought that her own would shortly be penetrated.

'A cherry, then,' Talithea said, pausing in her spanking.

Elethrine felt something round and soft press against her anus, which opened to admit it.

'Pop, up it goes,' Talithea giggled. 'Now, how about this nice fat plum?'

Sticking her bottom out for the insertion, Elethrine giggled and pulled her head back, only to have Aisla take her by the hair and once more stuff her face against her bottom. A new wave of submissive bliss went through Elethrine as she once more began to lick Aisla's bottom and her anus began to stretch to accommodate the plum. Halfway in the plum burst, squashing juice out to run down Elethrine's warm tuppenny. Talithea burst into giggles and once more started to spank her playmate's chubby bottom.

Elethrine felt her climax coming as the plum juice ran down over her fingers. Her mouth was full of the taste of Aisla's bottom and tuppenny, her own bottom hot and throbbing under Talithea's punishing slaps. She was nude, her buttocks were red from beating and a cherry had been pushed into her hole. Her tongue was up her maid's bottom and her face was being held hard in between the girl's bare bum cheeks. She felt her muscles tense as another hard slap caught the fattest part of her bottom. Suddenly she desperately needed her bottom filled and reached back, scrabbling for the fruit bowl even as she started to come. Talithea responded, changing hands to spank with her left. Elethrine felt something press against her anus, something even bigger than Drathor's cock.

'Take it, Pommette, come on it,' Talithea moaned. 'It's a little apple – just for your name.'

Elethrine relaxed her anus and felt it fill, stretching impossibly wide and then closing abruptly and starting to pulse as the apple Talithea had chosen was forced up her bottom. It felt huge in her rectum, and heavy, producing a delightful weight in her bowels as her climax hit her.

She began to buck her hips, lapping frantically at Aisla's proffered bottom. Dizzy with pleasure she felt the apple start to squeeze out of her bottom, stretching the ring as wide as it would go.

'Naughty, dirty slut,' Talithea breathed, smacking Elethrine's bottom furiously as her victim's buttocks clenched and then opened once more.

Elethrine gave a final long, choking scream as the apple popped from her anus at the very peak of her orgasm. Only then did she realise that both the others had been masturbating too and that neither had finished taking her pleasure.

They used her thoroughly, each taking full advantage of her body to enhance her own orgasm. Aisla maintained her grip in Elethrine's hair, forcing her to lick her anus until her gasps told Elethrine that the maid was coming. Talithea, meanwhile, was using one hand to masturbate and the other to molest Elethrine, with her thumb in the demoiselle's aching bottom ring and her hand cupping her tuppenny.

Held tightly and thoroughly used, Elethrine cupped her breasts in her hands and started to rub the nipples, knowing that only a little more stimulation was needed to bring her once more to orgasm. As Talithea's fingers found her clitty it happened, again making her tense and scream. The three girls came together in mutual ecstasy, inhibitions forgotten in their mutual lust.

Awash with drink and sex, the three of them cuddled together in the centre of the carpet. Completely isolated and safe from the outside world, they allowed their darkest and dirtiest fantasies to come to the fore, licking and probing every orifice of one another's bodies until each had come many times and was sore in several places. At some stage they beat Elethrine with a heavy wooden spoon that had been snatched up during their hasty departure. This left her bottom purple with bruises and provided yet another exquisite climax.

In the morning they awoke cold, sore and with a desperate need for fresh water. The carpet had drifted high and the world lay beneath them, a magnificent panorama of sea and barren wilderness. Directly ahead of them two great volcanoes rose on either side of a narrow strait, a feature which the map identified as the Rieve. To the west of this a tall line of cliffs ran away to the south, their strata exposed like the layers of an elaborate cake. Beyond the cliffs was an apparently endless wasteland of rock and sand. To the east the coastline swept away in a majestic curve of red-brown dunes, which they judged to be the seaboard of the Red Parch, or Ara Khum desert. Inland the red wilderness continued to the far horizon, broken only by a jagged line of mountains trailing away to the northeast.

'Beautiful,' Talithea said, quietly.

'Beautiful, yet dead,' Elethrine added.

'I want some water,' Aisla moaned.

Consulting the map, they discovered that the sea beyond the Rieve was the Ergan Deep, a circle of water shaped as if a pebble had been dropped into mud and encircled by mountains. The map also showed that they had travelled a great distance, despite the fact that the air on the carpet seemed completely still. Despite her thirst and throbbing head, Elethrine drew courage from this discovery.

'See,' she declared, pointing at the map, 'if the wind holds true, another two days' flight will bring us over the Aeg Roads, and once more to Aegmund, where, with luck, we might bring ourselves down within the principality of Ateron!'

'Where I will be immediately immured in a celibentuary,' Talithea pointed out.

'Not so!' Elethrine said, enthusiastically. 'We must be a league in the air and will cross perhaps three hundred leagues of central Aegmund. We are bound to pass over a witch's spire, where we may land, beg the restoration of your maidenhead and then transport to more civilised parts!'

'Perhaps,' Talithea replied.

'Water,' Aisla interrupted, 'below.'

Elethrine turned to look, finding that they had drifted over the western of the two volcanoes. Far below them, in pockets created by spent fumaroles, water reflected the blue of the sky among fields of grey and black rock. They descended quickly by lying on their bellies and dangling the skins of wine and mead over the side. The crater passed below them, a great bowl of black rock with a broad, steaming lake deep inside. Beyond was a long slope on which they managed to land. On impact

191

with the ground the carpet immediately deactivated and once they had emptied two of the three skins and filled them with clear, fresh water, they once more took to the air. One skin of heavy red wine they kept, sharing an unspoken agreement that the lust-filled events of the previous night were worth repeating.

All that day they drifted high over the Ergan Deep, resting, and slowly recovering from the excesses of the night. Dusk found Elethrine lying on her stomach and looking out over the sea to where a mountainous peninsula thrust out for the shore. On its westerly flanks the setting sun showed patches of green, the first vegetation they had seen from the air save yellow grass and straggling thorn bushes along the distant shores.

Idly, she began to pick at the frayed edge where the corsair's sword had cut the carpet and her thoughts turned to the pleasures which they might explore that evening. She had suffered a carefully constructed perfect indignity – a naked spanking while she licked her maid's bottom – and by mutual agreement it was now Talithea's turn to undergo and enjoy a similar fate. How, she wondered, to bring the Princess's humiliation to the perfect peak that would provide the same earth shaking climaxes that she herself had achieved?

Short of descending to the ground and staking Talithea out for goblins, it was hard to see how Elethrine's own experience could be topped. Glancing once more at the peninsula, she wondered if the sparse wood of its slopes harboured goblins, or whether it would be too dry. Of course, if they did stake Talithea out there would be a good chance of her and Aisla being caught too, and then she would be deflowered with a vengeance. Some fat green cock would be rammed into her tuppenny while she was made to suck and pull on others.

Blushing at the sheer filthiness of her thoughts, she turned her face down and noticed a curious phenomenon. From the slashed edge of the carpet, tiny golden flakes were drifting away, leaving the ruptured fibres like spray blown from a breaking wave. All day the carpet had shown a tendency to lose height, and twice it had been necessary to adjust the amount of weight that protruded from the sides. With a sudden flash of insight, Elethrine realised that in some way the carpet was losing its ability to remain aloft and that unless they managed to gain more height they would have difficulty in clearing the approaching peninsula.

'Bring things in!' she called to her friends.

Talithea and Aisla, who had been exploring each other's breasts amid giggles and suggestions for what degradation might appeal to the Princess, looked round in surprise. Elethrine explained hastily and they quickly had the carefully positioned skins pulled in. The carpet rose, but with a notable lack of urgency.

For the next hour they waited, unable to do more to control their fate. The map showed more sea beyond the peninsula, and it became a matter of debate whether to put down there and take their chances with possible goblins and other unknown perils rather than risk the certain fate of landing in the sea. Yet the map also marked a city – Port Ergan – some fifty leagues beyond the peninsula and it seemed at least possible that they might reach it. Finally they agreed to see if they could pass over the ridge of rock that lay directly ahead and then to land hurriedly if they seemed likely to come down in the sea.

Slowly the carpet lost height, seeming to aim precisely at the ridge. As they approached Elethrine saw movement and the prospect of a goblin's cock in her virgin tuppenny suddenly became very real and very alarming. Closer inspection revealed only small, shaggy goats and relief flooded through her as they crested the ridge with less than two man heights to spare. Beyond was a glittering expanse of sea with the coast sweeping away to the west and bordered not by cliffs, but by an expanse of mudflat and marsh. Judging their height and rate of descent, it seemed to Elethrine that they would come down on the land, and hopefully not too far from Port Ergan.

As they crossed out over the sea, once more the carpet began to falter, losing its ability to remain stable and starting to pitch and yaw alarmingly. It was clearly failing, as was the light. A lurch spilt the knife and one of the remaining apples over the side to tumble to the water far below. Fighting down her panic, Elethrine hung her arms over the edge and ordered Aisla to do the same on the opposite side while Talithea stayed in the exact centre to provide stability. Their descent became more rapid, and Elethrine watched the sun set with unnatural speed as they dipped towards the sea. For a moment it seemed that they would come down in the water, until a low-level current of air pulled them inshore and finally deposited them gently on a great expanse of glutinous brown mud.

Abandoning the carpet, they made their way to the narrow strip of pebbles that separated mud from marsh. Tired, scared and smeared with muck, they set off to the north, following the curve of the tide line until the last traces of light faded from the sky and they were forced to stop and camp.

In the morning they washed as best they could in a brackish stream and fashioned skirts and bras from reeds in order to cover Aisla's total nudity and the ragged remains of the drawers and pantalettes that were the sole remaining pieces of Elethrine's once magnificent attire.

By good fortune Port Ergan proved closer than the map suggested and they reached it at noon on the following day. It seemed a prosperous city, with fine stone houses lining the sea front and jetties running out into the sea to form the harbour. Many masts were visible and even the sterncastles of the bigger vessels, giving Elethrine new hope of a safe passage home. Still cautious, she ordered a halt to confer and study the map.

'Dwarven, or perhaps halfling, I suspect,' Talithea said, peering at the squat, plain architecture of the buildings.

'True,' Elethrine agreed. 'If dwarven we are at least safe from slavery. The map marks these lands as dwarven kingdoms, yet it is not necessarily accurate.'

'Well, we cannot stay here,' Aisla pointed out, 'and perchance those ships include traders from Opina.'

'Opina is now a thousand leagues to the south,' Elethrine replied, 'yet you are right. Our best course is to try and find a shipmaster who will allow us to work passage.'

They approached Port Ergan, filled both with trepidation and hope. As they had suspected, the population proved mainly dwarven, with many halflings and the occasional Hai. Reasoning that a Glass Coast trader might well touch at a port on the coast opposite Mund, the girls identified the crossed swords of Hai on a merchantman's flag and approached it. The shipmaster was seated at a table in the waist of the ship, enjoying a lunch of pickled fish and yellow wine. He showed only mild surprise at their approach, introduced himself as Yarath and offered bread and drink.

'We seek passage to Mund, and will work if necessary,' Elethrine stated, 'although should you be willing to sail to Thieron itself you would find yourself handsomely rewarded.'

'No, no,' Talithea broke in. 'Not direct to Thieron.'

'Sorry,' Elethrine corrected herself, 'the coast near Thieron.'

'Be it the city or be it the coast,' Yarath replied, 'I will not venture there.'

'Why so?' Elethrine demanded.

195

'First,' he answered, 'there are the Merim Islands that close off the Ergan Deep, each of which is home to a nest of pirates more dreadful than the last. Then there are the Grey Deans, where the Spine mountains break into a thousand islets and half-submerged rocks between Kora and Cypraya. A thousand hulks surround every rock and a hundred skulls fill each hulk. I do not wish to add the *Amaratine* – nor myself – to their number. The currents are also ferocious and the tides of such height that a mariner may moor in what he thinks is safety only to wake perched on a pinnacle of rock ten times the height of a man. Finally the area swarms with sea monsters with which I have no desire to become more closely acquainted. If, by some miracle, we win through these hazards, the privateers of the Mundic coast are rumoured to be no less murderous than the Merim pirates, and gigantic to boot.'

'These are our kin,' Talithea pointed out somewhat frostily, 'and would grant you passage at a word from me.'

'More like secure you and then loot and fire the *Amaratine*,' Yarath replied sceptically, 'but the point is moot, I will not attempt the Merim pirates nor yet the Grey Deans. My route is simple. I ply between An-Jhorai and Port Ergan, carrying Hai glass the one way, dwarven iron the other. You will find most ships here do the same, although some venture far to the south to the Sepia and Viridian coasts for goods of Opina and the Vendjome Empire. No, I can offer passage to An-Jhorai at the reasonable rate of fifty dwarven weights of iron apiece, or perhaps an equivalent.'

'Might we not work our passage?' Elethrine suggested.

'You look strong, yet I have no need of spare hands,' Yarath replied, 'nor do I want for cooks or seamstresses, while I find that ship's whores cause more distraction than satisfaction.'

'We thank you, then,' Elethrine said, colouring only slightly at his suggestion that they prostitute themselves – a suggestion that would have filled her with furious outrage only weeks before.

They left the *Amaratine* and began to try other ships, but with no success. Many, both dwarven and Hai, were willing to take them to An-Jhorai at a price, but only one offered them work, and that not only as ship's whores and general dogsbodies but on a voyage to Anjome, which was worse than useless. Finally it became evident that they would need to earn a minimum of one hundred weights of iron in order to obtain the cheapest passage to An-Jhorai. This infuriated them, as the map showed that the Hai city lay somewhat to the southeast and that the wild southern coast of Aegmund was no further off.

From An-Jhorai it would be possible to reach the north coast of Hai, with which Talithea was certain at least some trade took place with Mund. Unfortunately, being of royal blood, it was beneath her to have such crass commercial knowledge. With little choice in the matter, they decided to earn their passage money and returned to Yarath for advice, he having been the most loquacious of the shipmasters and mates they had spoken to.

'Two techniques suggest themselves,' he said when they had explained their needs, 'and from what I know of Mundic customs, both might be unacceptable to highborn ladies such as yourselves.'

'Aisla is but an artisan,' Elethrine answered, 'and Talithea and myself have learnt to place expediency before predilection.'

'Then,' Yarath continued, 'you might obtain employment as tavern wenches, stable girls or perhaps seamstresses, all of which earn perhaps three to four weights of iron per day.'

'We do not care to spend so long in Port Ergan,' Elethrine answered.

'Alternatively,' he went on, 'you might make use of your beauty and youth and sell your favours on the streets of Port Ergan. Mouth service would gain perhaps a weight of iron per time, cunt or anus three and five weights respectively – at present rates. There is no shortage of trade along the docks, nor shortage of competition. A week's work might earn you passage, if you ate sparingly and slept under the moons.'

'Better,' Elethrine replied, no more horrified at the prospect of sex with sailors and longshoremen than at that of menial work, 'but still a long time. Is there no quicker way to earn?'

'Are you beaten regularly?' Yarath queried. 'I understand that the Mundics make something of an art of flagellation.'

'I am caned when I am naughty,' Elethrine replied guardedly, 'and have occasionally suffered more humiliating punishments.'

'In Port Ergan it is considered perverse and forbidden by decree,' Yarath replied. 'We Hai enjoy whipping girls before coition and those who have settled here might pay well for a taste of home pleasures.'

'A good idea,' Elethrine answered, 'although if I am to be caned I prefer it to be by someone of high degree, perhaps a warrior. Who should we contact?'

'I forgo such pleasures when in Port Ergan,' Yarath stated. 'The penalties are harsh and the prices high, while in An-Jhorai it is easy to entice a fine plump wench to the pleasures of the whip and at no cost, save perhaps the price of a flagon of wine. You are in luck though. Look yonder – the lank-haired villain with the face of a hungry polecat. That is Kenion the Pimp, who will certainly help you, though at a price.'

'What is a pimp?' Elethrine asked.

'A sort of agent for girls of easy virtue and men who would pay to advantage themselves of such girls,' Yarath answered.

'Oh,' Elethrine answered, dubiously. 'Well, in any case, we thank you once more, and should you wish service in reward, Aisla here will oblige while Talithea and I speak with this pimp.'

Aisla giggled at the prospect of sex with the burly Yarath and went below while Elethrine and Talithea hurried to overtake Kenion, who was sauntering slowly away along the quayside. He showed some surprise at their request and was doubtful at first, but after a brief flash of Elethrine's still bruised buttocks in an alley, he decided that they were genuine. Once satisfied, he offered three alternatives. The first was an innkeeper of Hai origin whom Kenion reckoned might be prepared to go as high as thirty weights to cane and fuck all three girls, more if he could bugger them. The second was more tempting still, an offer from the rich widow of a long-dead Hai glass merchant who was prepared to pay high to be able to beat girls as she herself had been punished in her youth. Kenion estimated that sixty weights of iron might not be too much to hope for. Finally there was the best-priced offer, which was both bizarre and terrifying. A halfling nymph merchant by the name of Bormontal apparently had a captive troll which he used to keep the lusts of his stock satisfied. Having sold his nymphs in An-Jhorai, he was returning to Ythan, but the troll – deprived of its nightly glut of tight, willing vagina – was becoming irritable. He had told Kenion that he was willing to pay as much as one hundred and fifty weights to any human girl who would satisfy the troll, the bargain also involving a prior whipping to bring her on heat, with himself and his staff as an audience.

'We must consult,' Elethrine answered, when the pimp had finished explaining the alternatives.

The thought of indulging in such practices had made her tuppenny moist and left her limbs trembling, yet telling herself that it was for a good cause only partially allayed her shame at the sheer force of her own lust. Indulging in drunken orgies with Aisla and Talithea was one thing, but putting on a deliberate erotic display for an innkeeper or merchant's wife was quite another, let alone having sex with a great, shambling brute of a troll.

Not, she reminded herself, that it would be her who accepted the troll's member in her tuppenny. That would go to Talithea or Aisla, and indeed, as Talithea had already agreed to indulge in some exquisite erotic degradation, this might be a perfect opportunity. She suggested as much as they walked back to the *Amaratine*, the Princess returning a muted sob that Elethrine took as assent.

On the ship they found Aisla in Yarath's cabin with her grass skirt turned up over her bottom and a dozen neatly spaced cane lines decorating her pale skin. She was sighing and clearly ready for entry, so Elethrine and Talithea obliged by sucking Yarath's cock to full erection before he mounted the maid's freshly beaten bottom and inserted it into her. Aisla pulled her breasts free of her reed bra as she was humped and came with a finger on her clitty before the shipmaster had finished deep inside her.

'A cabin is reserved for you,' Yarath called, as they descended the gangplank of the *Amaratine*, 'and at but thirty weights the head.'

Highly excited, and as ready as they ever would be, the three girls walked back to the alley in which Kenion the Pimp waited. Moving furtively from alley to alley, he conducted them to a house well up the hill from the docks. After a whispered conversation with a servant they were admitted to a large upper chamber, where a heavily built halfling reclined on well-stuffed cushions of rich blue silk.

'Kenion?' the man – evidently Bormontal himself – queried.

'May I introduce Talithea of Mund,' Kenion

200

answered with a smirk, 'also her friends Elethrine and Aisla. Talithea has agreed to the proposition that we discussed three days ago.'

'You, a highborn lady of Mund, wish to satisfy the lust of a troll?' Bormontal asked Talithea in disbelief.

'Look on it as a debt of honour,' Talithea replied.

'I will certainly look on it with pleasure,' Bormontal answered, casting a lust-filled glance at the Princess, whose curves were barely concealed beneath her flimsy grass outfit and ruined pantalettes.

'For two hundred weights of iron,' Kenion put in quickly.

'Two hundred?' Bormontal answered without surprise. 'So be it, if her friends are willing to give mouth service while we watch the entertainment.'

Elethrine nodded, already wondering if halfling cock tasted as good as dwarven.

'Excellent,' Bormontal went on, 'very well, two hundred it is.'

He signalled to a servant who walked briskly to the end of the room and pulled aside a drape. Within was an iron cage and in it sat the troll, a bulky, hulking man-thing shaped like a giant goblin save for his skin being stone-grey in place of green and his genitals, fortunately, being in more reasonable proportion to his body. Stark bald, his head resembled nothing so much as a lump of granite, and Elethrine could see why the legend of trolls being made of rock had arisen. In height he was perhaps two heads above Aisla, while the breadth of his chest and his great, solid muscles spoke of enormous power.

'Meet Simooth,' Bormontal announced with pride, 'named after the great dwarven ore-crushing machine. Simooth, come, we have a pretty lady for you.'

The troll stood slowly, his bright, piggy eyes focusing on the girls with unmistakable lust. Elethrine swallowed, awed by the sheer power of the troll. Trolls were rare in

Mund and kept to the high peaks of the Spine, but the proudest triumph of Aisla's giant father, Uroth, was to have wrestled with a troll – and lived.

'Do not be scared,' Bormontal said blithely. 'He is tame and equates girls with erotic pleasure far too strongly to wish to harm you. Yet are you sure? I want a display of wanton passion, not the timid acceptance of a girl who seeks only money.'

'I am sure,' Talithea said thickly, 'but perhaps it would serve well to help me first.'

'In what way?' Bormontal queried.

'By bringing her to heat with a beating,' Elethrine put in.

'A fine idea, and one that is already part of the bargain,' Bormontal agreed, 'although such pleasures are not taken lightly here. Hefty fines attach to any man indulging himself, while girls who allow it for their pleasure are chained beneath the public latrine for a week. Still, we are among friends . . .'

He trailed off and Elethrine realised that he expected them to start immediately. Nodding to the merchant, the pimp, the three servants and finally the troll, she took Talithea by the ear, pulled her into the middle of the room and sat down on a large chest. Using the brisk, no-nonsense manner that she knew would humiliate Talithea most deeply, she pulled the Princess down across her knee, tore the grass skirt away and pulled the pantalettes down and off.

Bormontal licked his lips at the sight of Talithea's magnificent bottom and, reclining back on the cushions, signalled to Aisla. As Elethrine pulled Talithea's bra off to let the Princess's full breasts swing nude beneath her chest, Aisla knelt to accept the merchant's penis in her mouth. Elethrine felt the Princess shiver with the deep shame of full nudity and the knowledge that she was to be spanked by hand. As Aisla started to suck, Elethrine began to spank.

Talithea was soon groaning as her bottom began to colour, sticking it up to ensure that her humiliation be deepened by the full display of her pouted tuppenny. Seeing Talithea's eagerness, Elethrine paused to pull open the Princess's plump bottom cheeks and show the audience her tight anal aperture. Talithea moaned again and then gave a little choking sob as Elethrine went back to the task of spanking her.

With the Princess's bottom a warm ball of glowing flesh and Bormontal's cock a hard shaft in Aisla's mouth, Elethrine pushed her victim to the floor and stood up. Talithea stayed down, sobbing and red bottomed with her hips raised so that her wet tuppenny was on display to everyone. In the cage, Simooth was clearly aroused, pressing against the bars with a colossal grey erection thrust through into the room.

'Crawl and suck it,' Elethrine ordered, pointing to the monstrous cock.

Talithea crawled quickly to the troll's cage, hesitated only an instant, took hold of the troll's erection and popped it into her mouth. Simooth's hand came through the bars, enfolding Talithea's head and starting to fuck her mouth as she sucked his penis. Elethrine turned to find all three servants and the pimp with their cocks out and ready for her caresses. Walking to the pile of cushions, she made herself comfortable. Eager hands pulled her bra up as she took a servant's cock in each hand and began to masturbate them while they watched Talithea and the troll. A gentle pressure on her head made her turn, finding the pimp's cock pointing directly at her mouth. She took it in and began to suck, meanwhile keeping one eye on Talithea's blazing bottom and straining mouth.

'Put her in,' Bormontal ordered.

The third servant crossed the room, and, using an odd mixture of simple words and hand signals, indicated to Simooth that he was going to get more than just the use of Talithea's mouth. The troll pulled back, his lumpish face breaking into a huge grin. His penis was shiny with the Princess's saliva and so erect that the great veins along the shaft could be seen to throb. The servant operated the door mechanism and Talithea crawled inside, to be immediately grabbed by Simooth.

Elethrine watched around her mouthful of Kenion's cock, as her friend was mounted. Talithea was on her knees, bum high, tits swinging and thighs spread. Simooth loomed over her, his penis resting between her freshly-spanked buttocks as he held her by the hair. He took hold of his cock and pushed it between Talithea's bum cheeks, grunting as he sought entry. For an instant Elethrine thought he was going to try and bugger her, but then his penis disappeared into her body and the Princess's mouth opened in an 'O' of absolute bliss. As always when she watched another girl entered, Elethrine wondered how her own tuppenny would feel stretched around an intruding member. When back in Korismund with her maidenhead intact, she decided she would do her best to tempt an honourable ravishment. Until then, she had to content herself with sucking and stroking men, or perhaps allowing the penetration of her bottom ring.

Simooth was grunting loudly as he fucked Talithea. Nude, with his callused grey hand twisted in her pale hair, her plump pink breasts swinging in time to his thrusts and her reddened buttocks raised to meet him, she looked the perfect picture of female submission. A girl ravished by a troll, Elethrine thought, and began to suck harder on the pimp's cock at the idea. The halfling's cock had a gently musky taste, not strong enough to make her lose control, but enough to heighten her erotic pleasure.

The third servant had entered Aisla where she lay curled up on her side and busy with Bormontal's erection. The merchant was fondling one heavy breast, which quivered with each of the servant's thrusts into the maid's vagina. Elethrine's jealousy increased as she watched both her friends fucked and her need to be penetrated herself was rising alarmingly. Determined to come before she gave in and begged for entry, she slid a hand between her thighs. Pulling up her grass skirt she found the opening to her drawers and tugged them open. Inside her tuppenny was wet and ready, the lips swollen and parted, her clitty a hard bud in between.

Simooth had come in Talithea and was making her lick his cock clean while come dribbled from her gaping vagina. She had her bottom to the room, both holes showing clearly as she used her tongue on the troll's still hard penis. She had started to masturbate and her fingers could be seen working in the wet pink centre of her white, furred tuppenny. Suddenly the troll came again, unexpectedly and full in her face. Talithea gathered a handful of sperm, began to rub it over her stiff nipples and then went back to sucking and masturbating. The Princess was clearly close to orgasm, and as Elethrine's mouth filled with the pimp's sperm, both girls started to come.

As Kenion pulled back from Elethrine's mouth one of the servants replaced him, the other putting his hand on top of hers and helping her frig as she jerked at his cock. Across the room, Talithea was obviously in the middle of orgasm, while the troll had pushed thick grey fingers into her vagina and anus. Elethrine's own climax exploded in her head as another load of sperm erupted into her mouth. She swallowed, coming in an ecstasy of touch and visual stimulation as the cock in her hand splashed hot come over her bare breasts and her eyes locked on the sight of the troll's fingers in Talithea's holes.

Then it was over and she was lying back with come dribbling down her chin and splashed across her breasts. She turned, to see the servant who had entered Aisla pull out and spray come over the maid's buttocks and thighs. Bormontal groaned and sperm burst from Aisla's lips as he too came, deep in her mouth.

In the cage the troll was stroking Talithea's hair as she lay with her head in its lap, licking the last traces of come from its heavy balls. Bormontal, recovering his breath, ordered the Princess released. Talithea exited the cage with an abashed grin, leaving Simooth sitting back with a dopey, satisfied smile on his block-shaped face.

Bormontal ordered water and towels, the servants changing from fellow orgy participants back to their normal roles on the instant. Clean, and once again dressed, the three girls lay back on fresh cushions while Bormontal counted out the iron to Kenion and a servant fetched wine.

'For us men, fine red from the Lais Elain valley in Ythan, my homeland,' Bormontal said to Kenion as the servant returned with two flasks and five matching glasses. 'Served in matchless Hai glass, fashioned in Zihai itself. For the girls the same vessels but a different wine – sweet white Croisaine from the hills to the east of Jihai, rich yet pungent. I will vouch that you have never tasted the like.'

'To the contrary,' the once-more-serene Princess answered, as she took a glass, 'at Thieron it is occasionally served with peaches in jelly and other rich desserts.'

'Then perhaps you would prefer something different?' Bormontal asked.

Something about the speed of his response alerted Elethrine, even as Talithea was putting the glass beneath her dainty nose.

'This is not Croisaine,' the Princess stated, 'or if it is then there is something severely wrong with it.'

'Then to Barbrazel with it,' Bormontal said. 'Men, take them.'

Not wasting time with pointless protest, Elethrine

206

kicked out at the nearest servant, catching his tray and sending its precious burden crashing to the floor. Bormontal cursed and grabbed at her wrist, only to pull back as Aisla's arm locked around his podgy neck. The troll roared as a servant grappled Talithea and began to shake the bars of the cage. A single servant faced Elethrine, the other attempting to loosen Aisla's grip on his master's neck.

The man with Talithea grunted in pain as her elbow found his crotch. Elethrine jumped back to seize a heavy candelabrum as the slam of the door signalled the hasty departure of Kenion. Elethrine cursed, realising that the pimp still had the two hundred weights of iron. The window was beside her and for an instant she had the option of screaming for the watch. The thought of their well-whipped bottoms being discovered and the subsequent chaining beneath the latrine presented itself in forceful counter argument and instead she came forward, swinging the candelabrum. The servant backed away cautiously, only to trip over Aisla's leg and sprawl backwards onto the floor.

Elethrine struck out for the man who was trying to free Bormontal from Aisla's grip, catching him hard on the temple. He slumped on to the cushions, allowing Elethrine to turn and serve Talithea's antagonist the same way. The remaining servant backed away, wary of Elethrine's weapon. Bormontal's face was turning blue, and Aisla had the light of murder in her eyes.

'Leave him!' Elethrine ordered. 'Let us flee!'

Aisla obeyed on the instant, dropping the fat merchant and jumping to her feet. Amid a chorus of Simooth's roars, Bormontal's hoarse gasps and the servants' groans, they sped for the door and burst into the passage, only to find themselves faced by three guards with clubs held at the ready. Elethrine hurled herself forward, taking the middle guard down the stairs. She rolled, the man's heavy body throwing her off balance as she scrabbled for a hold. For an instant she was in free fall, then her head struck the floor and everything seemed to explode in a shower of sparks.

10

Nymph

Elethrine awoke with a sore head to find herself, Talithea and Aisla caged on the foredeck of a barge. They were near naked – Aisla alone retaining both top and skirt – although coarse-weaved rugs allowed some modesty, and each bore an anklet of iron securely locked and engraved with a cursive symbol that she knew related to Bormontal. A hurried inspection allowed Elethrine to discover that they still had the map, concealed with care in the complex folds of her drawers. A sweet-sour taste in her mouth suggested that she had been fed drugged wine after becoming unconscious.

The merchant himself approached when all three of them had revived. Offering water, he explained that they were captive and that they were on the river Lais-Elain. Despite their cold, angry response he seemed inclined to further explanation, only to be called away to answer some dispute between his guards and the crew. For the remainder of the day he failed to make an appearance, adding a feeling of unimportance to Elethrine's fury and shame.

On the second day on the Lais-Elain the barge reached the Elven city of Lai. Despite her misery Elethrine could not help but stare. Towers of some pale, near-white stone rose from within a high wall. Unlike the thick, round greystone towers of Mund, these were slender structures with an apparent fragility that appeared to belie their great height. Narrow spans connected them, one to another, creating a spider's web of glittering white. As they drew nearer she made out the elves themselves, tiny white-haired beings as fragile as their architecture. They strolled across the bridges and walked the top of the wall, apparently oblivious to the gulfs of air beneath them. Wary of their evil reputation, she stayed still, huddled into her blanket with everything but her face covered. The elves took no notice, even as the barges glided beneath the walls of Lai, held carefully in midstream by the boatswain.

Glancing up as they drifted past, Elethrine could make out the faces of the elves, their haughty visages like nightmares carved in bone, beautiful yet utterly cold. Both males and females were present, of similar size but the females even more slender and graceful than their male counterparts. Tiny, high breasts and slim waists marked the females, while both sexes had skin the colour of charta and hair of pure white. As they passed, one female looked directly at Elethrine with a gaze showing no more interest than a human might have bestowed on a rock.

The bargees stayed absolutely quiet, minding their tasks and ignoring the elves. Bormontal, alone, dared to watch the city, his expression one of concern as his eyes took in the view. Elethrine noticed that he seemed to be paying particular attention to various apertures in the otherwise featureless wall. From each one a long tube of some silvery-grey metal protruded, its shape alarmingly similar to the bombards of Vendjome and the *Black Joke*, only somehow conveying the potential for far greater destructive power. Only when the weird city had faded astern into the murk did Bormontal speak, blowing out his great cheeks in an expression of profound relief.

'An evil race,' he sighed as he turned to the

boatswain. 'Had I the power I would see them dead – every one.'

The boatswain gave a taciturn nod, adding his own opinion with an insulting gesture towards the distant towers.

'Still,' Bormontal continued, suddenly cheerful again, 'think of their fury if they knew what I plan, eh?'

'Your death would last ten thousand days,' the boatswain replied, glumly.

'Ha!' Bormontal laughed. 'How are they to find out when they never leave their high towers?'

The boatswain merely grunted.

'What do you plan?' Elethrine asked, aware that whatever scheme the fat merchant was plotting certainly involved herself and her friends.

'To become rich, immensely rich,' Bormontal answered, beaming at his captives.

'How so?' Talithea demanded.

'Through the use of your exquisite hair,' Bormontal replied.

'My hair?' Talithea asked, tugging worriedly at a strand of her ghost-pale locks.

'Well, principally yours,' Bormontal answered. 'I had best explain, as then you will the better understand what you must do and why.'

'I will never serve you,' Talithea answered.

'Oh, but you will, my precious,' Bormontal answered, 'and with pleasure. The scheme is this. As you know, I am a merchant and my principal trade is in nymphs. Together with a group of my fellow merchants, I have for years been pursuing a quest – the breeding of pale-skinned nymphs with yellow or red hair. Several times we have discussed a raid into Mund or Aegmund to secure tow-haired maidens to be bred into the stock, but have always been discouraged by the size and ferocity of the native barbarians, which is to say, your kin.'

211

He paused, chuckling as all three of the girls' faces set in anger.

'Then,' he continued, 'you three arrive at Port Ergan as if sent by the Gods. Not only do I get magnificent specimens of gold- and copper-haired maidens but also one whose hair is so white that she might be mistaken for an elf – were she not twice the height, pink skinned and rather too fully endowed. After years of trying, my colleagues and I have succeeded in breeding nymph stock with hair of a pale tawny and skin not wholly unlike yours. With your plasms added to the stock, I hope that in ten or at most twenty years, I will be able to offer for sale nymphs that resemble elves in all outward appearances. Can you imagine what the grandees of Vendjome, Oretes and Zihai would pay for such a creature?'

'A great deal, I have no doubt,' Elethrine replied haughtily, 'but you must exclude us from your sordid programme. Be assured that we will never submit ourselves to your bull-nymphs and that our strength is easily sufficient to resist them.'

'You had best abandon your depraved plan,' Talithea put in.

'Curious,' Bormontal remarked, 'that a girl who will encourage a troll to enter her objects to coition with a male nymph.'

'You do not understand,' Talithea replied. 'That was of my own choice, and served our purpose. You have taken us against our will and seek to enslave us. Yet I shall never surrender myself to your base intentions.'

Bormontal laughed and dipped a hand into his pouch to draw out a glass phial set in a web of ironwork.

'Were I to break this under your nose,' he said with great delight, 'you would be tearing at one another's clothes in your eagerness to enjoy one another's sex. As you did so you would be begging me to use you, and not just me, but every man available on the barge, from

212

Grathail the boatswain to Hombles, the imbecile who cleans the bilges and latrine chute – not to mention Simooth. It is goblin musk, distilled ten-fold.'

Elethrine gasped in horror, her reaction drawing a long peel of laughter from Bormontal.

'Be cheerful,' the fat merchant called as he turned away. 'As you are earmarked for the breeding programme you will be spared the attentions of Hombles, at least as long as you are good.'

The girls were left staring aghast as Bormontal retired below decks.

For days the barge drifted on the oil-smooth waters of the Lais-Elain. Unable to escape their cage, the three girls maintained a haughty detachment, refusing to rise to the taunts of the crew. Around them the landscape became gradually more arid, until the river formed an aisle of green in what was otherwise near desert.

At last they reached the confluence of the Lais-Elain with a yet larger river. On the isthmus of land between the two stood a city, really no more than a huddle of red mud-brick hovels clustered around a fortress of the same sun-baked clay. Consulting the map when no attention was on them, the girls decided that the larger river could only be the Ephraxis and the city Dry Ulan, most southerly of the cities of Ythan. With a sinking feeling Elethrine realised that this placed them no more than four hundred leagues to the north of Gora-Jome.

The barge turned north up the Ephraxis and after another half day's sailing docked at a dry gully filled with olives and feather-tree. Their cage was carried from the barge and through a screen of trees. Beyond stood a fine mansion, constructed of the same red mud-bricks as Dry Ulan, but heavily decorated and shaded beneath tall feather trees. Elethrine felt a shiver in her belly as she realised that the frieze depicted naked nymphs, some dancing, some striking lewd poses, but most engaged in frenzied copulation and other, more contrived, sexual acts.

'My domain – Gorangrove,' Bormontal declared proudly as he strolled over to their cage. 'Fine, is it not? Now, here you have two choices. First, you may remain caged and be treated in the same fashion as the rest of my stock. That is to say, not cruelly, but neither with any greater comfort than a nymph might expect. Secondly, should you wish, you may behave as my guests, the sole stipulation being that you behave with decorum and do not attempt escape. Before you make your choice I should point out that here we are barely north of the Eigora Khum. The surrounding lands are parched and hard to cross, while the people of Ythan will recognise you as my property by your anklets and simply return you here – after they have amused themselves with you, that is.'

Elethrine glanced at Talithea, receiving a resigned shrug in return. Clearly remaining caged was the poorer option, and, she reasoned, Bormontal had not actually demanded their oaths as highborn Mundics not to escape.

'We will behave,' she replied, sullenly.

'A wise choice,' Bormontal replied.

The girls were released from the cage and taken into the mansion. Within a side room they were helped to bathe by maids. These were small, black-haired women, by no means uncomely but meek and with none of the spirit that marked Mundic women. When washed, the girls were given short kirtles in place of their ragged clothing. These were in cloth of a mustard yellow and consisted of a simple length of material with a hole for the head. Strips of black ribbon allowed the garments to be fastened at waist height, pulling the material firmly against breasts that might otherwise have been at risk of exposure but causing the hems to rise and provide glimpses of the lower curves of bare bottoms. Given that her once beautiful drawers were now little more than a soiled rag that risked both buttocks and tuppenny showing, Elethrine decided to abandon modesty in favour of neatness. The map was also a concern, better concealed beneath the kirtle than in the ruins of her drawers. The others followed her example, leaving their bottoms peeping out from beneath the hems of their kirtles. They shared blushes and wry smiles and then walked into the hall.

Bormontal sat at the head of a great table of highly polished wood. Others ranked down the sides; short, burly men and petite women who Elethrine assumed to be the more senior of Bormontal's staff. To the merchant's right – in what was presumably the place of honour – sat a tall, saturnine man in a black robe. On the girls' entrance he turned to them, his dark eyes glittering with what Elethrine hoped was only carnal lust. Elethrine returned a polite nod and made for one of the empty places, allowing Talithea the one closest to the head.

She ate with absolute formality, replying to those questions directed to her with as much brevity as politeness allowed. Determined to make it quite clear that she considered their behaviour unacceptable, she initiated no conversations of her own and quelled Aisla with a glance when the maid responded too warmly to the attentions of one of the more handsome guards. Talithea, if anything, remained more frosty still, and Elethrine thought to recognise the same unnatural calm that the Princess had shown during the slave auction.

Bormontal accepted their cold behaviour with his normal indifference and spent the meal quaffing a strong red wine, gorging himself on spiced goat meat and talking merrily with his fellows. His remarks included his intentions for the girls, on which he expanded without the slightest consideration for their modesty or opinion.

When the spread of meats and savouries had been finished and a new one of sweets and fruit was being laid out, a servant appeared to announce the arrival of a late guest. This proved to be Ayapan, the nymph merchant whom the girls had last seen in Vendjome. He greeted Bormontal with the hearty openness of old friends, then caught sight of the girls and stopped, his mouth breaking into a wide grin.

'So, we meet again!' he boomed. 'I see my old friend Bormontal has succeeded where I failed.'

Elethrine, Talithea and Aisla greeted him with the formal nods appropriate for an old adversary.

'You know them?' Bormontal asked, his voice showing a trace of disappointment.

'So I do,' Ayapan replied. 'We first met at Fujome, where I fear I was sufficiently slow-witted not to attempt to take them into my custody. A little later I saw them at the Pelucidome in Vendjome, where the copper-haired glory sold for over one thousand imperials!'

'One thousand imperials!' Bormontal echoed.

'So it was,' Ayapan confirmed, 'and the others for only a little less. When I heard that you had captured three fine, northland barbars I hoped it might be them, and indeed it is. Beware the pale-haired one – she is what the northlanders call berserk and tends to leave tooth and claw marks on any who oppose her.'

'The same was true when I took them in Port Ergan,' Bormontal replied and then held up the vial of goblin musk. 'Still, she will be placid enough tonight, although placid is perhaps the wrong word; besides, I have pointed out to them that escape is an impossibility. After all, we are not in Vendjome with its vast population and myriad roads.'

'True,' Ayapan conceded, 'yet take care, the women of their race are no less ferocious than the males. Talking of Vendjome, how, girls, did you escape the Panjandrum's seraglio? After all, it is not as if you could blend with the crowds.'

216

'The Princess Talithea struck down two of their nobles,' Elethrine replied, unable to keep the pride from her voice. 'We then escaped from a high window at dusk and left the city concealed in jars of honey.'

'You see, Bormontal,' Ayapan stated, 'no girl of Ythan would have attempted such a feat, nor yet of Vendjome.'

'Perhaps,' Bormontal admitted, 'yet do not worry, we have many guards and also the revered D'jannith.'

Ayapan nodded to the man in black, who returned a thin, cruel smile. Evidently this was D'jannith, who had contributed little to the conversation during the meal but was evidently a warlock or sorcerer of some kind. Ayapan took a seat and began to help himself to a dish of pastries soaked in honey. Elethrine accepted a beaker of sweet orange wine, thinking to soothe herself and calm her fluttering nerves.

Finally the meal was over, and Elethrine felt her pulse rising. Bormontal had made it very clear what was going to happen. They would be taken out to the nymph pens and given a treatment by D'jannith, the details of which she was unsure of. The result would be to ensure that the three of them bore male children after they had been dosed with distilled goblin musk and mated with Bormontal's prize bull-nymph.

Rare essences were served when the last plate had been cleared, the company sipping and sniffing at their tiny glasses for what seem to Elethrine an interminable period. Finally the last drop had been drained and Bormontal rose to his feet.

'To work then,' he declared. 'There is light enough, the scent of thyme will be strong in the air and the evening, truly, is the best time for erotic encounters.'

Elethrine said nothing, but rose to her feet, determined to maintain the attitude of aloof pride appropriate to her station. The situation appeared hopeless, with barren and hostile lands on every side

217

and no apparent means of escape. After her experience with the dwarves she knew that once she had scented goblin musk she would have no control over her body and would allow the bull-nymph to mate her with every bit as much wanton lust as she had shown in the arms of her friends.

Outside, they walked to the pens, the two merchants, the warlock and two burly men-at-arms with their crossbows cocked and ready. Bormontal stopped by one of the largest cages and rattled the bars with an ornate cane he had collected at the door. Immediately the bull-nymph emerged from his hut, a man-thing no more than half Elethrine's height yet beautiful, exquisitely formed and undoubtedly masculine. A cock that would have done credit to a goblin hung between his legs, twitching in response to the girls.

'Golden Glory,' Bormontal announced with immense pride.

Elethrine swallowed, aware of an involuntary lust swelling within her. There was a scent to the bull-nymph, a musk not unlike that of dwarves but sharper, spicier and too weak to take much resistance. While she knew that, in Apraya, nymphs were considered erotic playthings for those who could afford them, in Mund the situation was very different. Nymphs were wild – fey, solitary man-things living in the depths of the great forests and high among mountains. For a girl to submit herself to a bull-nymph – which were small and easily resisted – was a disgrace worse even than allowing herself to be caught by goblins. After all, if a girl was surrounded by goblins she had little choice in the matter of her surrender, but bull-nymphs were solitary, and beautiful. The sight and scent of Golden Glory filled her with longing, yet it was a longing that rebelled against every dictum of her upbringing.

Beside her Talithea was quiet and appeared absolutely calm. Knowing the strength of both the Princess's lust and her ferocity, Elethrine wondered which would win. Talithea had surrendered her precious maidenhead to Kaulak with indecent eagerness, and indulged herself with the corsairs like a nymph in rut. Yet when her pride had been threatened she had taken a very different course.

As Bormontal drew the iron-bound vial from his robes, Elethrine realised that there was going to be no choice. With a head full of ten-fold distilled goblin musk, Talithea was likely to ravish Golden Glory rather than the other way around.

'First, the preparation,' Bormontal announced. 'Elethrine, Aisla, kindly step into the cage to your side. I wish no unseemly disturbances.'

Two crossbows moved to cover Elethrine and her maid and they obeyed with as much dignity as possible. The cage indicated contained several female nymphs, pretty creatures with skins the colour of pale honey, which chittered excitedly as the girls came into their cage. A guard snapped the catch into place and both moved to cover Talithea, with their backs to the cage but clear of Elethrine's reach.

'D'jannith, if you would be so good,' Bormontal continued.

Talithea tilted her chin up in arrogant pride as the warlock bent to the small black case he had been carrying. From it he produced a vial of murky, orange liquid and a curious device consisting of a glass tube with a long needle at one end and what appeared to be a plunger at the other. With great care he drew the fluid into the tube, then held it up to the pale evening sky and depressed the plunger, discharging air and a single drop of fluid from the needle's tip. Talithea stood immobile as D'jannith approached her, went to her rear and lifted the hem of her kirtle. Elethrine felt a tingle of shock and sensuality at the casual exposure of the Princess's bottom but Talithea remained immobile. Even as the warlock stabbed the needle suddenly into one full buttock she gave no more than an involuntary twitch of muscle. The warlock depressed the plunger, forcing whatever the tube held into Talithea's blood.

'We must wait a while for the emulsion to circulate,' D'jannith remarked, 'after which it may be guaranteed that the next child she produces will be male.'

'Splendid,' Bormontal answered. 'We proceed.'

All eyes were on Talithea, Elethrine's included. Evidently the warlock had implanted Talithea with some sort of potion to ensure the sex of her firstborn. The practice was not unknown in Mund, although few witches would do it and even then could not be relied upon to follow instructions. Whether they used needles to insert the fluid, she doubted. As she watched she felt a soft touch on the bare skin of her thigh. Looking down in sudden shock, she found that the female nymphs in the cage had crowded close. The boldest had reached out to stroke her thigh and was looking up with huge, beautiful eyes full of curiosity and longing. Elethrine patted the nymph's hand gently away, not wishing to hurt the fragile creature but also not wishing to be fondled and explored. The nymph moved back quickly, then turned to investigate the contents of her food trough as if embarrassed by the rejection. Elethrine immediately felt sorry and then noticed the trough.

'Very well, we are ready,' D'jannith announced.

Talithea stepped into Golden Glory's cage with the same calm disdain she had shown throughout. The bull-nymph immediately became excited, seizing its cock and beginning to jerk it frantically to erection. Bormontal popped the stopper on the vial of musk and shook a little into the cage. Elethrine and Aisla pushed close to the bars of their own cage, unable to resist watching. As she pressed up to the bars, Elethrine noticed the lock, a simple twist mechanism ample to restrain nymphs but far from sufficient for humans. Yet it was too late, had any resistance been practical in the first place.

Talithea had lowered herself into a squat and raised her kirtle, exposing her tuppenny to the now stiff penis of the bull-nymph. Elethrine swallowed hard, wondering if she herself would manage to submit with such dignity or whether she would grovel on her knees and present Golden Glory with her upturned bottom. The bull-nymph approached, flourishing his cock in delight at the Princess's proffered hole. Talithea took the cock in her hand and guided it towards her vagina. Briefly she rubbed the tip against her tuppenny to stimulate her clitoris. Every eye was on her as she guided the immense cock lower to find her vagina.

At that moment Elethrine realised that Talithea was holding her breath. With a sudden jerk the Princess swung the bull-nymph around by his cock, hurling it across the cage. Bormontal cried out in rage, stepping forward to intervene, the guards following. Seizing her chance, Elethrine twisted the lock of the cage. Bormontal was pulling furiously at the door held shut by a now purple-faced Talithea as Elethrine grabbed the long metal feeding trough from the ground. Kicking the door open, she swung the trough at the head of the nearest guard, catching him hard on the temple. His crossbow dropped from his hands and an instant later it was in Elethrine's.

It was Ayapan who first realised the danger and called out a warning. Elethrine was already bringing the crossbow up, and as she did so her father's voice came clear into her mind with a lesson instilled since childhood – when in a mêlée where magic might be used, always kill the warlock first; and shoot for the head, not the heart.

Even as the thought finished she released the catch. An iron bolt seemed to spring from D'jannith's forehead and he fell lifeless to the ground. The other guard was coming round, but the squat body of Ayapan blocked his aim. Elethrine threw herself to the side even as Aisla cannoned into the merchant to send him crashing back on to the guard. There was the twang of a crossbow string and a yell of pain. Ayapan rolled to the side, the misspent bolt embedded in one plump arm. Aisla scrambled back, away from the clutching fingers of the guard, as Talithea hurled herself out of the cage.

To a chorus of yells and the excited chittering of the nymphs, Elethrine jumped up, planted a vicious kick into Bormontal's midriff and sprang away. Aisla was squared off against the guard, her teeth bared in a snarl, he reluctant to come against her height and wild demeanour. Talithea grabbed up the needle and tube device and plunged it into Bormontal's fat backside as he staggered away from Elethrine's kick, drawing a yell of pain and fury. Three lay on the ground: Ayapan groaning, one guard unconscious, and D'jannith dead.

'Run! To the dock!' Elethrine screamed as she saw that Talithea intended to continue her assault on Bormontal.

Aisla obeyed immediately, leaping away from her adversary and speeding for the fringe of trees that hid the river. Talithea took no notice, but as Elethrine grabbed her arm and wrenched, she followed, throwing curses back at Bormontal as they went. The guard alone followed, Bormontal sinking to the ground with a loud groan. Long legged and unencumbered by clothing, the three girls sped across the lawn.

As they neared the wood Elethrine risked a backward glance to find, to her horror, the vast bulk of Simooth rushing headlong towards them. The guard was ahead of the troll and bringing up his crossbow. At that instant Talithea tripped and sprawled headlong on the ground. The guard altered his aim, pointing the wicked quarrel at the helpless Princess. Elethrine screamed and leapt to shield her friend, only to see Simooth sweep the guard aside with a single blow of his massive arm. Talithea scrambled to her feet, taking Elethrine's hand and once more dashing for the trees.

Gloom enveloped them as they entered the narrow wood, then they came once more into the evening light, with the sun throwing a red trail across the mighty Ephraxis. The dock stood to one side, several boats secured to its pillars. One alone had its sweeps in place, a long black vessel with a sharp prow and a blunt stern.

Elethrine leapt aboard without breaking pace, thrusting the oars into the water as Aisla and Talithea struggled with the painter. It came loose quickly and they pulled away. Simooth's roars sounded from beyond the trees, mingled with screams and angry cries, and as they pulled clear another guard burst from the trees. Elethrine pulled on the ludicrously short oars with all her strength, sending the slender boat cutting through the water. The guard levelled his weapon, fired, and the bolt thudded home into the side of the boat, a spare hand's breadth from Aisla fingers. Again he fired, but the bolt flew wide, his aim perhaps disturbed by the light of the setting sun. Once more he loaded, but then seemed to think better of the action and instead ran back into the trees.

Elethrine pulled for the centre of the placid Ephraxis, leaving Gorangrove rapidly astern. Even when the trees were no more than a jagged line coloured red by the setting sun, they could still hear the infuriated roars of the troll. Finally the domain was hidden from view behind a long scrub-covered island and Elethrine at last allowed herself to pause for breath.

'They will follow along the bank on horses,' Aisla said glumly, 'and perhaps also in sailing vessels.'

'It will be dark in moments,' Elethrine replied. 'Besides, we have but little option save to keep rowing and pray to our ancestors for a turn of fate.'

'When we tell our saga,' Talithea joked, attempting to

223

sound optimistic, 'Simooth had better become a great warrior who helped us from motives of pure honour.'

'Rather than a giant troll who helped us for the memory of a portion of willing tuppenny,' Elethrine answered, with a weak grin.

Dusk quickly faded to night, forcing them to ground the boat on one of the numerous low islands that broke the great Ephraxis into dozens of interlocking channels. After rowing against the current for so long, Elethrine was exhausted and quickly fell asleep, allowing Aisla to take the first watch.

She awoke to the first pale illumination of dawn and Aisla's excited announcement that they had discovered the boat's true method of propulsion. The truncated oars were clearly only for manoeuvring, while a curious device of black metal at the stern caused a jet of water to gush out beneath the surface. A lever allowed the strength and direction of the jet to be controlled, while a twist device could start it and shut it off. It was clearly a magical device and they declined to investigate more than its basic function. Instead they accepted its boon and once more set off upstream, travelling at a pace similar to that of a cantering horse.

All day they journeyed north, maintaining as much speed as possible between the sand banks and islands of the Ephraxis. Lone domains and villages became increasingly frequent and three times boats put out from the shore to intercept them. Each time their speed was sufficient to elude the pursuers, and by the third occasion their confidence had risen so far that they merely laughed at the Ythanites as they swept past. Once clear, Elethrine left Aisla to steer the boat and spread the map out on the rowing bench.

'Many problems still face us,' she stated, as Talithea moved into a squat beside her and put an arm around her waist. 'From here, sense suggests making for the north coast of Apraya, from where, with luck, we may take ship for Kora. See, the map shows the Ephraxis and its tributaries running from within a hundred leagues or so of the coast and other rivers lead north once we have crossed the watershed. Yet the best route would seem to take us past Ap-Ythan, which seems to be the capital of Ythan. Until north of there we will not be safe.'

'Especially with anklets marking us as the property of Bormontal,' Talithea added with disgust.

'We could pass Ap-Ythan at night,' Aisla suggested, 'and perhaps the pure dwarven kingdoms further north might prove more friendly.'

'Very likely,' Elethrine agreed. 'Until then we must forage as best we can and trust to the speed of this boat to keep us from harm.'

For days they continued north, feeding on river crustaceans and molluscs and stealing grapes, olives and other fruit from the lands they passed. Each night they would beach the boat on a lonely island and post watches. Their intimacy grew, until each was as familiar with the contours and responses of the others' bodies as she was with her own. They also indulged their love of erotic pain and humiliation without restraint, frequently spanking one another and taking turns to serve stripped and red bottomed in order to enjoy the sensation.

No longer did the Princess hold herself aloof from the maid, but would frequently serve her. This extended even to Talithea licking Aisla's anus while the maid squatted on the Princess's face and masturbated as Elethrine kissed her neck, face and breasts. Yet Talithea was far from alone in exploring the pleasures of submission. Frequently all three girls would go to sleep with warm, red bottoms and the taste of each other's juices in their mouths. Elethrine's vagina alone remained unpenetrated, her anus and the others' holes all frequently knowing the feeling of entry by fingers,

225

tongues and even the handles of the boat's small oars. The oars also proved excellent spanking implements, capable of bringing a girl's bottom to blazing heat with only a few well-aimed smacks.

Increasingly uninhibited and increasingly detached from the strictures of their upbringing, they admitted to deeper and darker fantasies. Typically Mundic, Talithea's favourite fantasy was to be captured and caged naked in a public square. After being pelted with refuse and humiliated in a hundred ingenious ways, she would be taken out, thrown in a pond to clean the worst of the muck from her body and then comprehensively ravished by the population. Cocks would be put in her vagina, mouth, anus and between her breasts while, in between sessions with groups of men, she would be spanked and made to lick the tuppennies of the womenfolk. Finally she would be given to the town dung gatherer, and used again and again on the floor of his filthy hovel.

In response, Elethrine admitted that she became excited at the thought of being ravished by goblins and that she sometimes came over the idea. The others listened with giggles of disgust and delight as she described her dream of being caught in the cherry orchard at Korismund, stripped and penetrated in every orifice. The confession also put all three of them thoroughly on heat and afterwards Elethrine was spanked in the nude and made to bring the others off under her tongue. Talithea then repeated the goblin fantasy back to Elethrine while all three of them masturbated.

Aisla, while less imaginative, had many true tales to tell, of secret and dirty liaisons with men-at-arms, dwarven mercenaries and other girls. To Elethrine's amazement the maid admitted that sex between the girls of Korismund Keep was not only commonplace but frequently took place in groups of three, four or more. Not only that, but Elethrine herself was often the object of their lust and several whippings that the Demoiselle had fondly imagined to be disciplinary had in fact been carefully engineered by their victims. The revelations earned Aisla a long and painful whipping with willow twigs, yet it was unashamedly erotic and led to another bout of intimate and passionate sex.

They left the Ephraxis a few leagues short of the city of Piran, moving on to a tributary almost as large, but which the map failed to name. Ap-Ythan was passed in the night, yet once more they had to outrun pursuing vessels. At noon of the next day they reached another confluence, immediately before which an octagonal tower stood on either bank and a great iron chain stretched across the river, supported on stout pillars. Suspecting that they had reached the northern border of Ythan, they stopped in the shadow of an island and consulted the map.

Having reached a decision, they waited for hours under the overhang of a willow. Then, when the chain was opened to allow a legitimate trading barge to pass, they shot out from concealment and drove hard for the gap. The ruse succeeded with laughable ease and they turned and waved merrily to the astonished guards as they spilt out of their towers to stare. Aisla even went so far as to stand and lift the back of her kirtle, displaying her bare bottom in taunting defiance of the guards, and of Ythan in general.

The following day they reached the city of Ar-Kian, a place black with the smoke of foundries and overhung with plumes of grey smoke. After careful reconnoitring, it proved to be dwarven and not hostile. A smith removed their anklets, cheerfully accepting the weight of the iron and the use of Talithea's vagina in payment. Unlike the last occasion on which they had bought the services of a smith, the Princess gave herself joyfully and without reserve, stripping off her kirtle and kneeling over the anvil to be taken from the rear.

Unfortunately the smith's wife appeared at the exact moment that he was coming deep inside Talithea. All three girls were forced to submit to ignominious over-the-knee spankings and left with sore red bottoms but were unable to restrain their giggles. As she scampered back to the boat with her kirtle held up to rub at a smarting cheek, Elethrine found herself wondering at the depth of the change within herself. Before their journey the very idea of a bare-bottom spanking over the knee of a dwarven woman would have been enough to send her into a spitting, blushing rage. Now it made her laugh for the humour of suffering it herself and the sight of seeing her friends get their bottoms warmed as well. Similar service gained food and drink, with Aisla giving a slow and expert suck to a dwarven shopkeeper while the others bent with their kirtles turned up at the back and their reddened bottoms on show.

Beyond Ar-Kian the countryside became rapidly bleaker. The valley narrowed, with grim hills closing in on either side, their slopes clad in coarse vegetation of a dull grey-green. Smoke-darkened dwarven towns gave way to villages and isolated communities centred on mines, then to farmsteads and lone houses set by quarries. The river also became shallower and faster, making navigation tricky. Twice they were forced to carry the boat past stretches of rapids, and finally to abandon it at the foot of a waterfall which marked the head of the valley.

Ahead of them the horizon was a flat line of moorland, with no discernible features. High mountains stood to the east and west, and the girls judged that they had at last reached the watershed of the vast Ephraxis basin. Wary of wild beasts and goblins, they climbed on to the moor, keeping to gullies and avoiding the skyline. Despite their worry, the place seemed entirely devoid of life and dusk found them unmolested in a dank hollow well into the moor.

They spent a miserable night huddled together in the lee of a rock and set off cold and wet in the morning. Abandoned buildings began to appear, squat grey structures each consisting of a tall chimney and a square room which they judged to be either abandoned mines or a peculiar type of stronghold. At noon they reached a scarp high above a lush, green countryside so similar to the coastal regions of Mund that Elethrine found tears in her eyes. A brook flowed out of the moor to the north, which they followed, scrambling down through stretches of grass and heather, then hawthorn and rowan and finally massive chestnuts. Presently the brook reached flatter ground and joined another to become a placid stream running between banks lined with willow, coffinwood and poplar. As the light was fading from the sky they came across a solitary cabin, by which a flat-bottomed skiff was moored. Appropriating the skiff with no more than a minor flush of guilt, they loaded what remained of their rations and set off to the north.

11

Strumpet

After two days of subsisting on a diet of stale bread and
raw crawfish, the girls found the sparse farmland and
woods beginning to give way to more heavily cultivated
areas. Late one afternoon they reached a city of huddled
houses built of some near-black wood with the massive
block-shaped dwarven foundries set behind them on a
low hill, each with its tall chimney belching smoke.
Consulting the map, they confirmed the place as the city
of Utan.

'I know Utan,' Elethrine declared, 'or rather I know
of Utan. It is the port from which dwarven mercenaries
embark for Kora.'

'Precious few, these days,' Talithea remarked. 'Still,
we may be lucky.'

'We can only try,' Elethrine agreed, 'and perchance
the river leads to the docks, where we must hope to find
a shipmaster who will give us passage.'

'A dwarf provide free passage?' Talithea answered,
dubiously.

'An Aeg, perhaps?' Elethrine put in.

'You would be ravished before we were out of
sight of land,' Talithea put in. 'I mean, the heiress to
the Barony of Korismund? What Aeg could resist
you?'

'None,' Elethrine admitted, 'but still, if he were
highborn –'

'A shipmaster?' Talithea retorted. 'Reeve at best, more like artisan or merchant peasant.'

Elethrine gave a sniff of distaste but made no reply. For all her acceptance of her sexual feelings, she was still a highborn lady of Mund, and while she might indulge her dirtiest fantasies and basest desires to the full if there was no chance of her actions becoming known to her people, the thought of marrying beneath her was nevertheless repugnant.

'Perhaps if we were to sell the skiff we might buy passage from a dwarf?' Aisla suggested. 'And see, beyond those low buildings, the masts of ships.'

'Possibly,' Elethrine agreed. 'Anyway, let us be cautious. Accept no liaisons that might put us in the power of an unscrupulous merchant. Take neither wine nor food that is offered as a gift and remain alert at all times.'

The buildings proved to be warehouses, beyond which the river turned abruptly and spilled out into a bay. The water immediately became choppy and the girls were forced to put into a slipway. Numerous dwarves were near and quickly had the skiff clear of the water. For the first time since their escape from Bormontal Elethrine became conscious of the paucity of her clothing and found herself blushing under the undisguised interest of the largely male crowd. The thought flashed briefly across her mind that none of the dwarves in the crowd might hold sufficient rank for her to speak to, only to be dismissed as both ridiculous and impractical. Wondering again at the amount she had changed while in Apraya, she decided that it was also unwise to broadcast her own rank in a city that might well contain Aeg warriors.

'Good folk,' she began, 'we are travellers seeking passage to Kora. Pray be so good as to direct us to a ship bound to the north.'

Several dwarves responded, each citing the merits of

a particular vessel, and Elethrine realised that many were in fact crew members of the various ships moored along the dock. Suggesting the exchange of the skiff for passage, she was disappointed to find an immediate lapse of interest.

'What then would be the cost of passage?' she demanded. 'And what will you offer for the skiff?'

'It is a dwarven skiff and probably stolen up river,' a stout, grey-bearded dwarf answered. 'I offer ten weights of iron. As to passage, I crew on the *Moran's Ghost* and you might have a hammock each for but twenty weights.'

'What of service?' Elethrine sighed, facing the prospect of another round of cock sucking and the use of her breasts and bottom with a mixture of resignation and relish. 'And whither is the *Moran's Ghost* bound?'

'To Aegerion itself,' the dwarf replied, 'bearing ironware and silk, for which we have guaranteed safe passage.'

'Aegerion would leave us needing to cross the full width of Aegmund,' Elethrine answered. 'Are none bound for Ateron?'

'I am, aboard the *North Wind*,' a burly dwarf spoke up, 'on which I am mate. Moreover we ask no passage fee as Captain Rhaiton is keen to employ one or more ship's whores to keep crew and passengers entertained on the crossing.'

'Ship's whores?' Elethrine echoed. 'But we are highborn Mundics. As you travel to Aegmund your must know this from the colour of our hair. How could we endure the stigma of having indulged our lust with you once we arrived at Ateron?'

'Simple,' he answered. 'All aboard are dwarven, both crew and the twenty warriors we take to teach the men of Ateron Keep the arts of dwarven warfare. We will say nothing and none need learn of what I realise is a disgrace to your bizarre way of thinking.'

232

'What of it?' Elethrine asked, turning to her friends.

'It would be disastrous if it were to become known that you and I worked passage as ship's trollops on a dwarven troop ship,' Talithea responded. 'Yet, I am disgraced already.'

'Come, let us do it,' Aisla urged. 'Dwarves are notorious for their lack of idle curiosity and never tittle-tattle or gossip.'

'What choice have we?' Elethrine added.

'Little,' Talithea admitted with a long sigh, 'and seeing as I seem to be doomed to spend my remaining days in a celibentuary in any case, I may as well allow myself a final expression of my lust.'

'We accept,' Elethrine informed the dwarven mate.

Tired and deeply homesick, she herself felt that another few cocks would be a small price to pay for her return home, and dwarven honour allowed the certainty of not having her tuppenny unexpectedly or forcefully penetrated. Moreover, for all that she ached to be back in Korismund Keep, she was aware that once there she would no longer be able to indulge the lustful pleasures that she had come to enjoy in Apraya. The ship would provide a final glut of thick cocks, well-filled ball sacks and the heady pleasure of musk. Until her ravishment that would be it, saving only that she could now expect to play freely with Aisla. Even that would have to wait for bath times and when Nurse Anaka was elsewhere, for once she returned to the keep the first thing that would happen would be that a new purity girdle was fixed on her.

Accepting their ten weights of iron for the skiff, the girls went into Utan and purchased a meal and thick woollen cloaks against the cold of the northern seas. In fact their brief kirtles had been becoming increasingly inadequate as they travelled north, and all three donned their cloaks immediately, glad to be free of the cold air. The way the breeze tended to lift the kirtles and provide sudden glimpses of their bare bottoms and the furry triangles of their lower bellies had also become irritating, not that they really objected to the exposure of their bodies any more, but because it was inconvenient to be constantly waylaid and fondled.

Warm, fed and at last with a reasonable prospect of safe return to Korismund, Elethrine found herself wanting to run or even skip as they walked down to the docks to find the *North Wind*.

Elethrine sat, legs splayed, on a dwarf's lap. She was nude and her bottom hole was stretched taut around his penis, onto which she had lowered herself after making a display of greasing her bottom with lard to open her anus. He was bouncing her on his cock, sending shocks of ecstasy through her as her naked breasts bounced in his hands, the nipples stiff between his callused fingers. He was the third to bugger her that evening, while four others had come in her mouth and one between the soft pillows of her breasts. Each she had accepted with delight, while her head swam with the scent of their musk and her and her friends' juices.

The main chamber of the *North Wind* was warm and alive with the sound of revelry and laughter. Outside a stiff breeze filled the sails and drove the ship hard through the swells of the Aeg Roads, but the dwarven troops were oblivious to it. Near to where Elethrine was being buggered, Aisla knelt on a chair with her slim buttocks thrust out for the attentions of two dwarves with dog whips. Her haunches and thighs were criss-crossed with red welts, while the end of a carrot protruded obscenely from her anus, its whip-tattered greenery sticking up like an absurd tail. Her vagina was wet and gaping, having been invaded again and again by dwarven cocks. Come dribbled down into the deep red hair of her mound while she had a finger working on her clitty, bringing her towards orgasm as she was whipped. Her mouth was agape around a thick penis, its owner mounted on a chest in order to reach the level of her head. Her face and breasts were splashed with come, evidence of the eight dwarves she had so far taken to orgasm. Her spare hand caressed the cock of one of those who had been first to come in her mouth and who would clearly soon be ready once more if the half-stiff state of his cock was anything to go by.

At the far end of the hall, Talithea had been strung up from a beam. Completely helpless, she was moaning in ecstasy as a dwarf buggered her with a lazy, casual rhythm. Her full bottom was thrust out into his lap, the plump cheeks red from the beating she had received after first being hung from the beam for punishment. Her whipping had been for no serious offence, but simply for failing to show sufficient zeal and deference when serving dinner earlier.

The girls served nude, and frequently found themselves being taken, either in kneeling positions or bounced on a dwarf's lap with his penis inside her. Talithea, eagerly sucking on one dwarf's cock while another filled her vagina, had failed to respond to a demand for wine and so it had been quickly agreed that she should be strung up and whipped later that evening. The dwarf she had failed to please now had his cock wedged firmly up her bottom and was playing with her clitoris to make her come while he was inside her. Several others had had her before she was strung up, using her vagina and mouth with abandon. The buggery was supposedly part of the punishment, although it would undoubtedly have happened anyway.

Elethrine gasped in pleasure as the cock in her bottom ejaculated. The dwarf lifted her off and she felt the wet sperm ooze out of her bottom. She had been masturbating and near orgasm, and as he turned her she opened her mouth willingly to suck clean the thick penis that had just been withdrawn from her back passage.

Making herself comfortable in a kneeling position, she again started to masturbate as she sucked, tasting herself mixed with the heady musk of dwarven come.

As she started to come another cock was pushed at her gaping, slimy bottom hole, easing in as her anus contracted firmly around its tip in the first spasm of her climax. The dwarf grunted and forced its erection deeper up her bottom, making her gag on her mouthful. As he started to bugger her she came with a long moan deep in her throat, lost in the ecstasy of having penes in her, front and rear.

Not that her orgasm meant that her service was over. Every one of the dwarven troops had come, and many of them twice. The more virile were still eager for the girls and had started to demand slower and more careful attention for their second and third orgasms. Again and again cocks were inserted into Elethrine's mouth and anus, until her belly was swollen with their come and her bottom ring was sore and throbbing. Finally she collapsed into a sweaty, sperm-sodden heap on the floor, at which the dwarves took pity on her. She was taken on deck and washed down with buckets of sea-water, then helped to her hammock. Talithea and Aisla were already asleep, reddened bottoms uppermost for comfort. Just as she was drifting off to sleep the watch changed and the sailor who had been in the crow's nest came down to have his cock sucked. Elethrine obliged, sleepily allowing him to feed his erection in and out of her mouth and then swallowing his sperm.

So the voyage continued, with the girls allowed to rest for most of each day but spending the night satisfying the eager troops and sailors. Not that the dwarves were inconsiderate. Each time a girl was whipped her bottom would be allowed to return to pristine condition before she was once more accused of some minor or wholly imaginary fault and punished again. They were also scrupulously honourable about allowing Elethrine to preserve her maidenhead, refraining from entering her vagina even when she was crawling naked on the floor and begging for use.

The dwarves also had a love of bizarre games, such as making the girls suck cock to see who came most rapidly to orgasm and giving them enemas to see who could retain a flagonweight of ale in their bowels for the longest. It was during one such game that the coast of Kora was first sighted. The three girls were naked on the foredeck and masturbating furiously. The first to come was to be rewarded with a night in the captain's bed, the last to be strapped to the main mast and dog-whipped. Elethrine was already feeling the first spasms of approaching orgasm when the lookout called. Distracted, she failed to come off properly and was duly fixed to the mast and beaten. Yet, even while her bottom burned under the stinging blows of the whip she had eyes only for the distant black peaks of western Aegmund.

Later that day a dragon-prowed ship pulled out from the shore to intercept them. Despite thrilling at the sight of an Aeg ship, the girls hurried below and waited while Rhaiton persuaded the Aeg captain of their guarantee of safe conduct. The Aeg ship finally left, perhaps more impressed by the twenty heavily armed dwarven warriors than by Prince Kavisterion's seal. Returning on deck, Elethrine watched until the low black hull disappeared behind a headland, suddenly more homesick than ever. Coming to her side, Aisla took her hand and led her below decks, where she was presently lost in the heady pleasure of her maid's tongue on her clitoris.

When Elethrine awoke the next morning after another riotous night of pleasuring the dwarves, she realised that the *North Wind* was no longer in motion. Coming on deck, she found that they had dropped anchor in a sheltered bay beneath a great mountain.

Around the edge of the bay lay the ruins of white marble structures, buildings, docks and a wall.

'Where are we?' she queried, approaching Rhaiton and a group that included both mates and the four dwarven handleaders.

'The island of Vraic,' Rhaiton answered, 'where, with your assistance, I intend to attempt a project that has come to mind.'

'How with my assistance?' Elethrine asked, cautiously.

'Because you are both wanton and virgin,' he stated, 'traits that are normally mutually exclusive.'

'Go on,' Elethrine said.

'On Vraic,' Rhaiton continued, 'lives the claviscar, a curious man-thing said to be a degenerate form of elf. They are intelligent, agile and near impossible to capture, yet they are said to be partial to virgin cunt, which they can scent from a league or more.'

'You will recall that you are honour bound not to take my maidenhead,' Elethrine said, 'and besides, why do you wish to capture such a creature?'

'You need not fear for your maidenhead,' he assured her, 'we dwarves have a cunning method of sealing a woman's cunt. As to why, you mentioned the other night that certain merchants of Ythan are intent on breeding elf-like nymphs. Clearly they have not heard of the claviscar, for they resemble elves to all outward appearance. They are untameable and so I had never thought to disturb them, yet I dare say one could be tempted to mount a nymph easily enough.'

'Perhaps,' Elethrine answered as she pondered the implications of Rhaiton's idea. On the one hand she would have to undergo the highly undignified and possibly dangerous process of attempting to lure the claviscar. Not that dignity was all that important anymore, when she had allowed herself to become so utterly abandoned under the influence of her own lust

238

and the power of dwarven musk. In Mund it would be a different matter, but she was not yet in Mund. On the other hand it was unlikely that Bormontal, Ayapan and their colleagues had abandoned their breeding program, and so, by helping to supply them with a claviscar, she might save some luckless pale-haired maiden from a life of slavery and degradation. Given that the highborn Mundics were all related to one another, she would in effect be defending a relative, which was her duty.

'So be it,' she said suddenly as her train of logic reached its end. 'But make sure your seal is tight, I have no wish to be ravished by this elven creature.'

'You are a fine wench,' Rhaiton said happily, the other dwarves nodding agreement. 'Come then, let us waste no time.'

Elethrine's vagina was sealed, a process no more humiliating or painful than buggery and strangely exciting as it reimposed the enforced chastity that she had known since coming of age.

They landed on the island – Elethrine, Aisla, Rhaiton and a party of sailors and troops – with shovels and nets. Climbing into the dense woods that covered the lower flanks of the mountain, they found a suitable fallen tree and set to work. A long pit was dug, covered with a net and disguised with leaves and twigs. Elethrine was then bound tightly across the trunk with her hands in the small of her back and her legs well spread. Her cloak and kirtle were turned up, exposing her bottom and the rear of her tuppenny. She was then masturbated by Aisla until her juice had started to run and the air was thick with the scent of excited girl. Only when she had started to moan and beg for orgasm did they leave her, retreating into the thick undergrowth. Grateful for the seal over her vagina yet half wishing she could be penetrated, she waited, her ears straining for any sound that might herald the approach of the claviscar.

For an hour she waited, aware of the scent of her own

sex and wondering if Rhaiton's optimism had been well founded. As they climbed the slopes of Vraic, she had suggested that claviscars might retain sufficient intelligence to realise that a virgin girl bound over a log was sure to be a trap. Rhaiton responded that the breed was said to have retained the arrogance of their elven ancestors, so a male would think her put out for his pleasure by superstitious men. His reasoning struck Elethrine as suspect to say the least, and she was more than half expecting to remain in her rude position until the light began to fade and they had to abandon the project. She had also been assured that neither trolls nor goblins inhabited the island, as either sort of man-thing would have made full use of her mouth and anus for their pleasure, trolls being too large and powerful to be trapped by the pit and goblins being too numerous for a whole tribe to be snared.

A faint crackle attracted her attention, the sound of dry leaves beneath a foot. Turning her head, she found herself looking directly at what could only be a claviscar. He stood about half her height, a pale-skinned, white-haired creature with all the cold beauty of an elf, yet without the fearful disinterest of the elves of Lai. Indeed he was evidently far from disinterested, for as he approached he opened his rough goatskin garment to expose his penis. Presumably stimulated by the scent of her virgin tuppenny, it was already fully erect – white, thin but extraordinarily long.

Elethrine felt a thrill of alarm. Instead of rushing headlong to mount her, the claviscar was being remarkably cautious. Rhaiton and the others had retreated far enough to ensure that they would not be scented and she found herself deeply grateful for the seal that prevented her from being ravished. The claviscar began to stroke his penis and a long tongue flicked out to moisten his thin, white lips. As he moved directly behind Elethrine her view was obscured by the material of her cloak, which had been bunched up on her back to leave her tuppenny fully exposed.

She waited for the sound of the trap being sprung, tense and shivering, very aware of her vulnerability. Nothing happened and then the claviscar appeared again, moving sideways and feeling the ground with long white toes. With a thrill of alarm Elethrine realised that he had discovered the existence of the pit, presumably having suspected a trap immediately. Her sense of helpless anticipation rose at he skirted the pit and then jumped onto the fallen tree trunk to run down it with a strange, prancing gait.

Elethrine sighed as the claviscar placed a delicate hand on her naked bottom, resigning herself to whatever he intended. He began to feel her, exploring her buttocks in detail and then transferring his attention to her tuppenny. She moaned as sensitive fingers found her clitoris and began to twiddle, using a motion similar to the one she liked to use when she masturbated. Then something soft and wet touched her thigh and she realised that she was going to be licked. The claviscar's tongue was long and muscular, flicking around her labia and clitoris with a maddening expertise. She was quickly moaning and thrusting up her bottom, filled with shame but unable to suppress her reaction.

The elf-thing's fingers touched the seal of her vagina, working at it in an effort to puzzle out how it was attached. Elethrine sighed, half grateful for the skill of the dwarven workmanship, half wishing the seal would come away so that she could be filled with long, white cock. Then his tongue left her clitty and dabbed against her anus, wetting the little hole for a very obvious purpose.

Elethrine gave a long sigh of resignation as she realised that she was going to be buggered. The claviscar's tongue had burrowed into her bottom hole, producing a sensation too exquisite to be denied. She

241

moaned, raising her bottom as best she could in her tight bonds and bracing herself for anal entry. The claviscar stopped exploring her anus with his tongue and mounted her, locking his long fingers on her hips and clasping the full width of her spread bottom between his knees. Elethrine felt the tip of his penis touch the damp ring of her anus and then ease inside, finding little difficulty with a ring that had been opened by the massive Drathor and so frequently stretched around fat dwarven cocks. She moaned deeply as the penis slid up her, deep, deep into her bowels. It was soon all in, and his stringy thighs were pressed against the soft flesh of her full buttocks. The elf-thing came forward, resting on her back and taking a plump breast in each hand. Then he began to hump her bottom, squeezing her breasts as he moved his erection in her anus and she moaned and panted out her ecstasy and humiliation.

Then the cock in her rectum began to move, wriggling about in the most extraordinary manner. Elethrine gave a cry of surprise as she felt the squirming movements begin. The claviscar was buggering her as an ordinary man might have, humping away against her buttocks with evident relish. He was also doing something very peculiar, making his cock wriggle inside her in a way that produced a sensation at once utterly obscene and completely irresistible. Elethrine began to squirm her toes and fingers in an agony of helpless pleasure not far short of orgasm.

The claviscar began to come, not the frantic, jerking eruptions of most males, but a steady stream of hot fluid that quickly began to fill out Elethrine's rectum. Breathless, panting hard, she could only let it happen. Knowing that her control of her bum hole was about to go and that the claviscar's cock was not thick enough to plug her, she shut her eyes in a state of ecstatic shame stronger even than when she had first been anally penetrated.

The come burst from her bottom, splashing against the claviscar's belly and running stickily down her thighs and over her tuppenny. She cried out, closer to orgasm than she had ever been without the stimulation of her clitoris. The claviscar – used only to his own type and usually their vaginas at that – abruptly moved back. He gave a strange cry, not unlike a squeal of alarm, then lost his balance on her upraised bottom. She felt his penis pulled suddenly from her rectum and heard the crash as he fell back into the pit, then the snap and whine of the net mechanism activating.

Aisla and the dwarves returned a while later, to find Elethrine still tied in place and the claviscar struggling furiously in the net. They immediately gave whoops of joy, which turned to laughter as they discovered that Elethrine's anus was still pulsing and oozing sperm.

Unable to resist, Rhaiton had Aisla suck him erect and immediately mounted Elethrine, buggering her happily while the maid rubbed at her mistress's tuppenny to give her a desperately needed orgasm. Having satisfied all the dwarves and Aisla, Elethrine was untied and carried down the hill to be welcomed on the *North Wind*. Somewhat uncomfortable, but distinctly proud of herself, she went below decks. Supper was due to be served and then the celebration of their success was bound to be long, riotous and require the full services of Talithea, Aisla and herself.

12

Maiden's End

Elethrine gazed in rapture at the grey-black towers of
Ateron, heedless of the waves that tossed the ship like a
paper doll. Salt spray blew hard in her face as the
seamen struggled to bring the ship around to face the
harbour, but she was scarcely aware of their cries, nor
of the howling wind. Instead she had eyes only for the
grim citadel, bastion of the Princes of Northern
Aegmund, a place that had housed the enemies of her
family for generations yet now seemed a place of
welcome and fellowship. Beyond the keep and town,
hills rose in ranks, blue-black in the dull light, their
outlines jagged with oak, black spruce, larch and
coffinwood. To the east a craggy line of faint grey hinted
at the Spine, on the flank of which her home lay.

'Get below, you fool trollop!' one of the mates roared,
but Elethrine ignored him, holding her place at the bow as
the ship made her slow, ponderous turn into the harbour.

Only when the *North Wind* had been drawn against
the quay by longshoremen and lashed to great
black-iron bollards did she leave her post, jumping onto
the quay and kissing the cold stone with far greater
fervour than she had shown any of the crew. As she rose
to her feet she discovered Aisla beside her, the maid's
face beaming with pleasure at being on the soil of Kora
once more. Talithea was still on the ship, her delicate
features set in a pensive frown.

'Why so glum, Moth?' Elethrine called up, shouting above the wind. 'Are we not home?'

Talithea returned a weak smile and started for the gangplank that the crew were moving into position.

'I am home, true,' the Princess announced as she joined them, 'and in truth I never thought to see this moment. Yet in ways I wish myself back in Apraya. Even the life of slave whore to Irqual's corsairs seems preferable to the disgrace that now faces me.'

Elethrine did not answer but placed an arm around Talithea's shoulders, suddenly feeling tactless for having shown so much pleasure at her homecoming. As soon as they announced themselves they would be taken to a matron for the inspection of their maidenheads. When it was discovered that Talithea was no longer virgin there would be a scandal. Her betrothal to Prince Kavisterion would be abandoned and she would be sent to some bleak celibentuary to live out her life as a shamed recluse. Elethrine, with her maidenhead intact, could confidently submit to inspection by Prince Kavisterion's matrons and then demand an honour guard to see her safe to Korismund Keep.

'If we could but find a witch,' Aisla suggested.

'A vain hope,' Talithea replied dejectedly. 'For we need a guard to reach a witch yet we cannot command a guard until after seeing a witch.'

'Perhaps that is not so,' Elethrine put in. 'Highborn of Korismund come here occasionally – to duel, challenge or perhaps seek a ravishment. Saving the last case, their colours will be displayed at the window of any tavern they occupy.'

'A kind thought,' Talithea answered, 'but hardly a practical one. No thane or squire with the courage to seek combat here would miss the opportunity to ravish the daughter of his Liege Lord, especially when she had not so much as a wooden girdle to guard her chastity.'

'He need not know that I am so vulnerable,' Elethrine said. 'Besides, in the heat of ravishment he might not notice that you lacked a maidenhead, while I would simply end up wedded to whatever fine knight achieved me.'

'You are generous,' Talithea said, 'and perhaps it is not such a foolish plan.'

'Better than confinement in a celibentuary,' Elethrine remarked, 'where rumour says the girls are spanked bare every night to remind them of their sins.'

'And made to scrub floors in the nude,' Aisla put in, 'with a lighted candle thrust in their deflowered tuppenny –'

'I have heard the rumours, thank you,' Talithea cut in, somewhat frostily. 'Very well, Pommette, let us try to reach a witch. Who knows – after what we have come through, perchance we might succeed.'

Wrapping their heavy cloaks around them and raising the cowls to obscure their features, they set off along the quay, ignoring the glances of curious fishermen and sailors. Ateron rose from the sea, a steep town with the quality of the houses improving as the hillside rose higher. By the docks was a jumble of warehouses and low taverns. Singing could be heard in one of these waterfront bars, a rude ditty the verses of which the female and male revellers sang alternately:

Four and twenty maidens, all in a line
Each so sweet and bashful, her innocence divine

Four and twenty longshoremen, each with a groat
Quite enough to tempt a maid to lift a petticoat

Four and twenty maidens, all in a rank
Every one so naughty that she deserves a spank

Four and twenty longshoremen, each with a stick
A maiden caught and made to kneel, by such a
    sneaky trick

Four and twenty maidens, all in a column
Their bottoms show, their tears run down and
  every one is solemn

Four and twenty longshoremen, each with a treat
A bottom plump and nude and round, his very
  own to beat

Four and twenty maidens, all in a row
Dresses up and drawers apart and bottoms all aglow

Four and twenty longshoremen, each with a smirk
A punished girl with willing hands to hold his cock
  and jerk

Four and twenty maidens, all in a queue
Each with a handsome cock to lick and wondering
  how it grew

Four and twenty longshoremen, each with a grunt
As virtue's lost, his prick invades her sopping little
  cunt

Four and twenty maidens, all in a file
With fannies wide and cocks inside – on every face
  a smile

Elethrine found herself smiling. It was a variation of a
common taproom song, in which the identity of the
males varied but the essence was always the same – the
tricking of maidens into a beating and then the loss of
their maidenheads. Before, the ditty had always
infuriated her. This was partly because it implied that
maidens were so stupid that they could be lured by the
trick of offering a groat for a flash of underwear and
then be tripped into a spanking position. Worse, it
implied that once a girl's bottom was hot she would
cheerfully submit to cock sucking and defloweration. As
she now knew, the latter part at least was close to the
truth, and hearing the ditty once more brought only
amusement and a fresh surge of joy at being home.

Above the docks was a commercial district with the shops and houses of artisans, then the houses of rich merchants and the lesser highborn with a few inns of quality among them and finally the keep itself, home to the Prince and his immediate circle.

The girls walked rapidly up the steeply cobbled streets, Talithea nervous and moody, Aisla and Elethrine unable to suppress their excitement at their homecoming. There was also no longer the strange feeling of being taller than everybody else, for during the entire period of their exile no more than a handful of those they had met had equalled their height. As they climbed they left behind the worst of the stench of fish and rotting seaweed that had shrouded the harbour and came into areas with purer air and a generally more refined atmosphere.

'Twice only have I been here,' Elethrine announced as they reached the broad, semi-circular street that ran beneath the walls of the keep, 'and was of course lodged in the keep. Some of our retinue, I believe, occupied a fine inn.'

'The *Black Cock*,' Aisla replied. 'It is to the left.'

They turned, feeling intensely conspicuous as they moved among the crowds, not one of whom had their face covered or walked with anything but confidence, be they an errand boy or a thane. The *Black Cock* proved to be a timbered building five stories in height and two gables wide, with the upper stories leaning far out over the street. Elethrine scanned the windows nervously, hoping to see a familiar banneret.

'Luck is with us,' Aisla said suddenly. 'See, in the side window, the green and bronze of the house Mirone. Squire Hathrul himself is perhaps within.'

'Luck indeed,' Elethrine answered, moving to where Aisla was peering down a narrow side alley. 'He is young and doubtless comes to duel, yet he is married, having taken Leitea, the daughter of a reeve, some four years past. He is perfect.'

'Let us greet this Hathrul, then, and quickly,' Talithea said with a nervous glance to a pair of men-at-arms high above on the walls of the keep.

Inside the inn an enquiry yielded the information that Squire Hathrul was indeed in residence and had gone up to his room no more than an hour before. Thanking the innkeeper, Elethrine led the girls up the steep staircase of wood polished smooth by generations of use. Her rap on the door produced an almost instant response, a handsome young man wearing only a surcoat of deep green and bronze throwing the door wide with a look of annoyance that faded to be replaced by amazement as he realised the identity of his visitors.

'Demoiselle Elethrine!' he exclaimed. 'And the Princess Talithea?'

'Squire Hathrul,' Elethrine replied coolly. 'Seeing your colours and being distant from fair Korismund, we chose to greet you. It is agreeable to chance upon the squire of a liege house when in a foreign city.'

'I am honoured,' Hathrul replied, stumbling over his words in his haste to speak. 'But how come you here? Where is your retinue? I heard that a great demon had swept you off to the south and I feared for the House of Korismund!'

'At a later date I shall be pleased to favour you with our saga,' Elethrine answered. 'For the instant, the Princess and I require an honour guard.'

'I shall oblige, of course,' he answered. 'One moment.'

He disappeared back into the room, Elethrine following to find a golden-haired girl sitting on the bed and struggling with the fastenings of her drawers. Her chemise was still undone, and as she attempted a curious cross between a curtsy and a bow her heavy breasts fell clear of the material.

'Leitea,' Elethrine greeted her, unable to resist a smile at the girl's frantic efforts to cover her breasts.

'But won't you be visiting Prince Kavisterion?' Hathrul asked of Talithea.

'Without proper escort? Unthinkable!' Elethrine answered, quickly. 'When will you be able to leave?'

'Now, in the circumstances,' Hathrul replied. 'We had come here in the hope that I might gain some advantage on the duelling field, but the Aeg seem ill-disposed to sport at present. Your venture takes precedence in any case. We can be ready as soon as my men-at-arms can be fetched from the taverns and pleasure houses, begging your pardon, Demoiselle . . . Princess.'

'Granted,' Elethrine replied, 'merely hurry.'

Within an hour the group were assembled in the courtyard, twelve mounted men-at-arms and Leitea's maid in addition to the five of them. New clothes had been fetched at their order, and once more they were clad according to their station as citizens of Mund. The three girls kept their faces swathed in cloth as the troop clattered out along the broad street and through the wall gate of Ateron. Only when the road divided and they took the smaller, eastern fork towards Korismund did they reveal their faces, Elethrine's tension fading as if the act of displaying her features was in itself a guarantee of safety.

Ahead of them the land rose in great broad hills, swathed in thick forest and cut by occasional gorges. The road followed ridges, crossing into valleys only when necessary. At first they passed occasional small holdings, then remote keeps, each perched on its spire of rock. Elethrine felt a strange pride, born of the knowledge that the vast efforts that had gone into making the keeps so strong was largely the result of the threat posed over the centuries by her own family.

The path became wilder and more narrow, finally giving way to a single track running beneath the overhanging foliage of great oaks and coffinwoods. Twice Elethrine thought to detect the faint waft of goblin musk and noted Leitea shiver in apprehension – or just possibly anticipation.

All the rest of the day they rode, moving ever deeper into the forest, until Hathrul ordered an encampment made in the lee of a great bluff that marked the start of the true foothills of the Spine. A tent was erected for her and Aisla, in which Talithea presently joined them, the three girls sleeping in each other's arms without thought for the gossip it might cause if they were discovered.

At noon on the following day they came within sight of Aurora's spire, a needle of grey stone that seemed to grow from the living rock itself. They passed within a league of it and Elethrine requested a halt. Hathrul obeyed, his position with respect to Elethrine preventing him from either countermanding her order or inquiring why she might wish to visit the witch.

Leaving the others at the base of the slope, Elethrine, Talithea and Aisla walked up towards the spire. As she approached, Elethrine found a knot of fear building in her throat despite her feelings of righteous indignation at the way she had been treated. While Aurora had the reputation for being well disposed, and particularly sympathetic to maidens, their errand was not an easy one, and the witch's sheer power was sufficient to make the prospect of demanding anything from her daunting to say the least. Talithea evidently did not share her qualms, but walked with a brisk, eager step. She also had the dangerous glitter in her eyes that Elethrine had come to know so well.

'Let me speak, Moth, please,' Elethrine said, mindful of the chaos that Talithea's temper had caused before.

'I wish to have words with the brat Ea,' Talithea answered, 'as should you, Pommette, and you too, Aisla.'

'We do,' Elethrine answered, 'yet please remember that while Ea may be a brat she is also a sorceress of some power. In any case, let us see to the restoration of your maidenhead before attempting any redress of the balance of justice.'

251

'Very well, but I will not be thwarted,' Talithea replied. 'First I shall have the brat stripped, then I shall take her across my knee and spank her impudent little rump. When you have both done the same, we will have her cast to the Glissades – as we were.'

'Thank you,' Elethrine responded as they reached the base of the spire. 'As to the punishment, we can only hope that Aurora agrees to its justice.'

A single door opened into the spire, quite unguarded, which was in itself a sign of the witch's indifference to the dangers of the outside world. The door was unadorned, with no handle or other instrument of entry, yet it swung open as they approached it. Steeling herself, Elethrine stepped within, to find a bare circular room from which a stair rose to a higher level. They took this, rising to find themselves in a tall cone illuminated by slits set high in the spire above. In the centre was a dais covered in white fur and pillows of thick white velvet. On this Aurora reclined, as languid as a cat and stark naked. With one hand the witch was stroking the jet black hair of her apprentice, whose head rested on her thigh. Ea was also naked and her black-in-black eyes regarded the three girls with an insolent calm. A round mirror lay on the bed beside them.

Elethrine stopped, her carefully judged greeting lost in her astonishment at the two witches' nudity. For a woman of Mund to go naked was a thing of extraordinary shame, and during the spanking that had caused all their troubles Ea had been as outraged at the prospect of being stripped as Elethrine herself would have been. Suddenly the idea of forcing Ea to accept a naked, over-the-knee spanking as punishment seemed less satisfying than it had a moment before.

'The answer to your question,' Aurora said casually, 'is that Ea did not object so much to being nude as to the significance that you yourselves placed on her nudity. She is, after all, a mixture of black Koran, Rai

Isle highlander and nymph, and so understands little of Mundic propriety. What's more, you, Aisla, were going to give her what was undoubtedly an unjust spanking.'

'I – I'm sorry,' Aisla stammered.

'No matter, you have been punished and perhaps have learnt to curb your arrogance,' Aurora continued, her calm, authoritative tone making Elethrine feel small, silly and anything but righteous.

'Yet do you consider our punishment just, merely for a girlish prank?' she managed, balancing her words to express her true feelings, without showing arrogance.

'Indeed not,' Aurora replied, greatly to Elethrine's surprise. 'If you ask to have Ea punished I must concede the justice of your demands.'

'I humbly request that she may be punished,' Elethrine said quickly, before Talithea could speak.

'Very well,' Aurora answered. 'So it shall be. But do you not have a more pressing matter than mere revenge?'

'How –?' Elethrine began, to be cut off by Aurora's silvery laugh.

'We have been watching you,' the witch explained, holding up the mirror which Elethrine now saw to show not a reflection, but her own image and that of Talithea and Aisla as if viewed from across the room.

Instinctively she looked up to where the viewpoint in the mirror appeared to come from. Nothing was apparent, save possibly an odd disjunction of light. Then the full implications of what Aurora had said came home to her and the blood rose to her cheeks in a furious blush. They might have watched her suck dwarven cocks – worse, groan out her ecstasy with a good two hands-breadths of corsair's cock up her bottom – perhaps worse still, watched her masturbate while Talithea and Aisla smacked her bare bottom with their hands. Ea laughed, adding to the fury of Elethrine's blushes.

'Yet I have a natural sympathy with deflowered maidens,' Aurora continued after a pause that was clearly designed to allow the girls to appreciate the full significance of having been watched. 'Did you know that I myself fled the celibentuary at Kavas-Arion before being apprenticed to the witch Hespera? No? Well, I did, after being confined there for allowing myself to succumb to the lust of a wild bull-nymph. Thus you may rely on both my cooperation and my silence. Still, it is a simple process and may be concluded once you have had Ea punished. You may even choose her punishment, but choose carefully, for you must be satisfied with what she takes. Ea, do you have anything to say?'

'I confess that my reaction was unjustified, mistress,' Ea answered quietly, 'and submit myself freely to justice.'

'What, then, would you have done to her?' Aurora asked, turning back to the three girls.

'Hurl her to the Glissades so that she too may cross leagues of burning desert and empty sea and endure the perils of Apraya!' Talithea demanded, hotly.

'Hardly a punishment,' Aurora replied. 'She would simply order the demon to return her in safety.'

'Then present her as a chattel to some roaring, drunken corsair, that she may learn the full function of each orifice of her body,' Elethrine suggested.

'Again, hardly practical when with a word she may destroy any who cross her.'

'Then throw her in a pit of goblins, with a vial of musk to ensure her arousal,' Aisla tried.

'A better idea,' Aurora replied. 'Ea, do you accept this as just punishment?'

'I do,' Ea replied quietly.

'Are all satisfied?' Aurora asked.

'Yes,' Elethrine and Talithea answered, simultaneously.

'Then so be it,' Aurora said. 'Come, Ea, justice must be done.'

There was something subtly mocking in the witch's tone, yet Elethrine set her qualms aside, instead content to delight in the prospect of watching the petite apprentice ravished by goblins. She found herself trembling with eagerness and knew that her tuppenny had started to juice. The pleasure, she knew to her shame, would come from more than just exacting her revenge – she actively wanted to see the goblins' huge, misshapen cocks and watch them work inside Ea's body.

Elethrine had imagined that the preparations would be complex. After all, it was scarcely imaginable that the two witches kept goblins on the premises when either of them might be mounted and penetrated unexpectedly at any instant. Aurora, however, simply led them downstairs and said a few quiet words. The centre of the floor immediately rearranged itself, folding according to a symmetry beyond Elethrine's understanding to form a deep pit the sides of which sloped inwards from the base. A low wall surrounded it, save in one place. After being splashed with musk by Aurora, Ea jumped down into the pit without hesitation and walked to the middle to stand naked and ready, apparently quite without fear. She made a gesture and was suddenly dressed in full, conventional Mundic style. With a mocking bow to the girls she lifted her dress to show that she wore petticoats and drawers beneath, all in black silk and heavily trimmed with lace.

Aurora then flung the door wide, revealing not the slope of scree and thin grass that Elethrine knew to be outside, but a swirling white mist. The witch began to speak, a quiet, insistent chant that held no meaning for Elethrine but yet managed to convey an urgent and obscene sexuality. As the girls watched, figures began to form in the mist – squat, lumpy and less than half the height of a man.

255

Aisla screamed and all three of them backed away as a goblin stepped out of the mist. Its bulbous eyes darted from side to side and, as its gaze found the girls, it licked its lips in an unmistakably lewd gesture. Pulling its grotesque cock free of the leather pouch between its bowed legs, it began to advance.

'This was not part of the bargain!' Elethrine squeaked, clutching at the front of her skirts and backing hurriedly away.

Aurora laughed and made a simple motion of her hand, as if to guide someone through a door. The goblin immediately changed course, looked at Ea in the pit and, with a lustful croak, leapt down. Another came close behind it, and a third, neither sparing the girls more than a glance before leaping down to join their companion. Presently Ea was surrounded by eight goblins, each one with its penis held ready in its hand. Aurora made another gesture and they came forward, tongues lolling from their mouths and running spittle as their fingers groped for their prize.

Eager green fingers grabbed Ea, pawing at her clothes in their haste to get at the juicy prize beneath. A squat, heavy-bellied goblin grabbed her hair and thrust its grotesque penis at her mouth. Ea gaped without hesitation, her lips stretching wide around the thick shaft. The goblin pushed hard, making her gag as its penis was jammed into her throat. Others already had her skirt up and were fighting to get at her bare flesh. More by luck than judgement they found the openings to her drawers and pantalettes simultaneously, tearing them open to expose the sweet white peach of her bottom. Elethrine could see the girl's tuppenny, pink and open in its nest of black hair; also her anus, a dark spot down between the firm little buttocks.

Ea made no effort to resist, but came up on her knees and flourished her naked bottom, almost as if seeking ravishment by the four goblins who were frantically disputing the right to use her vagina first. The biggest managed to push the others aside, its cock going straight to Ea's tuppenny. With an obscene grunt it forced it in, the fat green shaft looking impossibly big in Ea's tiny hole. It took hold of her buttocks with its long, splay-ended fingers and began to hump her even as its companions turned their attention to stripping away her remaining clothes.

The one in her mouth was coming, white jism spurting out around her lips as it pumped frantically into her. Then it pulled back, Ea gaping for it as if for a lost sweetmeat. Another thrust its cock into her sperm-stained mouth and her eyes closed in bliss again. Her bodice was torn open as she once more began to suck, the goblin's fingers groping eagerly for her tiny breasts.

Elethrine found herself smiling. Repulsion and delight warred within her as she watched the tiny apprentice ravished, both she and the goblins becoming increasingly heated as their ardour rose. The scent of musk was also strong, filling her with an urge to jump down and take her share of fat green cock. A finger was in Ea's bottom ring, the hole stretched pink and taut around the rough black-green digit. She had gone down low, supported on the hands of goblins groping her breasts. One of her hands was on a cock, the fingers not meeting around the thick shaft. The other was cupping the heavy, leathery scrotum of the one whose cock was in her mouth, kneading the balls as she sucked without restraint.

The one in her vagina came, pulling back at the last instant to spray come all over her bottom, cackling with bawdy glee as it emptied its load in between her pert, girlish cheeks. The one with its finger in her anus immediately pulled its digit free and leapt up to mount her, placing its bloated knob against the sperm-sodden cup of her slowly closing bottom ring.

'It's going to bugger her!' Talithea declared in a voice rich with satisfaction and disgust.

Elethrine watched as the goblin forced its massive penis slowly up Ea's back-passage, stretching the tiny pink ring until it seemed impossible that it had not split. With perhaps half of its two-foot length in her rectum, it began to bugger her, her anal skin moving in and out with the pushes. The one in her mouth pulled out, leaving her grunting with the effort of accommodating the monstrous organ in her bottom. Another goblin had slid itself beneath her and was licking eagerly at her tuppenny, bring a new note to her groans of pleasure before they were suddenly stilled by the insertion of yet another cock into her mouth. The one beneath her slid itself onto its back and pulled her down so that her tuppenny met its cock and filled, causing a grunt of annoyance from the one up her back-passage.

With cocks in mouth, vagina and anus, Ea began to come, her body starting to jerk and then going into spasm. Her tight little bottom bucked, writhing on the two cocks inside her from the rear as if trying to get more purchase. Her legs kicked and her hands jerked frantically at the two cocks which she was now holding. One came, spraying her back and upturned buttocks with come. Her whole body tensed, then she rammed her bottom out onto the intruding penes, intentionally stuffing them as far inside herself as they would go. Sperm erupted from around her lips as the one in her mouth came. It pulled free, leaving her open mouth full of bubbling white come. The one up her bottom jerked and she cried out as perhaps a full cup of jism was ejected into her bowels. Another, which had been using her long black hair to masturbate itself, pushed in and stuffed its erection into her gaping, sperm-soaked mouth.

Elethrine saw that Aisla had her skirt lifted and her hand inside her drawers. Her face wore an expression of

258

rapture and she was clearly playing with her tuppenny while she watched Ea ravished. Talithea was little better, with the same expression on her face and her hand pushed against her belly to rub herself through the folds of her skirts. Abandoning herself, Elethrine cocked a leg up onto the wall of the pit, pulled up her skirts and delved into the split of her drawers. Inside her pantalettes her tuppenny was warm and moist; she began to masturbate, ignoring Aurora's cool, knowing smile.

Ea had been rolled over onto her back. A goblin was beneath her, its prick wedged deep up her bottom. Another was mounted on her, its thighs entwined with hers, its muscular little buttocks stuck out and its wrinkled scrotum bouncing in time with its thrusts. Two were by her head, cocks thrust out over her mouth while she sucked on them in turn. Her whole body was sodden with sperm, particularly her face, belly and breasts. The expression on her face was one of absolute, unrestrained bliss, and Elethrine managed to feel cheated even as she pushed her own belly forward to get better friction on her clitty. Her eyes were fixed on the scene below her as her pleasure rose. A goblin came in Ea's mouth, the apprentice eagerly gulping down the sperm as clot after clot splashed out. Elethrine focused on the huge, pulsing cock and her muscles began to tense. Her breath came sharply as another goblin's cock erupted over Ea's breasts. Ea dropped the cocks to get her fingers to her tuppenny. Both girls came, Elethrine with a long sigh of pleasure, Ea with a bubbling cry muffled by her mouthful of come.

Even as Elethrine's orgasm tore through her she was vaguely aware that Aurora had taken Talithea in her arms. The witch's hand was between the Princess's legs, kneading her tuppenny. Turning, Elethrine saw her friend's face, the eyes wide with pleasure. Aurora was working her hand in Talithea's drawers, the motions

259

evidently expert and strangely similar to those she had used to draw the goblins. Talithea sighed and then gasped, giving the characteristic sound that Elethrine knew meant that she had come. Beside them Aisla had her skirts pulled high and her drawers open, masturbating blatantly as she watched Ea.

Aisla came as the largest goblin stuffed its balls into Ea's mouth at the same instant that the one in her vagina came. All eight had now come at least twice, some three times, and their ardour was beginning to lapse. Ea, however, showed no signs of flagging and was doing her best to bring off the one whose balls were in her mouth while she stroked the scrotum of the one whose penis was up her bottom. Elethrine sat down, dizzy with reaction from the scent of musk and her own orgasm.

'They can come three, perhaps four times,' Aurora said, her voice quite steady and calm, 'then they must eat. See, the old, fat one who took her first is already beginning to turn its thoughts from Ea's body to the pleasures of fungi and succulent leaves.'

Elethrine nodded faintly, still somewhat weak from her own orgasm. For a moment Aurora's words seemed ludicrously out of place, and then Elethrine realised that she was being teased. The scent of musk was still strong, and she found her pleasure building again as she watched the goblins finish off. The big one gave up first, simply losing interest and wandering off as if nothing had happened. One by one they followed suit, until Ea was left lying on a bed of sperm-sodden clothing, her thighs spread as she took herself to a final, helpless orgasm.

'Remember this scene well,' Aurora remarked cryptically, as her apprentice tensed and writhed in her orgasm.

Once Ea had come the goblins were released and the room returned to order. Once more they went upstairs,

Ea now clean and once more completely naked. She favoured the girls with an insolent smile as she spread herself out at her mistress's feet, kissing each and then relaxing into the soft white fur of the dais.

'What of my maidenhead?' Talithea asked, somewhat uncertainly.

'It is whole,' Aurora answered, 'see for yourself.'

Talithea cast a single half-pleased, half-embarrassed glance at Elethrine and delved under her skirts. A moment later her face broke into a smile.

'It was done as your climax came,' Aurora said. 'Now, would you converse further, or continue on your way?'

'I think we should go,' Elethrine said quietly, 'but we thank you, and trust that equity of justice has now been regained.'

'More or less,' Aurora replied, not deigning to give the required response to the formal statement.

They left hurriedly, Aurora conducting them to the door. As they reached it Ea's laugh floated down to them, a sound both mocking and amused. The door opened, revealing not mist but the slope of the mountain, on to which they stepped. The door shut behind them, leaving Elethrine feeling not revenged, but puzzled, cheated and distinctly foolish. Technically they had subjected Ea to a revenge that – if not quite in proportion to what they had been through – should have made a lasting impression on her. Instead she had enjoyed the experience, indeed she had revelled in it, even to the extent of seeming game for more when the goblins had been spent. Still, Elethrine reminded herself, Talithea's maidenhead was once more intact and that in itself was a fine and necessary achievement.

Below Aurora's spire the ground sloped quickly away to where Hathrul, Leitea, the maid Orina and the twelve men-at-arms were waiting patiently. Elethrine, Talithea and Aisla rejoined them, the Princess now once more cool and regal with her maidenhead renewed and no further fear of suffering the drudgery of the celibentuary.

In the distance the peak Kor, on an outcrop of which Korismund Keep stood, was clearly visible, no more than twenty leagues away across a carpet of thick forest. Other mountains of the Spine reared to their left, grey-black and seeming to brood over the landscape. Moving smoothly into formation, the column set off, plunging into a forest that quickly cut off the sight of both the witch's spire and the Spine itself.

Trees rose up on all sides, massive oaks with their great boles encrusted with black-green algae, dusky-leafed holly and the occasional jet-black coffinwood. Gloom surrounded them on all sides, only occasional rays of sunlight managing to penetrate the canopy high above. Woodland scents reached Elethrine's nose: leaf mould, flowers, fungi and a faint musk that might just have been goblin.

'Let us canter,' she addressed Hathrul. 'I am eager to see Korismund Keep once more.'

'Demoiselle, the path is treacherous,' the Squire objected, 'besides which, a canter is an unsuitable gait for an honour guard, lest it be taken for flight.'

'A trot, then,' she insisted, 'but perhaps we could ride higher on the slope where the woods are less thick?'

'The higher slope is strewn with loose rocks,' he answered. 'Yet if you insist?'

'No, let us simply hurry,' she answered, now aware that the scent very definitely was goblin.

For all the assurance provided by Hathrul and his men-at-arms, she felt far from secure. Not because there was the slightest risk of the column being overcome by goblins, but because the musky scent was making her want to run into the woods, strip naked and lay herself down for their attention. The image of Ea in a state of musk-induced ecstasy kept coming back to her, along

262

with the nagging certainty that the tiny apprentice had reached her climax at least five times while she was being ravished. It was impossible not to think of herself in the same situation, coming under a goblin's tongue while others made good use of her tuppenny, bottom ring, mouth, breasts and hands.

The column increased its pace, only to be forced to slow as a mist rose out of the valley beneath them. Soon it was impossible to see more than a few yards, and Elethrine's nervousness rose as they were forced to slow and finally to dismount.

'Possibly we should camp, mistress?' Aisla suggested from behind her.

'No, let us press on,' Elethrine insisted. 'Hathrul, let us move up the slope. Any amount of loose rocks are preferable to this mist.'

There was no answer.

'Hathrul?' Elethrine demanded, but again nobody replied.

'Who can hear me?' she called loudly, sure that many of the column must still be within earshot.

'I am here, mistress,' Aisla assured her.

'And I,' Talithea's voice came out of the mist.

No others answered, not even Leitea who had been riding directly to Elethrine's rear. She felt a pang of alarm that intensified as she once more smelt the earthy musk of goblin.

Without warning her horse started, rearing with a whinny of fear and aggression. Elethrine clutched at the reins, felt herself slipping and the next instant had landed with a bump on the forest floor. The horse disappeared into the mist with a muffled clatter of hooves. Then something else moved where the horse had been, a small, hunched form. The goblin scent came stronger and Elethrine felt her nipples pop up to erection within her bodice. Despite the mist, the path was discernible, a beaten line of mud and leaves among the thick undergrowth. A sound caught her attention, a hiss as of air expelled between teeth, a hiss that spoke of raw lust. Now was the time to run, blindly, risking scratches and bruises for the sake of her precious maidenhead.

Now was the time, but she could no more run than fly. For a moment the mist swirled aside and Elethrine gasped. A goblin stood in the path, under half her height, its mottled hide blotched black and green, its legs bowed around a pair of massive testicles above which protruded a colossal penis; thick, fleshy and gnarled with the fat, pinkish-green knob protruding from the foreskin almost at the level of the goblin's mouth. It was grinning at her and caressing its monstrous cock as if offering it to her.

Elethrine stayed stock still, everything she had ever been taught warring with every natural instinct. Her poniard was in its sheath, a weapon more than capable of dispatching the small goblin and as many of its fellows as chose to follow. She made no move to draw it, instead sinking slowly to her knees, her eyes locked on the huge, rigid penis in front of her. The goblin stepped forward, flourishing its cock for her. Elethrine groaned, trying with one last effort to pull herself away from it but finding her mouth opening and her body leaning forward despite herself.

The goblin gave what might have either been a laugh or a grunt of delight and held its cock to her face, inches from her open mouth. Hardly believing what she was doing, Elethrine leant forward, slowly, her parted lips gaping to encompass the fat penis head, her nostrils full of its rich, irresistible scent, like the scent of dwarf cock, but a hundred times stronger. Then it was in her mouth and she was sucking on a goblin's cock, not with the disgust that she had been sure she would feel, but with an eager, wanton delight.

The goblin began to masturbate into her mouth,

grunting with glee as two of its companions emerged from the fog behind it. Elethrine lifted her haunches, knowing exactly what was going to happen to her and powerless to resist her body's demands for pleasure. They were going to ravish her, to strip her bare and broach her precious maidenhead. They would bugger her too and make her swallow their come and use her breasts and hands and buttocks as slides for their grotesque green cocks. They would use her in every hole and cover her in sticky, slimy sperm, just as Ea had been used, and, just like Ea, she would relish every moment of the experience.

The two new arrivals had got behind her and were pulling up her skirts, chittering in pleasure and anticipation as her dress and then her petticoats were lifted one by one. Yet another appeared, its long fingers scrambling at her bodice, first squeezing her breasts through the cloth and then starting to wrench at the fastenings. The one in her mouth had taken her by the hair and was holding her head, fucking her pursed lips with its swollen knob while it jerked itself furiously into her mouth. Hands were on her buttocks, fondling, squeezing, pulling in an effort to get at the ripe prize beneath. Elethrine groaned in bliss and despair as they found the slit and pulled her drawers wide even as her bodice and chemise were tugged open and her breasts fell, bare and heavy, into eager, waiting hands.

An erect cock bumped against her arm and she took it in hand, revelling in the feel of the hard shaft in her fingers as she began to pull at it. The goblin grunted and grabbed at her breasts, pawing the plump flesh and making her nipples pop out, firm and excited. Two were holding her drawers wide, revealing her bottom in just frilly pantalettes while a third investigated the draw-strings. Its fingers probed, touching her between her buttocks, close to her anus. Then it discovered how the bows worked and began to tug them open, one by one,

265

exposing her most intimate parts and slowly removing the final barrier to her ravishment.

She could hear them chittering excitedly as her buttocks came on show. Fingers touched her flesh, prodding the girlish swell of her cheeks as if testing the quality, tickling her down between her crease, ever closer to the damp opening of her anal passage, an opening that they were sure to want to take advantage of. One touched it, making it open automatically, then they found her tuppenny and began to rub at her.

Helpless in the musk-induced ecstasy and held firm in the web of their groping arms, Elethrine raised her bottom, offering herself for entry. A tiny voice in her mind was screaming that she was offering her virgin tuppenny to a goblin, the most depraved of acts. The rest of her wanted it desperately, and as she spread her thighs in eager anticipation of being deflowered she felt the rounded head of a cock bump against her vulva. With her head held firm and her mouth full of cock it was impossible to turn and watch, yet she could imagine the grotesque body of the goblin mounted up on her raised bottom, its penis probing for her vagina.

Twice it pushed and missed, its cock sliding in among the wet folds of her tuppenny. Then it found the hole and its knob was straining against her maidenhead, pushing in, stretching her, forcing entry.

Elethrine gasped on her mouthful of cock as her maidenhead burst with a sharp stab of pain. Then the cock was sliding up her and the pain was forgotten. Uncontrollable ecstasy flooded into her brain as for the first time her vagina filled with penis. She began to suck yet more frantically as she was fucked, revelling in every sensation of her body. Her breasts were out and being groped, the nipples swollen and sensitive under long, green fingers. Her mouth was full of thick, hard penis, redolent of musk and surely about to erupt sperm into her. Her bottom was high and spread, eager fingers groping her full buttocks. Best of all there was a cock inside her, a fat, lumpy cock that created a sensation of breathless rapture as it moved in and out.

Pulling a hand free of a cock that she had barely been aware of holding, Elethrine put her hand back between her legs and started to masturbate. As she frigged, the goblin's balls slapped on her hand, faster and faster as it gathered pace inside her. She wanted to come desperately, to reach her orgasm while the first ever cock to penetrate her was still inside her. Her masturbation became frantic as the goblin humped her with ever greater urgency. Her clitty began to burn, then the muscles in her thighs tightened and she knew it was going to happen. The cock in her mouth erupted, filling her throat with sperm. She gagged, swallowing come as she tried to scream out her ecstasy. The cock inside her jerked even as her climax exploded in her head. The balls slapped a final time on her hand and then something wet and sticky was running down her tuppenny. She continued to frig, rubbing the sperm into herself as her climax faded. She sighed deeply as the cocks were pulled free of her mouth and hole at the same time and more come began to trickle down her chin and the insides of her thighs.

Yet already a second goblin had moved to take advantage of her now easy vagina. Another thrust its cock at her mouth and Elethrine went back to sucking as she was once more penetrated. As they used her, her senses slipped into a dizzy, half-awake state of bliss. Again and again her vagina and mouth were used. Occasionally she would be rolled over on to her back and one or more would do it between her plump breasts. Then it would be back on her knees for a better view of her bottom. In addition to their cocks she was frequently made to suck their balls and lick come from penes that had recently been in her deflowered tuppenny.

After a while one penetrated her anally, forcing the

full length of its monstrous prick into her rectum and buggering her as she grunted and squealed in abandoned joy. When it had come it moved to her head to have its cock sucked, which she accepted with pleasure even as another inserted its penis into her now open and ready bottom.

She quickly lost count of how many had taken her and everything became a blur of hot bodies, come and her own frequent orgasms. Finally the goblins began to tire and one after another lost interest, each shambling away when it had shed its final load over her body or into her mouth, vagina or anus. As the last one came deep in her tuppenny she found herself reaching out for it, desperate for more. It paid no heed, simply wiping its cock on her ruined dress and shuffling away. Still on her knees, she gave herself a final, lingering orgasm with her fingers.

Elethrine collapsed to the forest floor so dizzy with pleasure that she could barely see. She was naked, every orifice of her body oozing sperm, which also coated her skin and was caked in her hair. Dimly she was aware that it had stopped and that she should be glad, even though her true feelings were of deep regret.

Near her she heard someone sigh, a long, satisfied sound of perfect contentment. A shape showed faintly through the mist, its contours just discernible as female and naked.

'Moth?' she asked, as the movement of a tendril of fog revealed the shape of a breast.

'Yes,' Talithea answered, the word coming as a long sigh that mixed rapture, exhaustion and melancholy.

'Aisla?' Elethrine said, glancing around for any sign of her maid.

'Here, mistress,' Aisla said faintly from further off.

'That – I –' Elethrine tried and then trailed off, unable to find words to express her feelings.

'It was paradise,' Talithea said from out of the fog, 'yet for paradise there is a price.'

For a long moment there was silence, each girl's senses slowly returning to normal. Finally it was Aisla who spoke.

'We must return to Aurora,' she said. 'It can be no more than the journey of two hours by foot.'

'Let us hasten, then,' Talithea answered, 'for we can ill afford to come across Hathrul while we are in this state.'

Elethrine sat up, forcing herself to clear her thoughts despite her experience. Something was wrong. The air was different, fresher and cooler, without the strong earthy aromas of the deep forest. The scent of goblin was still there, but mainly from her own body and it was fading on a breeze that had definitely not been there before. Glancing down, she noticed that the bed of leaves on which she had been so thoroughly ravished were not oak and coffinwood but cherry and she was lying not on damp soil but on grass.

'I am not sure we are where you think,' she said, quietly.

A swirl in the mist caught her attention. For a moment she expected to once more see the grotesque figure of a goblin but instead the parting vapour exposed the bole of a tree. The wood was a rich, glossy brown and set with horizontal ridges, clearly cherry. As she rose unsteadily to her feet, the images of her dream of ravishment by goblins came back to her. It had been in the cherry orchard – always in the cherry orchard.

Clasping her soiled gown hastily to herself she realised that it had come true, and then as the mist dispersed she found herself standing, all but naked, not a quarter league from the gates of Korismund Keep. Both Talithea and Aisla were nearby, both in the same sorry state and both gaping in blushing embarrassment at the burly peasant standing not twenty yards away with a cherry basket in either hand, and a mouth open in astonishment.

Epilogue

Elethrine sipped delicately at her silver cup, tasting the subtle, faintly sweet flavour of the wine. She was half turned to the side, watching Talithea declaim their saga to a rapt audience that filled the great hall of Korismund Keep. Occasionally she herself would rise, to cover a part of the story that reflected credit on Talithea. Between herself and the Princess sat her parents and Prince Kavisterion, all three of them listening with the same pride and fascination as the lowest peasants in the hall.

'. . . as the terrible Irqual slumped lifeless in his chair,' Talithea was saying, 'the mate of the corsairs, Drathor, rose roaring to his feet. He was a terrible man, black visaged and cruel, a giant among his fellows. With a bellow of rage he drew his great sword from its sheaf and swung a merciless cut at Aisla's head. She ducked, an instant before the blade would have severed her head from her shoulders, then rose, as swift as a striking eagle, to plunge her dagger beneath Drathor's ribs. Like his master, he died without a sound . . .'

Elethrine smiled quietly to herself as Talithea continued. No mention had been made of Irqual and Drathor's sexual habits, especially of the fact that they had bedded the girls nightly. As far as the assembly knew, she, Talithea and Aisla had fought their way out of Apraya without succumbing to the lustful intent of the natives. While the achievement had been greeted with a pride that fell only just short of disbelief, the inspection of their maidenheads by Nurse Anaka had borne out their story. Not that Elethrine had expected to pass the inspection. When they had limped into the keep, sore and naked under coarse blankets, she had anticipated immediate disgrace. It had, after all, been obvious that they had fallen foul of goblins, and while she had said nothing, it was clear that the matron would find her deflowered.

Only she hadn't been. Perhaps as many as twenty goblins had pushed their huge penes into her vagina, and there had also been no shortage of exploration with fingers and long, muscular tongues. By any rights her maidenhead should have been torn and broken, clear testimony to her ravishment and disgrace. But it had not been, a fact that had astonished Elethrine even more than it had the matron. Rallying, she claimed she had managed to protect her tuppenny during ravishment, an assertion which the matron was forced to accept despite the feat being unheard of.

Her family had been more than glad to put their doubt at her achievement to the back of their minds, accepting it with the pride such a magnificent defence warranted. Talithea had also proved virgin, and was as astonished as Elethrine at the fact. Making the best of good fortune, she had accepted their praises, and if anybody wondered why Aisla – who had never claimed to be chaste in the first place – was also apparently virgin, then they were too tactful to remark on the point.

NEW BOOKS

Coming up from Nexus, Sapphire and Black Lace

Sandra's New School by Yolanda Celbridge
December 1999   £5.99   ISBN: 0 352 33454 1

Nude sunbathing and spanking with a lesbian, submissive girlfriend lead hedonistic Sandra Shanks to the rigours of Quirk e's school, where adult schoolgirls are taught old-fashioned submission, in the stern modesty of too-tight uniforms. In a school without males, the dormitory fun of 'all girls together' is as deliciously naughty as Sandra imagined – until she learns sadistic Miss Quirke's own guilty secret.

Tiger, Tiger by Aishling Morgan
December 1999   £5.99   ISBN: 0 352 33455 X

Aishling Morgan's third novel is a study in gothic eroticism. Her world is populated by strange half-human creatures, like Tian-Sha, the tigranthrope, a beautiful blend of girl and tiger. In this bizarre fantasy world a complex plot of erotic intrigue is played out against a background of arcane ritual and nightmare symmetry.

Sisterhood of the Institute by Maria del Rey
December 1999   £5.99   ISBN: 0 352 33456 8

The strict Mistress Shirer has always kept the residents of the Institute on a tight rein. Her charges are girls whose behaviour is apt to get out of hand and who need special discipline. Now they've opened a male dormitory and all manner of strange goings-on have come to her attention. Determined to restore order, Mistress Shirer sends Jaki, her cross-dressing slave, into the dormitories to find out exactly what is going on. A Nexus Classic.

Discipline of the Private House by Esme Ombreux
January 2000   £5.99   ISBN: 0 352 33459 2

Jem Darke, Mistress of the secretive organisation known as the Private House, is bored – and rashly accepts a challenge to submit to the harsh disciplinary regime at the Chateau, where the Chatelaine and her depraved minions will delight in administering torments and humiliations designed to make Jem abandon the wager and relinquish her supreme authority.

The Order by Nadine Somers

January 2000   £5.99   ISBN: 0 352 33460 6

The Comtessa di Diablo is head of the Order, an organisation devoted to Mádrofh, demonic Mistress of Lust. At an archaeological site in the West Country, the search is on to recover the fabled Nhaomhé Chalice, possession of which will allow the Comtessa to unleash a tidal wave of depravity across the world. Tamara Knight and Max Creed are agents for Omega, a secret government body charged with investigating the occult. As they enter the twilight world of depraved practices and unspeakable rituals, the race is on to prevent the onset of the Final Chaos, the return of Mádrofh and the ushering in of a slave society over which the Comtessa and her debauched acolytes will reign supreme.

A Matter of Possession by G.C. Scott

January 2000   £5.99   ISBN: 0 352 33468 1

Under normal circumstances, no woman as stunning as Barbara Hilson would have trouble finding a man. But Barbara's requirements are far from the normal. She needs someone who will take complete control; someone who will impose himself so strongly upon her that her will dissolves into his. Fortunately, if she can't find a man to give her what she wants, Barbara has other options: an extensive collection of bondage equipment, an imagination that knows no bounds, and, in Sarah, an obliging and very debauched friend.

A new imprint of lesbian fiction

Getaway by Suzanne Blaylock
October 1999   Price £6.99   ISBN: 0 352 33443 6
Brilliantly talented Polly Sayers had made two big life shifts
concurrently. She's had her first affair with a woman, and she's also
stolen the code of an important new piece of software and made her
break, doing a runner all the way to a seemingly peaceful coastal
community. But things aren't as tranquil as they appear in the haven,
as Polly becomes immersed in an insular group of mysterious but
very attractive women.

No Angel by Marian Malone
November 1999   £6.99   ISBN 0 352 33462 2
Sally longs to test her limits and sample forbidden pleasures, yet she's
frightened by the depth of her yearnings. Her journey of self-
discovery begins in the fetish clubs of Brighton and ultimately leads
to an encounter with an enigmatic female stranger. And now that
she's tasted freedom, there's no way she's going back.

BLACK
lace

The Best of Black Lace **edited by Kerri Sharp**
December 1999 £5.99 ISBN: 0 352 33452 5
This diverse collection of sizzling erotic texts is an 'editor's choice'
compilation of extracts from Black Lace books with a contemporary
theme. The accent is on female characters who know what they want
– in bed and in the workplace – and who have a sense of sexual
adventure above and beyond the heroines of romantic fiction. These
girls kick ass!

Stripped to the Bone **by Jasmine Stone**
December 1999 £5.99 ISBN: 0 352 33463 0
Annie is a fun-loving, free-thinking American woman who sets
herself the mission of changing everything in her life. The only snag
is, she doesn't know when to stop changing things. Every man she
encounters is determined to find out what makes her tick, but her
playful personality means that no one can get a hold on her. Her sexual
magnetism is electrifying, and her capacity for the unusual and experi-
mental sides of sex play have her lovers in a spin of erotic confusion.

Doctor's Orders **by Deanna Ashford**
January 2000 £5.99 ISBN: 0 352 33453 3
When Dr Helen Dawson loses her job at a state-run hospital, she is
delighted to be offered a position at a private clinic. The staff at the
clinic do far more than simply care for the medical needs of their
clients, though – they also cater for their sexual needs. Helen soon
discovers that this isn't the only secret – there are other, far darker
occurrences.

Complicity **by Stella Black**
January 2000 £5.99 ISBN: 0 352 33467 3
When Stella Black decides to take a holiday in Arizona she doesn't
bargain on having to deal with such a dark and weird crowd: Jim,
the master who likes his SM hard; Mel, the professional dominatrix
with a background in sleazy movies; Rick, the gun-toting cowboy
with cold blue eyes; and his psychotic sidekick Bernie. They're not
the safest individuals, but that's not what Stella wants. That's not
what she's come for.

Nexus

NEXUS BACKLIST

All books are priced £5.99 unless another price is given. If a date is supplied, the book in question will not be available until that month in 1999.

CONTEMPORARY EROTICA

THE ACADEMY	Arabella Knight	
AMANDA IN THE PRIVATE HOUSE	Esme Ombreux	
BAD PENNY	Penny Birch	
THE BLACK MASQUE	Lisette Ashton	
THE BLACK WIDOW	Lisette Ashton	
BOUND TO OBEY	Amanda Ware	
BRAT	Penny Birch	
DANCE OF SUBMISSION	Lisette Ashton	Nov
DARK DELIGHTS	Maria del Rey	
DARK DESIRES	Maria del Rey	
DARLINE DOMINANT	Tania d'Alanis	
DISCIPLES OF SHAME	Stephanie Calvin	
THE DISCIPLINE OF NURSE RIDING	Yolanda Celbridge	
DISPLAYS OF INNOCENTS	Lucy Golden	
EMMA'S SECRET DOMINATION	Hilary James	
EXPOSING LOUISA	Jean Aveline	
FAIRGROUND ATTRACTIONS	Lisette Ashton	
GISELLE	Jean Aveline	Oct
HEART OF DESIRE	Maria del Rey	
HOUSE RULES	G.C. Scott	Oct
IN FOR A PENNY	Penny Birch	Nov
JULIE AT THE REFORMATORY	Angela Elgar	
LINGERING LESSONS	Sarah Veitch	

THE GOVERNESS AT ST AGATHA'S	Yolanda Celbridge		
THE MASTER OF CASTLELEIGH	Jacqueline Bellevois		Aug
PRIVATE MEMOIRS OF A KENTISH HEADMISTRESS	Yolanda Celbridge	£4.99	
THE RAKE	Aishling Morgan		Sep
THE TRAINING OF AN ENGLISH GENTLEMAN	Yolanda Celbridge		

SAMPLERS & COLLECTIONS

EROTICON 4	Various		
THE FIESTA LETTERS	ed. Chris Lloyd	£4.99	
NEW EROTICA 3			
NEW EROTICA 4	Various		
A DOZEN STROKES	Various		Aug

NEXUS CLASSICS
A new imprint dedicated to putting the finest works of erotic fiction back in print

THE IMAGE	Jean de Berg	
CHOOSING LOVERS FOR JUSTINE	Aran Ashe	
THE INSTITUTE	Maria del Rey	
AGONY AUNT	G. C. Scott	
THE HANDMAIDENS	Aran Ashe	
OBSESSION	Maria del Rey	
HIS MASTER'S VOICE	G.C. Scott	Aug
CITADEL OF SERVITUDE	Aran Ashe	Sep
BOUND TO SERVE	Amanda Ware	Oct
BOUND TO SUBMIT	Amanda Ware	Nov
SISTERHOOD OF THE INSTITUTE	Maria del Rey	Dec

Please send me the books I have ticked above.

Name ....

Address ....

....

....

.... Post code..................

Send to: **Cash Sales, Nexus Books, Thames Wharf Studios, Rainville Road, London W6 9HT**

US customers: for prices and details of how to order books for delivery by mail, call 1-800-805-1083.

Please enclose a cheque or postal order, made payable to **Nexus Books**, to the value of the books you have ordered plus postage and packing costs as follows:

UK and BFPO – £1.00 for the first book, 50p for the second book and 30p for each subsequent book to a maximum of £3.00;

Overseas (including Republic of Ireland) – £2.00 for the first book, £1.00 for the second book and 50p for each subsequent book.

We accept all major credit cards, including VISA, ACCESS/ MASTERCARD, AMEX, DINERS CLUB, SWITCH, SOLO, and DELTA. Please write your card number and expiry date here:

....

Please allow up to 28 days for delivery.

Signature ....